Buffy the Vampire Slayer™

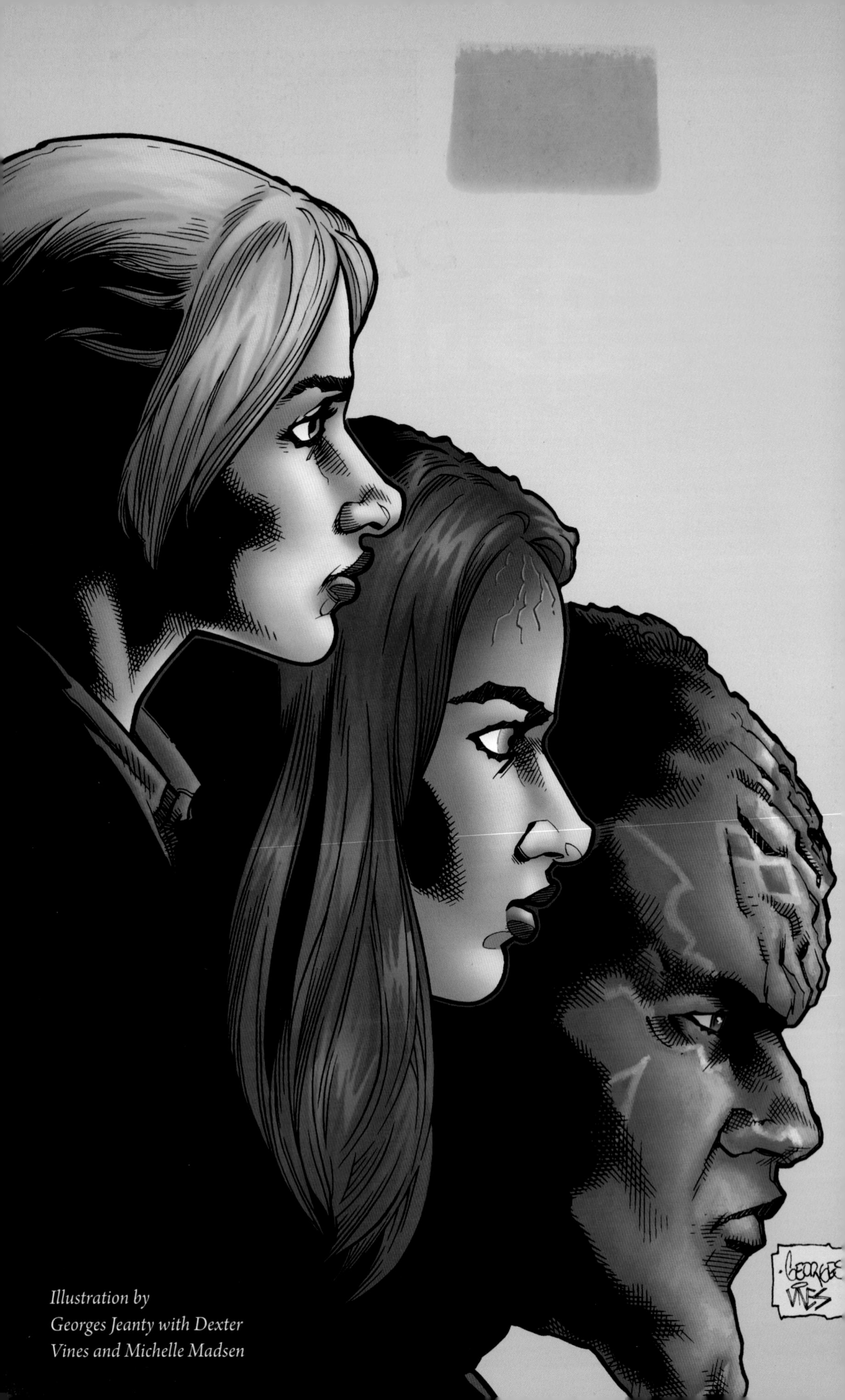

*Illustration by
Georges Jeanty with Dexter
Vines and Michelle Madsen*

Buffy the Vampire Slayer™

SEASON 9 · VOLUME 4

SCRIPT
ANDREW CHAMBLISS

WELCOME TO THE TEAM

PENCILS
GEORGES JEANTY

INKS
DEXTER VINES

THE WATCHER

PENCILS
KARL MOLINE

INKS
ANDY OWENS

COLORS
MICHELLE MADSEN

LETTERS
RICHARD STARKINGS
& Comicraft's JIMMY BETANCOURT

CHAPTER BREAK ART
PHIL NOTO

COVER ART
JO CHEN

EXECUTIVE PRODUCER
JOSS WHEDON

DARK HORSE BOOKS

President & Publisher
MIKE RICHARDSON

Editors
SCOTT ALLIE & SIERRA HAHN

Assistant Editor
FREDDYE LINS

Collection Designer
JUSTIN COUCH

Published by Dark Horse Books
A division of Dark Horse Comics, Inc.
10956 SE Main Street
Milwaukie, OR 97222

DarkHorse.com

International Licensing: (503) 905-2377
To find a comics shop in your area,
call the Comic Shop Locator Service toll-free at (888) 266-4226

First edition: October 2013
ISBN 978-1-61655-166-7

10 9 8 7 6 5 4 3 2 1
Printed in China

This story takes place after the events of *Buffy the Vampire Slayer* Season 8, created by Joss Whedon.

Special thanks to Lauren Winarski at Twentieth Century Fox, and Daniel Kaminsky.

This volume reprints the comic-book series *Buffy the Vampire Slayer* Season 9 #16–#20 from Dark Horse Comics.

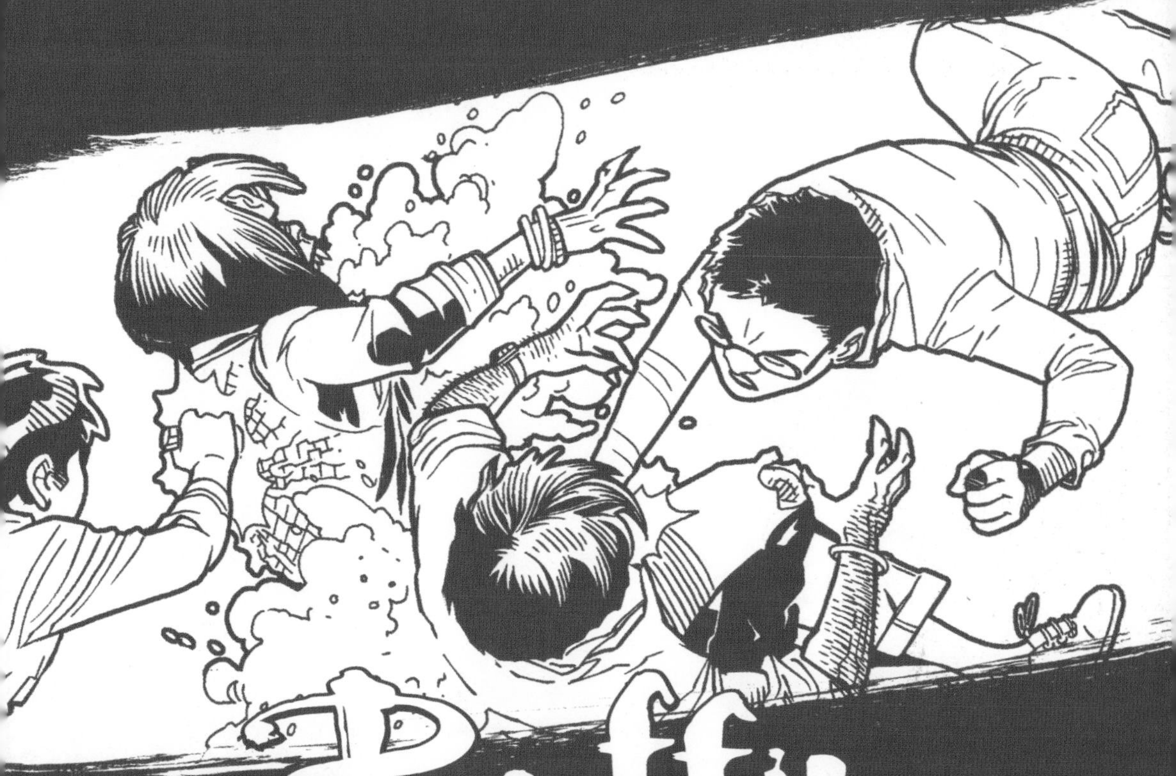

Buffy the Vampire Slayer™

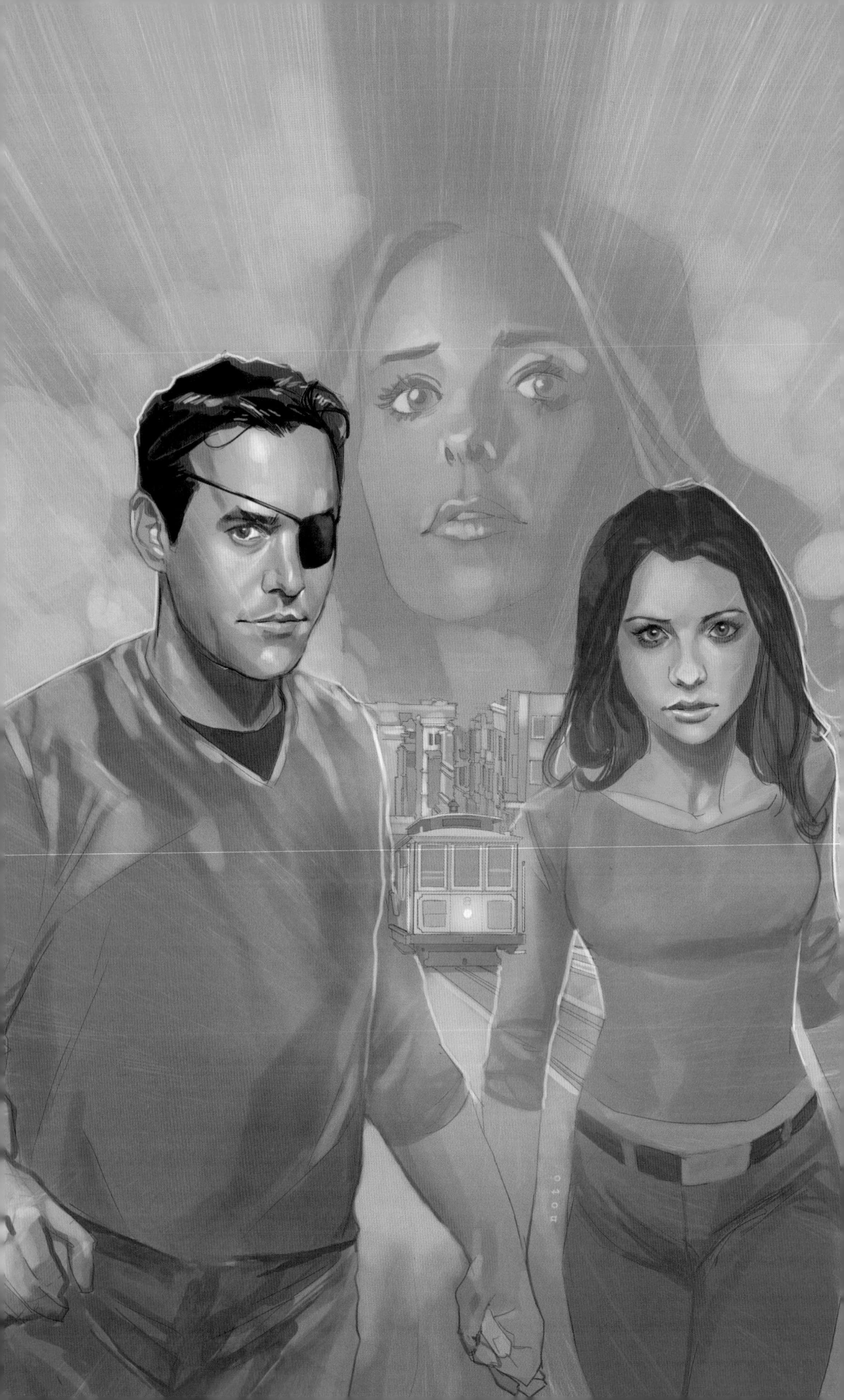

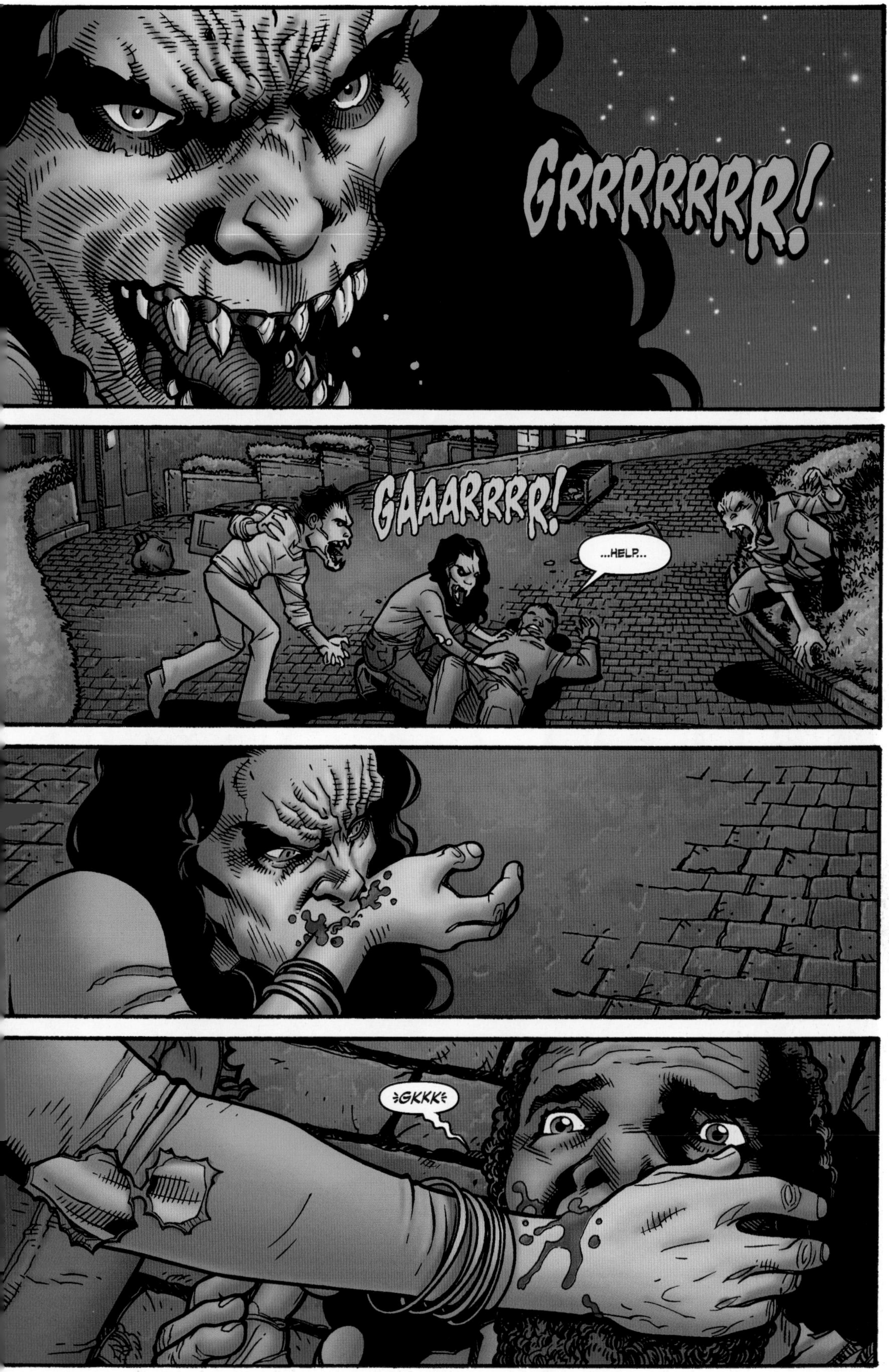
GRRRRRRRR!
GAAARRRR!
...HELP...
GKKK

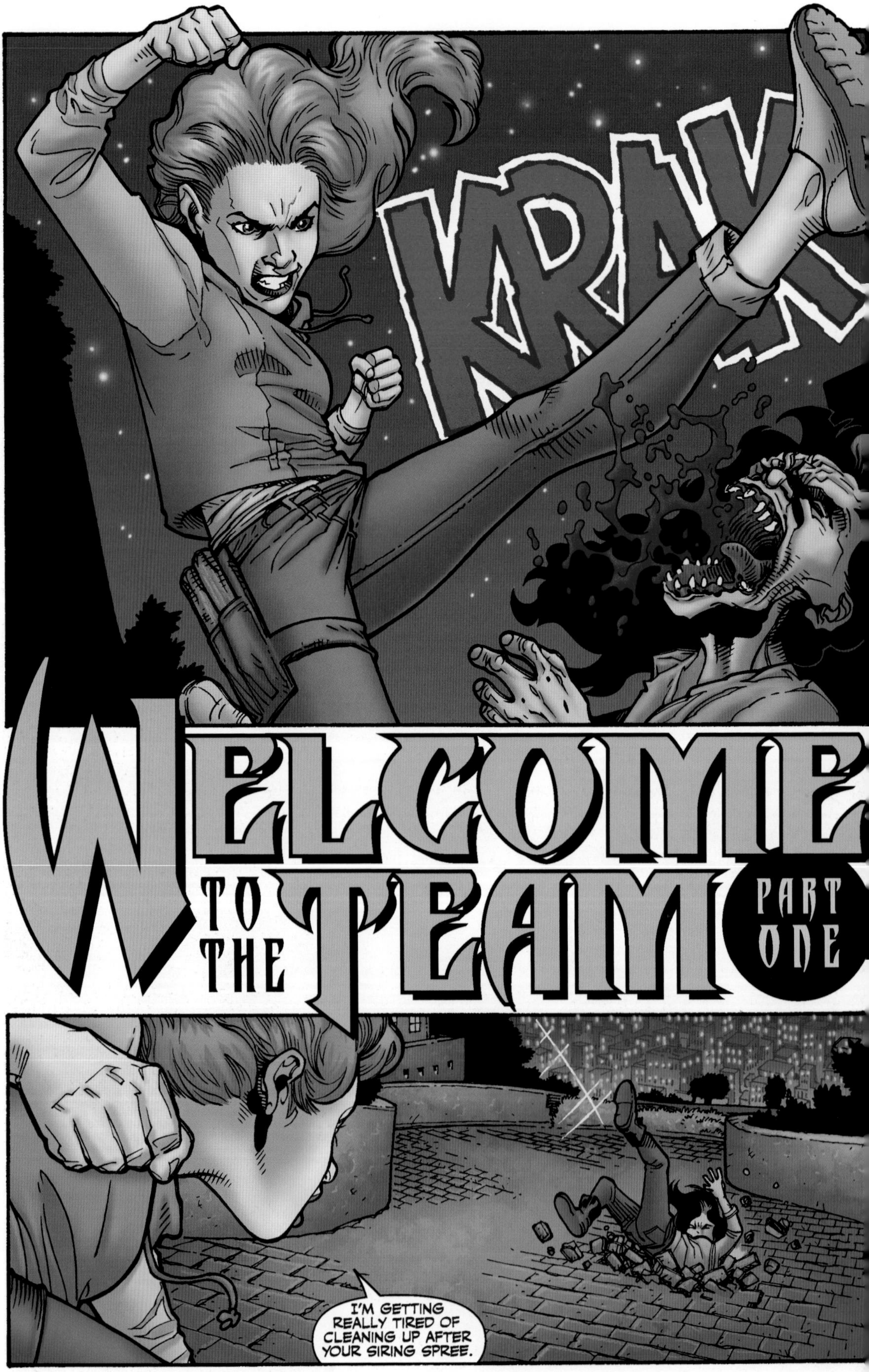
KRAK
WELCOME TO THE TEAM
PART ONE
I'M GETTING REALLY TIRED OF CLEANING UP AFTER YOUR SIRING SPREE.

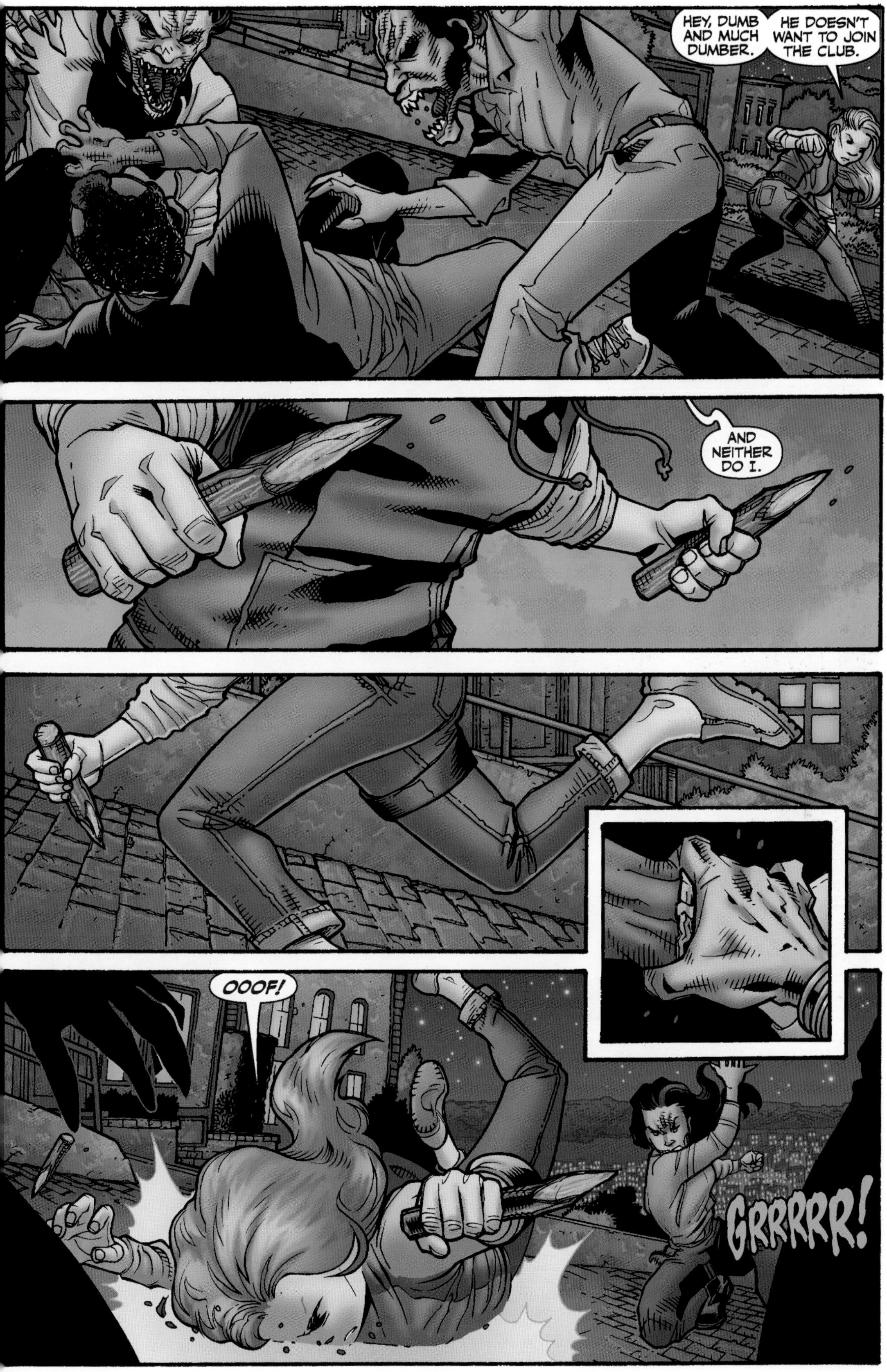
HEY, DUMB AND MUCH DUMBER.
HE DOESN'T WANT TO JOIN THE CLUB.
AND NEITHER DO I.
OOOF!
GRRRRR!

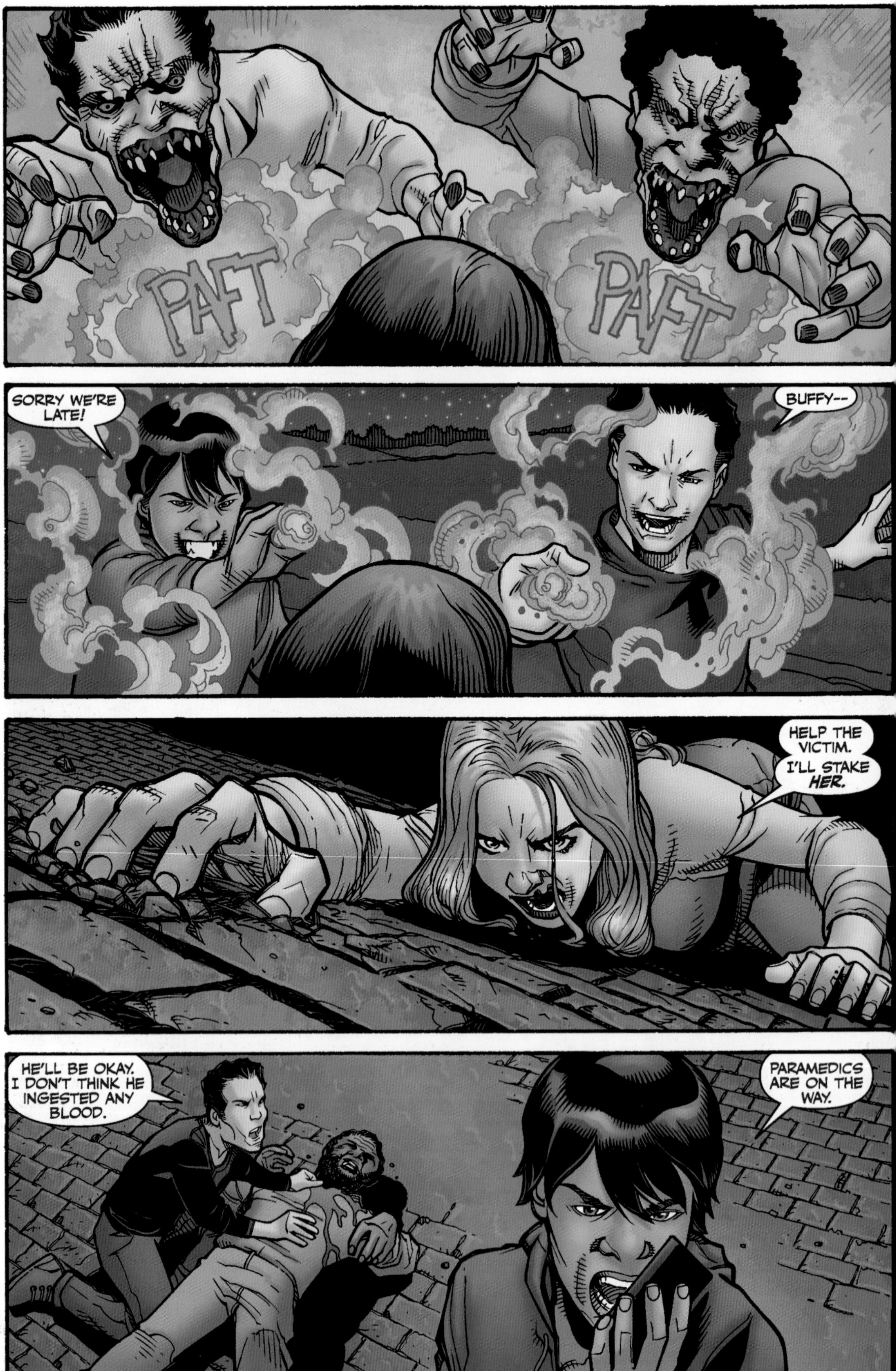
PAFT
PAFT
SORRY WE'RE LATE!
BUFFY--
HELP THE VICTIM. I'LL STAKE *HER.*
HE'LL BE OKAY. I DON'T THINK HE INGESTED ANY BLOOD.
PARAMEDICS ARE ON THE WAY.

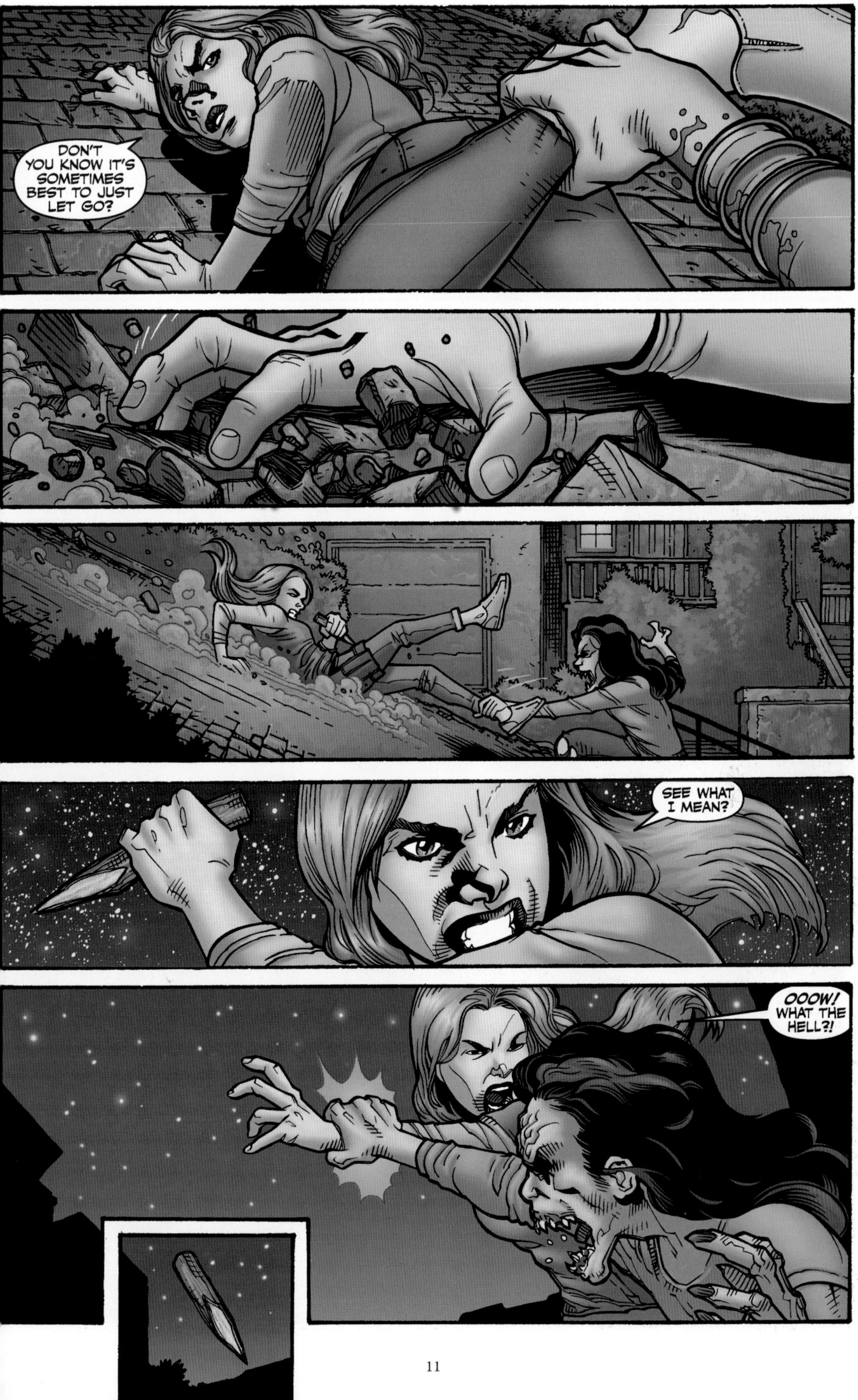
DON'T YOU KNOW IT'S SOMETIMES BEST TO JUST LET GO?
SEE WHAT I MEAN?
OOOW! WHAT THE HELL?!

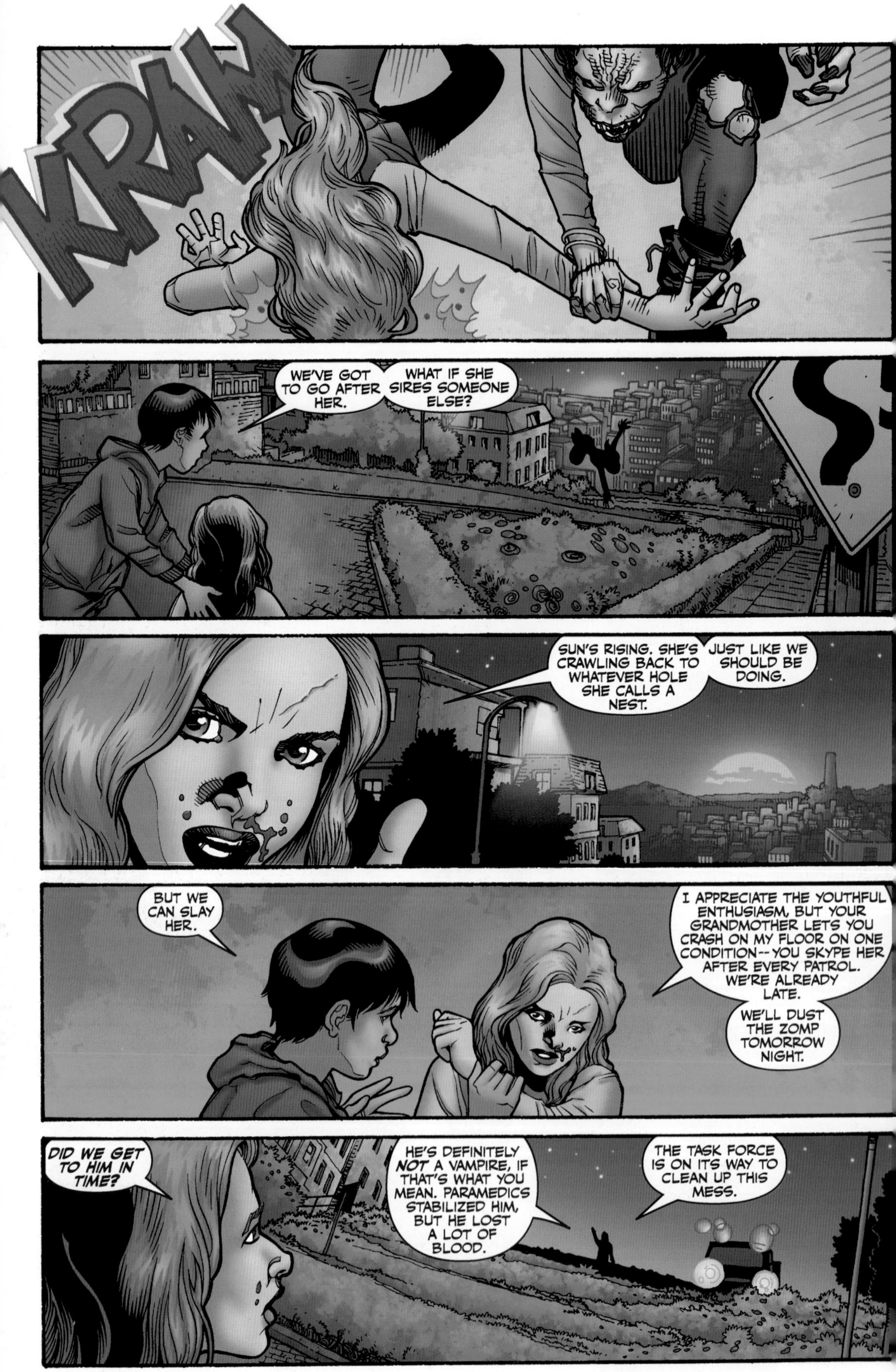
KRAW
WE'VE GOT TO GO AFTER HER.
WHAT IF SHE SIRES SOMEONE ELSE?
SUN'S RISING. SHE'S CRAWLING BACK TO WHATEVER HOLE SHE CALLS A NEST.
JUST LIKE WE SHOULD BE DOING.
BUT WE CAN SLAY HER.
I APPRECIATE THE YOUTHFUL ENTHUSIASM, BUT YOUR GRANDMOTHER LETS YOU CRASH ON MY FLOOR ON ONE CONDITION--YOU SKYPE HER AFTER EVERY PATROL. WE'RE ALREADY LATE.
WE'LL DUST THE ZOMP TOMORROW NIGHT.
DID WE GET TO HIM IN TIME?
HE'S DEFINITELY NOT A VAMPIRE, IF THAT'S WHAT YOU MEAN. PARAMEDICS STABILIZED HIM, BUT HE LOST A LOT OF BLOOD.
THE TASK FORCE IS ON ITS WAY TO CLEAN UP THIS MESS.

YOU WANT THE PARAMEDICS TO TAKE A LOOK AT YOU?

WHY?

YOU'RE HOLDING YOUR ARM LIKE SOMEONE JUST TORE IT OFF.

TRUST ME, I'VE HELD MY ARM LIKE SOMEONE'S JUST TORN IT OFF, AND IT DOESN'T LOOK LIKE THIS.

I'M FINE.

BUT THAT ZOMPIRE *WAS* ALL KINDS OF STRONG. EVEN FOR THE POST-SEED VARIETY.

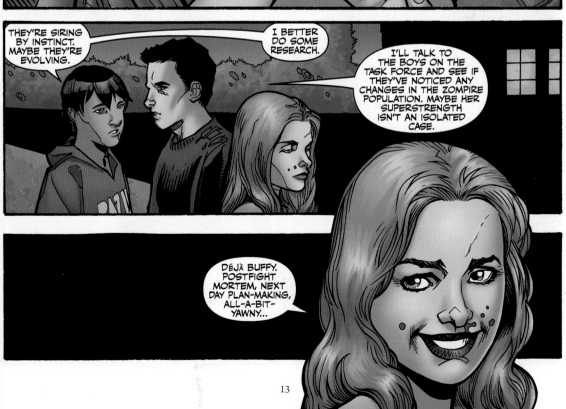

THEY'RE SIRING BY INSTINCT. MAYBE THEY'RE EVOLVING.

I BETTER DO SOME RESEARCH.

I'LL TALK TO THE BOYS ON THE TASK FORCE AND SEE IF THEY'VE NOTICED ANY CHANGES IN THE ZOMPIRE POPULATION. MAYBE HER SUPERSTRENGTH ISN'T AN ISOLATED CASE.

DÉJÀ BUFFY. POSTFIGHT MORTEM, NEXT DAY PLAN-MAKING, ALL-A-BIT-YAWNY...

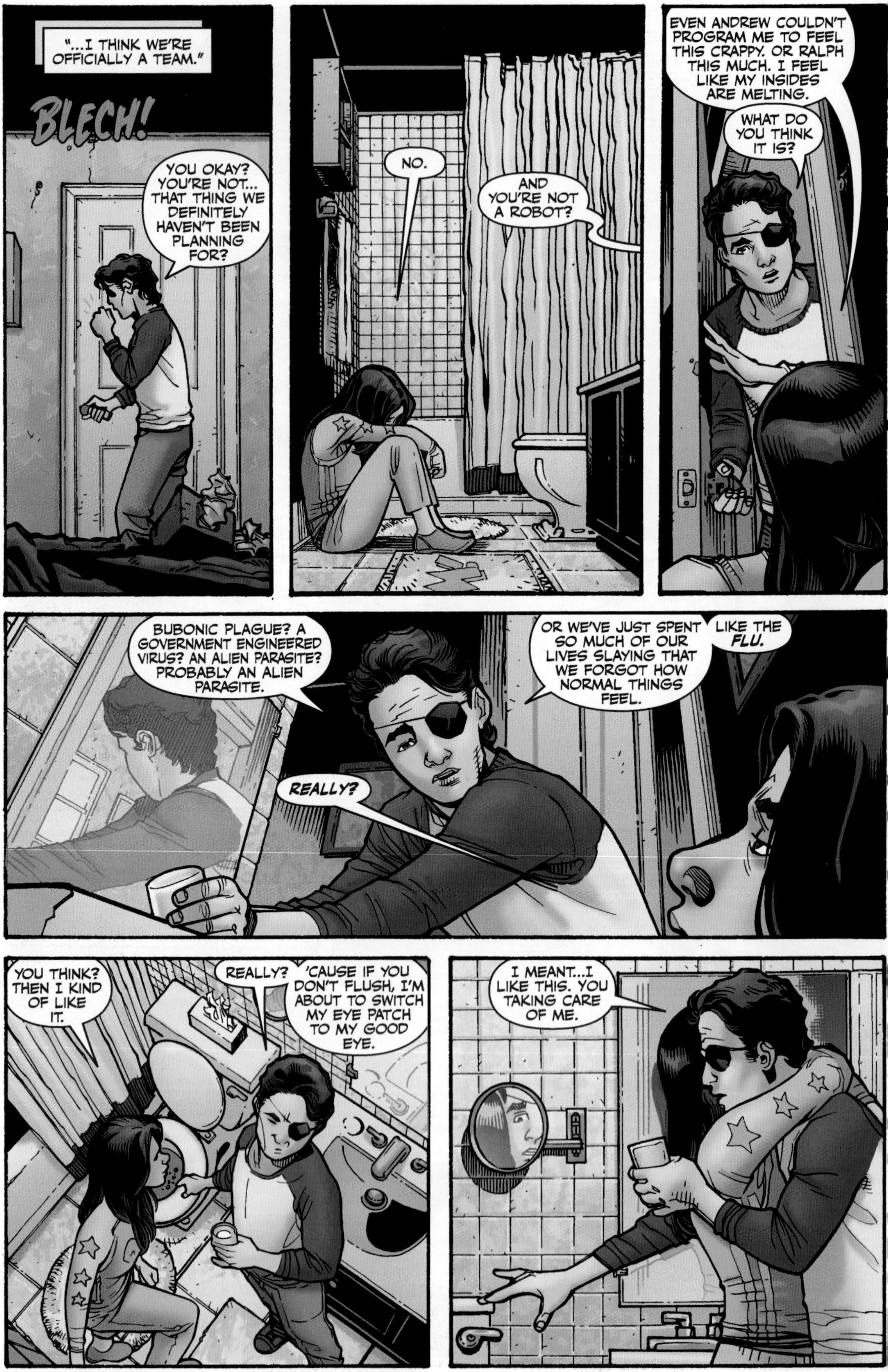
"...I THINK WE'RE OFFICIALLY A TEAM."
BLECH!
YOU OKAY? YOU'RE NOT... THAT THING WE DEFINITELY HAVEN'T BEEN PLANNING FOR?
NO.
AND YOU'RE NOT A ROBOT?
EVEN ANDREW COULDN'T PROGRAM ME TO FEEL THIS CRAPPY. OR RALPH THIS MUCH. I FEEL LIKE MY INSIDES ARE MELTING.
WHAT DO YOU THINK IT IS?
BUBONIC PLAGUE? A GOVERNMENT ENGINEERED VIRUS? AN ALIEN PARASITE? PROBABLY AN ALIEN PARASITE.
OR WE'VE JUST SPENT SO MUCH OF OUR LIVES SLAYING THAT WE FORGOT HOW NORMAL THINGS FEEL.
LIKE THE FLU.
REALLY?
YOU THINK? THEN I KIND OF LIKE IT.
REALLY?
'CAUSE IF YOU DON'T FLUSH, I'M ABOUT TO SWITCH MY EYE PATCH TO MY GOOD EYE.
I MEANT...I LIKE THIS. YOU TAKING CARE OF ME.

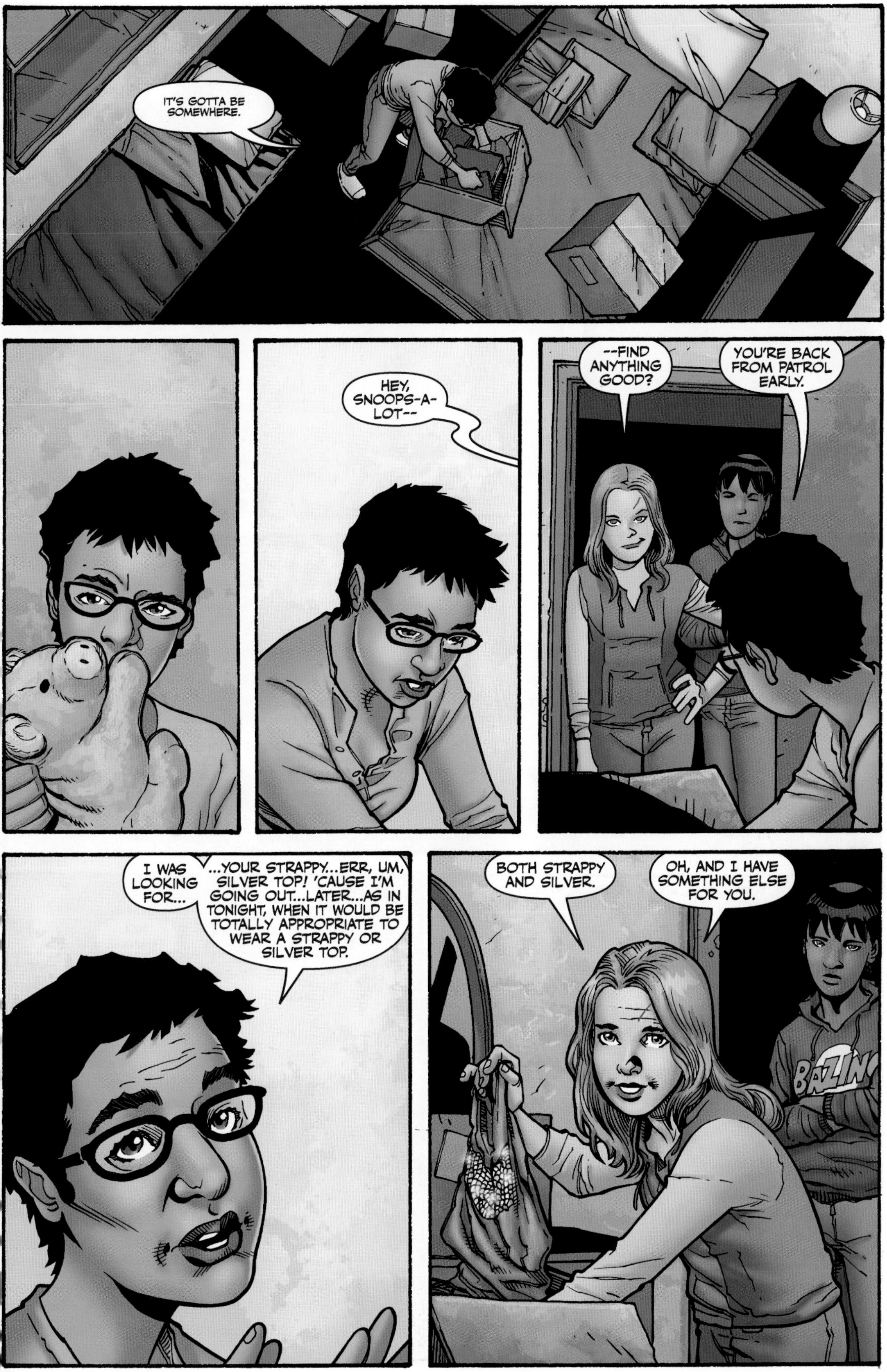
IT'S GOTTA BE SOMEWHERE.
HEY, SNOOPS-A-LOT--
--FIND ANYTHING GOOD?
YOU'RE BACK FROM PATROL EARLY.
I WAS LOOKING FOR...
...YOUR STRAPPY...ERR, UM, SILVER TOP! 'CAUSE I'M GOING OUT...LATER...AS IN TONIGHT, WHEN IT WOULD BE TOTALLY APPROPRIATE TO WEAR A STRAPPY OR SILVER TOP.
BOTH STRAPPY AND SILVER.
OH, AND I HAVE SOMETHING ELSE FOR YOU.
BAZING

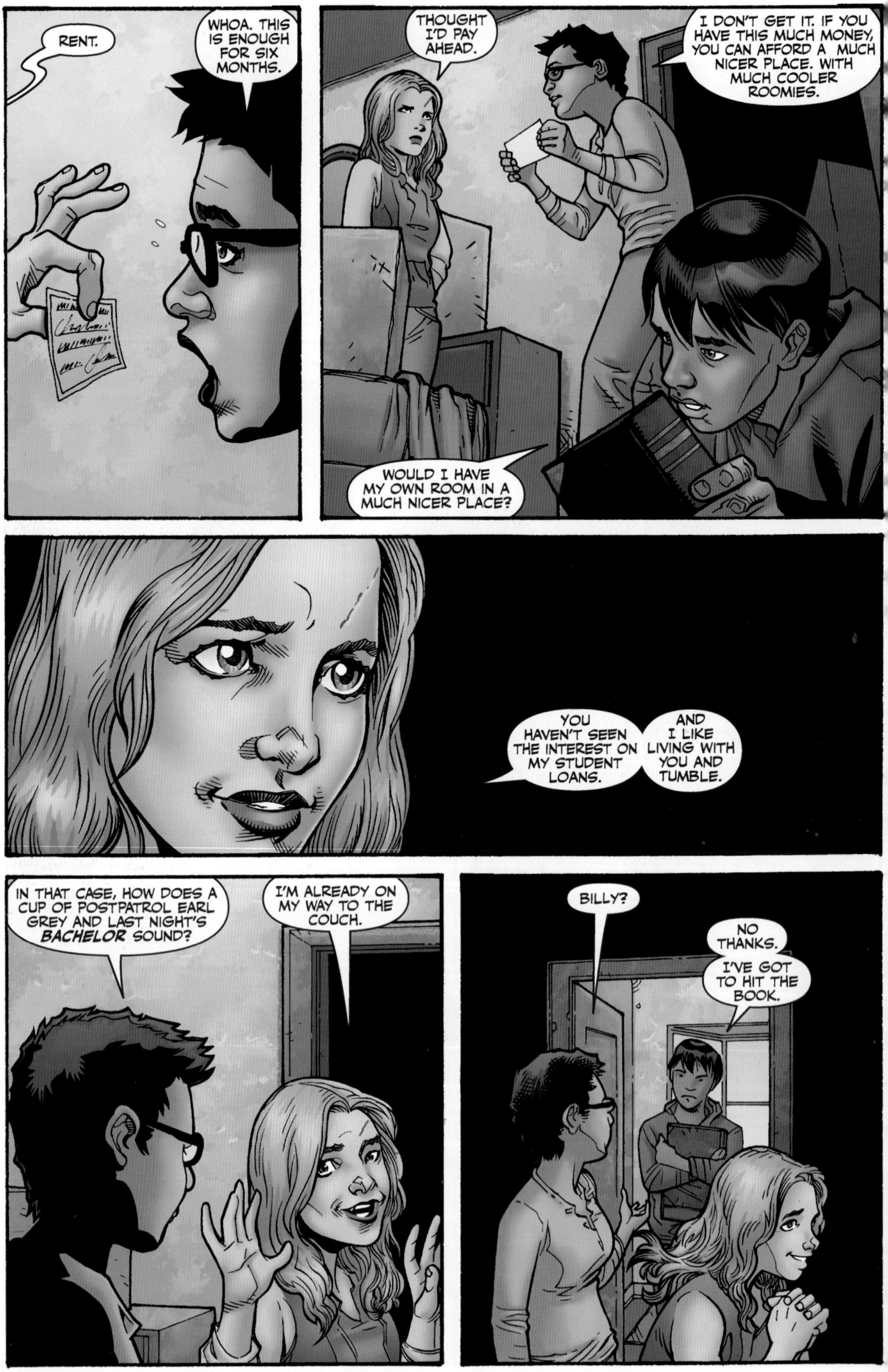
RENT.
WHOA. THIS IS ENOUGH FOR SIX MONTHS.
THOUGHT I'D PAY AHEAD.
I DON'T GET IT. IF YOU HAVE THIS MUCH MONEY, YOU CAN AFFORD A MUCH NICER PLACE. WITH MUCH COOLER ROOMIES.
WOULD I HAVE MY OWN ROOM IN A MUCH NICER PLACE?
YOU HAVEN'T SEEN THE INTEREST ON MY STUDENT LOANS.
AND I LIKE LIVING WITH YOU AND TUMBLE.
IN THAT CASE, HOW DOES A CUP OF POSTPATROL EARL GREY AND LAST NIGHT'S *BACHELOR* SOUND?
I'M ALREADY ON MY WAY TO THE COUCH.
BILLY?
NO THANKS.
I'VE GOT TO HIT THE BOOK.

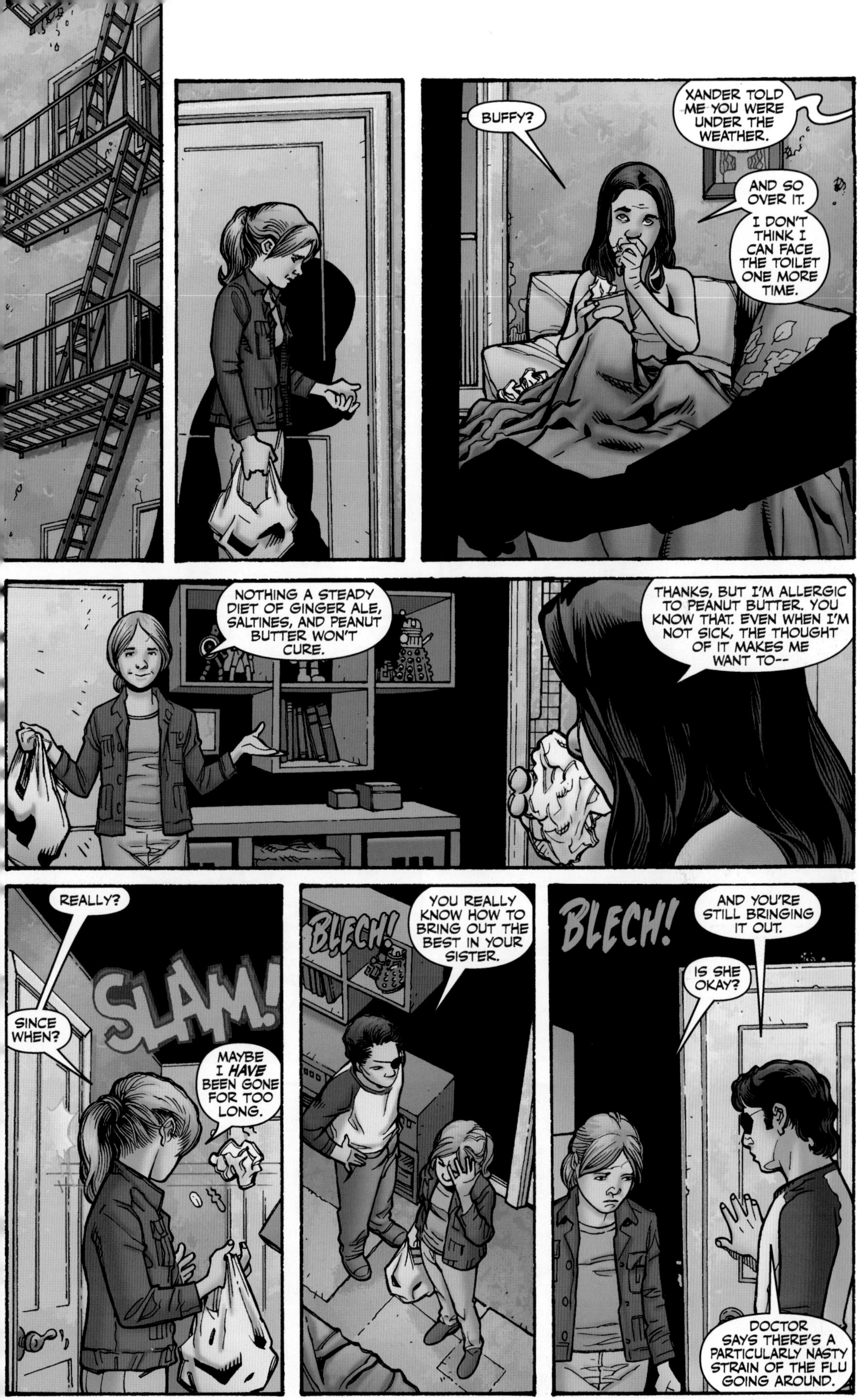
BUFFY?
XANDER TOLD ME YOU WERE UNDER THE WEATHER.
AND SO OVER IT.
I DON'T THINK I CAN FACE THE TOILET ONE MORE TIME.
NOTHING A STEADY DIET OF GINGER ALE, SALTINES, AND PEANUT BUTTER WON'T CURE.
THANKS, BUT I'M ALLERGIC TO PEANUT BUTTER. YOU KNOW THAT. EVEN WHEN I'M NOT SICK, THE THOUGHT OF IT MAKES ME WANT TO--
REALLY?
SINCE WHEN?
SLAM!
MAYBE I *HAVE* BEEN GONE FOR TOO LONG.
BLECH!
YOU REALLY KNOW HOW TO BRING OUT THE BEST IN YOUR SISTER.
BLECH!
AND YOU'RE STILL BRINGING IT OUT.
IS SHE OKAY?
DOCTOR SAYS THERE'S A PARTICULARLY NASTY STRAIN OF THE FLU GOING AROUND.

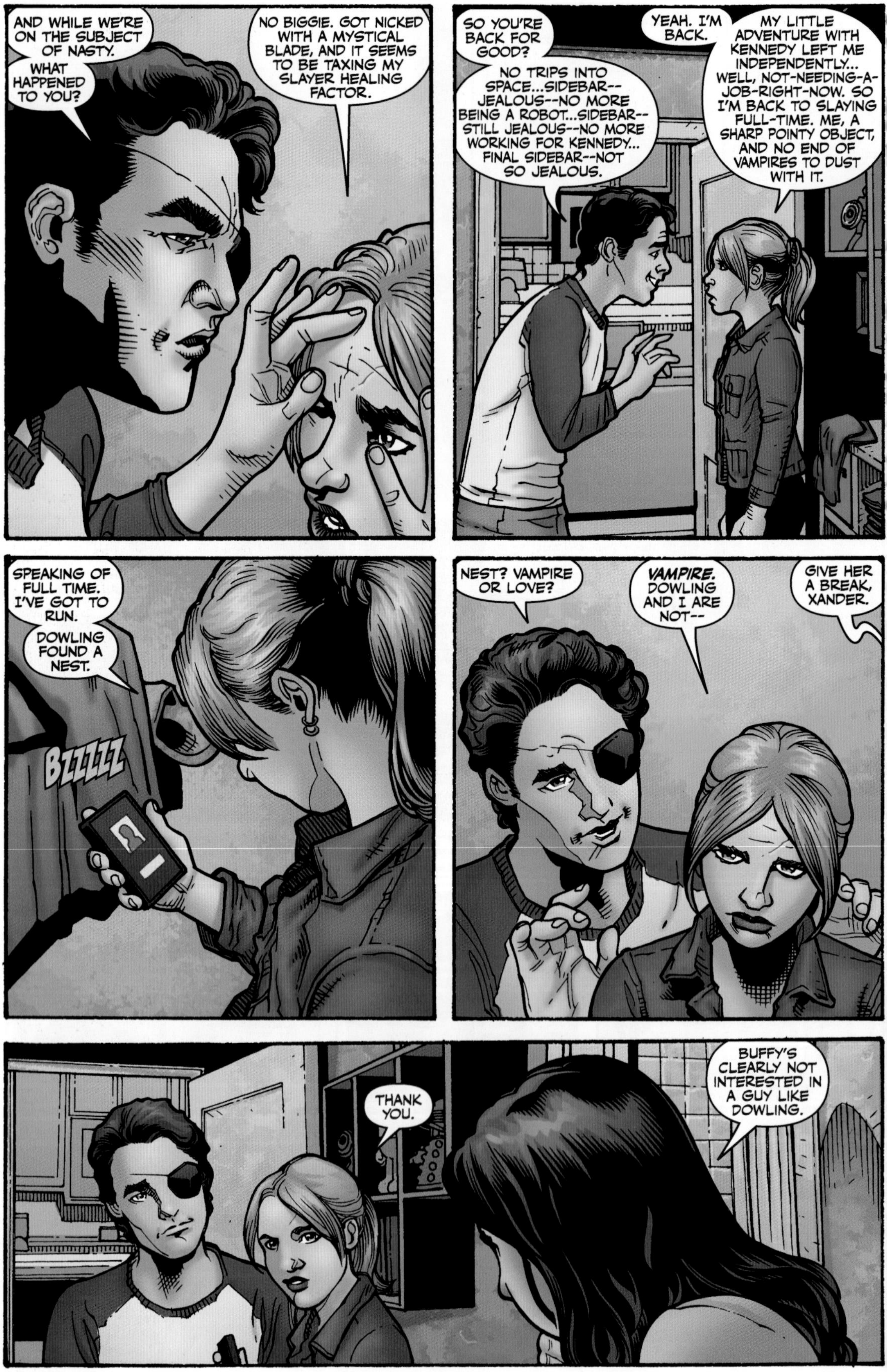
AND WHILE WE'RE ON THE SUBJECT OF NASTY.
WHAT HAPPENED TO YOU?
NO BIGGIE. GOT NICKED WITH A MYSTICAL BLADE, AND IT SEEMS TO BE TAXING MY SLAYER HEALING FACTOR.
SO YOU'RE BACK FOR GOOD?
NO TRIPS INTO SPACE...SIDEBAR--JEALOUS--NO MORE BEING A ROBOT...SIDEBAR--STILL JEALOUS--NO MORE WORKING FOR KENNEDY... FINAL SIDEBAR--NOT SO JEALOUS.
YEAH. I'M BACK.
MY LITTLE ADVENTURE WITH KENNEDY LEFT ME INDEPENDENTLY... WELL, NOT-NEEDING-A-JOB-RIGHT-NOW. SO I'M BACK TO SLAYING FULL-TIME. ME, A SHARP POINTY OBJECT, AND NO END OF VAMPIRES TO DUST WITH IT.
SPEAKING OF FULL TIME. I'VE GOT TO RUN.
DOWLING FOUND A NEST.
BZZZZZ
NEST? VAMPIRE OR LOVE?
VAMPIRE. DOWLING AND I ARE NOT--
GIVE HER A BREAK, XANDER.
THANK YOU.
BUFFY'S CLEARLY NOT INTERESTED IN A GUY LIKE DOWLING.

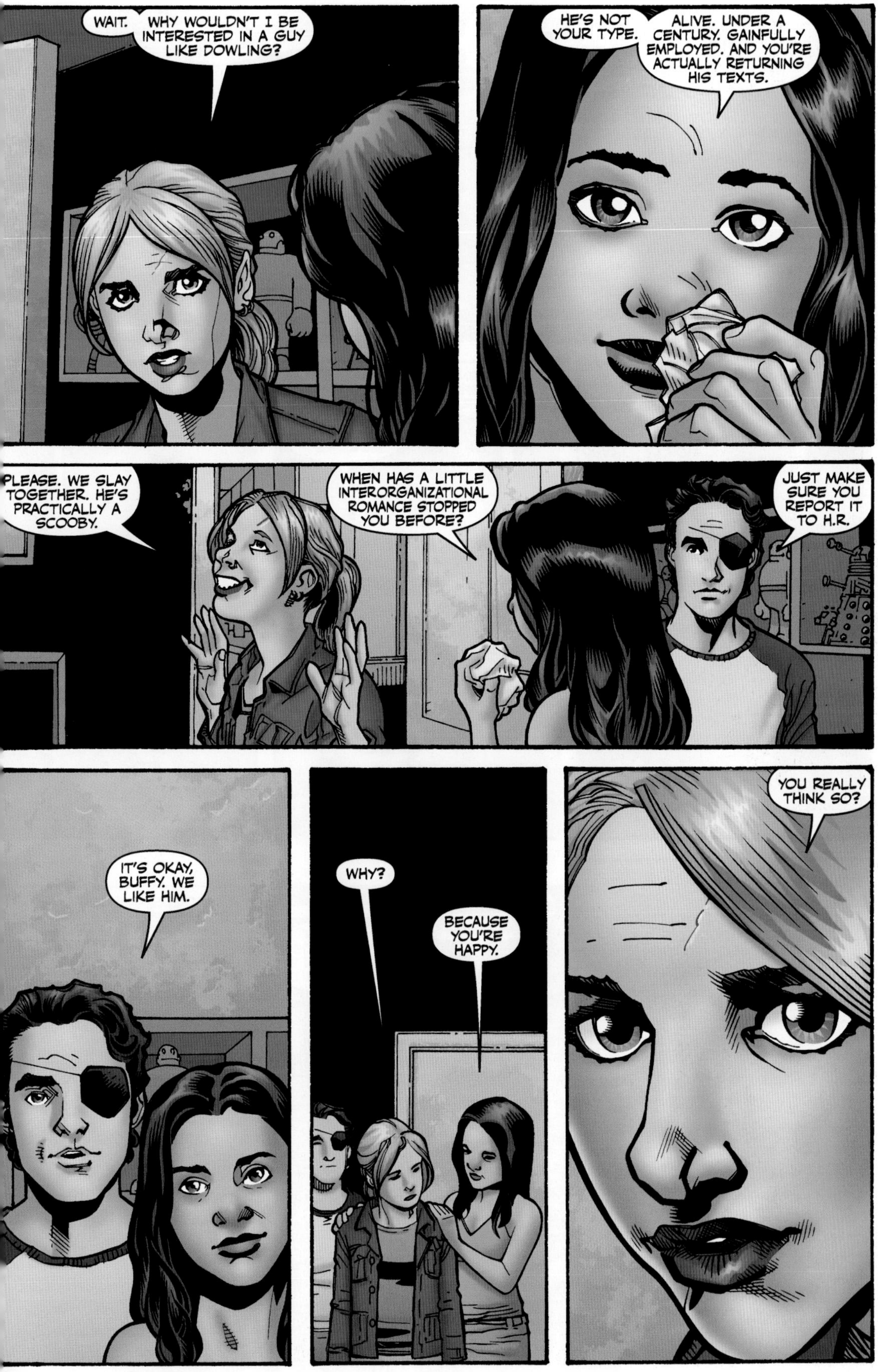
WAIT.
WHY WOULDN'T I BE INTERESTED IN A GUY LIKE DOWLING?
HE'S NOT YOUR TYPE.
ALIVE. UNDER A CENTURY. GAINFULLY EMPLOYED. AND YOU'RE ACTUALLY RETURNING HIS TEXTS.
PLEASE. WE SLAY TOGETHER. HE'S PRACTICALLY A SCOOBY.
WHEN HAS A LITTLE INTERORGANIZATIONAL ROMANCE STOPPED YOU BEFORE?
JUST MAKE SURE YOU REPORT IT TO H.R.
IT'S OKAY, BUFFY. WE LIKE HIM.
WHY?
BECAUSE YOU'RE HAPPY.
YOU REALLY THINK SO?

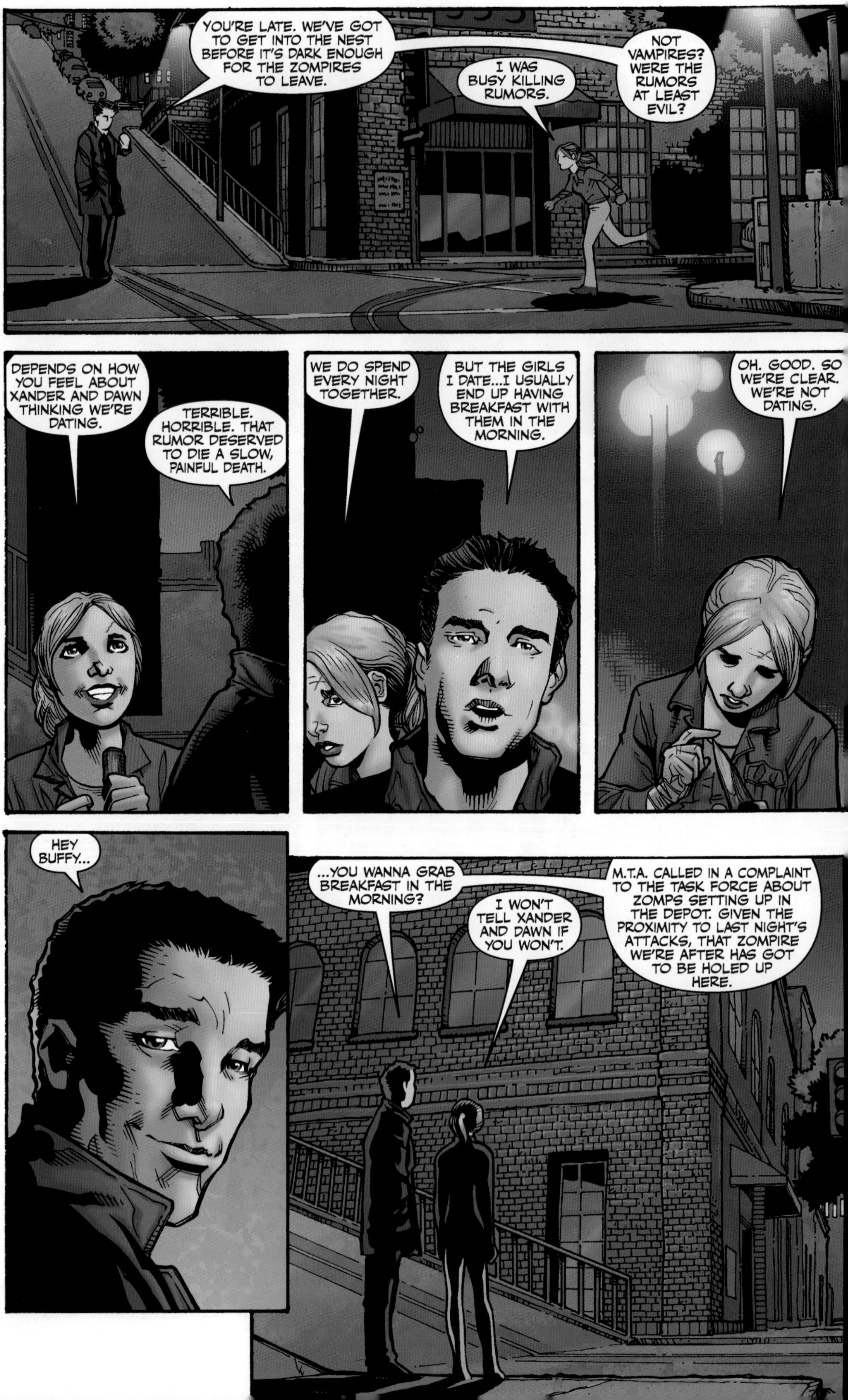
YOU'RE LATE. WE'VE GOT TO GET INTO THE NEST BEFORE IT'S DARK ENOUGH FOR THE ZOMPIRES TO LEAVE.
I WAS BUSY KILLING RUMORS.
NOT VAMPIRES? WERE THE RUMORS AT LEAST EVIL?
DEPENDS ON HOW YOU FEEL ABOUT XANDER AND DAWN THINKING WE'RE DATING.
TERRIBLE. HORRIBLE. THAT RUMOR DESERVED TO DIE A SLOW, PAINFUL DEATH.
WE DO SPEND EVERY NIGHT TOGETHER.
BUT THE GIRLS I DATE...I USUALLY END UP HAVING BREAKFAST WITH THEM IN THE MORNING.
OH. GOOD. SO WE'RE CLEAR. WE'RE NOT DATING.
HEY BUFFY...
...YOU WANNA GRAB BREAKFAST IN THE MORNING?
I WON'T TELL XANDER AND DAWN IF YOU WON'T.
M.T.A. CALLED IN A COMPLAINT TO THE TASK FORCE ABOUT ZOMPS SETTING UP IN THE DEPOT. GIVEN THE PROXIMITY TO LAST NIGHT'S ATTACKS, THAT ZOMPIRE WE'RE AFTER HAS GOT TO BE HOLED UP HERE.

YOU SLAYERS MUST HAVE SUPER-STRENGTH JUST SO YOU CAN HAUL ALL YOUR GEAR AROUND.

WHAT'S IN THE BAG?

ROPE SOAKED IN HOLY WATER. I READ ABOUT IT IN THE BIG BOOK O' VAMPYR.

IF WE CATCH THE STRONG ONE, MAYBE WE CAN FIGURE OUT WHAT'S GIVING HER THAT EXTRA PEP IN HER STEP.

IT'S TOO DANGEROUS. WE'VE GOT TO DUST HER.

I WENT INTO A *CHURCH* TO GET HOLY WATER. I CAN HANDLE AN UBERZOMP.

THE KID'S RIGHT. IF THERE'S A NEW KIND OF ZOMPIRE IN TOWN, WE NEED TO KNOW EVERYTHING WE CAN ABOUT IT.

BUT THE DETECTIVE IS RIGHT, TOO. IT'S DANGEROUS.

YOU CLEAR THE DECK. I'LL WRANGLE LITTLE MISS STAY-OUT-OF-THE-SUNSHINE.

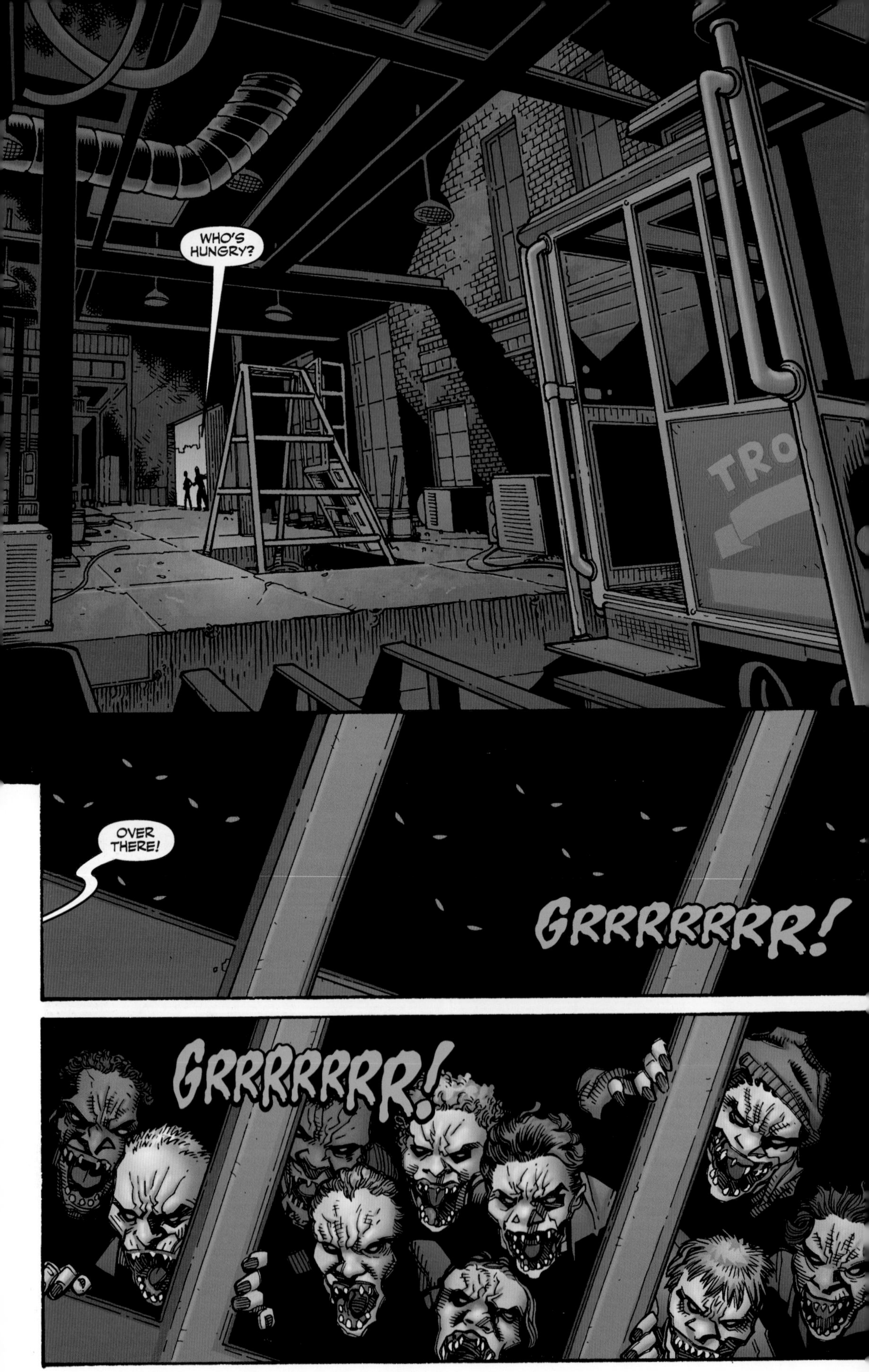
WHO'S HUNGRY?
TRO
OVER THERE!
GRRRRRRR!
GRRRRRRR!

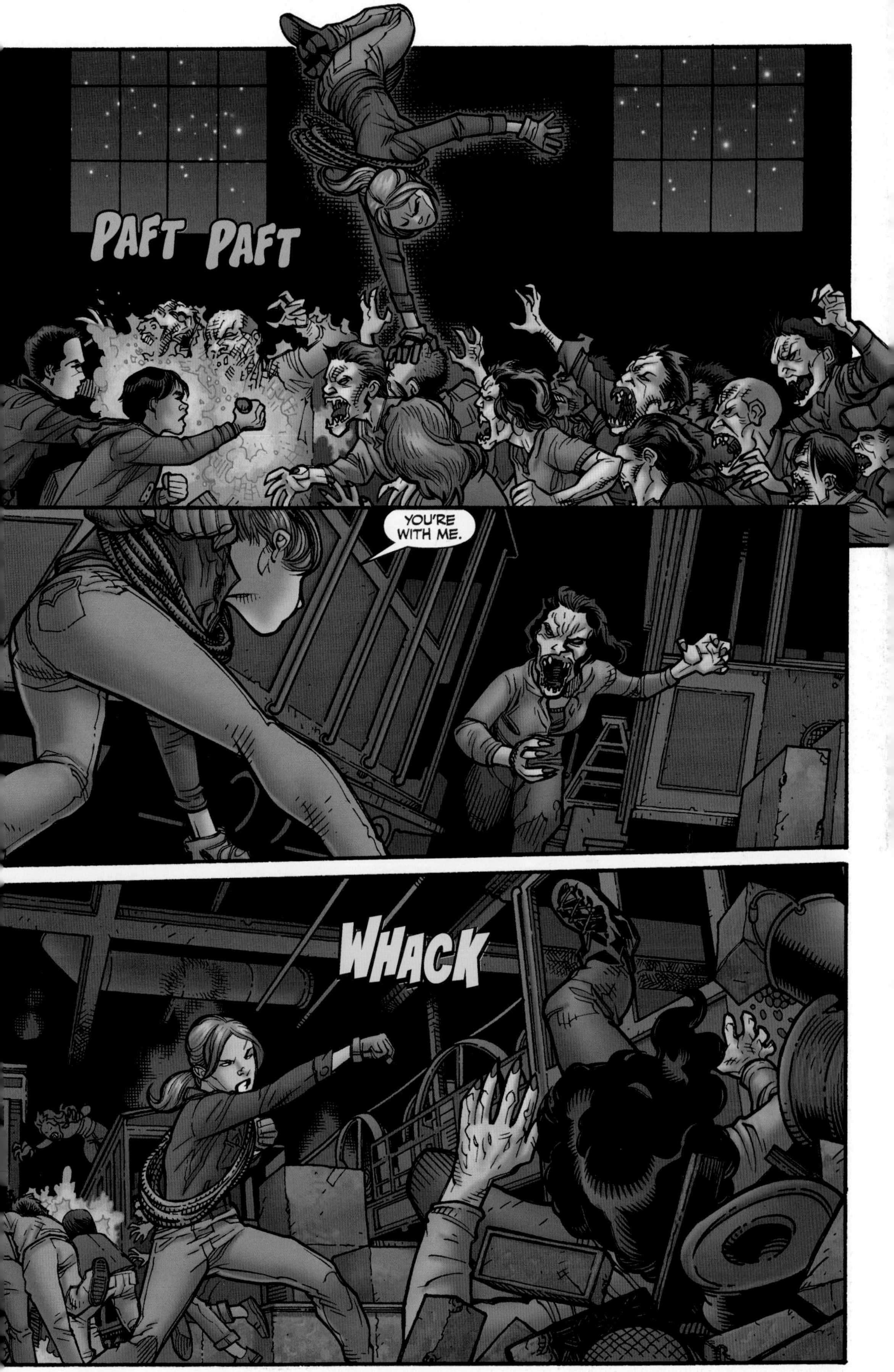
PAFT PAFT
YOU'RE WITH ME.
WHACK

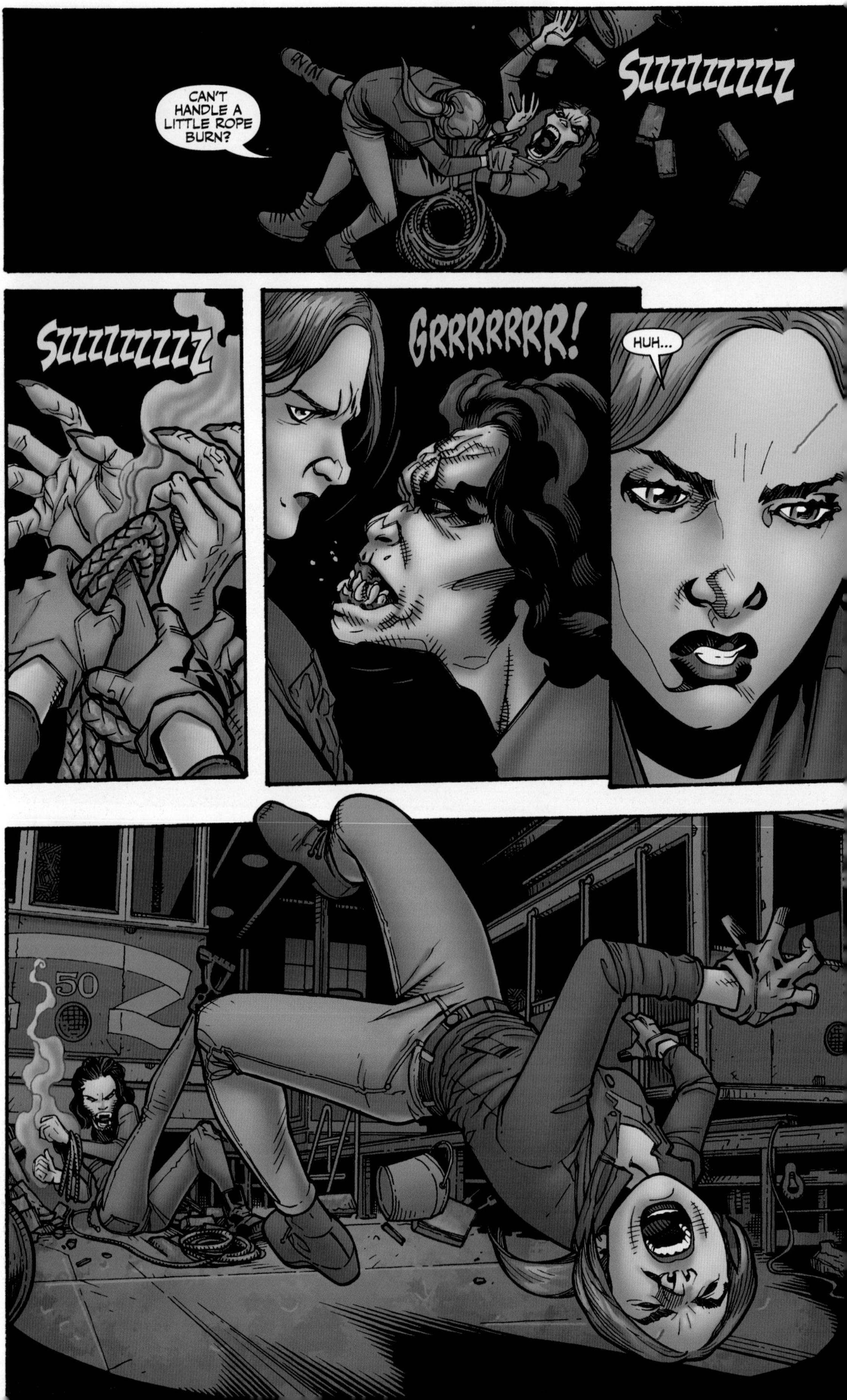
CAN'T HANDLE A LITTLE ROPE BURN?
SZZZZZZZZZ
SZZZZZZZZZ
GRRRRRRR!
HUH...
50

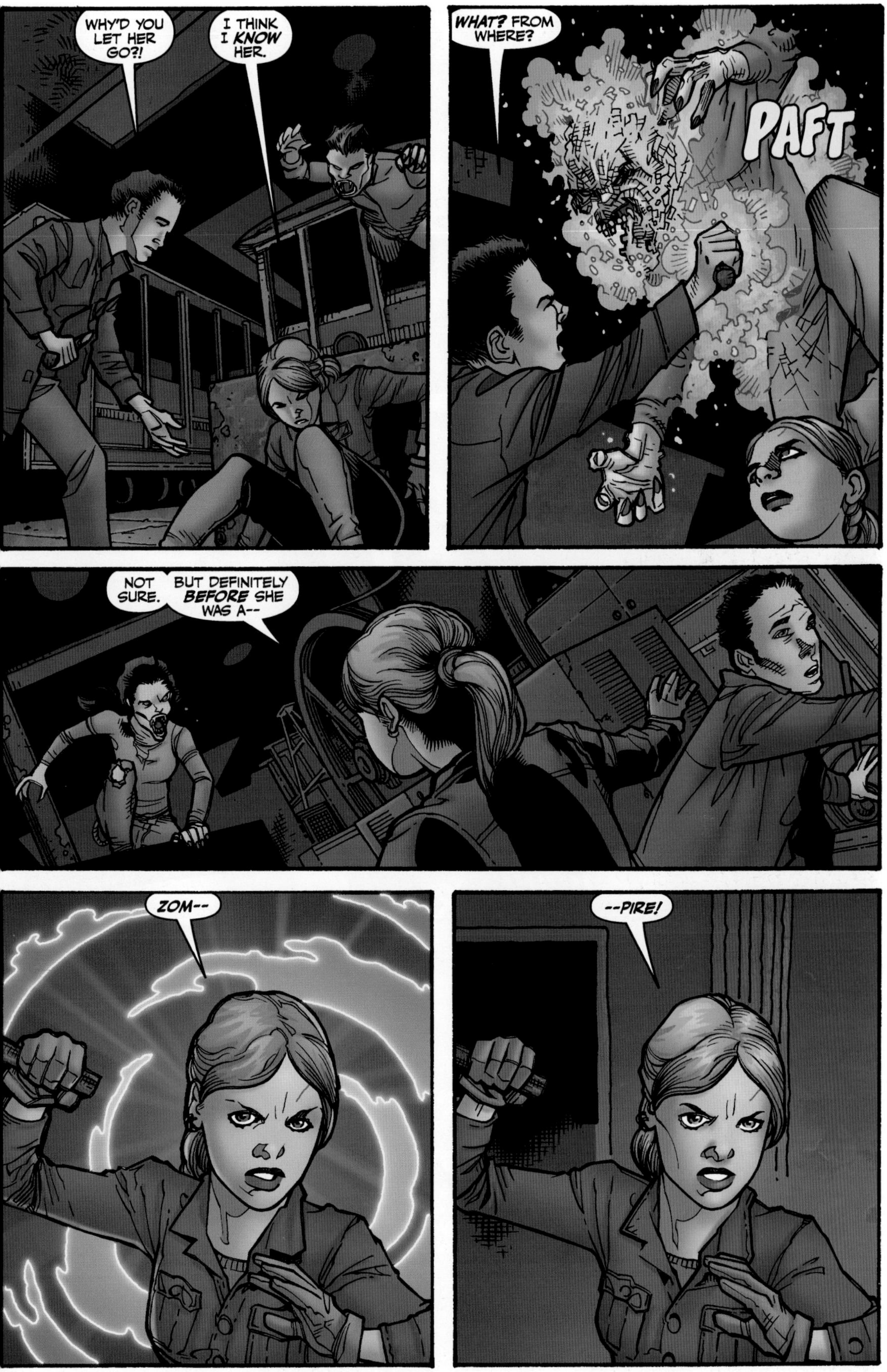
WHY'D YOU LET HER GO?!
I THINK I KNOW HER.
WHAT? FROM WHERE?
PAFT
NOT SURE.
BUT DEFINITELY BEFORE SHE WAS A--
ZOM--
--PIRE!

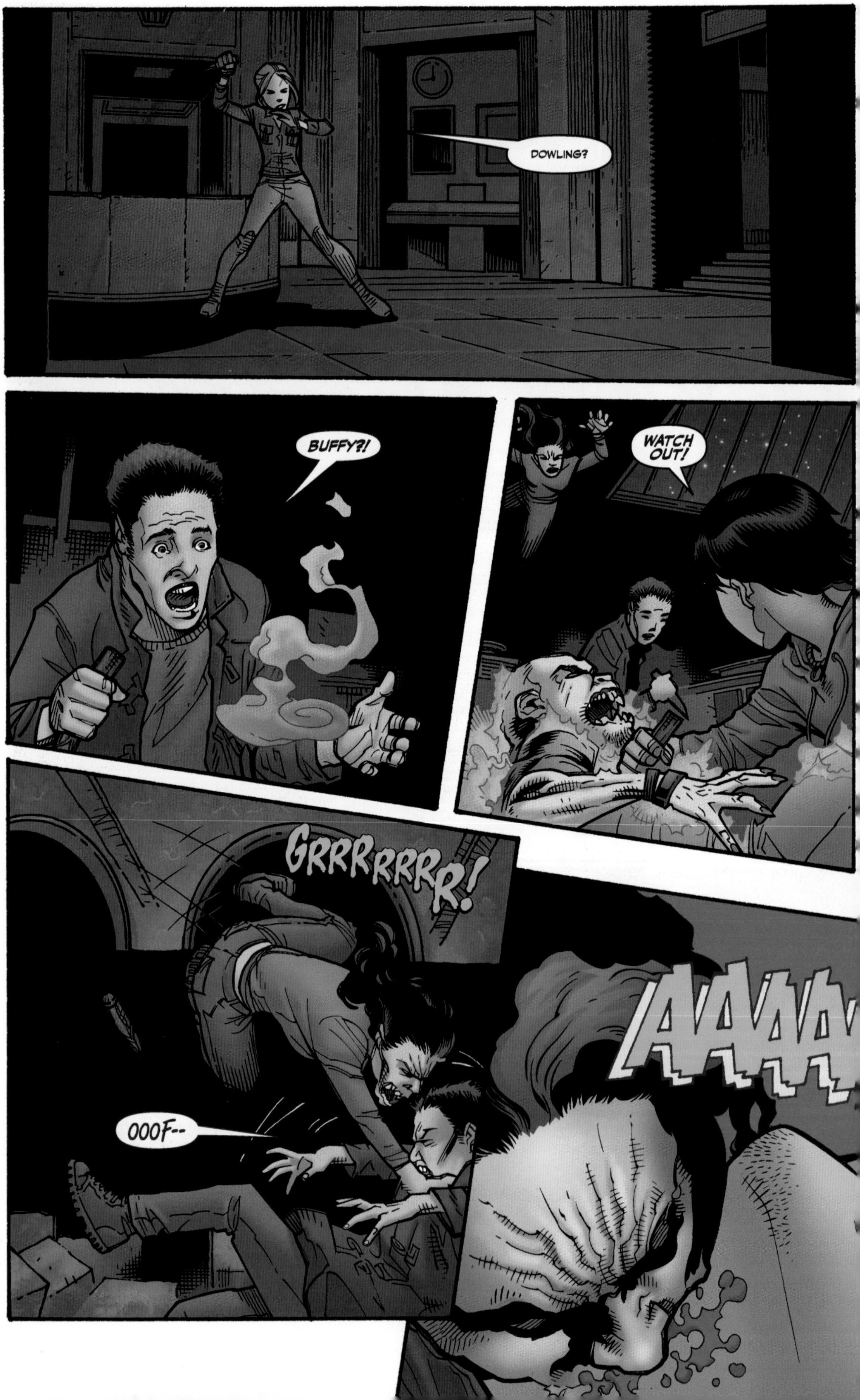
DOWLING?
BUFFY?!
WATCH OUT!
GRRRRRRR!
OOOF--
AAAA

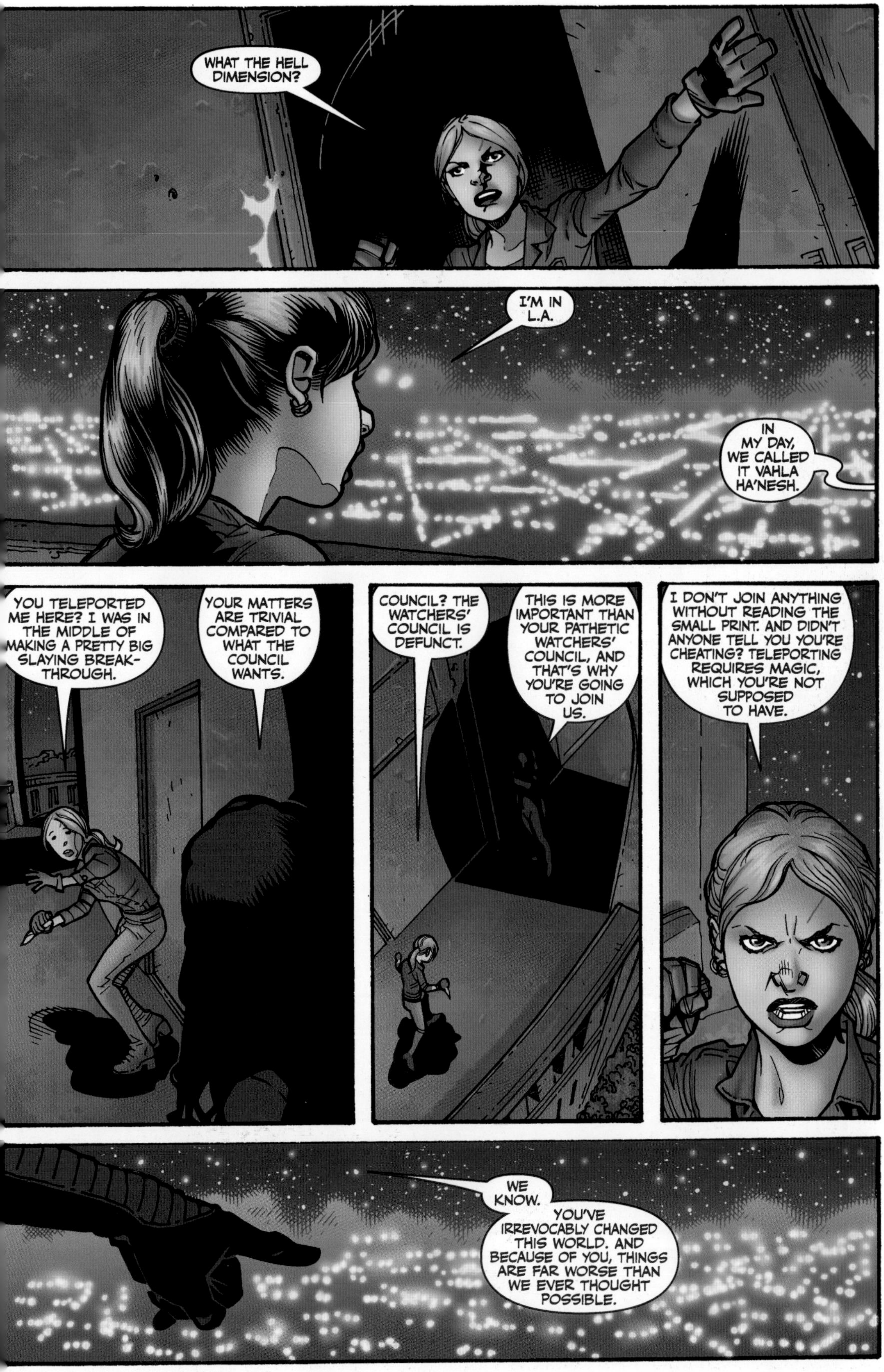
WHAT THE HELL DIMENSION?
I'M IN L.A.
IN MY DAY, WE CALLED IT VAHLA HA'NESH.
YOU TELEPORTED ME HERE? I WAS IN THE MIDDLE OF MAKING A PRETTY BIG SLAYING BREAK-THROUGH.
YOUR MATTERS ARE TRIVIAL COMPARED TO WHAT THE COUNCIL WANTS.
COUNCIL? THE WATCHERS' COUNCIL IS DEFUNCT.
THIS IS MORE IMPORTANT THAN YOUR PATHETIC WATCHERS' COUNCIL, AND THAT'S WHY YOU'RE GOING TO JOIN US.
I DON'T JOIN ANYTHING WITHOUT READING THE SMALL PRINT. AND DIDN'T ANYONE TELL YOU YOU'RE CHEATING? TELEPORTING REQUIRES MAGIC, WHICH YOU'RE NOT SUPPOSED TO HAVE.
WE KNOW.
YOU'VE IRREVOCABLY CHANGED THIS WORLD. AND BECAUSE OF YOU, THINGS ARE FAR WORSE THAN WE EVER THOUGHT POSSIBLE.

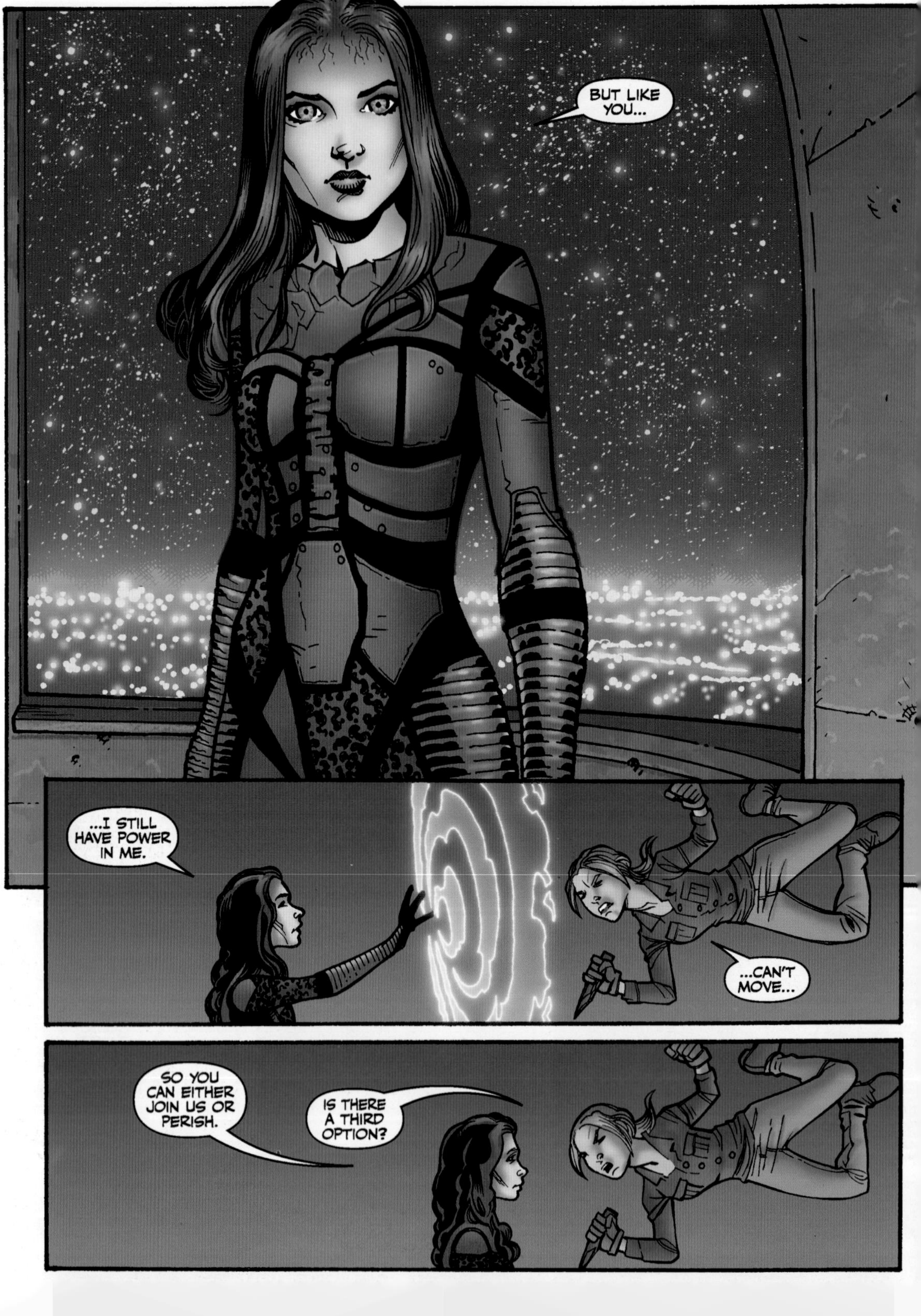
BUT LIKE YOU...
...I STILL HAVE POWER IN ME.
...CAN'T MOVE...
SO YOU CAN EITHER JOIN US OR PERISH.
IS THERE A THIRD OPTION?

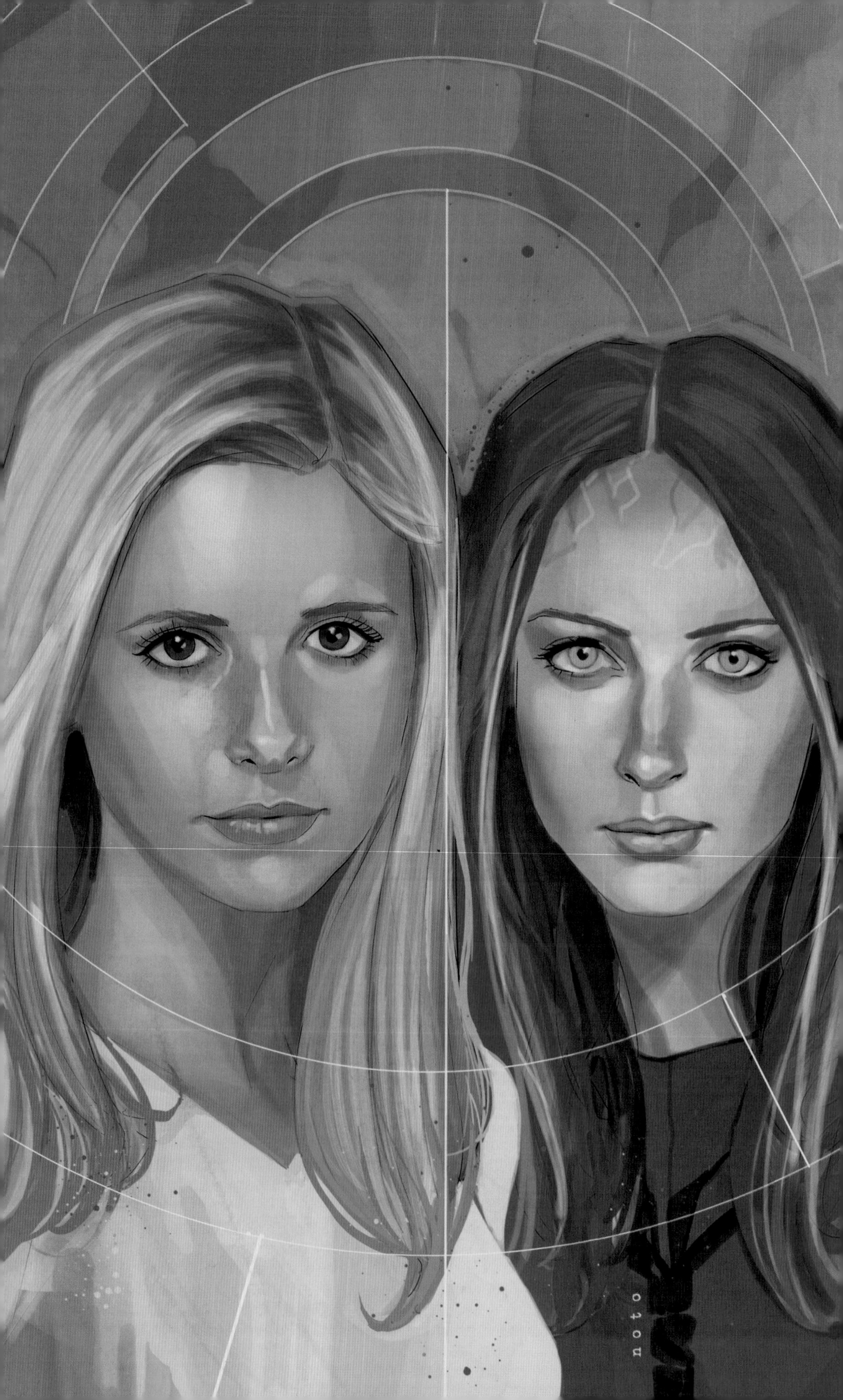
noto

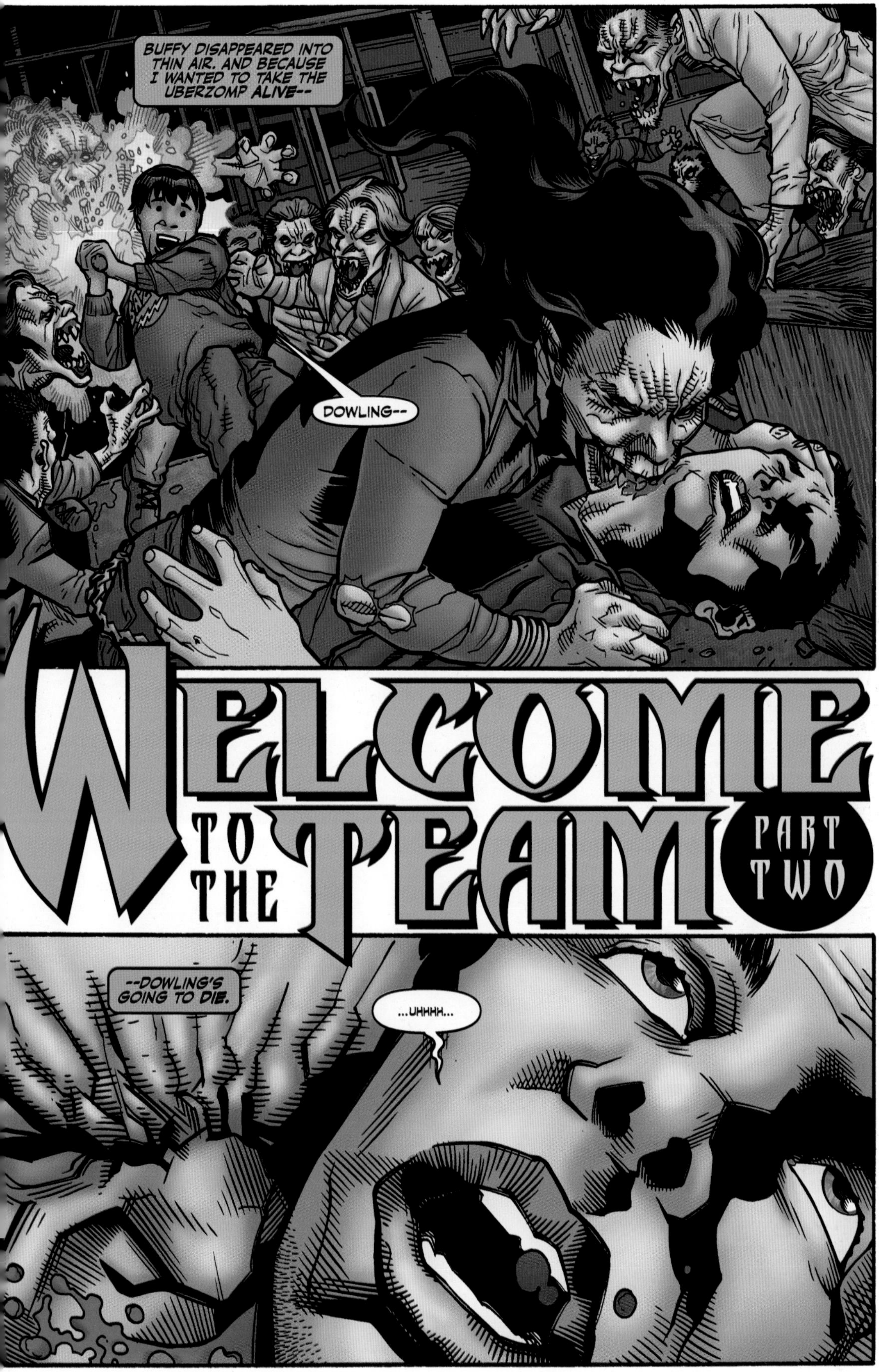
BUFFY DISAPPEARED INTO THIN AIR. AND BECAUSE I WANTED TO TAKE THE UBERZOMP ALIVE--
DOWLING--
WELCOME TO THE TEAM
PART TWO
--DOWLING'S GOING TO DIE.
...UHHHH...

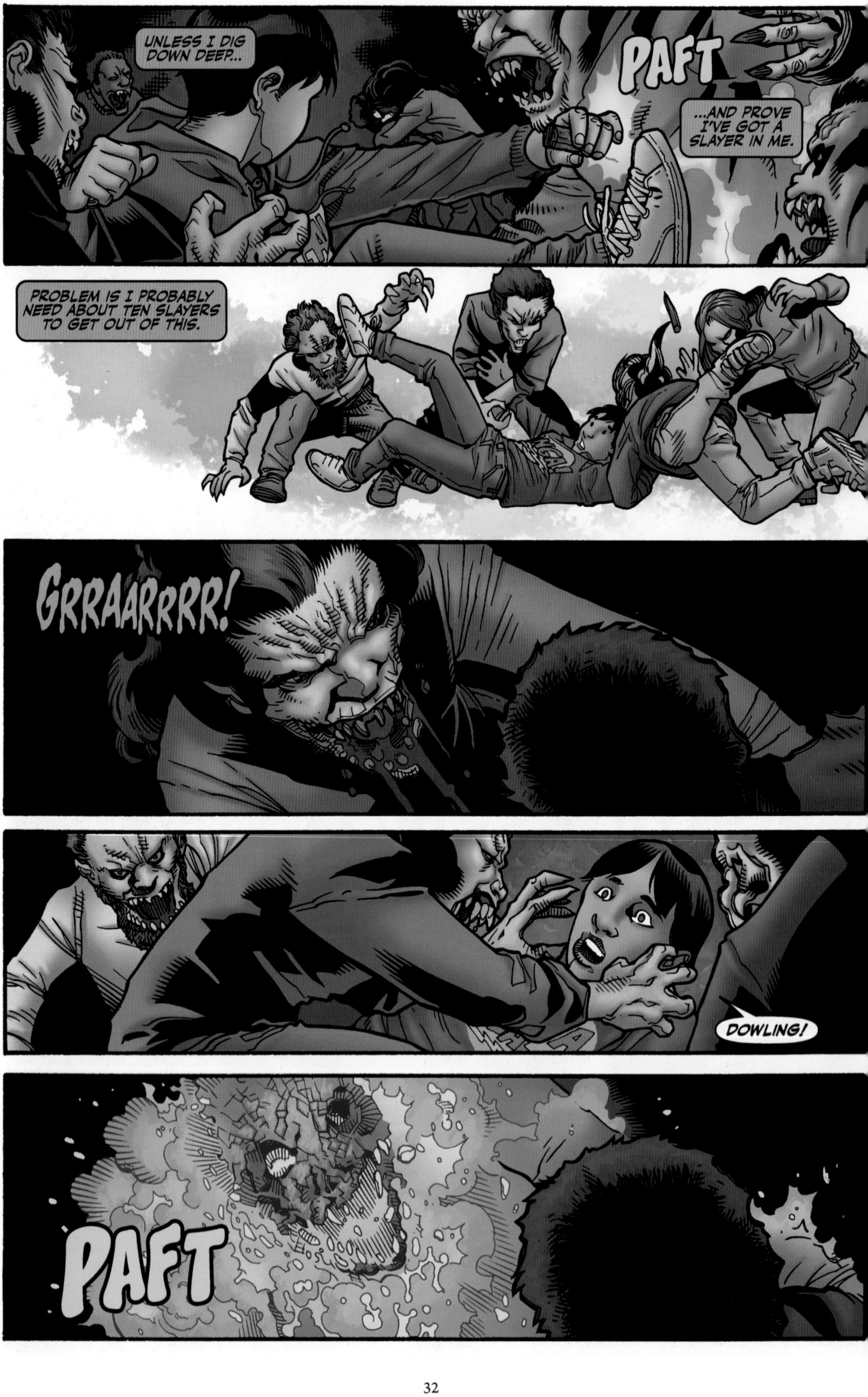

UNLESS I DIG DOWN DEEP...
PAFT
...AND PROVE I'VE GOT A SLAYER IN ME.
PROBLEM IS I PROBABLY NEED ABOUT TEN SLAYERS TO GET OUT OF THIS.
GRRAARRRR!
DOWLING!
PAFT

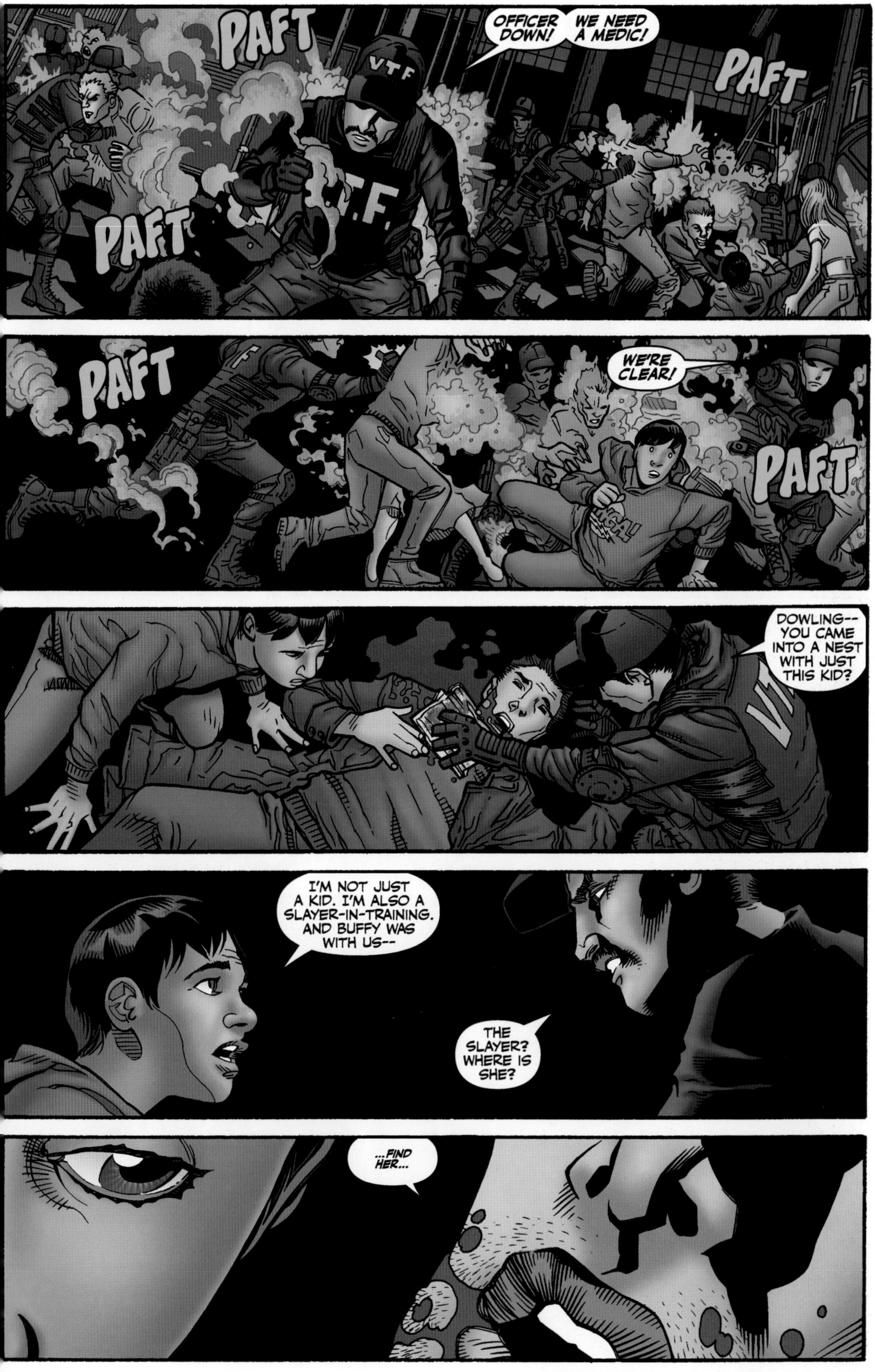
PAFT
OFFICER DOWN!
WE NEED A MEDIC!
PAFT
PAFT
PAFT
WE'RE CLEAR!
PAFT
DOWLING-- YOU CAME INTO A NEST WITH JUST THIS KID?
I'M NOT JUST A KID. I'M ALSO A SLAYER-IN-TRAINING. AND BUFFY WAS WITH US--
THE SLAYER? WHERE IS SHE?
...FIND HER...

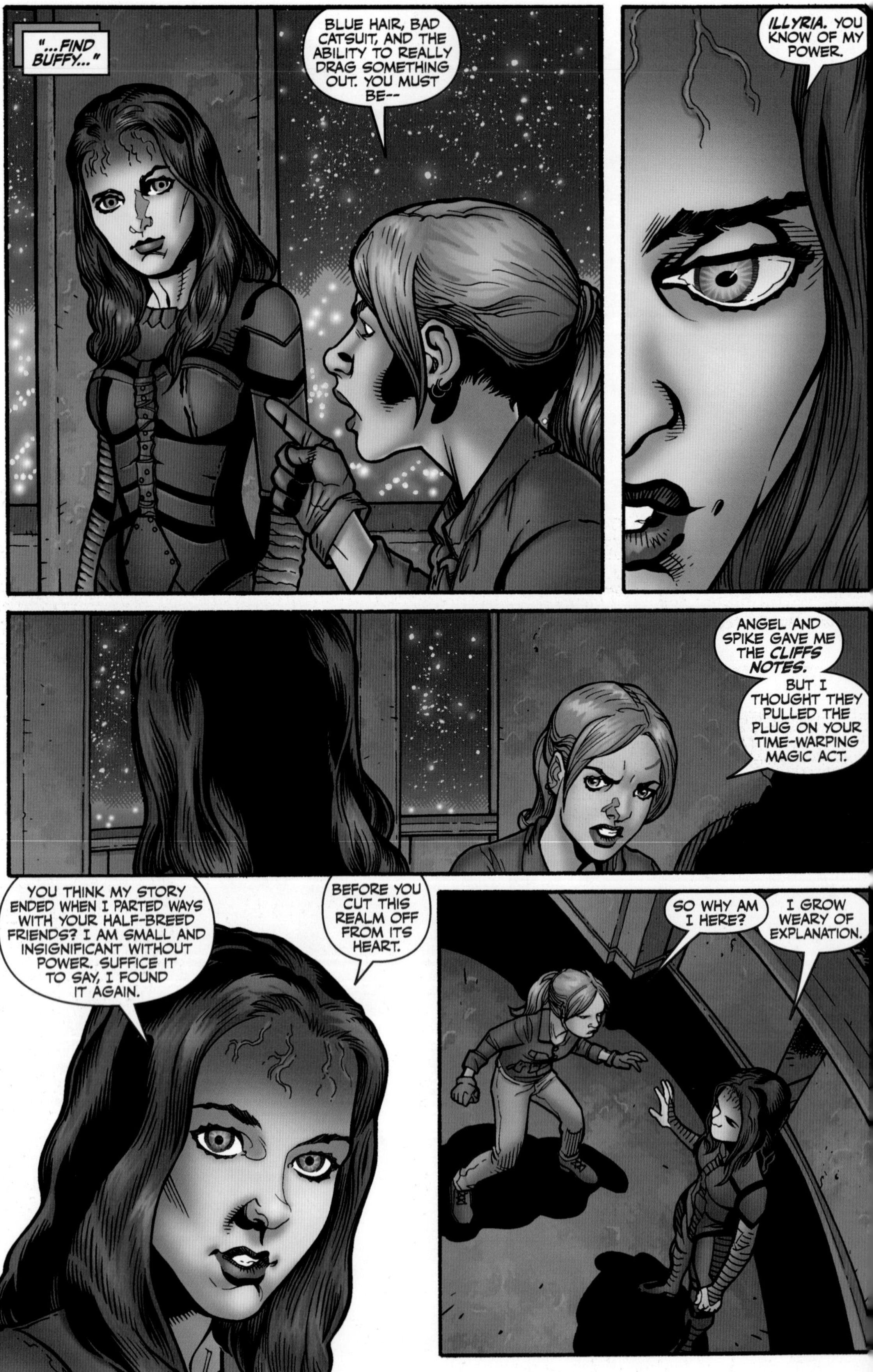
"...FIND BUFFY..."
BLUE HAIR, BAD CATSUIT, AND THE ABILITY TO REALLY DRAG SOMETHING OUT. YOU MUST BE--
ILLYRIA. YOU KNOW OF MY POWER.
ANGEL AND SPIKE GAVE ME THE CLIFFS NOTES.
BUT I THOUGHT THEY PULLED THE PLUG ON YOUR TIME-WARPING MAGIC ACT.
YOU THINK MY STORY ENDED WHEN I PARTED WAYS WITH YOUR HALF-BREED FRIENDS? I AM SMALL AND INSIGNIFICANT WITHOUT POWER. SUFFICE IT TO SAY, I FOUND IT AGAIN.
BEFORE YOU CUT THIS REALM OFF FROM ITS HEART.
SO WHY AM I HERE?
I GROW WEARY OF EXPLANATION.

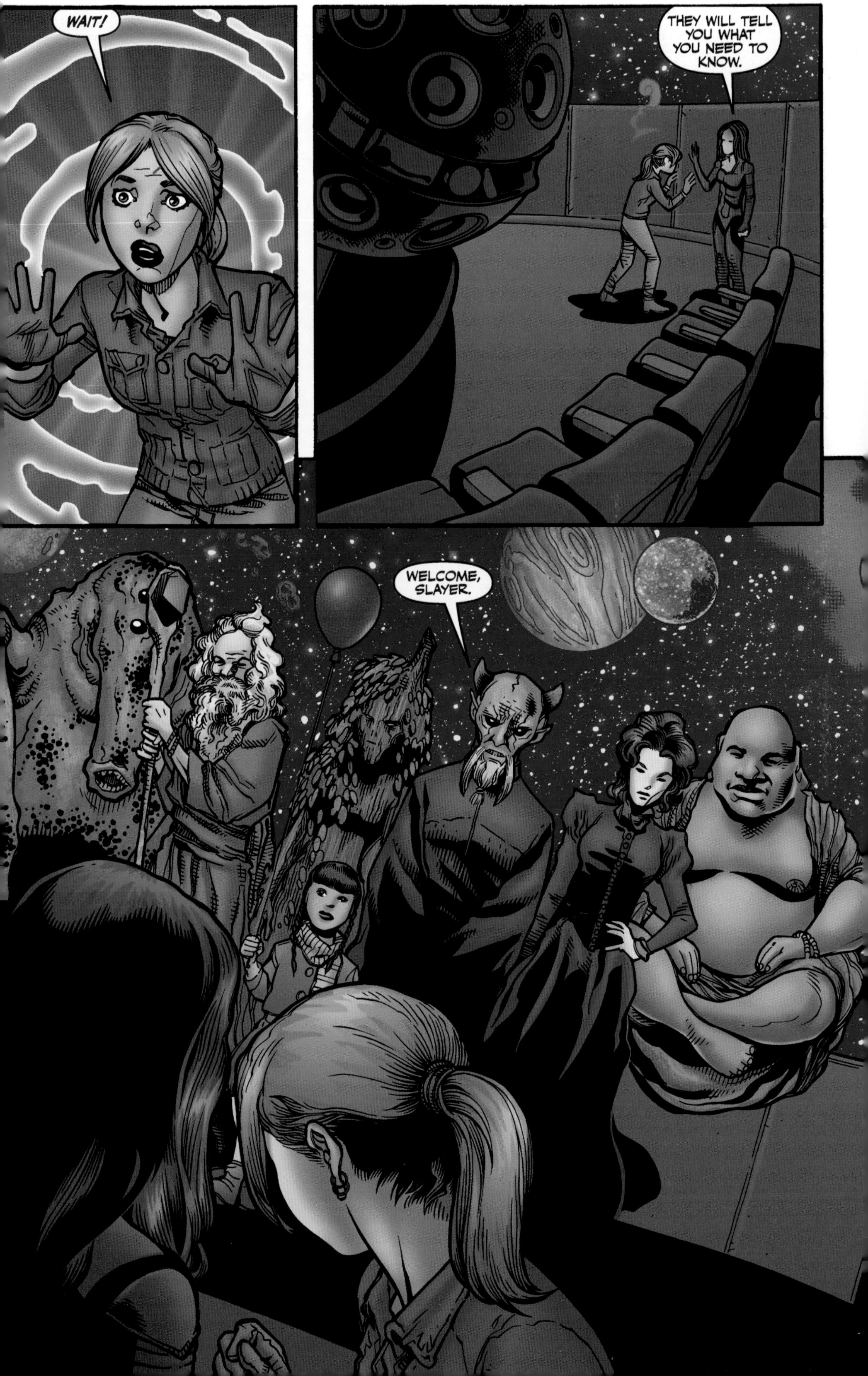
WAIT!
THEY WILL TELL YOU WHAT YOU NEED TO KNOW.
WELCOME, SLAYER.

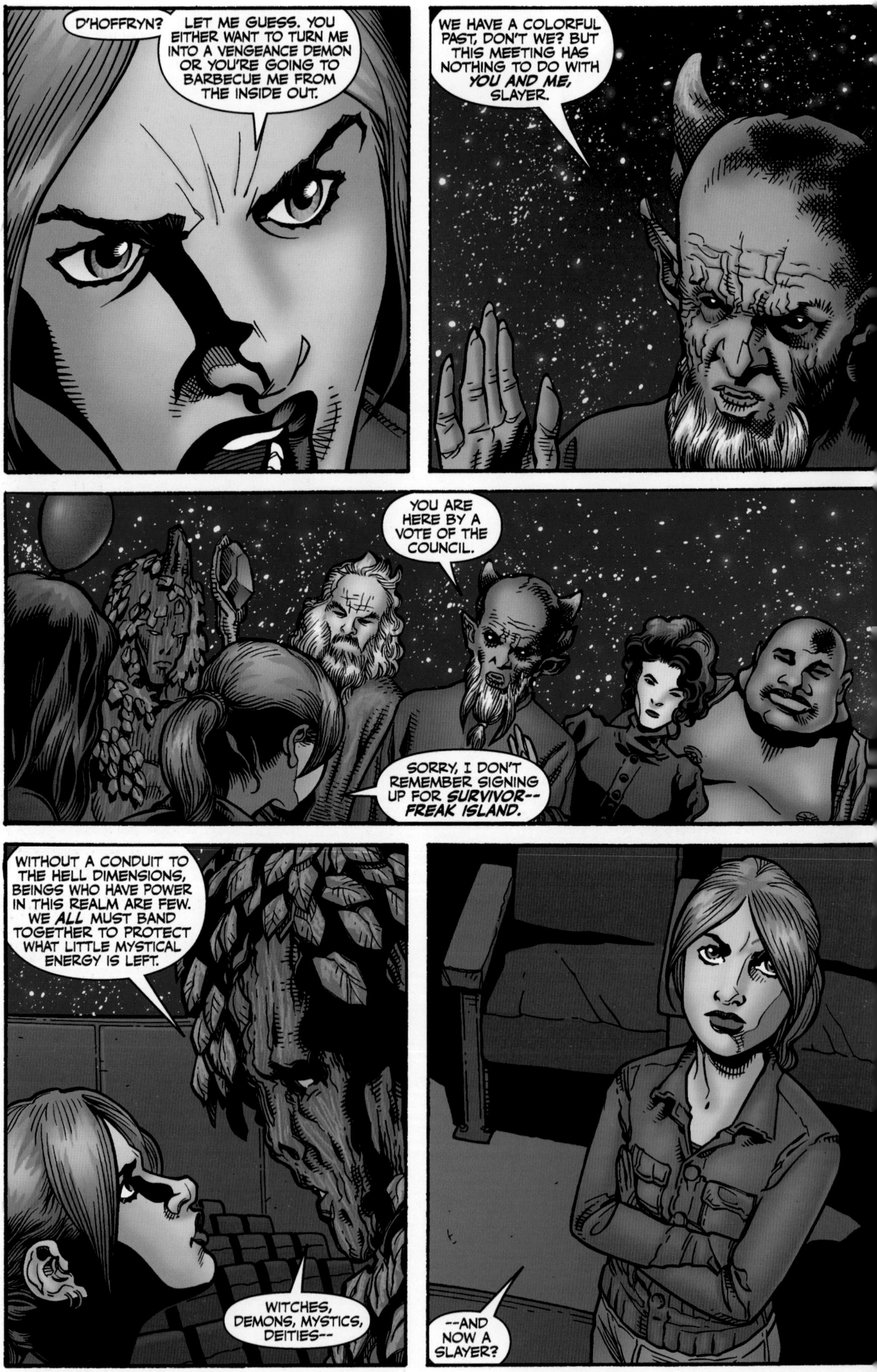
D'HOFFRYN?
LET ME GUESS. YOU EITHER WANT TO TURN ME INTO A VENGEANCE DEMON OR YOU'RE GOING TO BARBECUE ME FROM THE INSIDE OUT.
WE HAVE A COLORFUL PAST, DON'T WE? BUT THIS MEETING HAS NOTHING TO DO WITH *YOU AND ME,* SLAYER.
YOU ARE HERE BY A VOTE OF THE COUNCIL.
SORRY, I DON'T REMEMBER SIGNING UP FOR *SURVIVOR--FREAK ISLAND.*
WITHOUT A CONDUIT TO THE HELL DIMENSIONS, BEINGS WHO HAVE POWER IN THIS REALM ARE FEW. WE *ALL* MUST BAND TOGETHER TO PROTECT WHAT LITTLE MYSTICAL ENERGY IS LEFT.
WITCHES, DEMONS, MYSTICS, DEITIES--
--AND NOW A SLAYER?

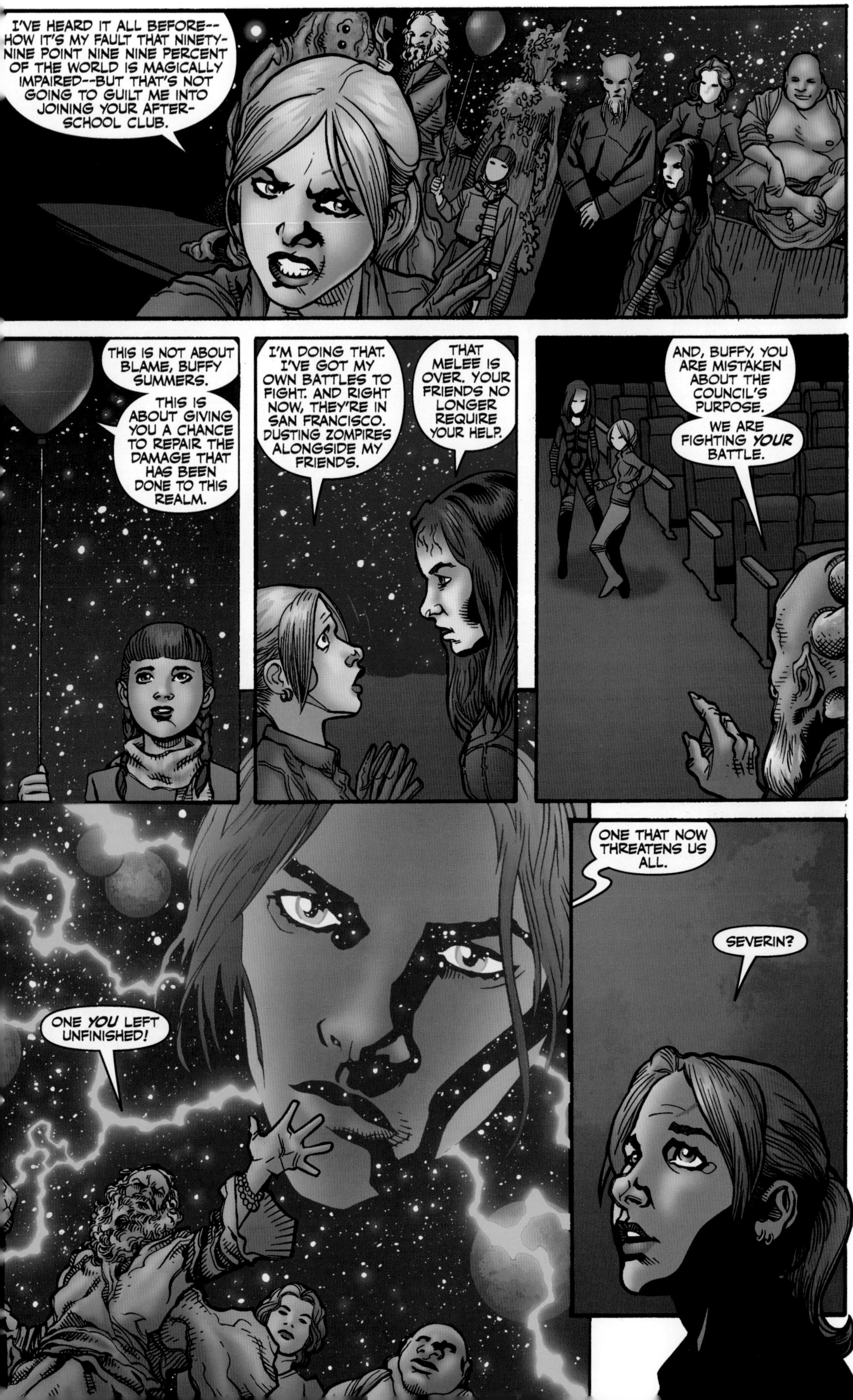
I'VE HEARD IT ALL BEFORE--HOW IT'S MY FAULT THAT NINETY-NINE POINT NINE NINE PERCENT OF THE WORLD IS MAGICALLY IMPAIRED--BUT THAT'S NOT GOING TO GUILT ME INTO JOINING YOUR AFTER-SCHOOL CLUB.
THIS IS NOT ABOUT BLAME, BUFFY SUMMERS.
THIS IS ABOUT GIVING YOU A CHANCE TO REPAIR THE DAMAGE THAT HAS BEEN DONE TO THIS REALM.
I'M DOING THAT. I'VE GOT MY OWN BATTLES TO FIGHT. AND RIGHT NOW, THEY'RE IN SAN FRANCISCO. DUSTING ZOMPIRES ALONGSIDE MY FRIENDS.
THAT MELEE IS OVER. YOUR FRIENDS NO LONGER REQUIRE YOUR HELP.
AND, BUFFY, YOU ARE MISTAKEN ABOUT THE COUNCIL'S PURPOSE.
WE ARE FIGHTING YOUR BATTLE.
ONE THAT NOW THREATENS US ALL.
ONE YOU LEFT UNFINISHED!
SEVERIN?

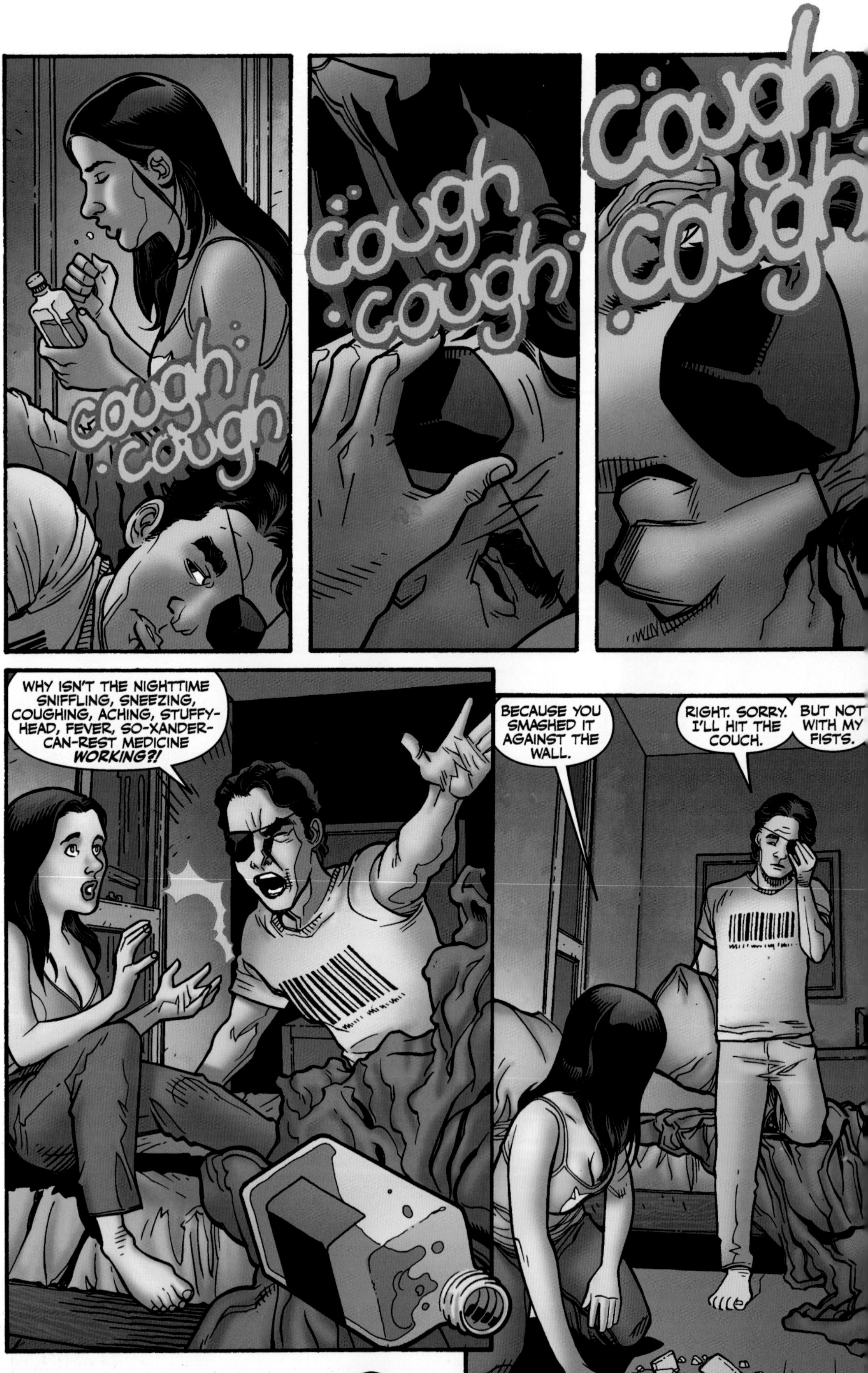

cough cough
cough cough
cough cough
WHY ISN'T THE NIGHTTIME SNIFFLING, SNEEZING, COUGHING, ACHING, STUFFY-HEAD, FEVER, SO-XANDER-CAN-REST MEDICINE *WORKING?!*
BECAUSE YOU SMASHED IT AGAINST THE WALL.
RIGHT. SORRY. I'LL HIT THE COUCH.
BUT NOT WITH MY FISTS.

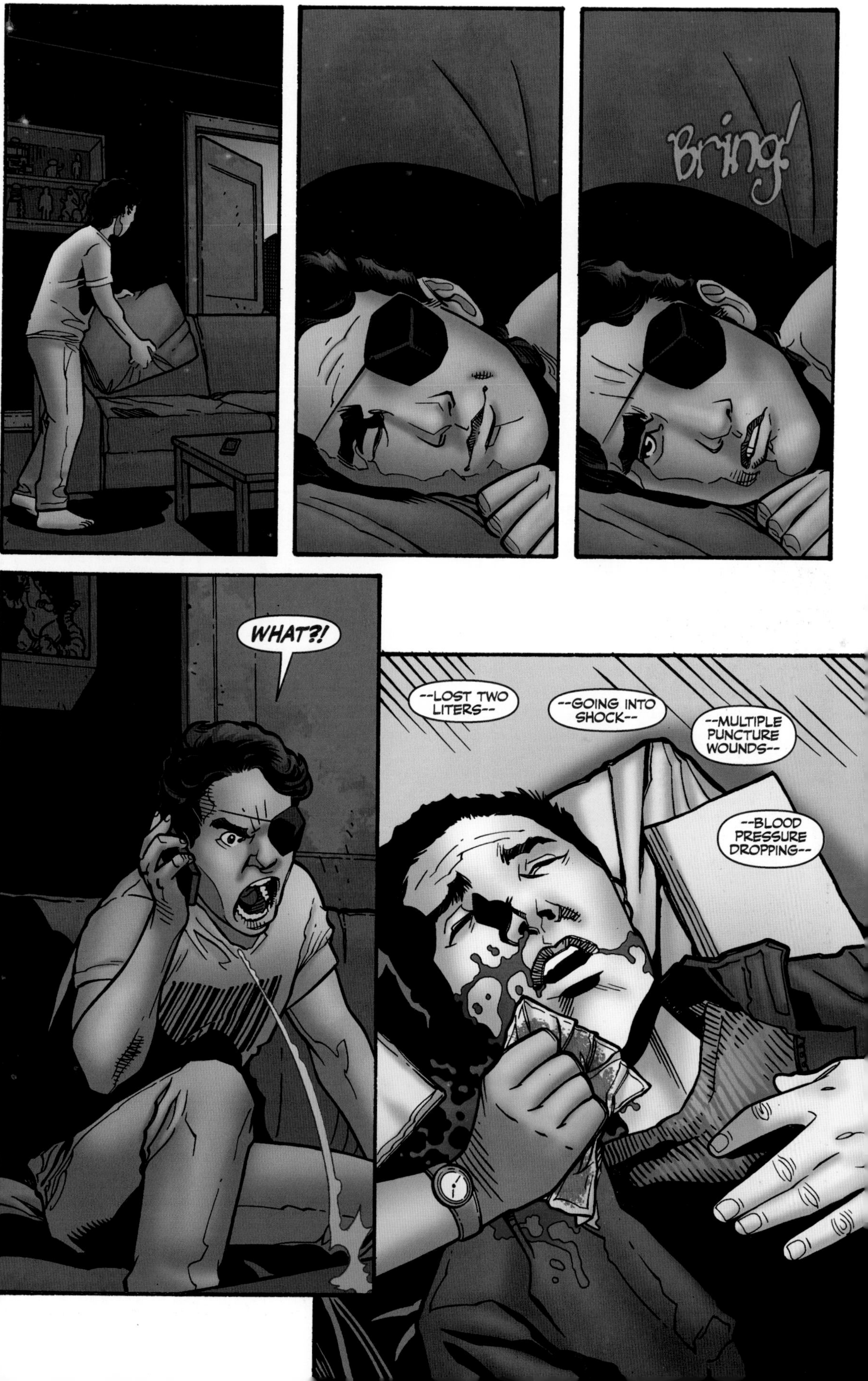

Bring!
WHAT?!
--LOST TWO LITERS--
--GOING INTO SHOCK--
--MULTIPLE PUNCTURE WOUNDS--
--BLOOD PRESSURE DROPPING--

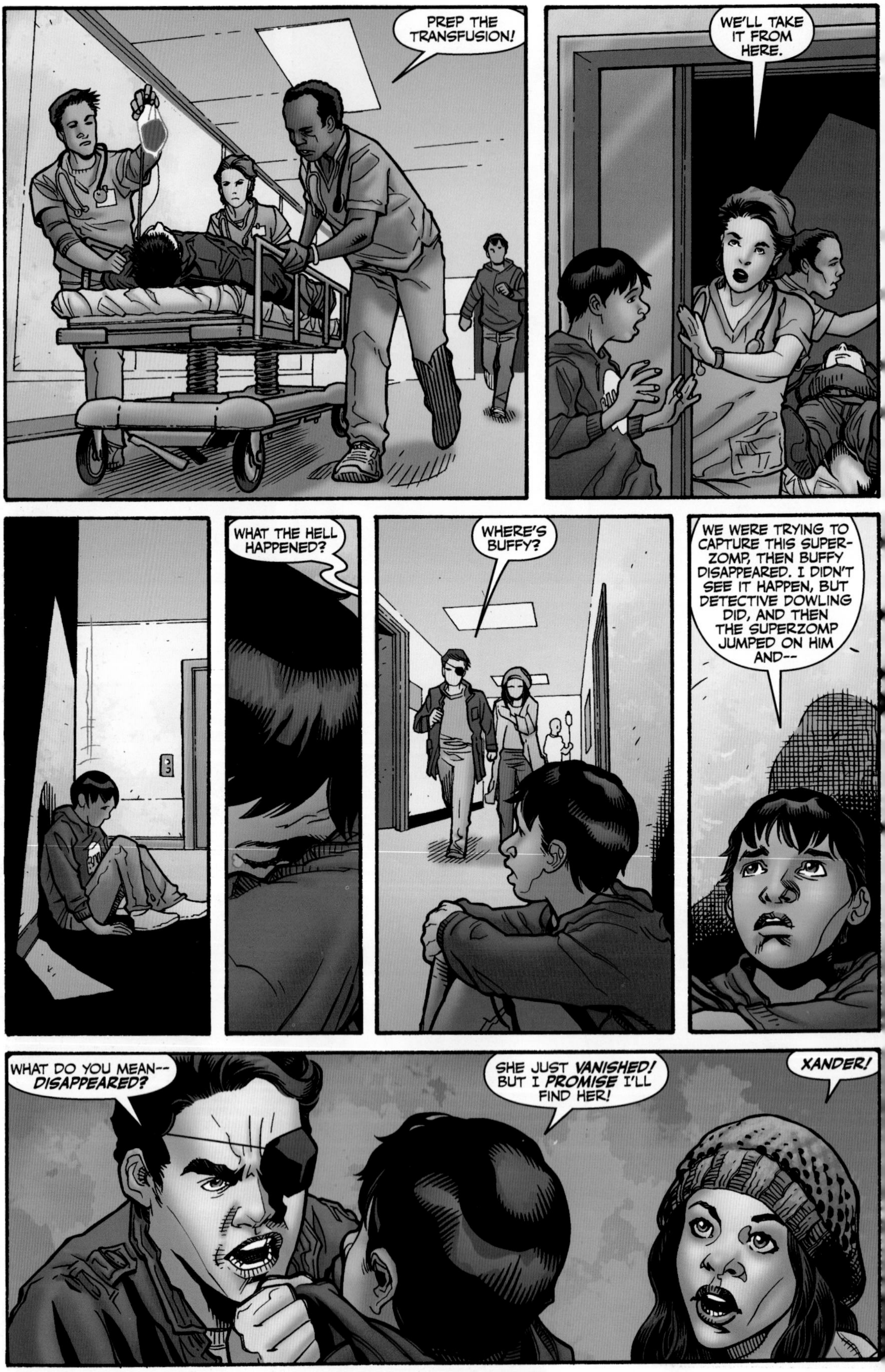
PREP THE TRANSFUSION!
WE'LL TAKE IT FROM HERE.
WHAT THE HELL HAPPENED?
WHERE'S BUFFY?
WE WERE TRYING TO CAPTURE THIS SUPER-ZOMP, THEN BUFFY DISAPPEARED. I DIDN'T SEE IT HAPPEN, BUT DETECTIVE DOWLING DID, AND THEN THE SUPERZOMP JUMPED ON HIM AND--
WHAT DO YOU MEAN-- DISAPPEARED?
SHE JUST VANISHED! BUT I PROMISE I'LL FIND HER!
XANDER!

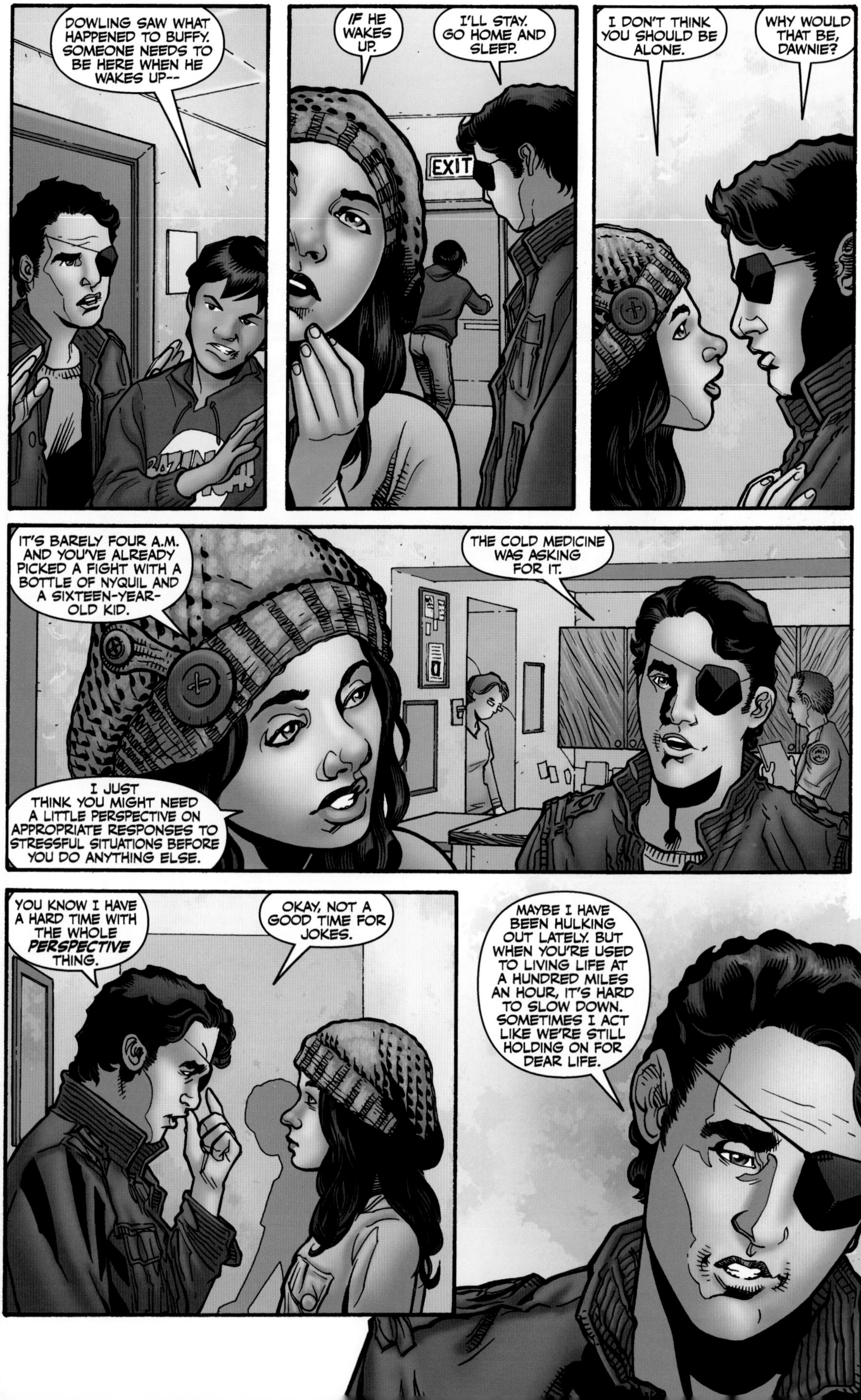

DOWLING SAW WHAT HAPPENED TO BUFFY. SOMEONE NEEDS TO BE HERE WHEN HE WAKES UP--
IF HE WAKES UP.
I'LL STAY. GO HOME AND SLEEP.
EXIT
I DON'T THINK YOU SHOULD BE ALONE.
WHY WOULD THAT BE, DAWNIE?
IT'S BARELY FOUR A.M. AND YOU'VE ALREADY PICKED A FIGHT WITH A BOTTLE OF NYQUIL AND A SIXTEEN-YEAR-OLD KID.
THE COLD MEDICINE WAS ASKING FOR IT.
I JUST THINK YOU MIGHT NEED A LITTLE PERSPECTIVE ON APPROPRIATE RESPONSES TO STRESSFUL SITUATIONS BEFORE YOU DO ANYTHING ELSE.
YOU KNOW I HAVE A HARD TIME WITH THE WHOLE *PERSPECTIVE* THING.
OKAY, NOT A GOOD TIME FOR JOKES.
MAYBE I HAVE BEEN HULKING OUT LATELY. BUT WHEN YOU'RE USED TO LIVING LIFE AT A HUNDRED MILES AN HOUR, IT'S HARD TO SLOW DOWN. SOMETIMES I ACT LIKE WE'RE STILL HOLDING ON FOR DEAR LIFE.

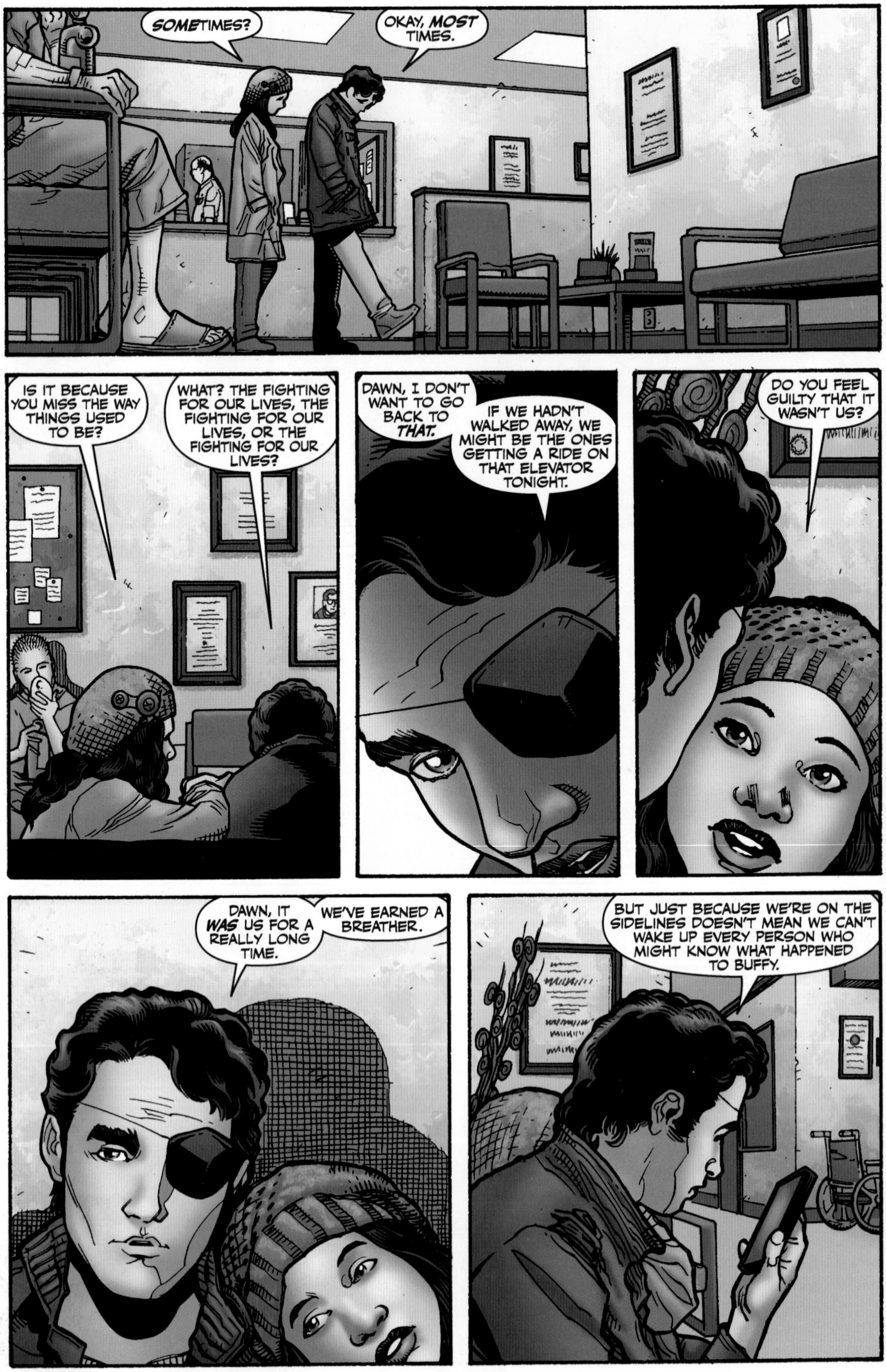
SOMETIMES?
OKAY, MOST TIMES.
IS IT BECAUSE YOU MISS THE WAY THINGS USED TO BE?
WHAT? THE FIGHTING FOR OUR LIVES, THE FIGHTING FOR OUR LIVES, OR THE FIGHTING FOR OUR LIVES?
DAWN, I DON'T WANT TO GO BACK TO THAT.
IF WE HADN'T WALKED AWAY, WE MIGHT BE THE ONES GETTING A RIDE ON THAT ELEVATOR TONIGHT.
DO YOU FEEL GUILTY THAT IT WASN'T US?
DAWN, IT WAS US FOR A REALLY LONG TIME.
WE'VE EARNED A BREATHER.
BUT JUST BECAUSE WE'RE ON THE SIDELINES DOESN'T MEAN WE CAN'T WAKE UP EVERY PERSON WHO MIGHT KNOW WHAT HAPPENED TO BUFFY.

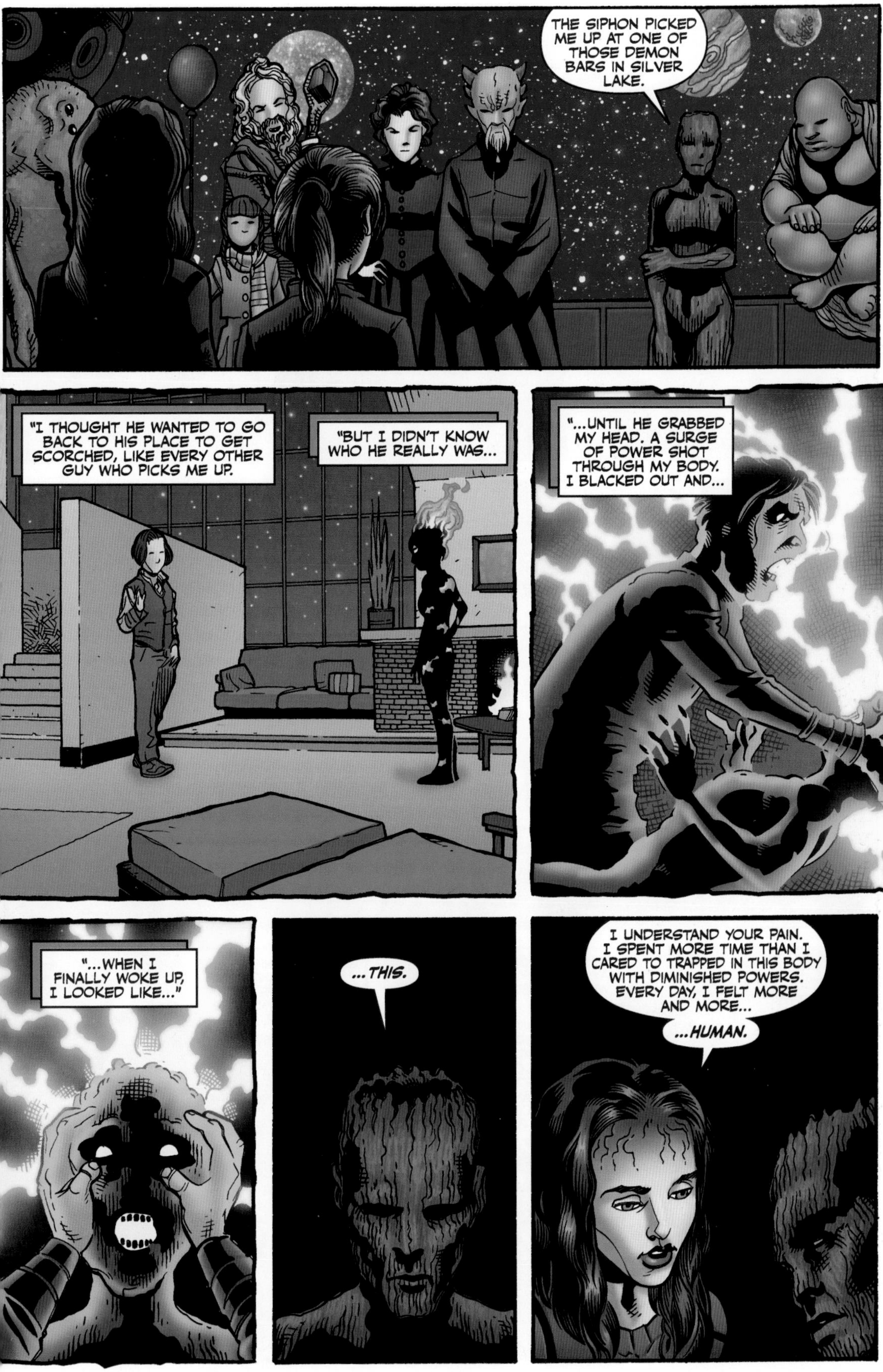

THE SIPHON PICKED ME UP AT ONE OF THOSE DEMON BARS IN SILVER LAKE.
"I THOUGHT HE WANTED TO GO BACK TO HIS PLACE TO GET SCORCHED, LIKE EVERY OTHER GUY WHO PICKS ME UP.
"BUT I DIDN'T KNOW WHO HE REALLY WAS...
"...UNTIL HE GRABBED MY HEAD. A SURGE OF POWER SHOT THROUGH MY BODY. I BLACKED OUT AND...
"...WHEN I FINALLY WOKE UP, I LOOKED LIKE..."
...THIS.
I UNDERSTAND YOUR PAIN. I SPENT MORE TIME THAN I CARED TO TRAPPED IN THIS BODY WITH DIMINISHED POWERS. EVERY DAY, I FELT MORE AND MORE...
...HUMAN.

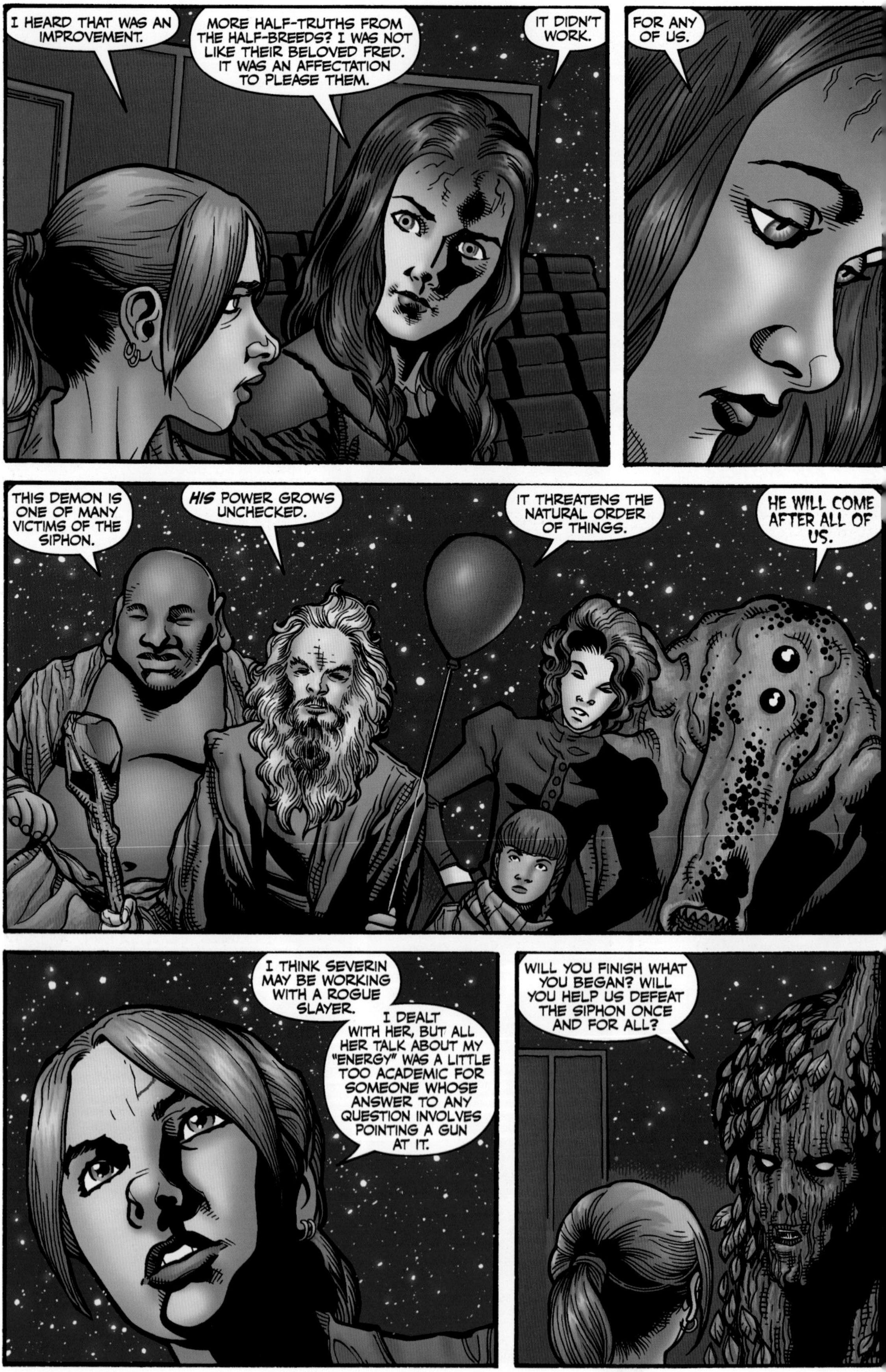
I HEARD THAT WAS AN IMPROVEMENT.
MORE HALF-TRUTHS FROM THE HALF-BREEDS? I WAS NOT LIKE THEIR BELOVED FRED. IT WAS AN AFFECTATION TO PLEASE THEM.
IT DIDN'T WORK.
FOR ANY OF US.
THIS DEMON IS ONE OF MANY VICTIMS OF THE SIPHON.
HIS POWER GROWS UNCHECKED.
IT THREATENS THE NATURAL ORDER OF THINGS.
HE WILL COME AFTER ALL OF US.
I THINK SEVERIN MAY BE WORKING WITH A ROGUE SLAYER.
I DEALT WITH HER, BUT ALL HER TALK ABOUT MY "ENERGY" WAS A LITTLE TOO ACADEMIC FOR SOMEONE WHOSE ANSWER TO ANY QUESTION INVOLVES POINTING A GUN AT IT.
WILL YOU FINISH WHAT YOU BEGAN? WILL YOU HELP US DEFEAT THE SIPHON ONCE AND FOR ALL?

USUALLY I'M THE ONE SNUFFING OUT MATCHSTICK DEMONS.

NO OFFENSE.

NONE TAKEN.

BUT SEVERIN'S CHARGING UP FOR A REASON.

WE NEED TO FIND OUT WHY.

I'M IN.

"I DON'T THINK I BELONG ON THE TEAM ANYMORE."

KNOCK IT OFF, BILLY.

BUFFY ASKED YOU TO BE A PART OF HER SQUAD BECAUSE SHE THINKS YOU CAN HANDLE IT.

BEFORE SHE DISAPPEARED. BEFORE I LET DOWLING GET MAULED BY A SUPERZOMP.

HOW MANY ZOMPIRES DID YOU TAKE OUT TRYING TO SAVE HIM?

I DON'T KNOW, DEVON. THREE OR FOUR.

THAT'S THREE OR FOUR WHO WON'T BE FEASTING ON THE FINE PEOPLE OF SAN FRANCISCO TONIGHT.

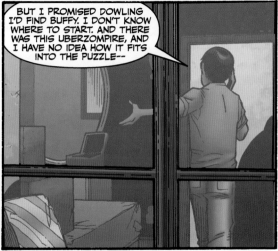

BUT I PROMISED DOWLING I'D FIND BUFFY. I DON'T KNOW WHERE TO START. AND THERE WAS THIS UBERZOMPIRE, AND I HAVE NO IDEA HOW IT FITS INTO THE PUZZLE--

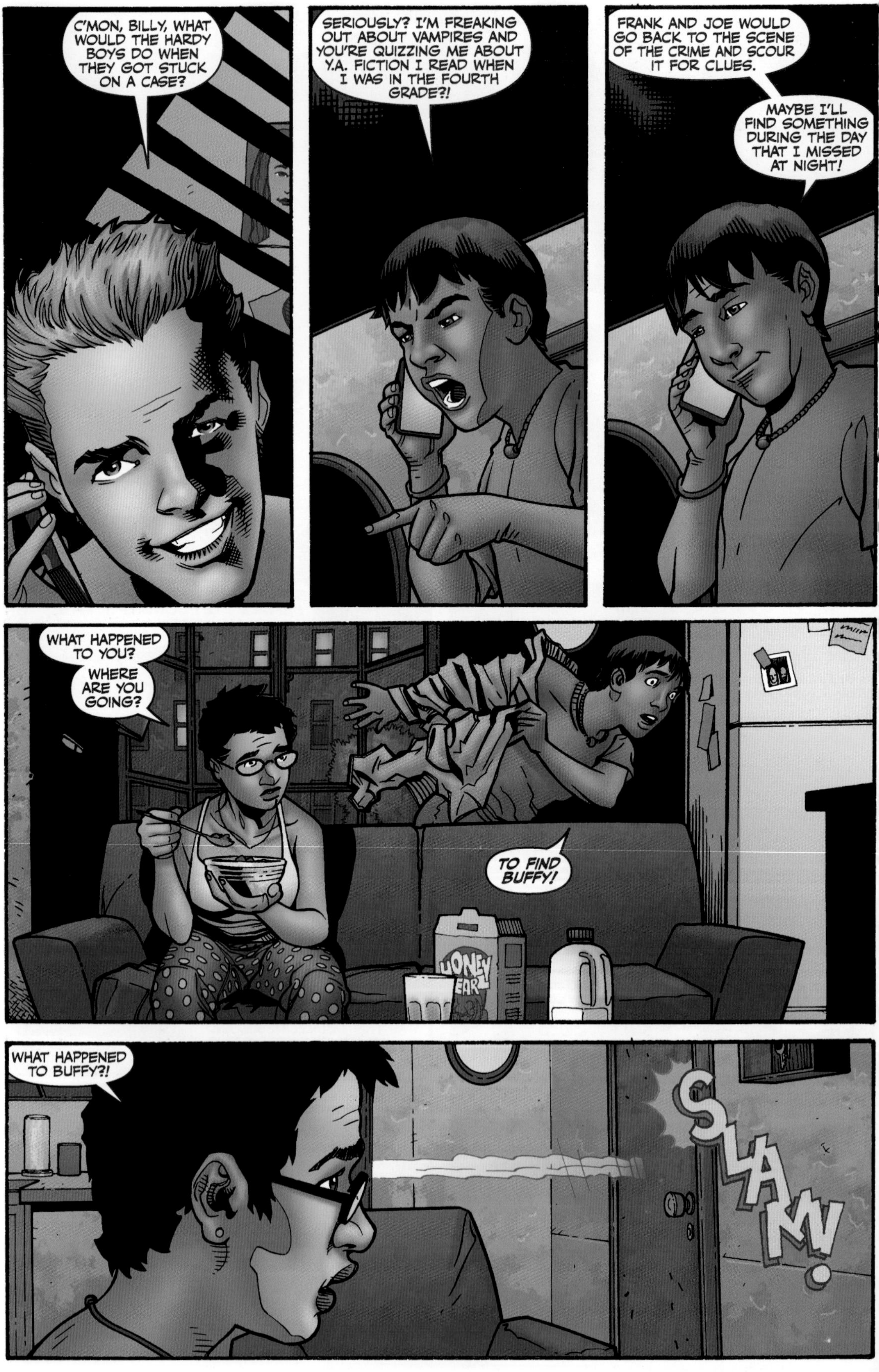
C'MON, BILLY, WHAT WOULD THE HARDY BOYS DO WHEN THEY GOT STUCK ON A CASE?
SERIOUSLY? I'M FREAKING OUT ABOUT VAMPIRES AND YOU'RE QUIZZING ME ABOUT Y.A. FICTION I READ WHEN I WAS IN THE FOURTH GRADE?!
FRANK AND JOE WOULD GO BACK TO THE SCENE OF THE CRIME AND SCOUR IT FOR CLUES.
MAYBE I'LL FIND SOMETHING DURING THE DAY THAT I MISSED AT NIGHT!
WHAT HAPPENED TO YOU? WHERE ARE YOU GOING?
TO FIND BUFFY!
HONEY BEAR
WHAT HAPPENED TO BUFFY?!
SLAM!

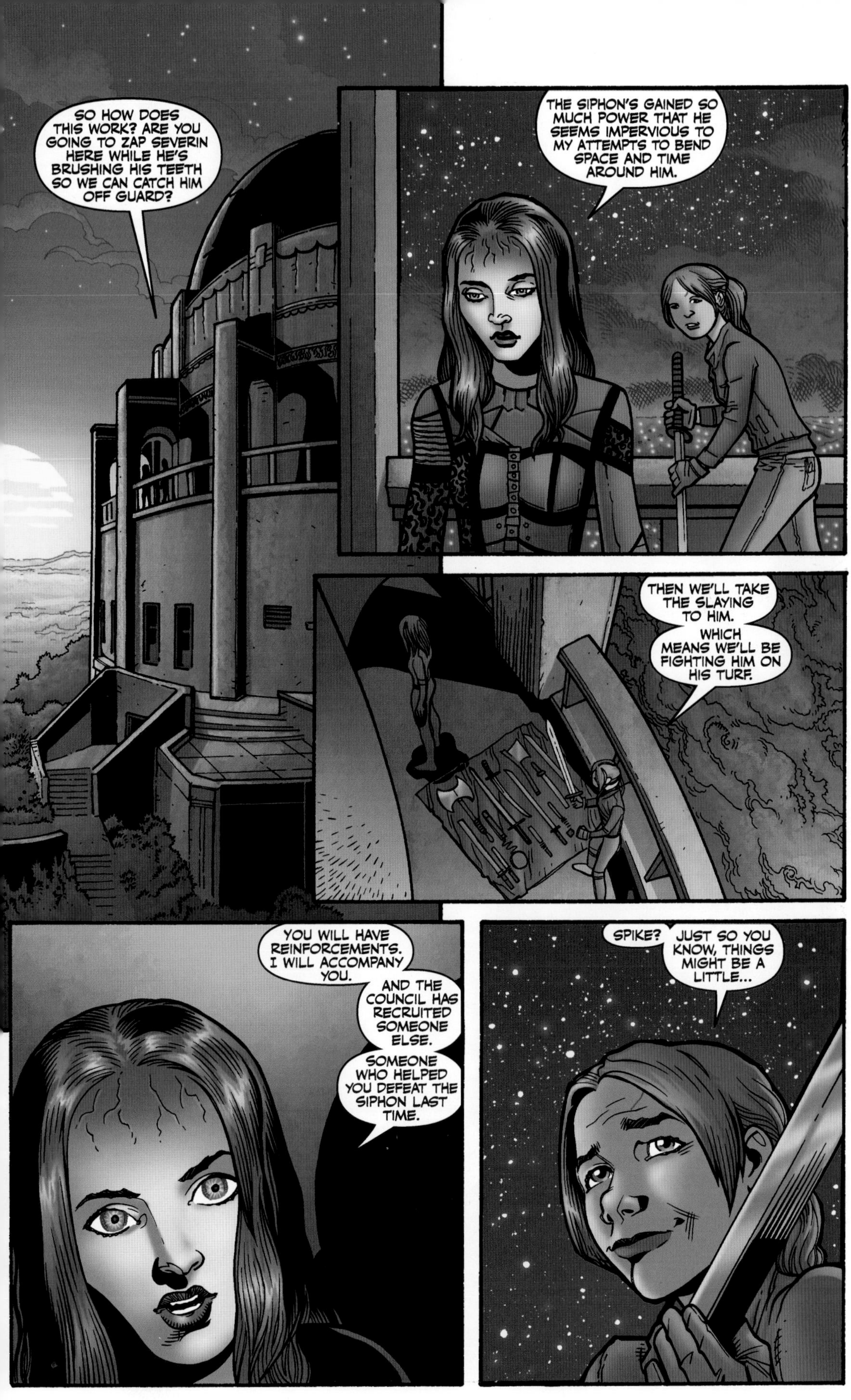
SO HOW DOES THIS WORK? ARE YOU GOING TO ZAP SEVERIN HERE WHILE HE'S BRUSHING HIS TEETH SO WE CAN CATCH HIM OFF GUARD?
THE SIPHON'S GAINED SO MUCH POWER THAT HE SEEMS IMPERVIOUS TO MY ATTEMPTS TO BEND SPACE AND TIME AROUND HIM.
THEN WE'LL TAKE THE SLAYING TO HIM.
WHICH MEANS WE'LL BE FIGHTING HIM ON HIS TURF.
YOU WILL HAVE REINFORCEMENTS. I WILL ACCOMPANY YOU.
AND THE COUNCIL HAS RECRUITED SOMEONE ELSE.
SOMEONE WHO HELPED YOU DEFEAT THE SIPHON LAST TIME.
SPIKE?
JUST SO YOU KNOW, THINGS MIGHT BE A LITTLE...

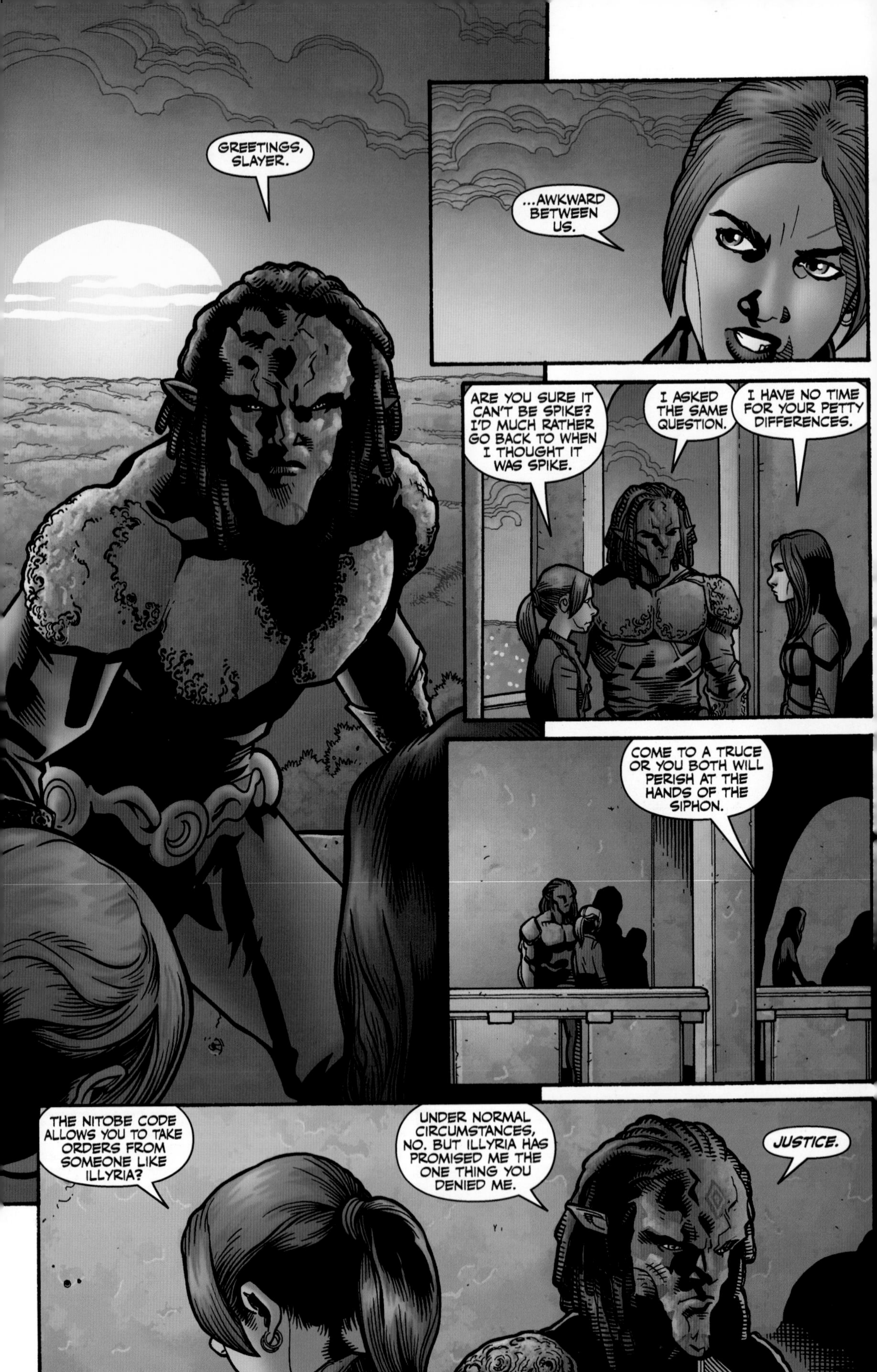
GREETINGS, SLAYER.
...AWKWARD BETWEEN US.
ARE YOU SURE IT CAN'T BE SPIKE? I'D MUCH RATHER GO BACK TO WHEN I THOUGHT IT WAS SPIKE.
I ASKED THE SAME QUESTION.
I HAVE NO TIME FOR YOUR PETTY DIFFERENCES.
COME TO A TRUCE OR YOU BOTH WILL PERISH AT THE HANDS OF THE SIPHON.
THE NITOBE CODE ALLOWS YOU TO TAKE ORDERS FROM SOMEONE LIKE ILLYRIA?
UNDER NORMAL CIRCUMSTANCES, NO. BUT ILLYRIA HAS PROMISED ME THE ONE THING YOU DENIED ME.
JUSTICE.

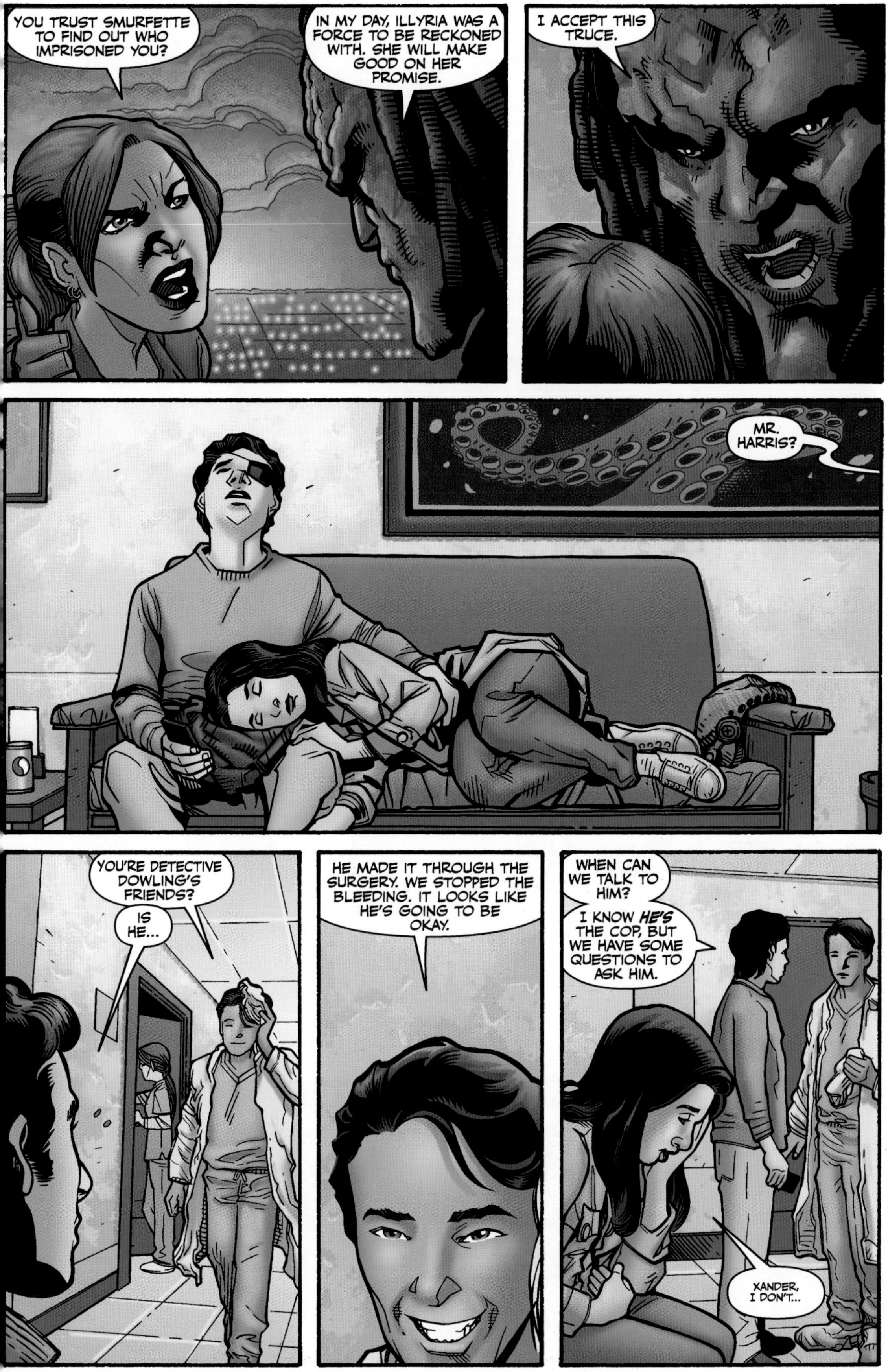
YOU TRUST SMURFETTE TO FIND OUT WHO IMPRISONED YOU?
IN MY DAY, ILLYRIA WAS A FORCE TO BE RECKONED WITH. SHE WILL MAKE GOOD ON HER PROMISE.
I ACCEPT THIS TRUCE.
MR. HARRIS?
YOU'RE DETECTIVE DOWLING'S FRIENDS?
IS HE...
HE MADE IT THROUGH THE SURGERY. WE STOPPED THE BLEEDING. IT LOOKS LIKE HE'S GOING TO BE OKAY.
WHEN CAN WE TALK TO HIM?
I KNOW *HE'S* THE COP, BUT WE HAVE SOME QUESTIONS TO ASK HIM.
XANDER, I DON'T...

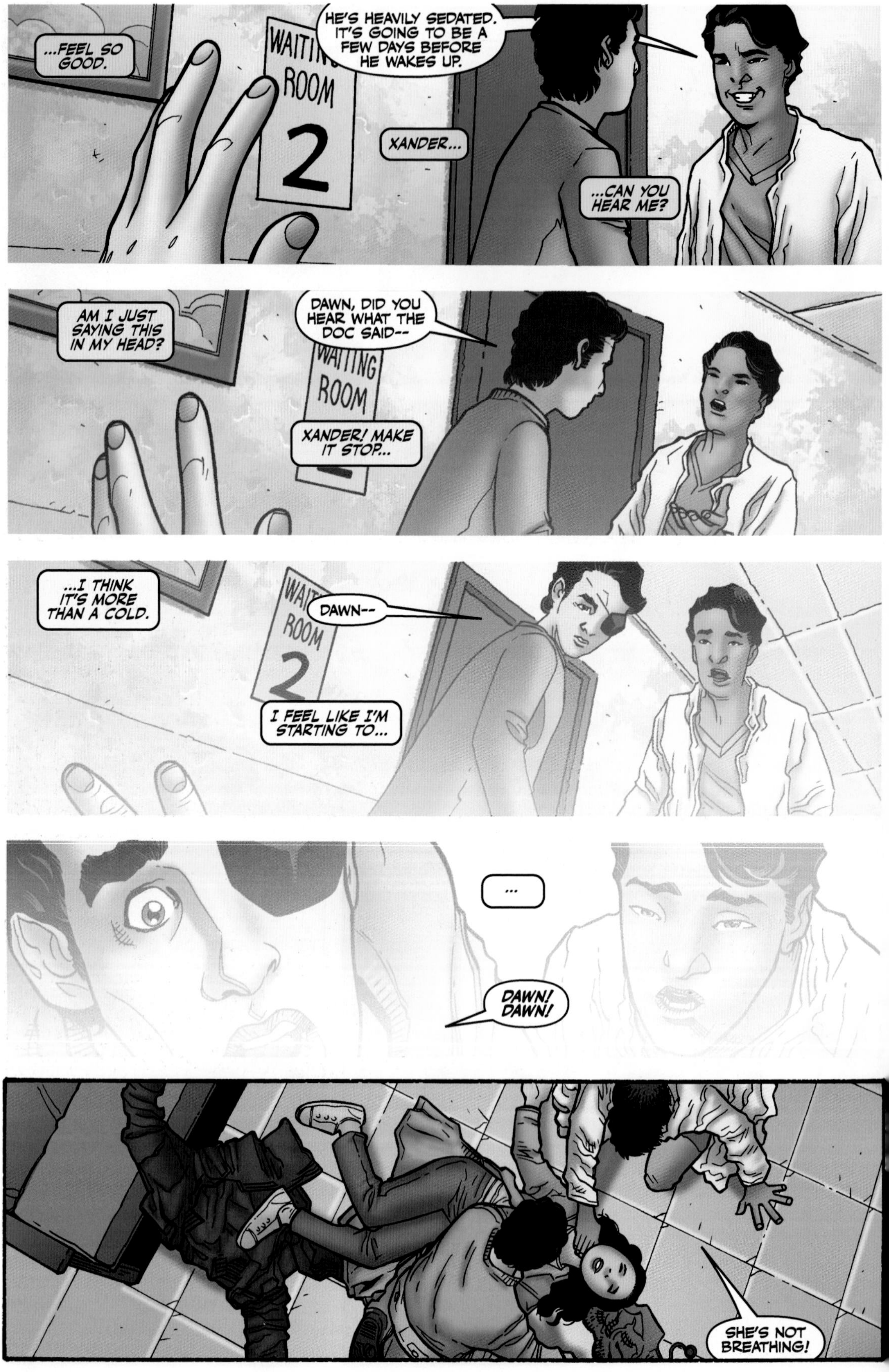
...FEEL SO GOOD.
HE'S HEAVILY SEDATED. IT'S GOING TO BE A FEW DAYS BEFORE HE WAKES UP.
WAITING ROOM 2
XANDER...
...CAN YOU HEAR ME?
AM I JUST SAYING THIS IN MY HEAD?
DAWN, DID YOU HEAR WHAT THE DOC SAID--
XANDER! MAKE IT STOP...
...I THINK IT'S MORE THAN A COLD.
DAWN--
I FEEL LIKE I'M STARTING TO...
...
DAWN! DAWN!
SHE'S NOT BREATHING!

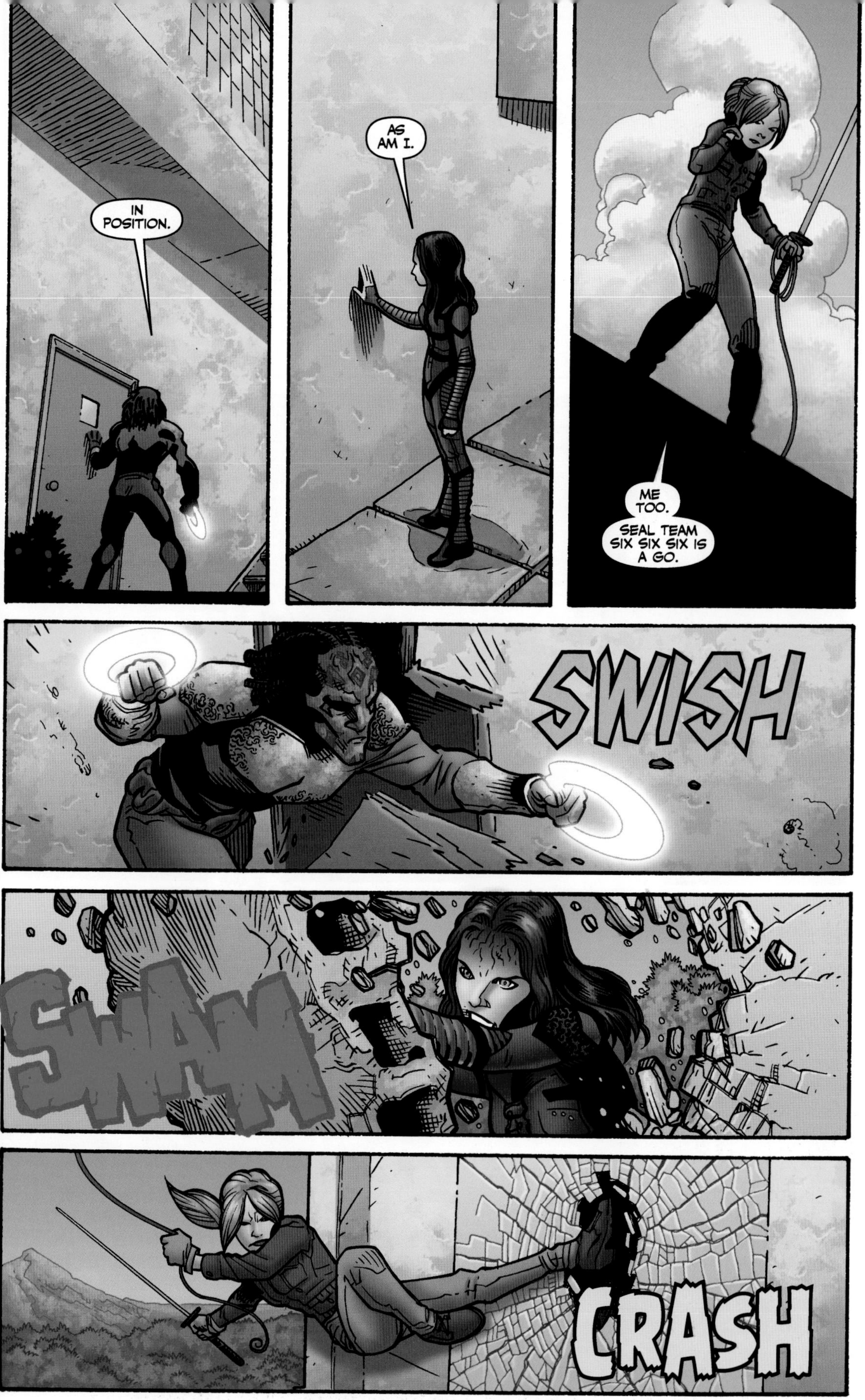
IN POSITION.
AS AM I.
ME TOO.
SEAL TEAM SIX SIX SIX IS A GO.
SWISH
SWAM
CRASH

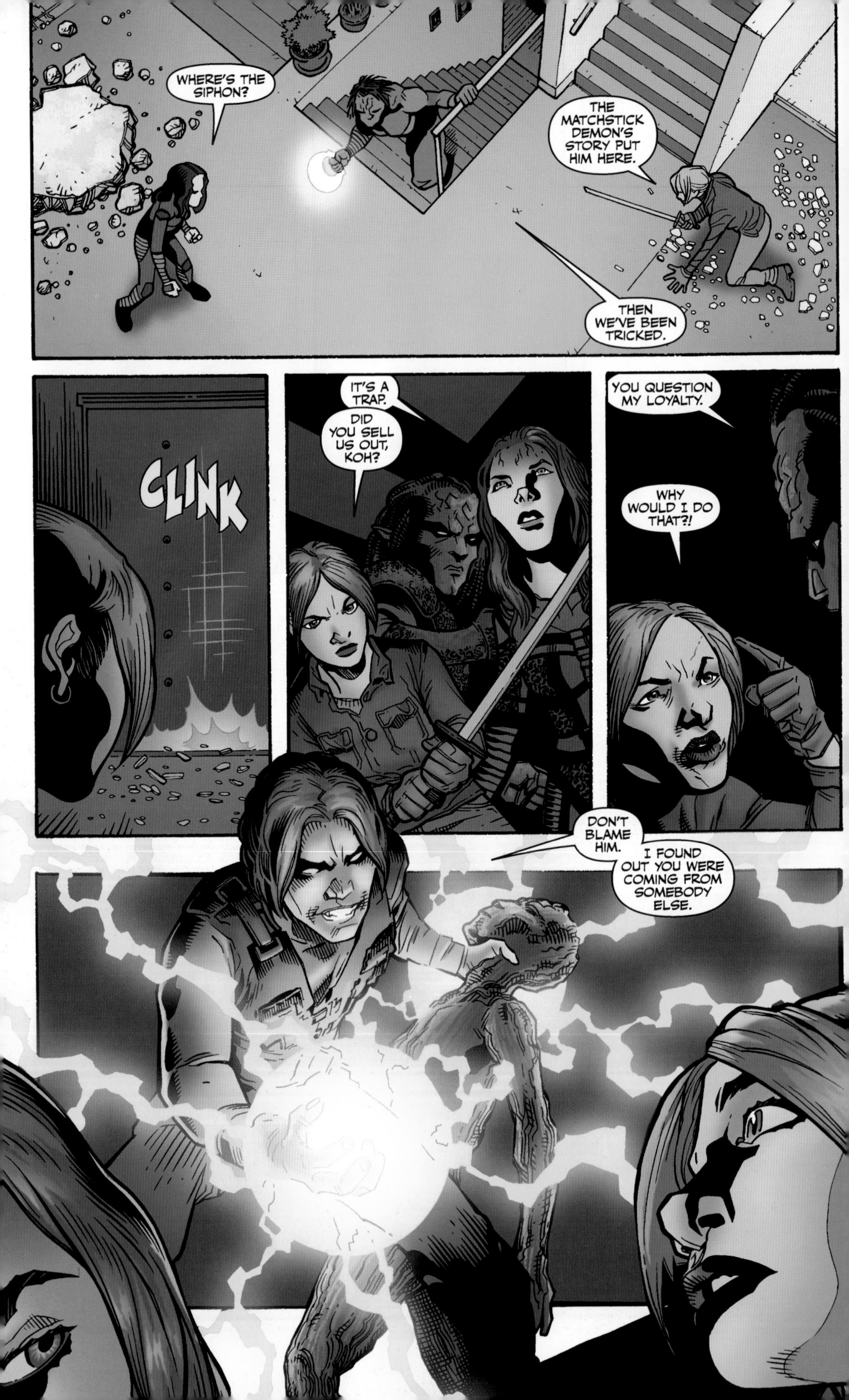
WHERE'S THE SIPHON?
THE MATCHSTICK DEMON'S STORY PUT HIM HERE.
THEN WE'VE BEEN TRICKED.
CLINK
IT'S A TRAP.
DID YOU SELL US OUT, KOH?
YOU QUESTION MY LOYALTY.
WHY WOULD I DO THAT?!
DON'T BLAME HIM.
I FOUND OUT YOU WERE COMING FROM SOMEBODY ELSE.

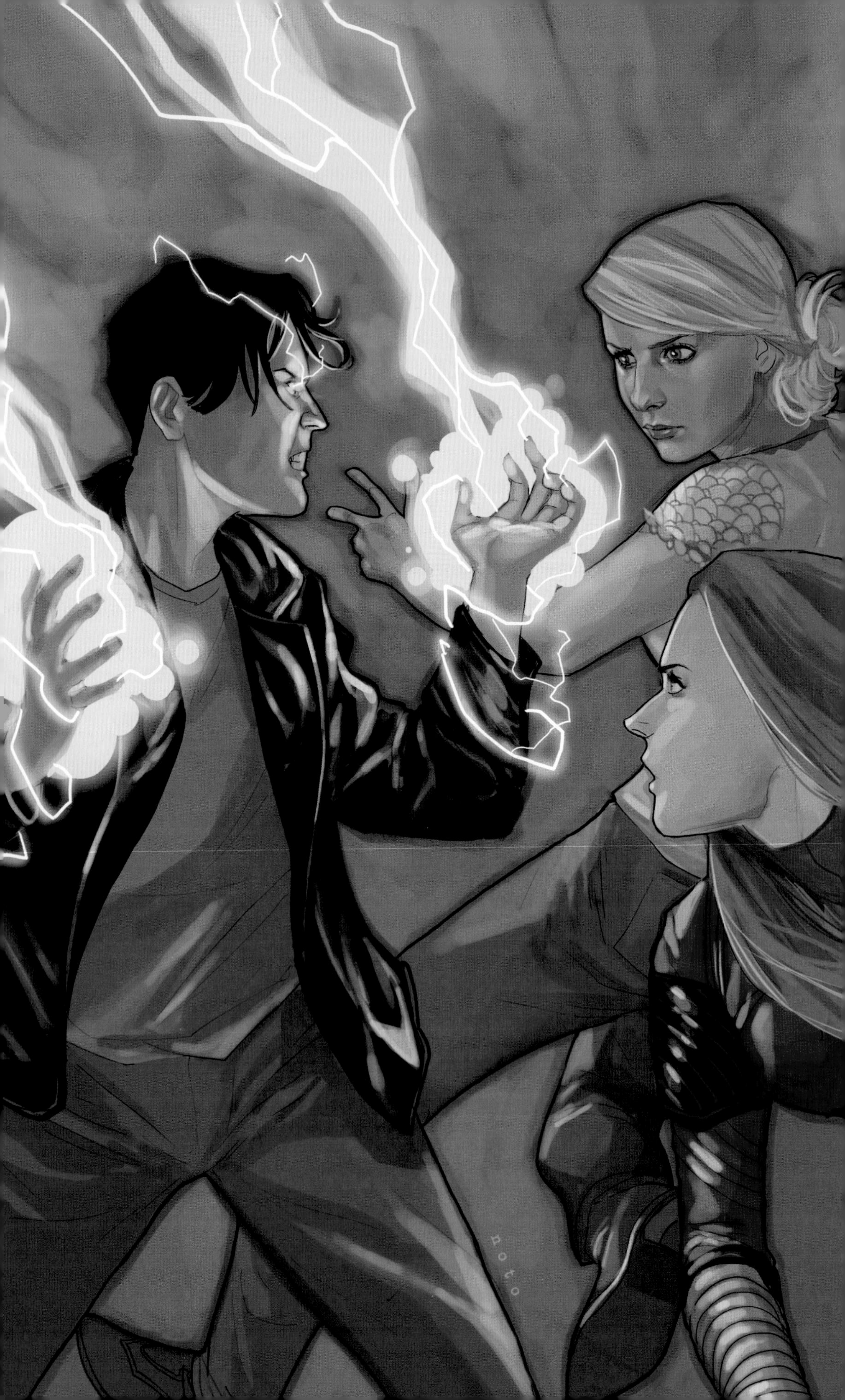
noto

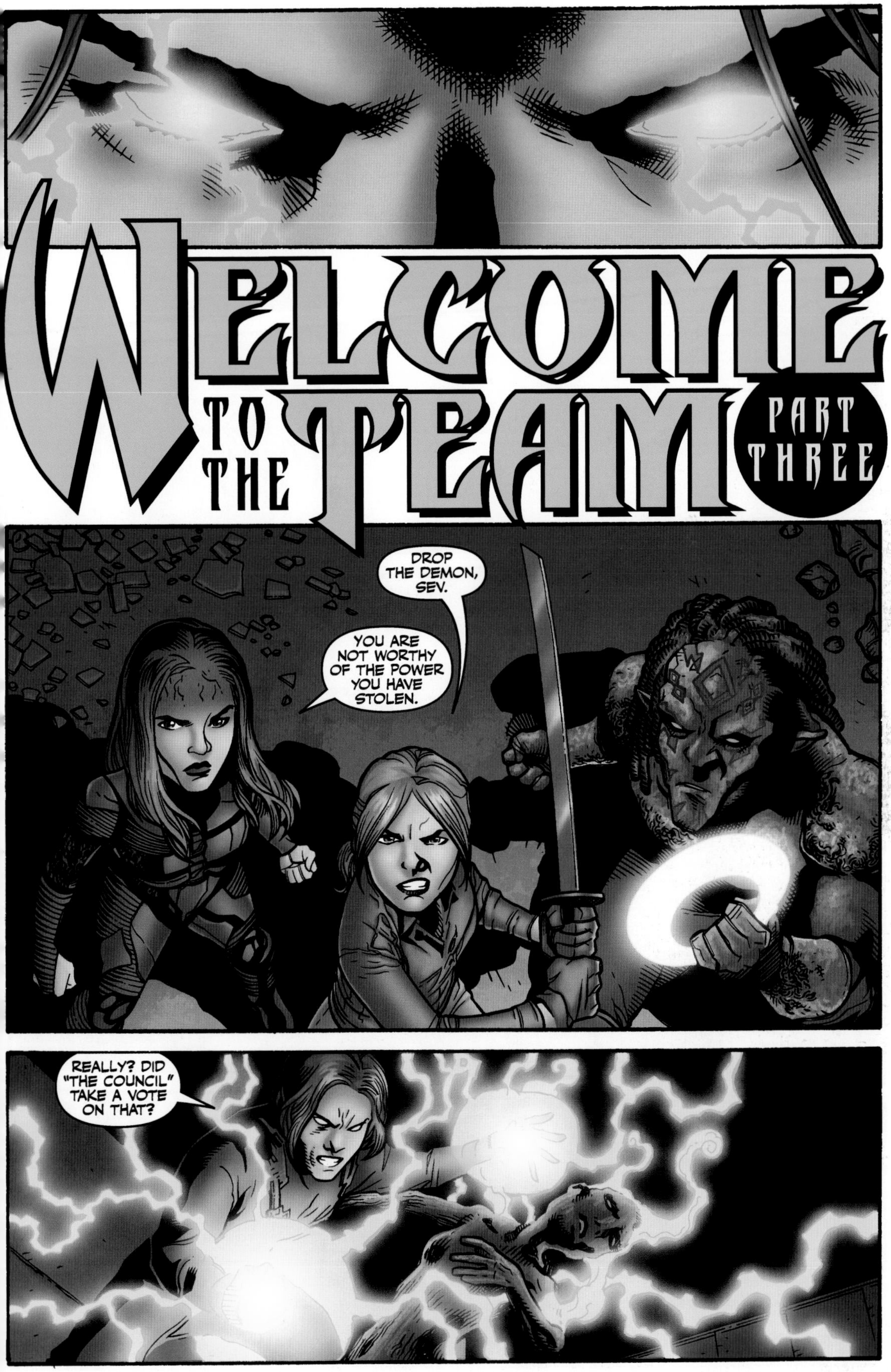
WELCOME TO THE TEAM
PART THREE
DROP THE DEMON, SEV.
YOU ARE NOT WORTHY OF THE POWER YOU HAVE STOLEN.
REALLY? DID "THE COUNCIL" TAKE A VOTE ON THAT?

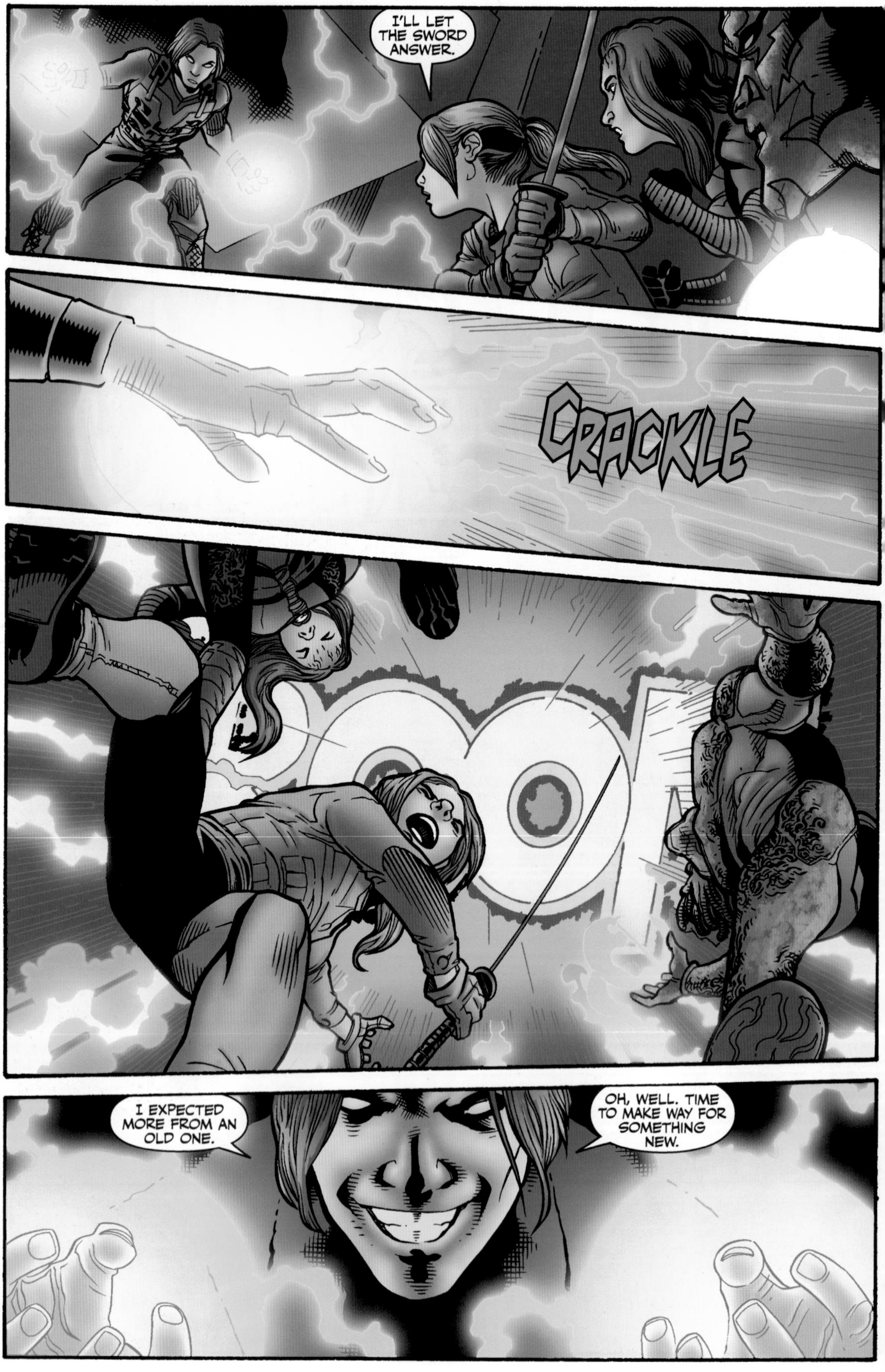
I'LL LET THE SWORD ANSWER.
CRACKLE
I EXPECTED MORE FROM AN OLD ONE.
OH, WELL. TIME TO MAKE WAY FOR SOMETHING NEW.

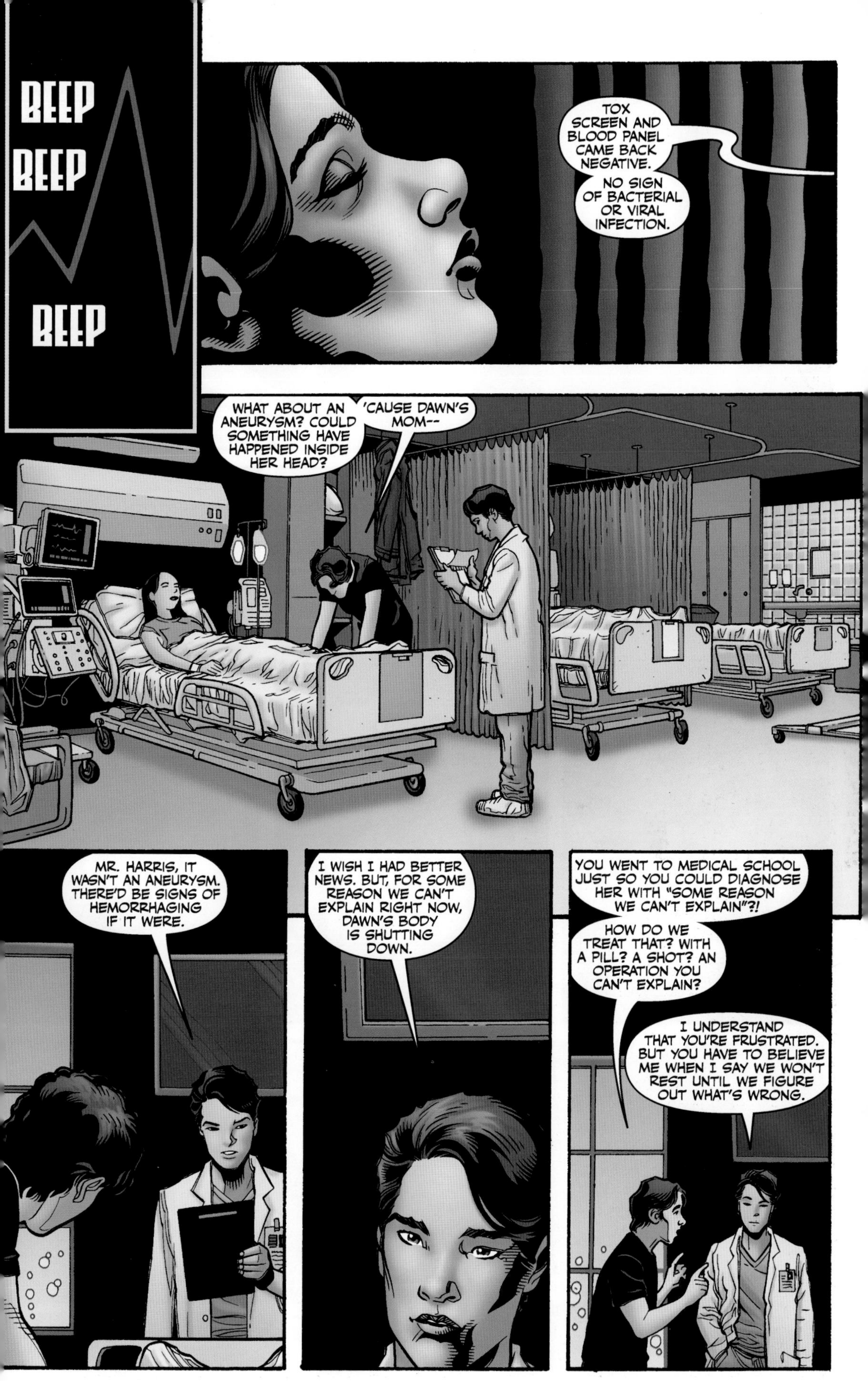
BEEP
BEEP
BEEP
TOX SCREEN AND BLOOD PANEL CAME BACK NEGATIVE.
NO SIGN OF BACTERIAL OR VIRAL INFECTION.
WHAT ABOUT AN ANEURYSM? COULD SOMETHING HAVE HAPPENED INSIDE HER HEAD?
'CAUSE DAWN'S MOM--
MR. HARRIS, IT WASN'T AN ANEURYSM. THERE'D BE SIGNS OF HEMORRHAGING IF IT WERE.
I WISH I HAD BETTER NEWS. BUT, FOR SOME REASON WE CAN'T EXPLAIN RIGHT NOW, DAWN'S BODY IS SHUTTING DOWN.
YOU WENT TO MEDICAL SCHOOL JUST SO YOU COULD DIAGNOSE HER WITH "SOME REASON WE CAN'T EXPLAIN"?!
HOW DO WE TREAT THAT? WITH A PILL? A SHOT? AN OPERATION YOU CAN'T EXPLAIN?
I UNDERSTAND THAT YOU'RE FRUSTRATED. BUT YOU HAVE TO BELIEVE ME WHEN I SAY WE WON'T REST UNTIL WE FIGURE OUT WHAT'S WRONG.

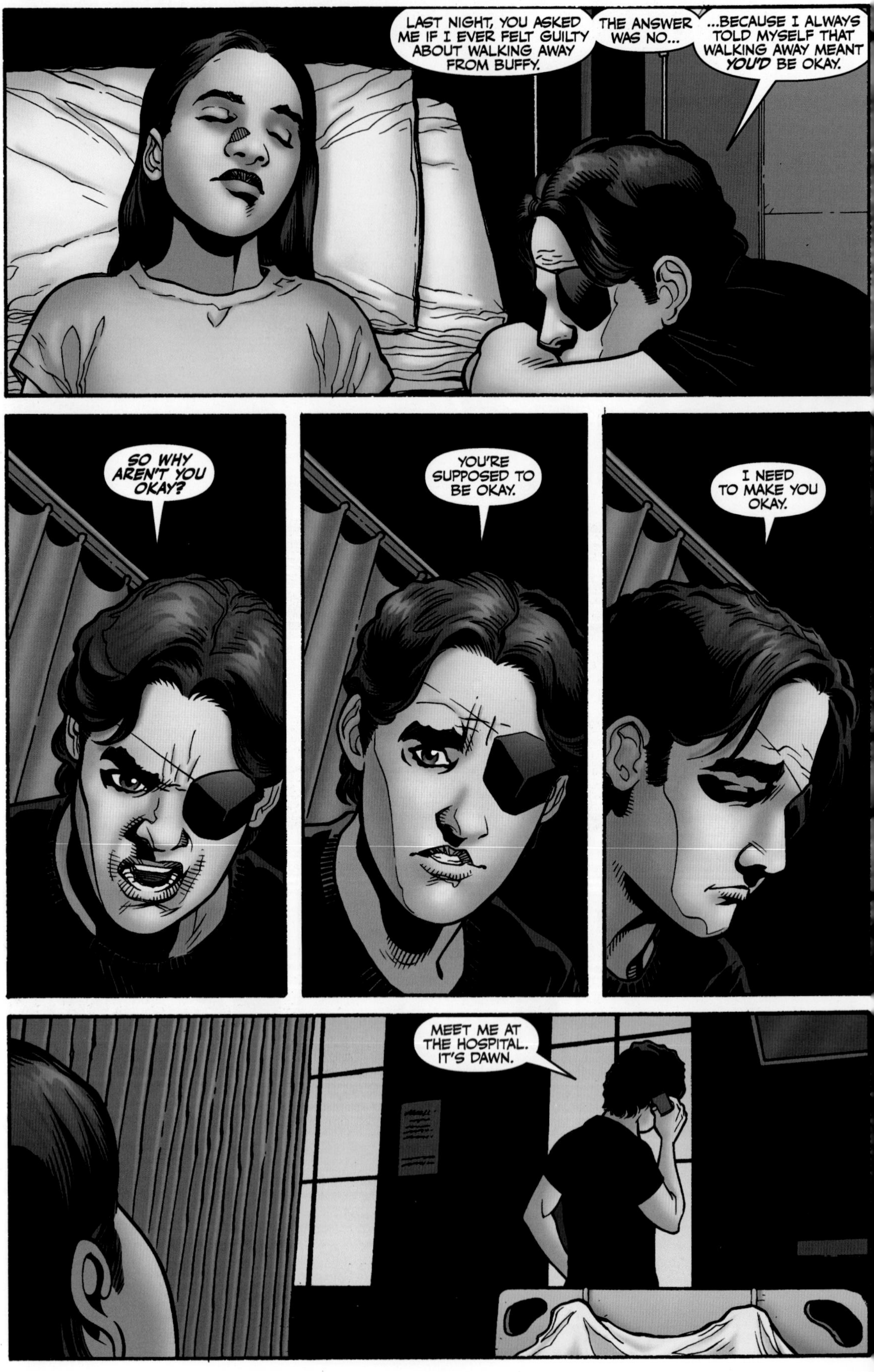
LAST NIGHT, YOU ASKED ME IF I EVER FELT GUILTY ABOUT WALKING AWAY FROM BUFFY.
THE ANSWER WAS NO...
...BECAUSE I ALWAYS TOLD MYSELF THAT WALKING AWAY MEANT YOU'D BE OKAY.
SO WHY AREN'T YOU OKAY?
YOU'RE SUPPOSED TO BE OKAY.
I NEED TO MAKE YOU OKAY.
MEET ME AT THE HOSPITAL. IT'S DAWN.

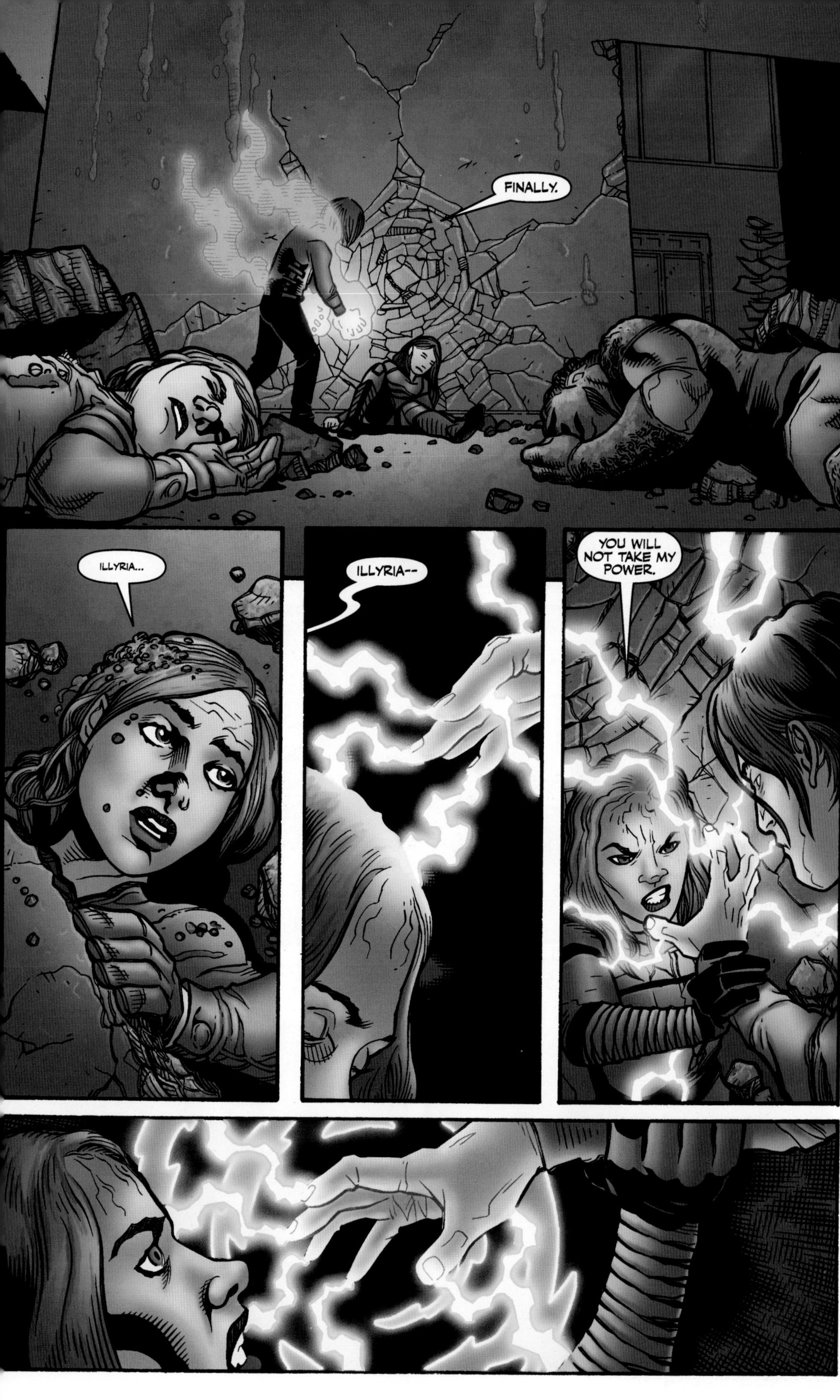
FINALLY.
ILLYRIA...
ILLYRIA--
YOU WILL NOT TAKE MY POWER.

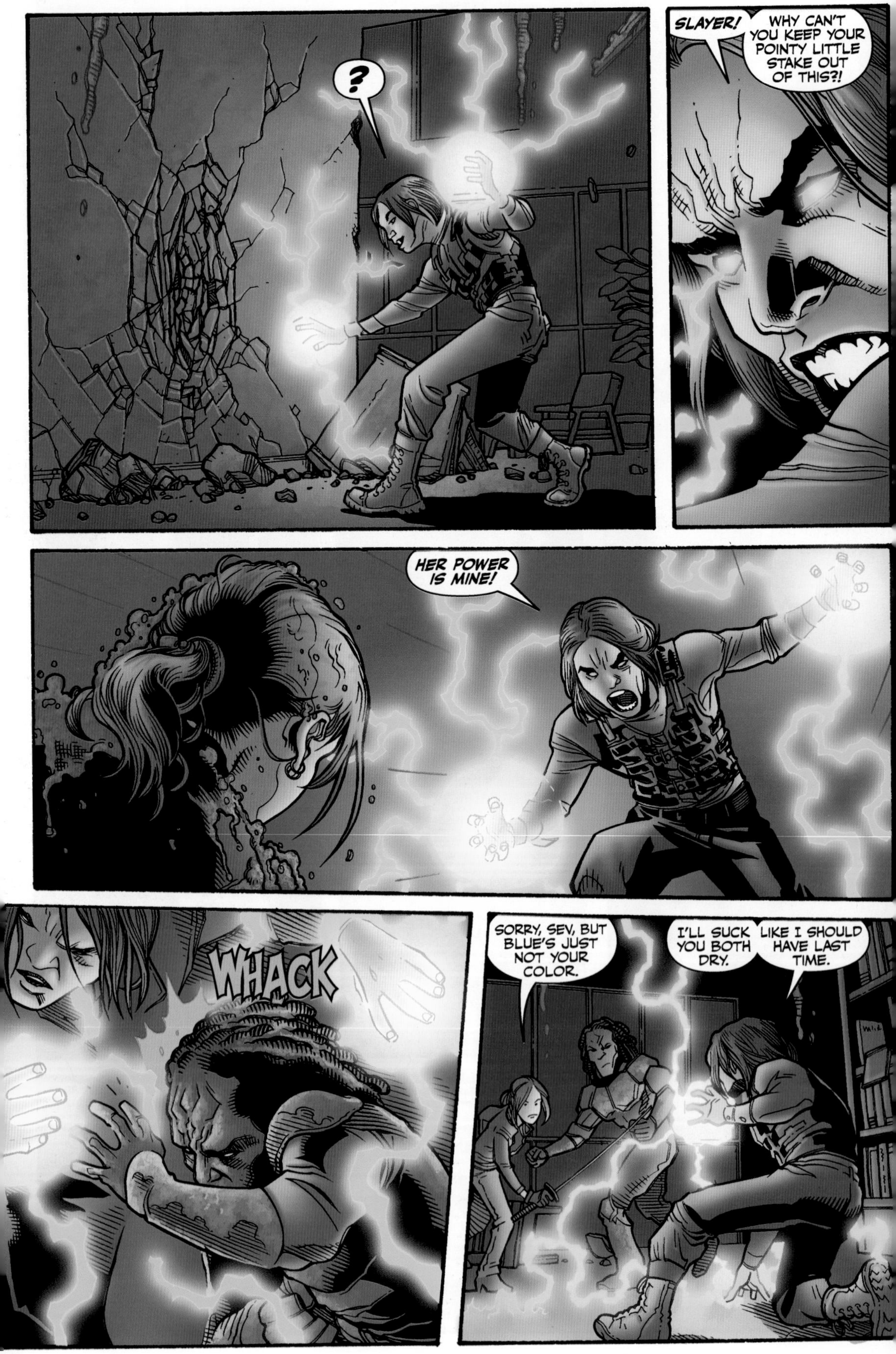
?
SLAYER!
WHY CAN'T YOU KEEP YOUR POINTY LITTLE STAKE OUT OF THIS?!
HER POWER IS MINE!
WHACK
SORRY, SEV, BUT BLUE'S JUST NOT YOUR COLOR.
I'LL SUCK YOU BOTH DRY.
LIKE I SHOULD HAVE LAST TIME.

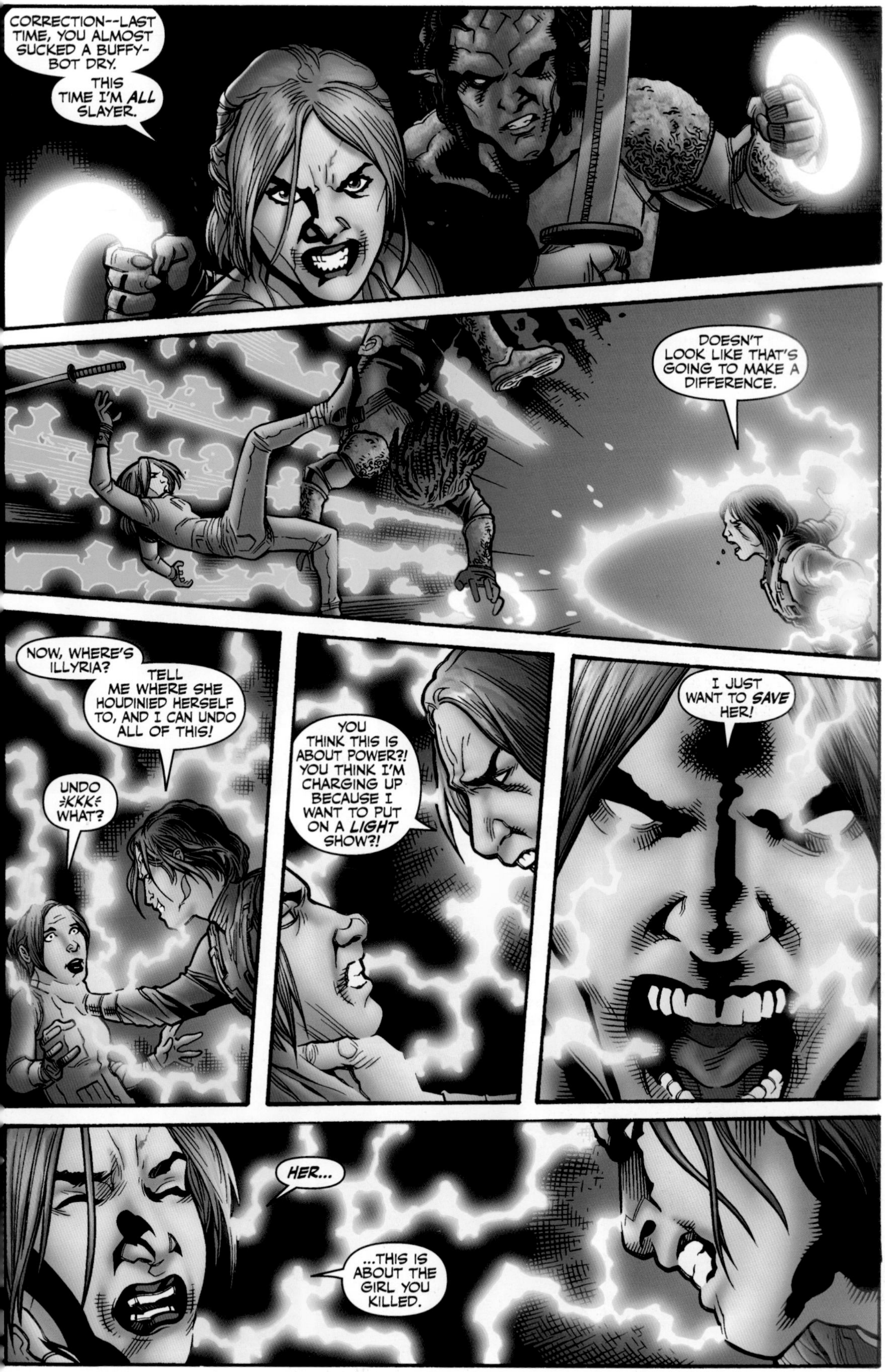
CORRECTION--LAST TIME, YOU ALMOST SUCKED A BUFFY-BOT DRY.
THIS TIME I'M ALL SLAYER.
DOESN'T LOOK LIKE THAT'S GOING TO MAKE A DIFFERENCE.
NOW, WHERE'S ILLYRIA?
TELL ME WHERE SHE HOUDINIED HERSELF TO, AND I CAN UNDO ALL OF THIS!
UNDO *KKK* WHAT?
YOU THINK THIS IS ABOUT POWER?! YOU THINK I'M CHARGING UP BECAUSE I WANT TO PUT ON A LIGHT SHOW?!
I JUST WANT TO SAVE HER!
HER...
...THIS IS ABOUT THE GIRL YOU KILLED.

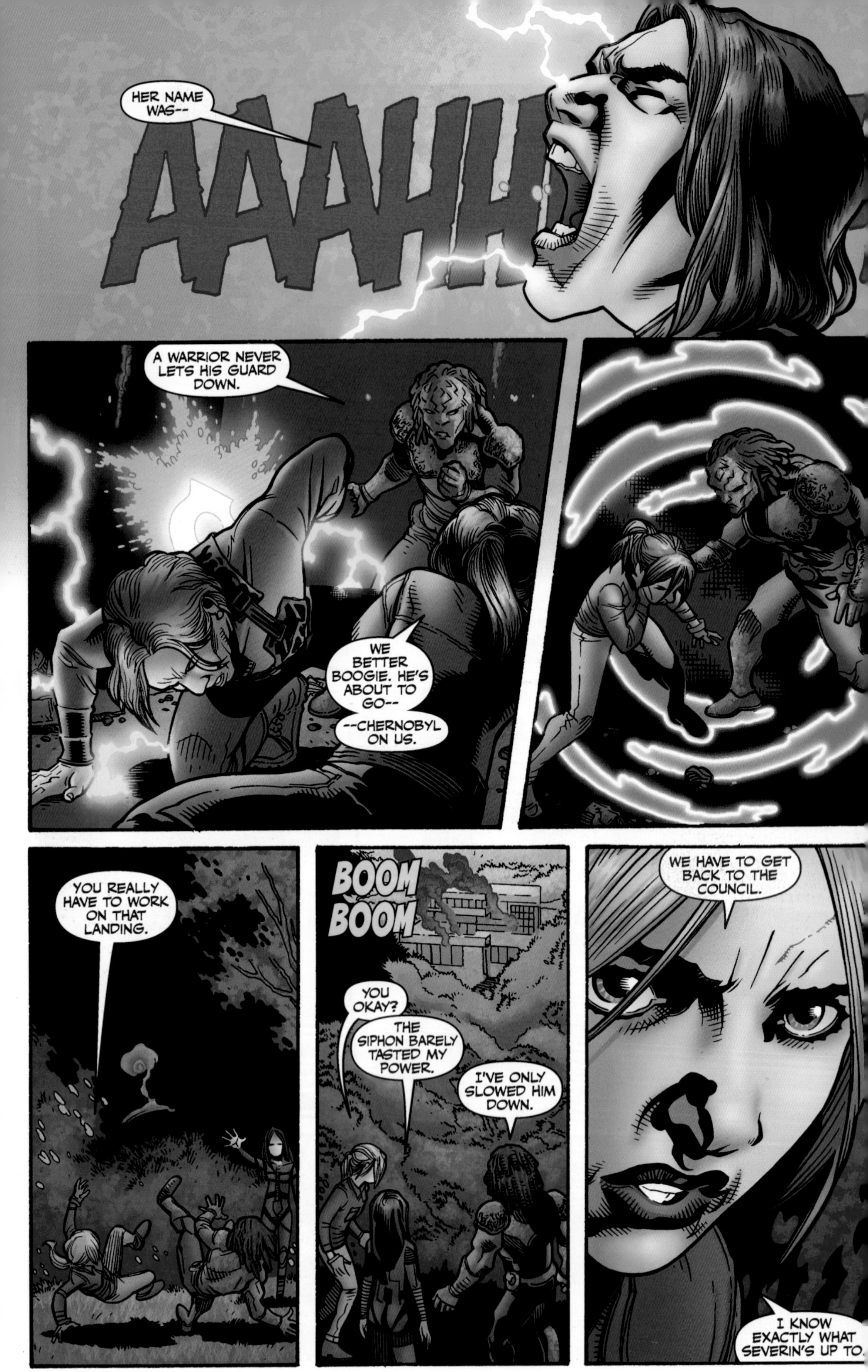

HER NAME WAS--
AAAHH
A WARRIOR NEVER LETS HIS GUARD DOWN.
WE BETTER BOOGIE. HE'S ABOUT TO GO--
--CHERNOBYL ON US.
YOU REALLY HAVE TO WORK ON THAT LANDING.
BOOM
BOOM
YOU OKAY?
THE SIPHON BARELY TASTED MY POWER.
I'VE ONLY SLOWED HIM DOWN.
WE HAVE TO GET BACK TO THE COUNCIL.
I KNOW EXACTLY WHAT SEVERIN'S UP TO.

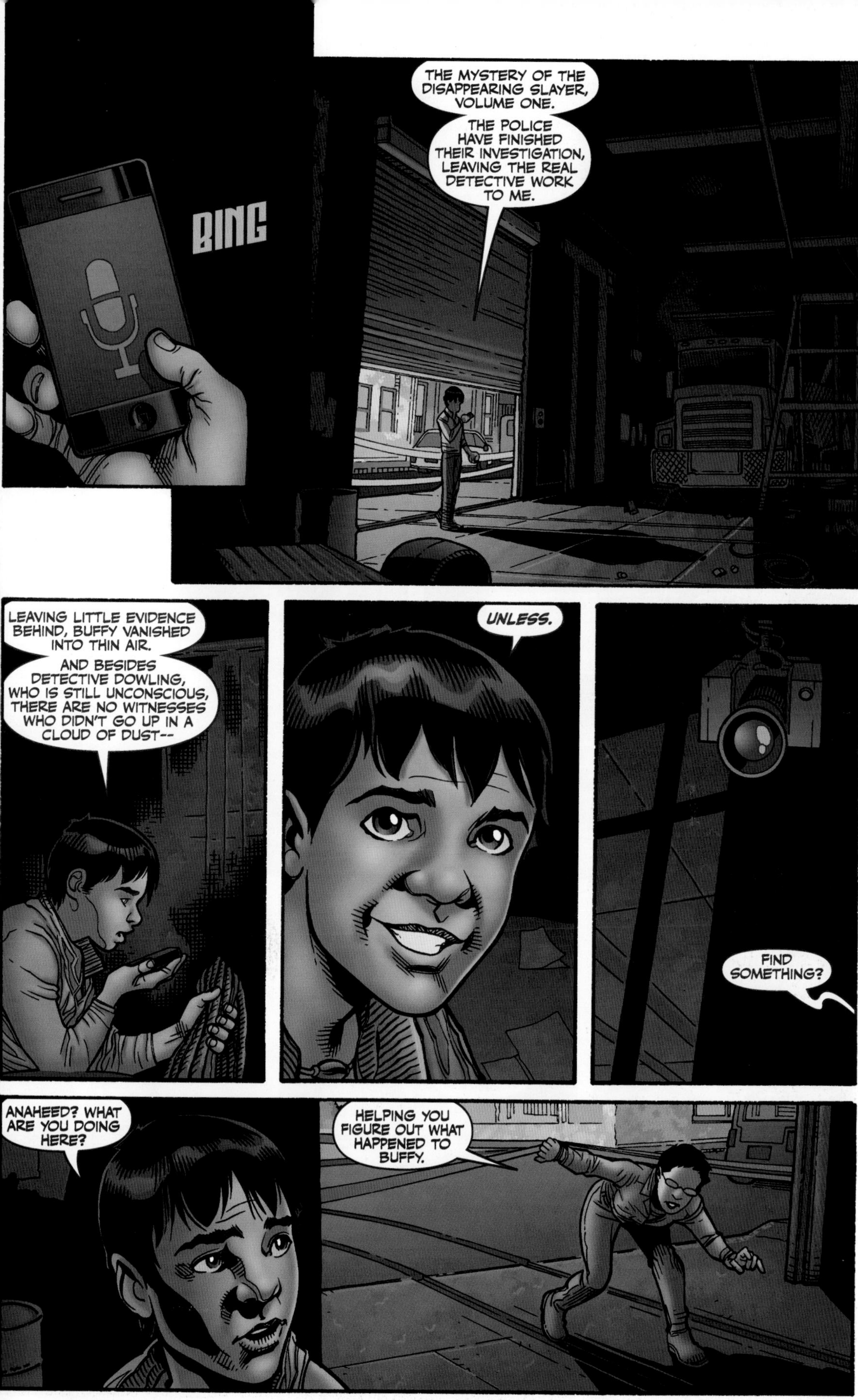
BING
THE MYSTERY OF THE DISAPPEARING SLAYER, VOLUME ONE.
THE POLICE HAVE FINISHED THEIR INVESTIGATION, LEAVING THE REAL DETECTIVE WORK TO ME.
LEAVING LITTLE EVIDENCE BEHIND, BUFFY VANISHED INTO THIN AIR.
AND BESIDES DETECTIVE DOWLING, WHO IS STILL UNCONSCIOUS, THERE ARE NO WITNESSES WHO DIDN'T GO UP IN A CLOUD OF DUST--
UNLESS.
FIND SOMETHING?
ANAHEED? WHAT ARE YOU DOING HERE?
HELPING YOU FIGURE OUT WHAT HAPPENED TO BUFFY.

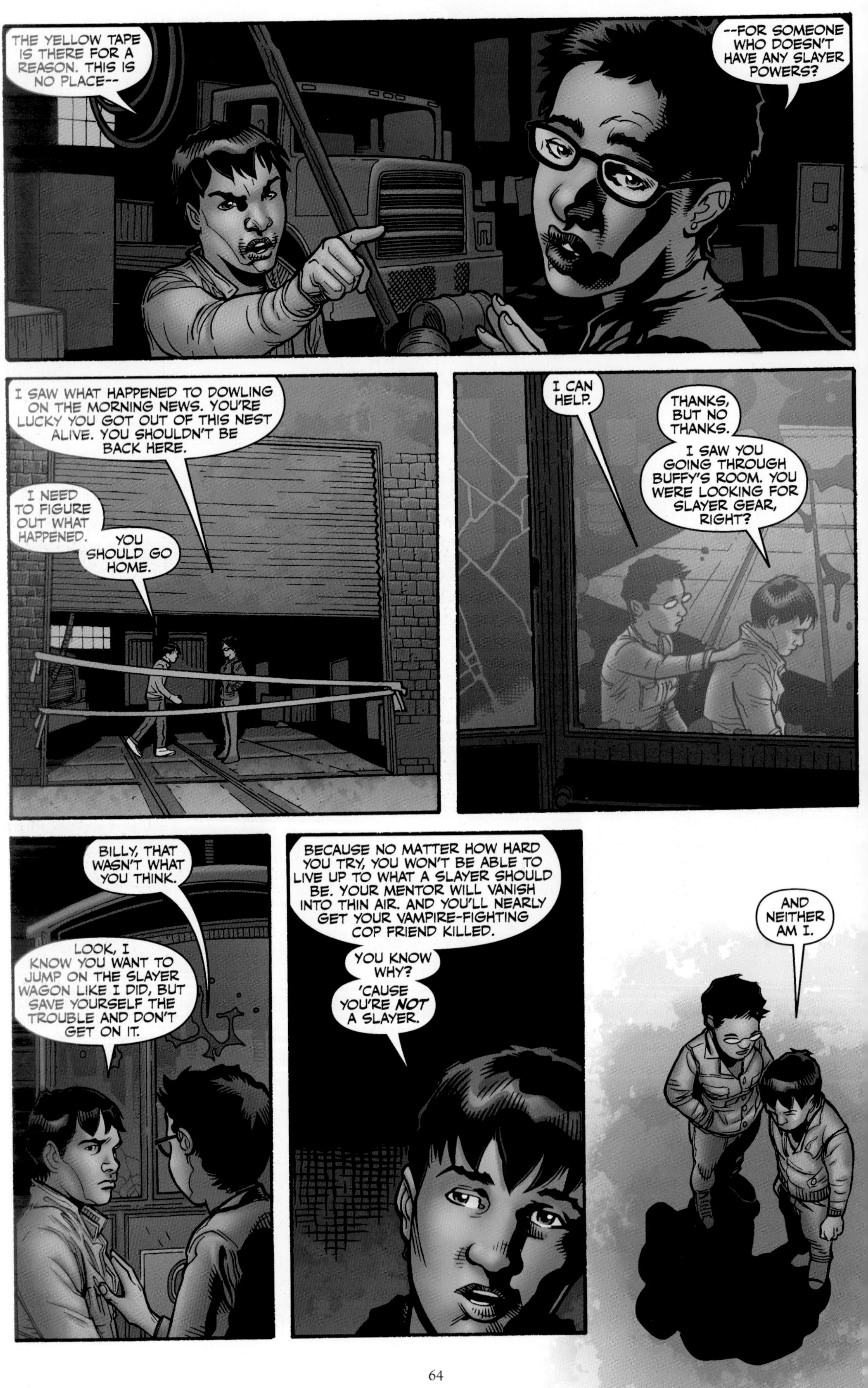
THE YELLOW TAPE IS THERE FOR A REASON. THIS IS NO PLACE--
--FOR SOMEONE WHO DOESN'T HAVE ANY SLAYER POWERS?
I SAW WHAT HAPPENED TO DOWLING ON THE MORNING NEWS. YOU'RE LUCKY YOU GOT OUT OF THIS NEST ALIVE. YOU SHOULDN'T BE BACK HERE.
I NEED TO FIGURE OUT WHAT HAPPENED.
YOU SHOULD GO HOME.
I CAN HELP.
THANKS, BUT NO THANKS.
I SAW YOU GOING THROUGH BUFFY'S ROOM. YOU WERE LOOKING FOR SLAYER GEAR, RIGHT?
BILLY, THAT WASN'T WHAT YOU THINK.
LOOK, I KNOW YOU WANT TO JUMP ON THE SLAYER WAGON LIKE I DID, BUT SAVE YOURSELF THE TROUBLE AND DON'T GET ON IT.
BECAUSE NO MATTER HOW HARD YOU TRY, YOU WON'T BE ABLE TO LIVE UP TO WHAT A SLAYER SHOULD BE. YOUR MENTOR WILL VANISH INTO THIN AIR. AND YOU'LL NEARLY GET YOUR VAMPIRE-FIGHTING COP FRIEND KILLED.
YOU KNOW WHY?
'CAUSE YOU'RE **NOT** A SLAYER.
AND NEITHER AM I.

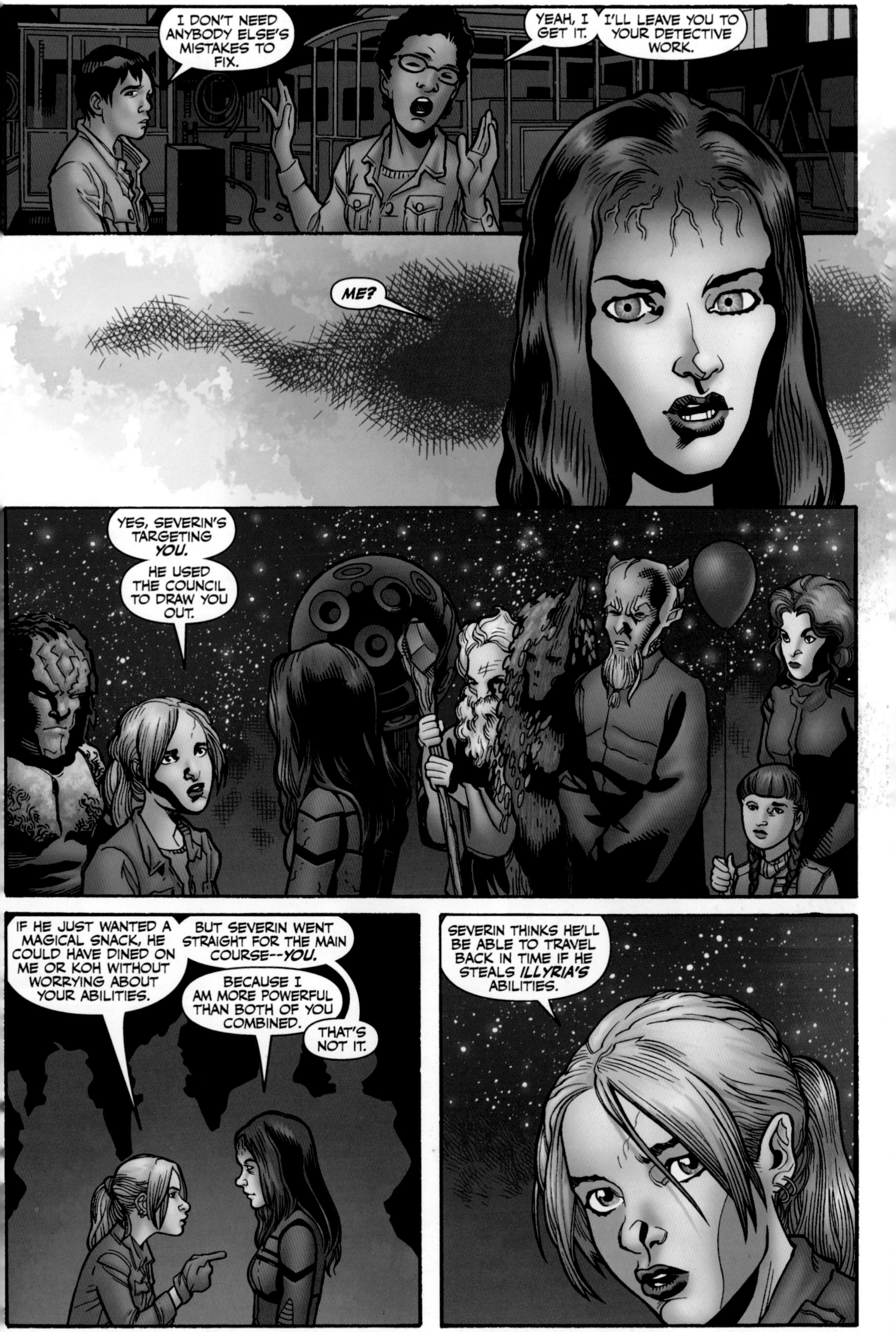
I DON'T NEED ANYBODY ELSE'S MISTAKES TO FIX.
YEAH, I GET IT.
I'LL LEAVE YOU TO YOUR DETECTIVE WORK.
ME?
YES, SEVERIN'S TARGETING YOU.
HE USED THE COUNCIL TO DRAW YOU OUT.
IF HE JUST WANTED A MAGICAL SNACK, HE COULD HAVE DINED ON ME OR KOH WITHOUT WORRYING ABOUT YOUR ABILITIES.
BUT SEVERIN WENT STRAIGHT FOR THE MAIN COURSE--YOU.
BECAUSE I AM MORE POWERFUL THAN BOTH OF YOU COMBINED.
THAT'S NOT IT.
SEVERIN THINKS HE'LL BE ABLE TO TRAVEL BACK IN TIME IF HE STEALS ILLYRIA'S ABILITIES.

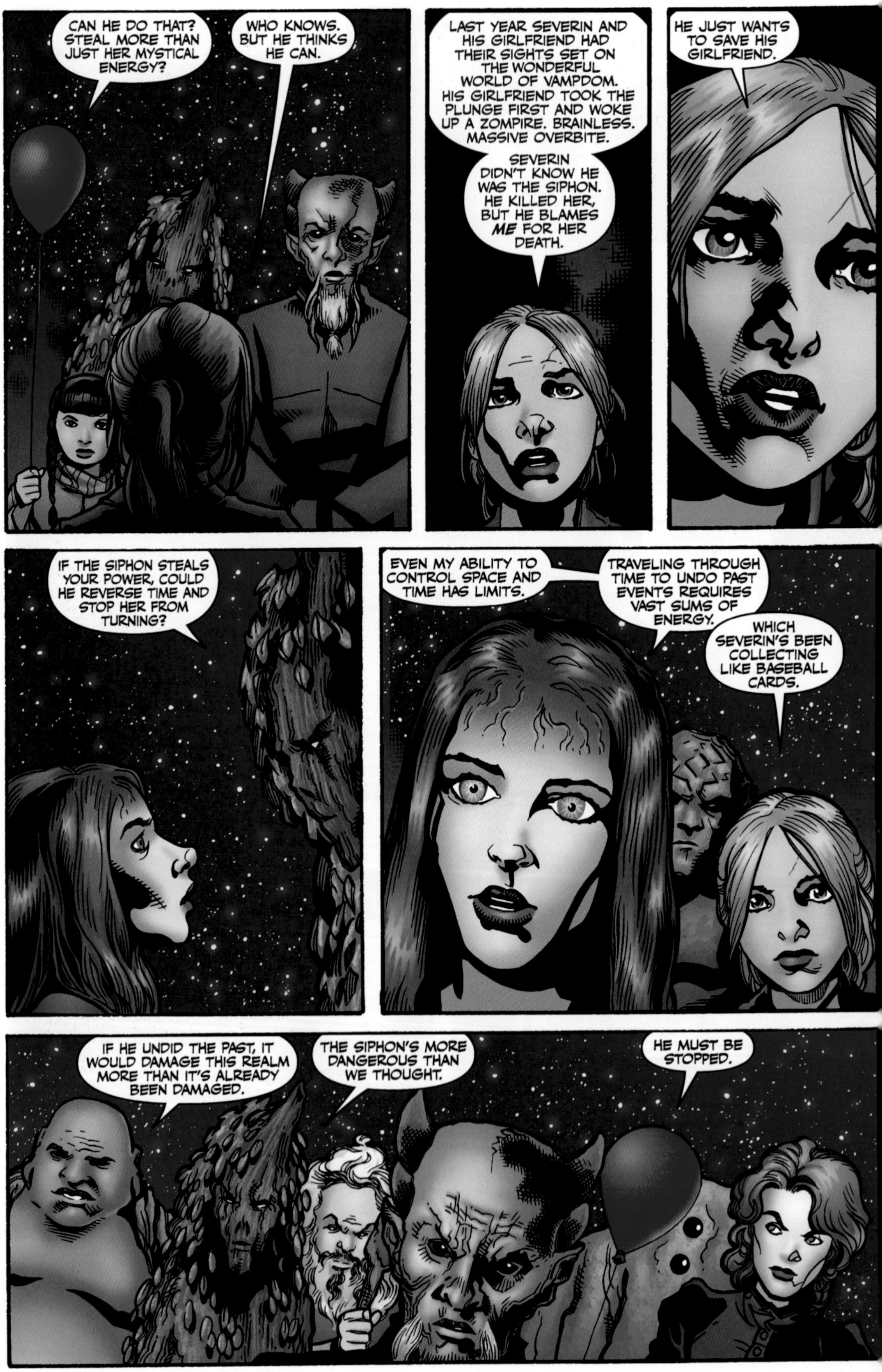
CAN HE DO THAT? STEAL MORE THAN JUST HER MYSTICAL ENERGY?
WHO KNOWS. BUT HE THINKS HE CAN.
LAST YEAR SEVERIN AND HIS GIRLFRIEND HAD THEIR SIGHTS SET ON THE WONDERFUL WORLD OF VAMPDOM. HIS GIRLFRIEND TOOK THE PLUNGE FIRST AND WOKE UP A ZOMPIRE. BRAINLESS. MASSIVE OVERBITE.
SEVERIN DIDN'T KNOW HE WAS THE SIPHON. HE KILLED HER, BUT HE BLAMES *ME* FOR HER DEATH.
HE JUST WANTS TO SAVE HIS GIRLFRIEND.
IF THE SIPHON STEALS YOUR POWER, COULD HE REVERSE TIME AND STOP HER FROM TURNING?
EVEN MY ABILITY TO CONTROL SPACE AND TIME HAS LIMITS.
TRAVELING THROUGH TIME TO UNDO PAST EVENTS REQUIRES VAST SUMS OF ENERGY.
WHICH SEVERIN'S BEEN COLLECTING LIKE BASEBALL CARDS.
IF HE UNDID THE PAST, IT WOULD DAMAGE THIS REALM MORE THAN IT'S ALREADY BEEN DAMAGED.
THE SIPHON'S MORE DANGEROUS THAN WE THOUGHT.
HE MUST BE STOPPED.

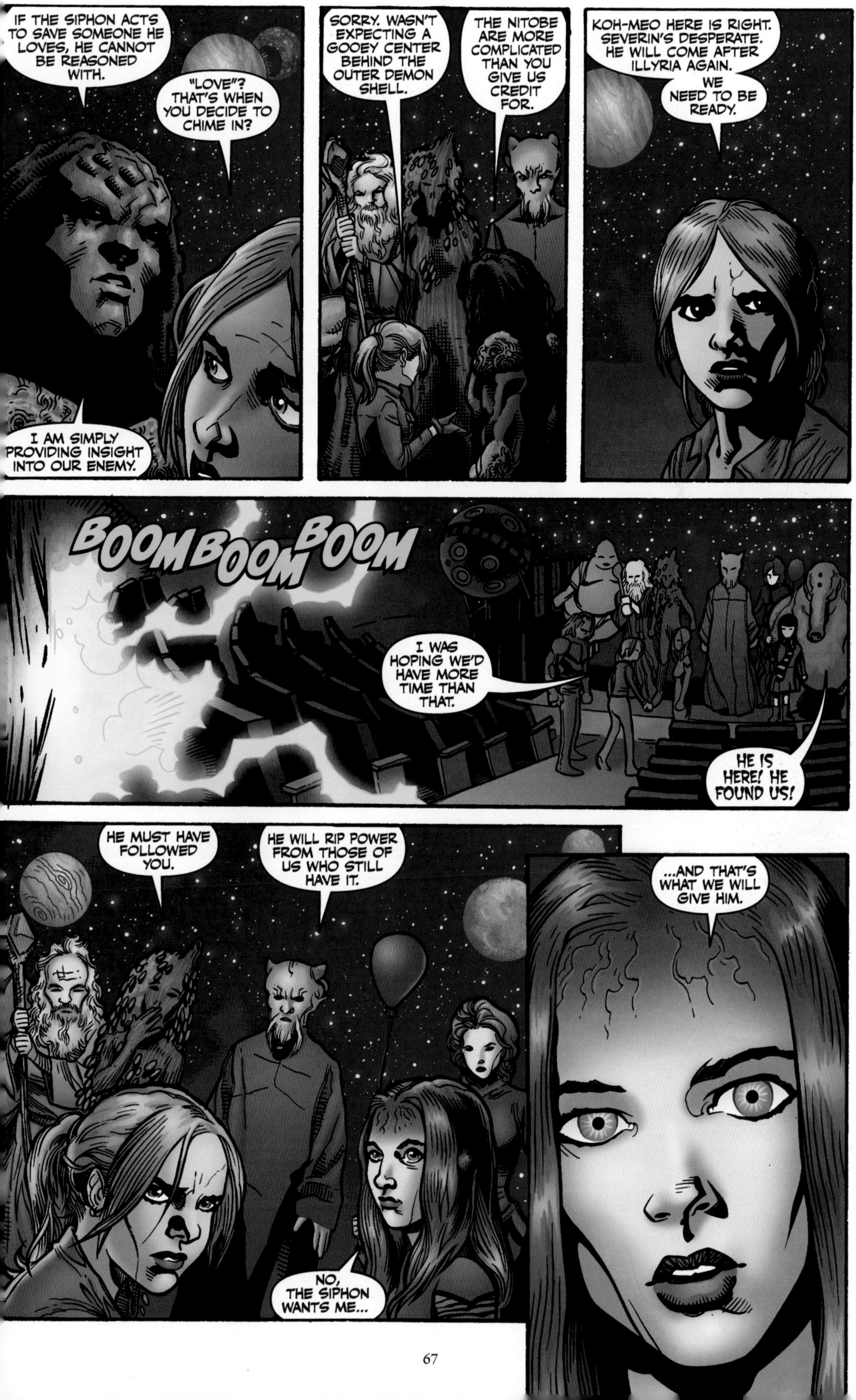
IF THE SIPHON ACTS TO SAVE SOMEONE HE LOVES, HE CANNOT BE REASONED WITH.
"LOVE"? THAT'S WHEN YOU DECIDE TO CHIME IN?
I AM SIMPLY PROVIDING INSIGHT INTO OUR ENEMY.
SORRY. WASN'T EXPECTING A GOOEY CENTER BEHIND THE OUTER DEMON SHELL.
THE NITOBE ARE MORE COMPLICATED THAN YOU GIVE US CREDIT FOR.
KOH-MEO HERE IS RIGHT. SEVERIN'S DESPERATE. HE WILL COME AFTER ILLYRIA AGAIN.
WE NEED TO BE READY.
BOOMBOOMBOOM
I WAS HOPING WE'D HAVE MORE TIME THAN THAT.
HE IS HERE! HE FOUND US!
HE MUST HAVE FOLLOWED YOU.
HE WILL RIP POWER FROM THOSE OF US WHO STILL HAVE IT.
NO, THE SIPHON WANTS ME...
...AND THAT'S WHAT WE WILL GIVE HIM.

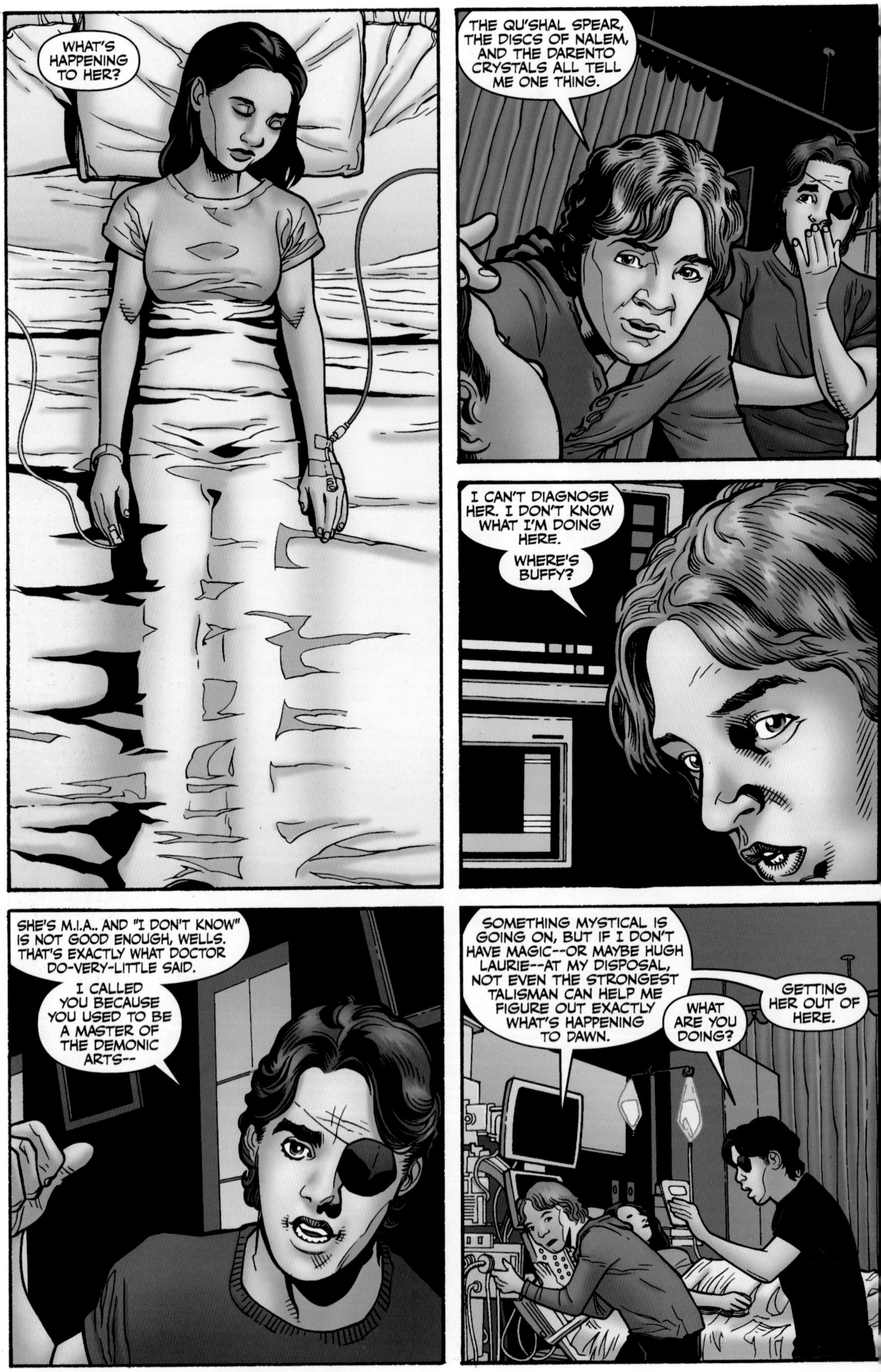

WHAT'S HAPPENING TO HER?
THE QU'SHAL SPEAR, THE DISCS OF NALEM, AND THE DARENTO CRYSTALS ALL TELL ME ONE THING.
I CAN'T DIAGNOSE HER. I DON'T KNOW WHAT I'M DOING HERE.
WHERE'S BUFFY?
SHE'S M.I.A.. AND "I DON'T KNOW" IS NOT GOOD ENOUGH, WELLS. THAT'S EXACTLY WHAT DOCTOR DO-VERY-LITTLE SAID.
I CALLED YOU BECAUSE YOU USED TO BE A MASTER OF THE DEMONIC ARTS--
SOMETHING MYSTICAL IS GOING ON, BUT IF I DON'T HAVE MAGIC--OR MAYBE HUGH LAURIE--AT MY DISPOSAL, NOT EVEN THE STRONGEST TALISMAN CAN HELP ME FIGURE OUT EXACTLY WHAT'S HAPPENING TO DAWN.
WHAT ARE YOU DOING?
GETTING HER OUT OF HERE.

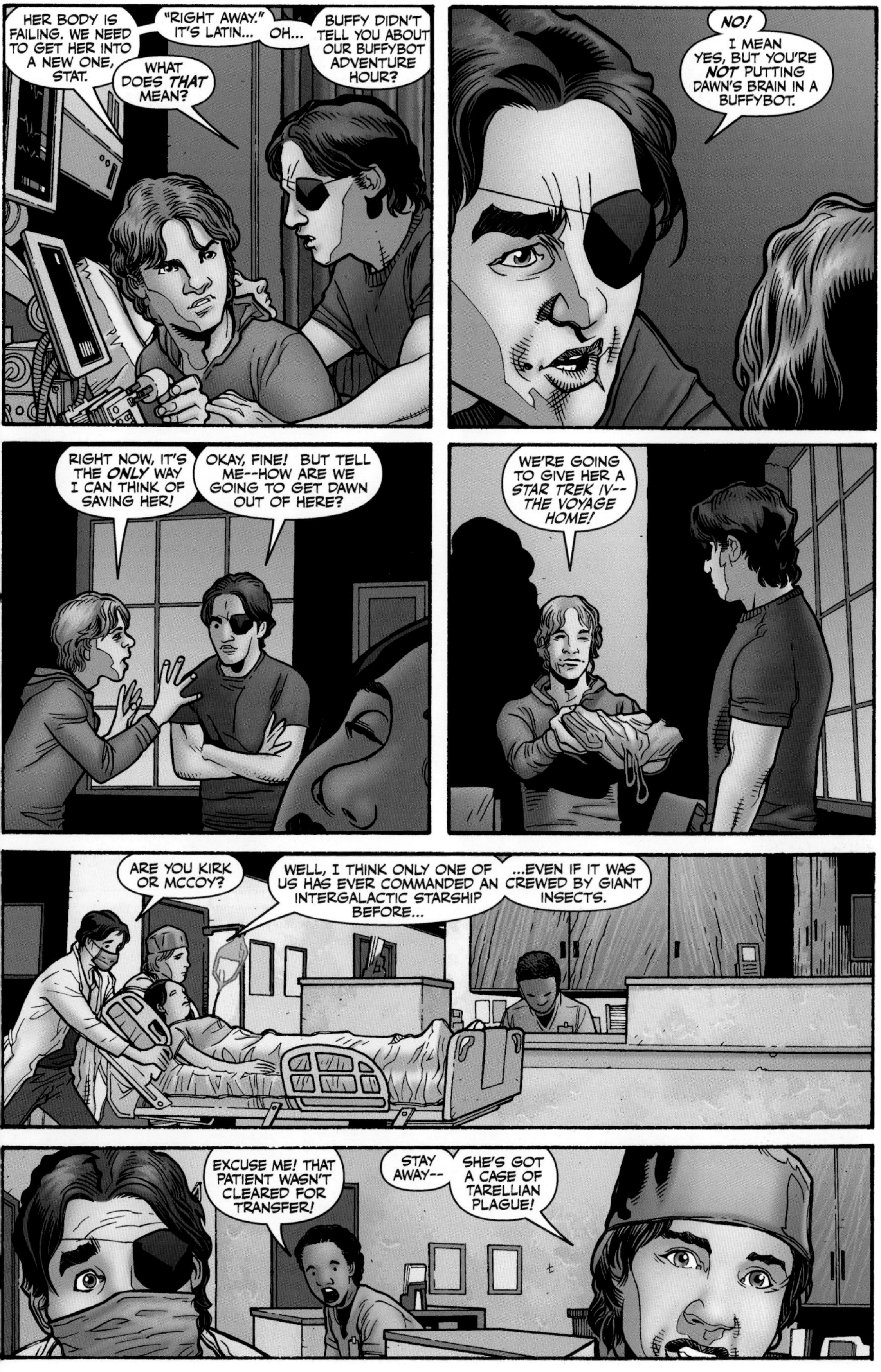
HER BODY IS FAILING. WE NEED TO GET HER INTO A NEW ONE, STAT.
WHAT DOES THAT MEAN?
"RIGHT AWAY." IT'S LATIN... OH...
BUFFY DIDN'T TELL YOU ABOUT OUR BUFFYBOT ADVENTURE HOUR?
NO!
I MEAN YES, BUT YOU'RE NOT PUTTING DAWN'S BRAIN IN A BUFFYBOT.
RIGHT NOW, IT'S THE ONLY WAY I CAN THINK OF SAVING HER!
OKAY, FINE! BUT TELL ME--HOW ARE WE GOING TO GET DAWN OUT OF HERE?
WE'RE GOING TO GIVE HER A STAR TREK IV-- THE VOYAGE HOME!
ARE YOU KIRK OR MCCOY?
WELL, I THINK ONLY ONE OF US HAS EVER COMMANDED AN INTERGALACTIC STARSHIP BEFORE...
...EVEN IF IT WAS CREWED BY GIANT INSECTS.
EXCUSE ME! THAT PATIENT WASN'T CLEARED FOR TRANSFER!
STAY AWAY--
SHE'S GOT A CASE OF TARELLIAN PLAGUE!

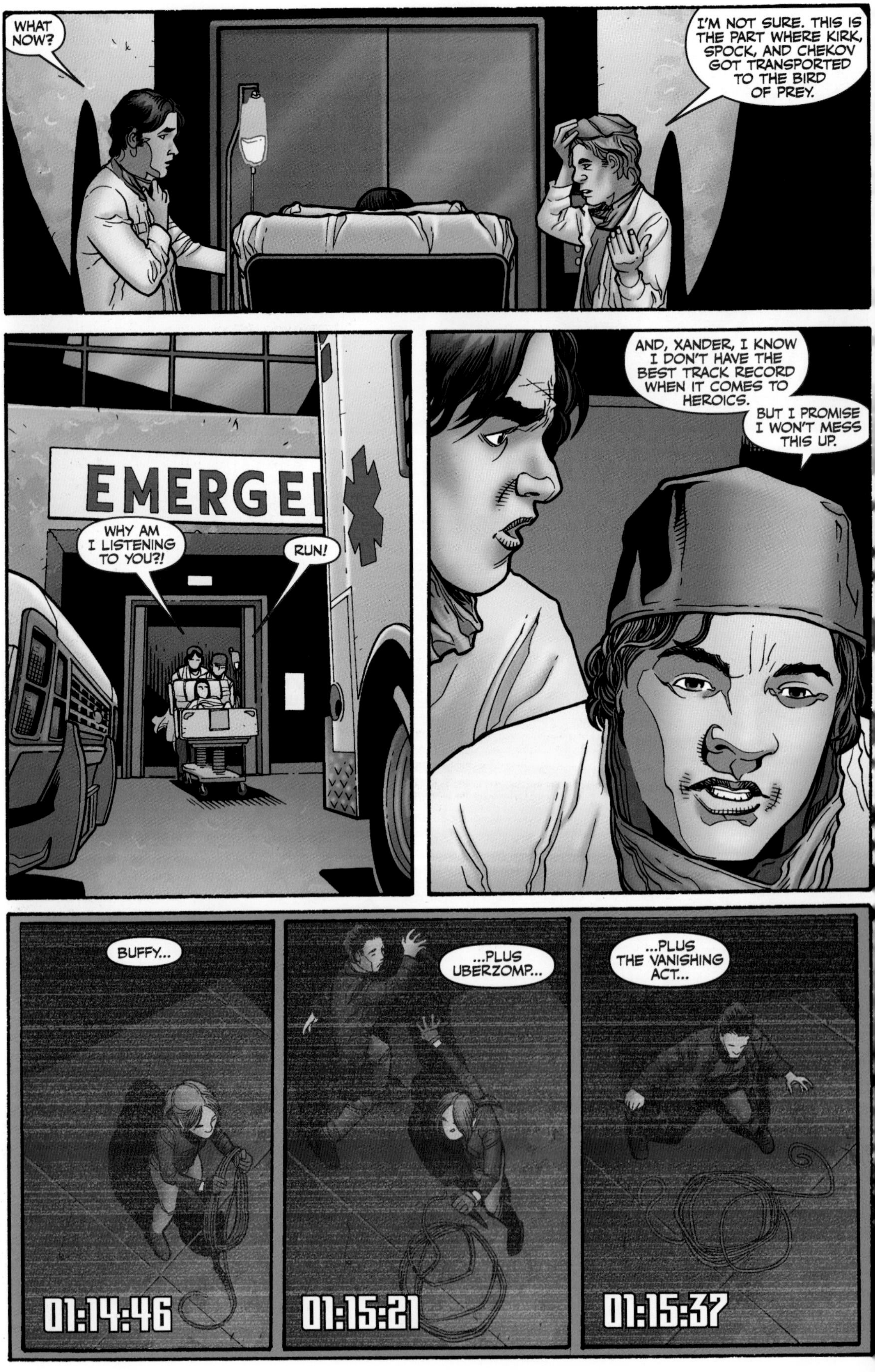
WHAT NOW?
I'M NOT SURE. THIS IS THE PART WHERE KIRK, SPOCK, AND CHEKOV GOT TRANSPORTED TO THE BIRD OF PREY.
EMERGE
WHY AM I LISTENING TO YOU?!
RUN!
AND, XANDER, I KNOW I DON'T HAVE THE BEST TRACK RECORD WHEN IT COMES TO HEROICS.
BUT I PROMISE I WON'T MESS THIS UP.
BUFFY...
01:14:46
...PLUS UBERZOMP...
01:15:21
...PLUS THE VANISHING ACT...
01:15:37

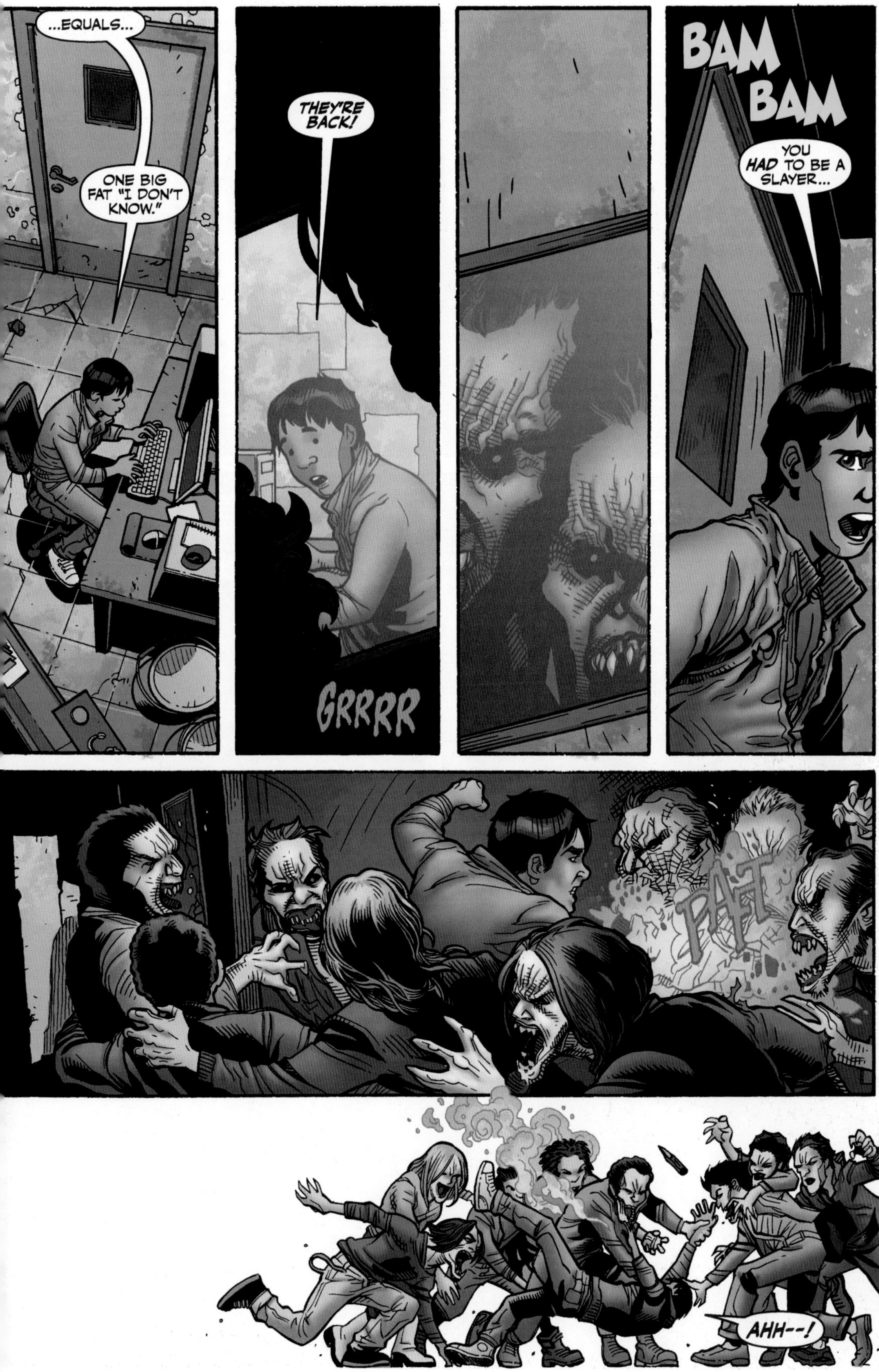

...EQUALS...
ONE BIG FAT "I DON'T KNOW."
THEY'RE BACK!
GRRRR
BAM
BAM
YOU HAD TO BE A SLAYER...
PAF
AHH--!

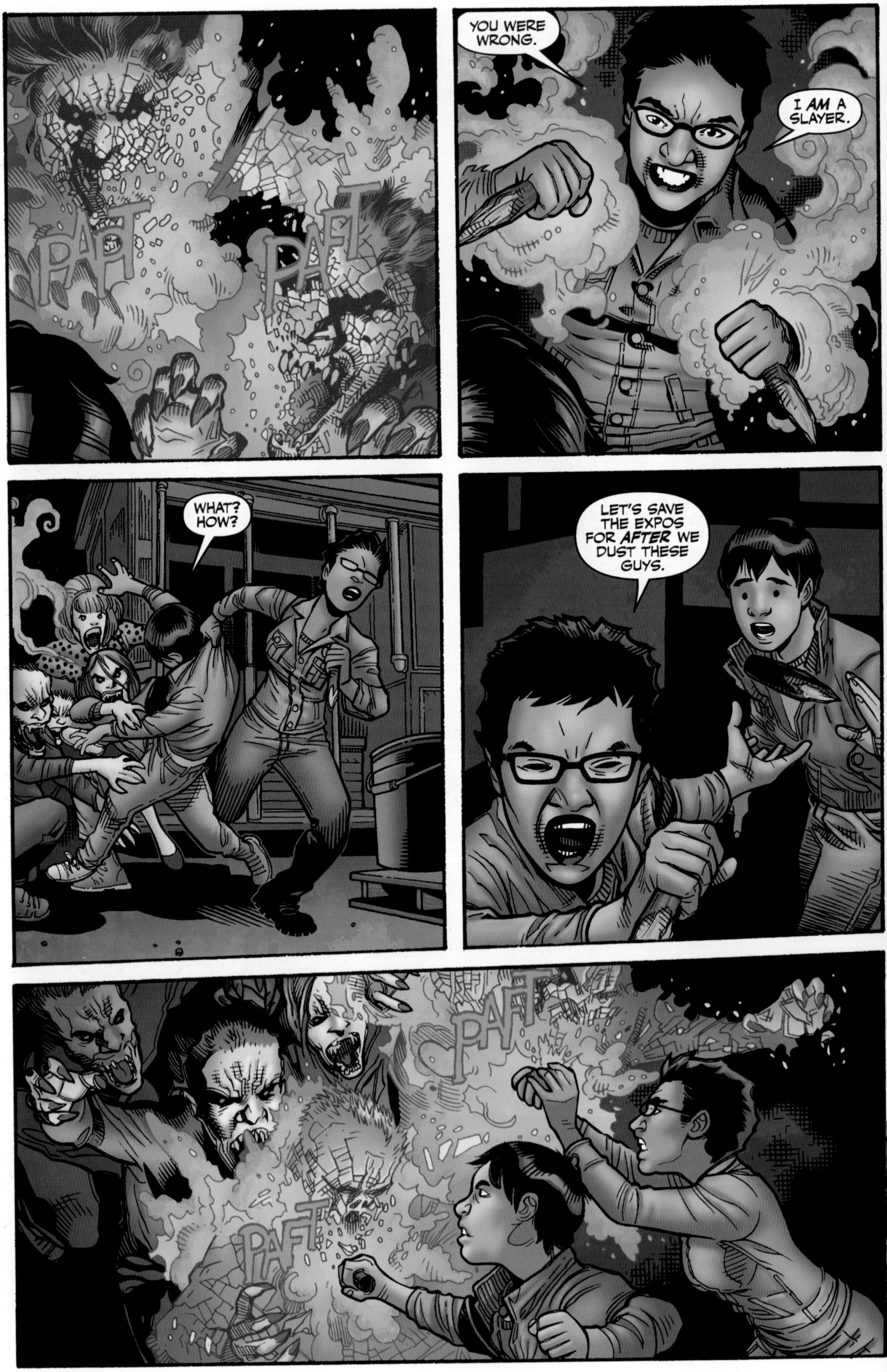
PAFT
PAFT
YOU WERE WRONG.
I AM A SLAYER.
WHAT? HOW?
LET'S SAVE THE EXPOS FOR AFTER WE DUST THESE GUYS.
PAFT
PAFT

WE CANNOT HOLD THE SIPHON OFF FOREVER.

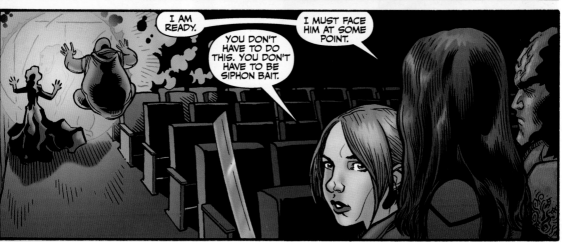

I AM READY.

YOU DON'T HAVE TO DO THIS. YOU DON'T HAVE TO BE SIPHON BAIT.

I MUST FACE HIM AT SOME POINT.

AND I CAN DISTRACT HIM LONG ENOUGH FOR YOU AND ELDRE KOH TO DO WHAT WE BROUGHT YOU HERE TO DO.

SLAY HIM.

HIS GUARD WILL BE DOWN WHEN HE TRIES TO STEAL YOUR ENERGY. THAT IS WHEN WE MUST STRIKE.

LISTEN. I WILL TELEPORT YOU TO MY SIDE WHEN HE PLACES HIS HANDS ON ME.

DON'T WORRY. WE'LL SLAY HIM *BEFORE* HE SUCKS AN OUNCE OF YOUR MOJO.

I DO NOT FEAR LOSING MY POWER.

I HAVE FACED THAT BEFORE. WHAT IT'S LIKE TO FEEL SMALL AND INSIGNIFICANT. TO EXPERIENCE PAIN AND LOSS.

TO BE HUMAN.

I CAN HANDLE IT. BUT THE SIPHON...

73

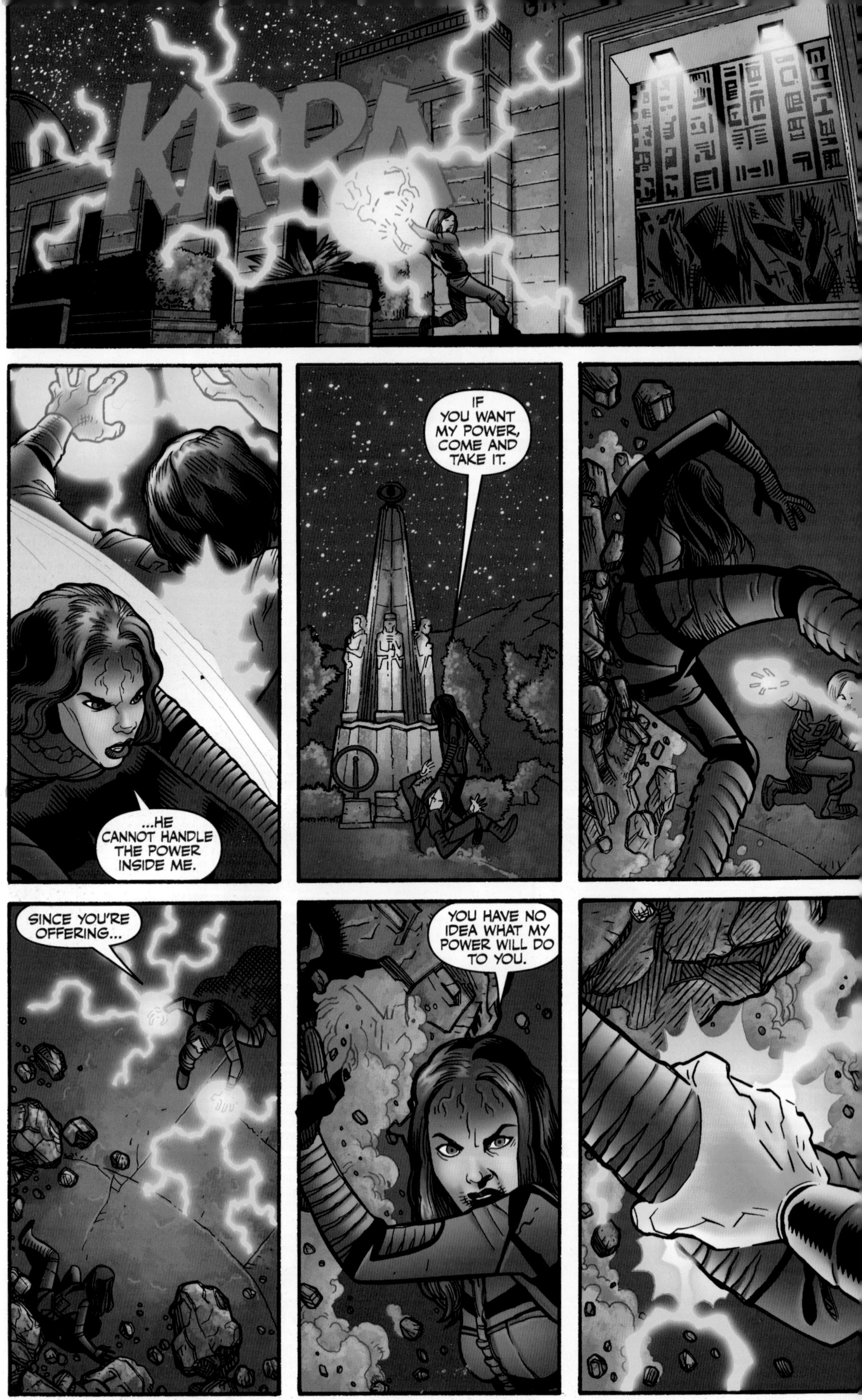
KRRA
...HE CANNOT HANDLE THE POWER INSIDE ME.
IF YOU WANT MY POWER, COME AND TAKE IT.
SINCE YOU'RE OFFERING...
YOU HAVE NO IDEA WHAT MY POWER WILL DO TO YOU.

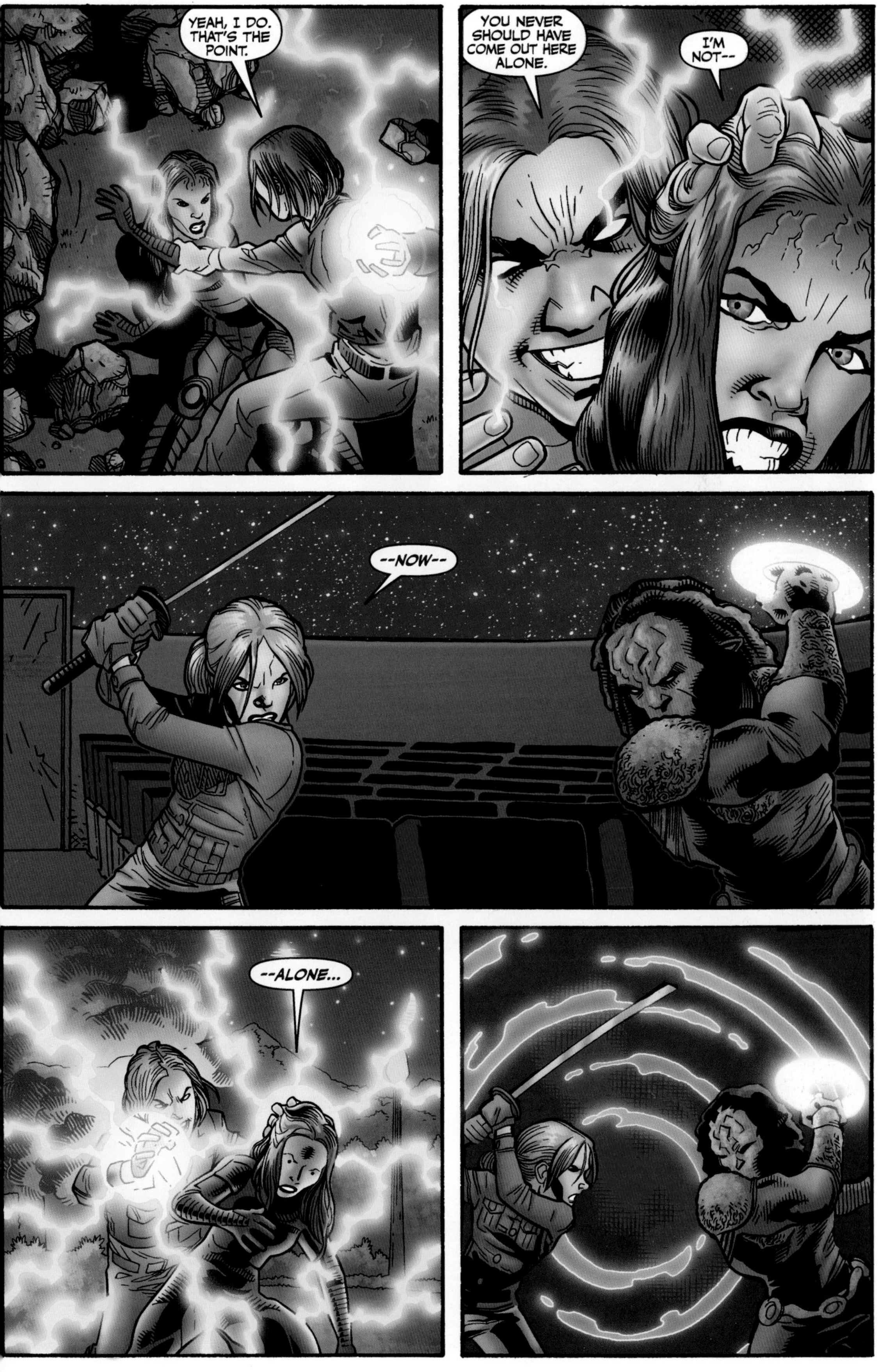
YEAH, I DO. THAT'S THE POINT.
YOU NEVER SHOULD HAVE COME OUT HERE ALONE.
I'M NOT--
--NOW--
--ALONE...

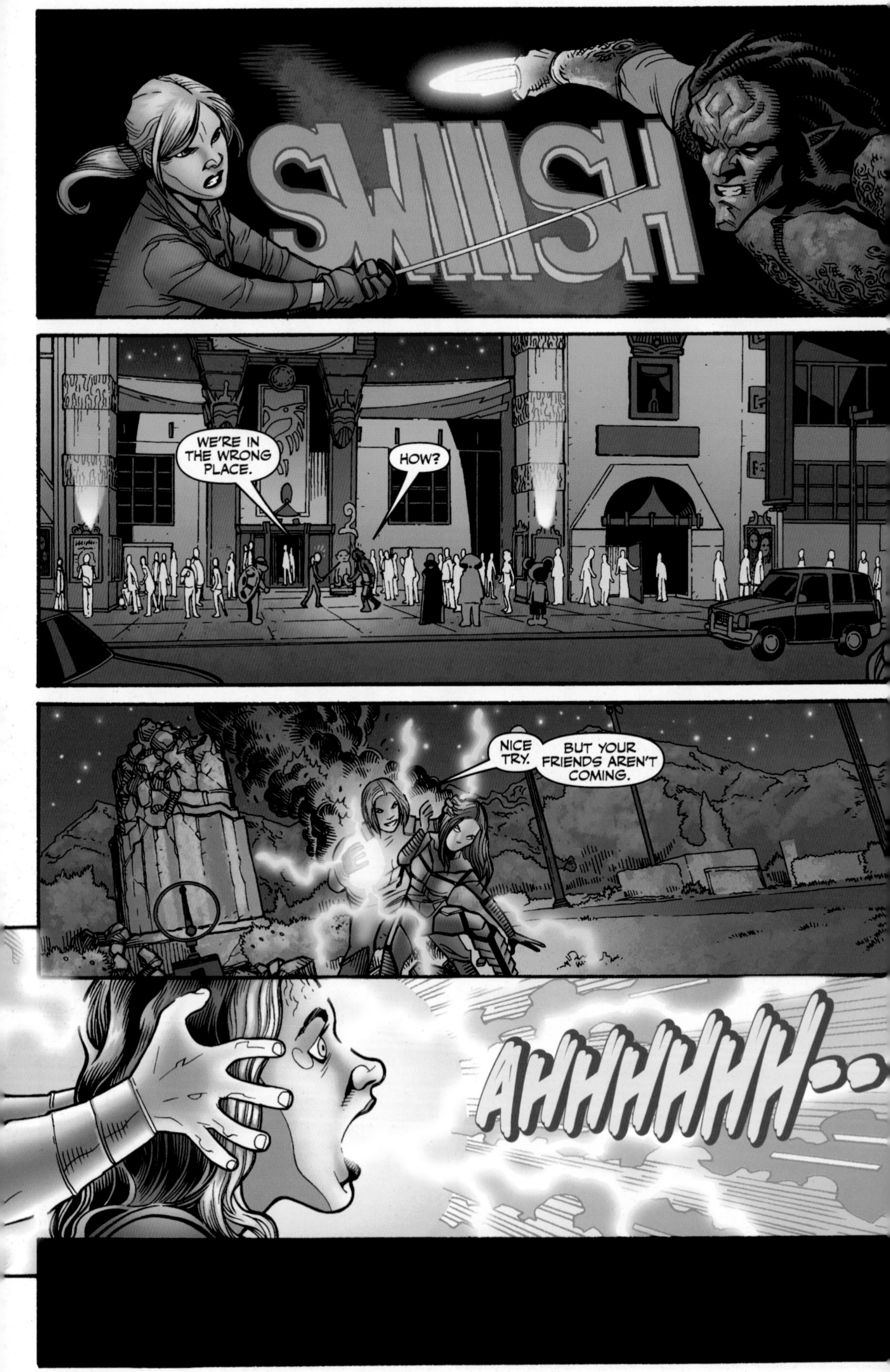
SWIISH
WE'RE IN THE WRONG PLACE.
HOW?
NICE TRY.
BUT YOUR FRIENDS AREN'T COMING.
AHHHHHHH--

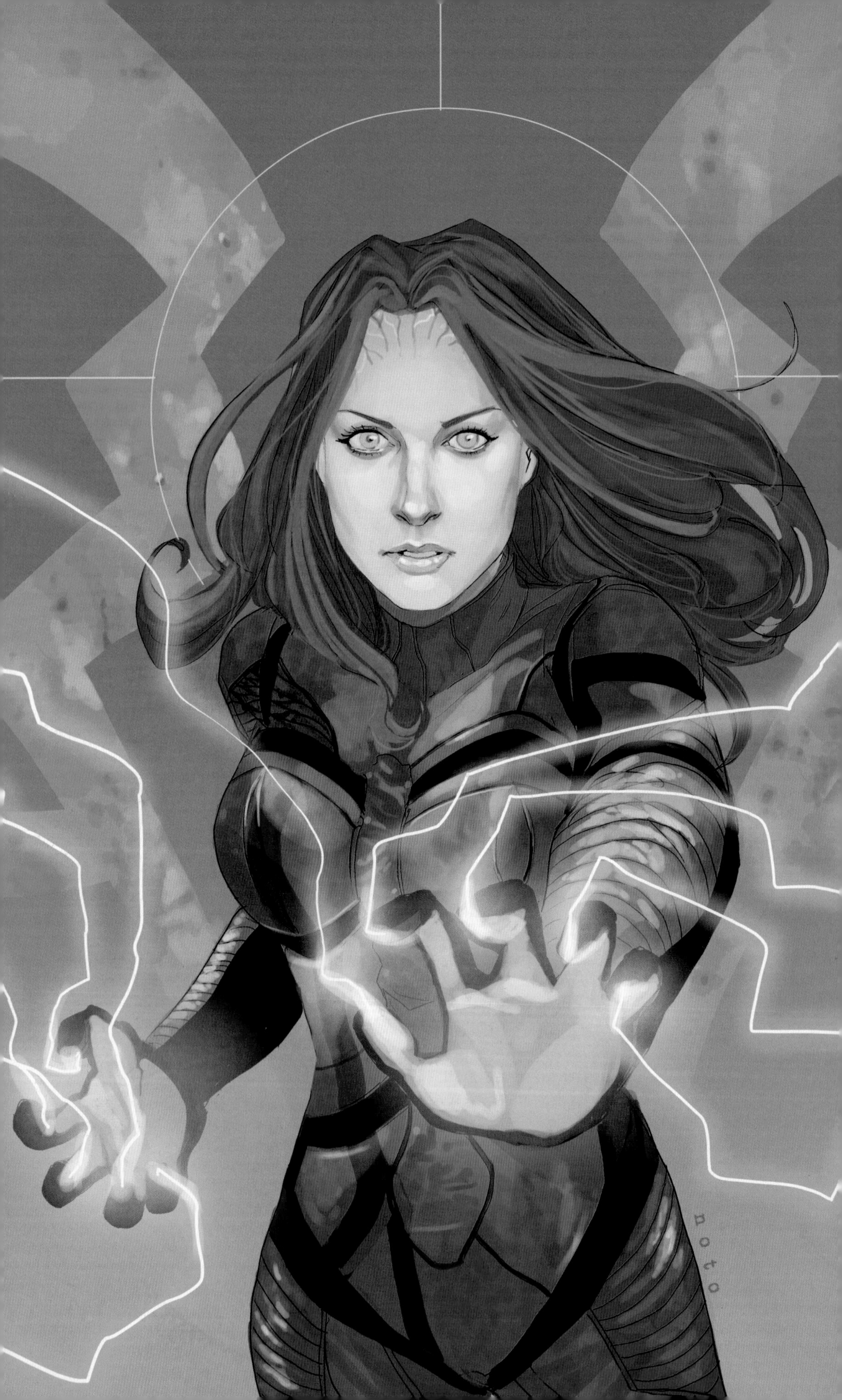
noto

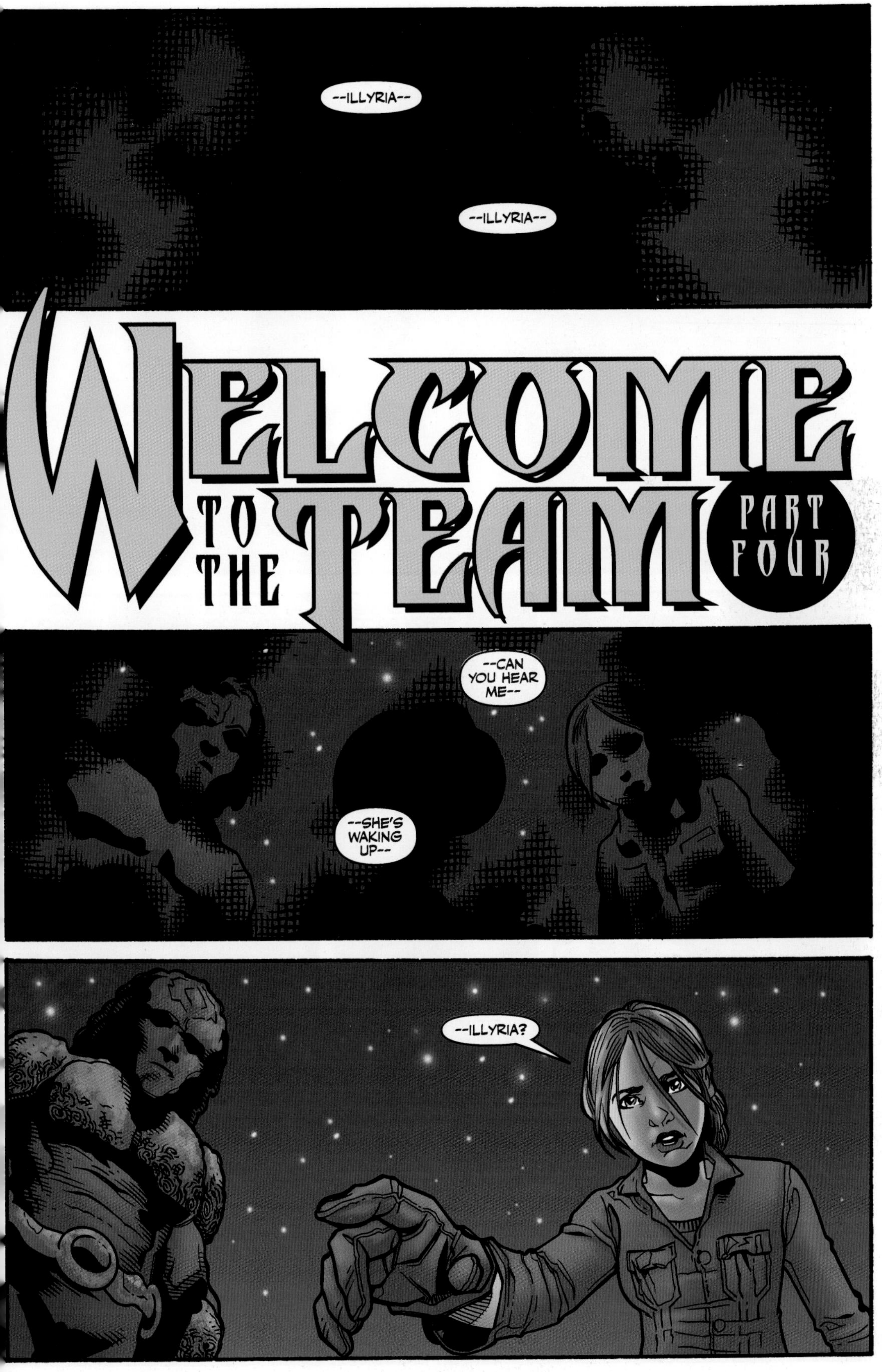
--ILLYRIA--
--ILLYRIA--
WELCOME TO THE TEAM
PART FOUR
--CAN YOU HEAR ME--
--SHE'S WAKING UP--
--ILLYRIA?

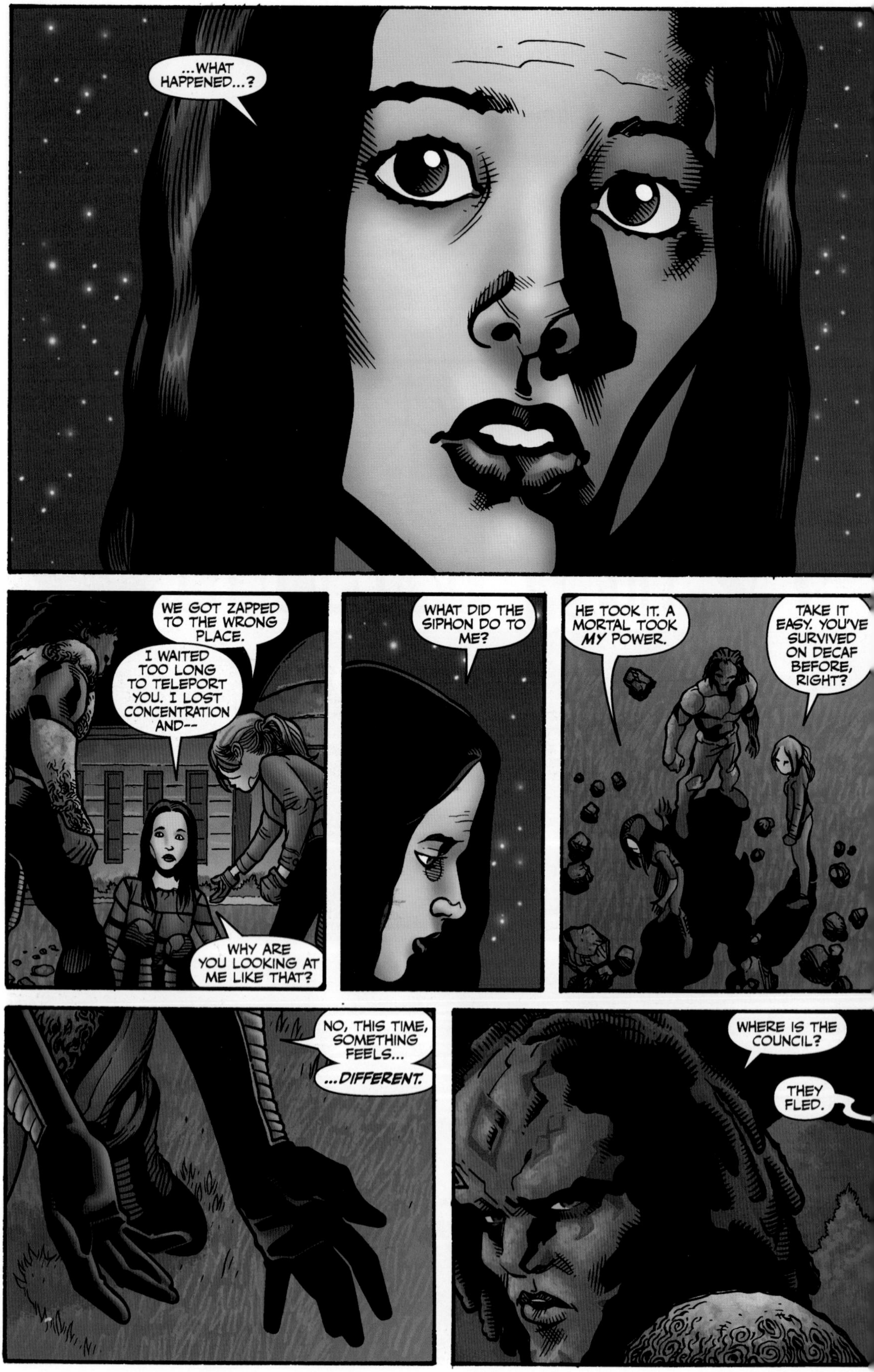
...WHAT HAPPENED...?
WE GOT ZAPPED TO THE WRONG PLACE.
I WAITED TOO LONG TO TELEPORT YOU. I LOST CONCENTRATION AND--
WHY ARE YOU LOOKING AT ME LIKE THAT?
WHAT DID THE SIPHON DO TO ME?
HE TOOK IT. A MORTAL TOOK MY POWER.
TAKE IT EASY. YOU'VE SURVIVED ON DECAF BEFORE, RIGHT?
NO, THIS TIME, SOMETHING FEELS...
...DIFFERENT.
WHERE IS THE COUNCIL?
THEY FLED.

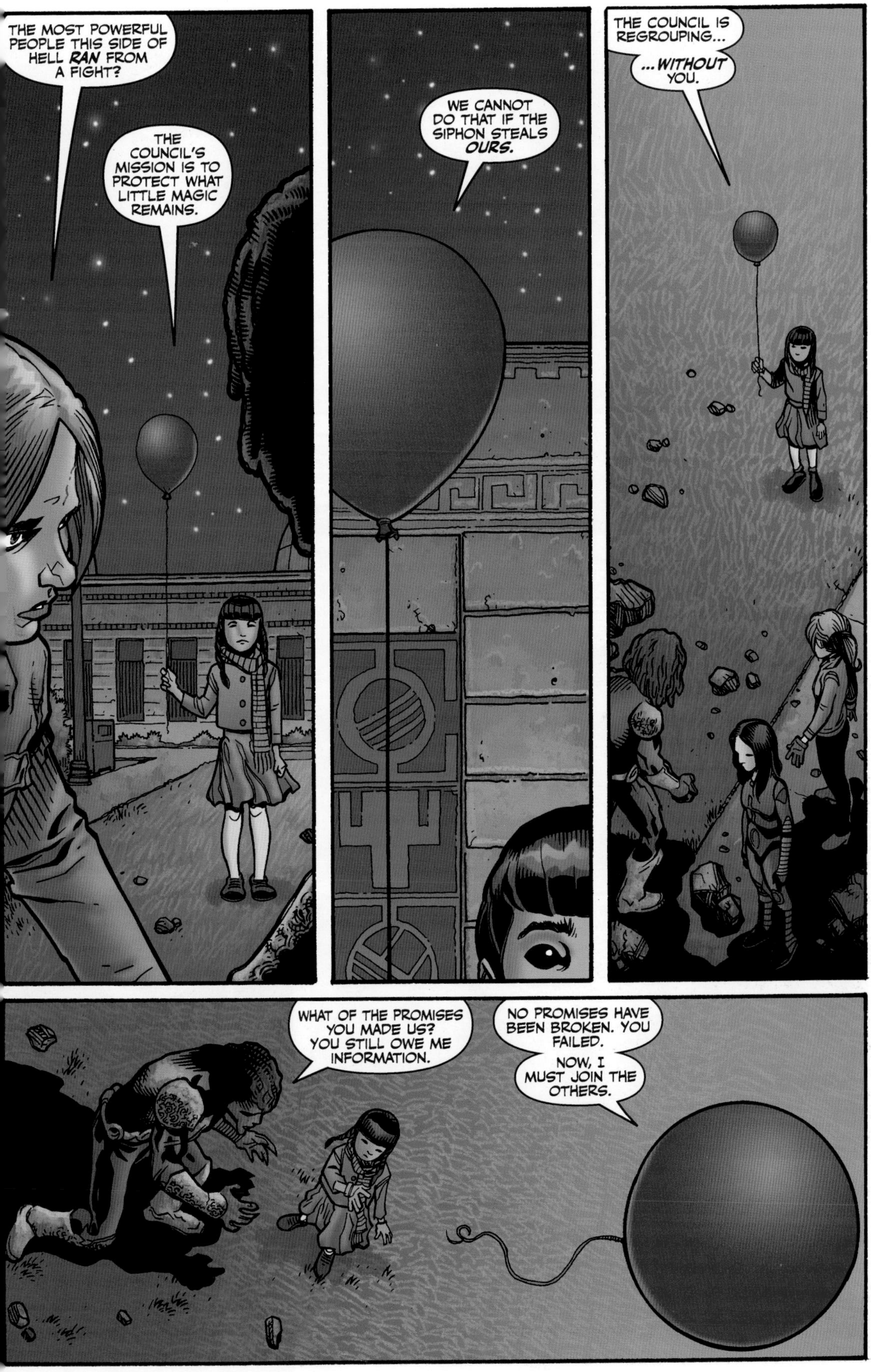
THE MOST POWERFUL PEOPLE THIS SIDE OF HELL *RAN* FROM A FIGHT?
THE COUNCIL'S MISSION IS TO PROTECT WHAT LITTLE MAGIC REMAINS.
WE CANNOT DO THAT IF THE SIPHON STEALS *OURS.*
THE COUNCIL IS REGROUPING...
...*WITHOUT* YOU.
WHAT OF THE PROMISES YOU MADE US? YOU STILL OWE ME INFORMATION.
NO PROMISES HAVE BEEN BROKEN. YOU FAILED.
NOW, I MUST JOIN THE OTHERS.

WE'VE GOT BIGGER PROBLEMS THAN FINDING WHO THREW YOU IN JAIL, KOH. AND THE PARTY BALLOON'S RIGHT. WE FAILED BIG TIME.

SORRY ABOUT THAT, ILLYRIA.

I DO NOT REQUIRE AN APOLOGY, SLAYER.

I AM MORE CONCERNED WITH WHAT THE SIPHON WILL DO WITH MY POWER.

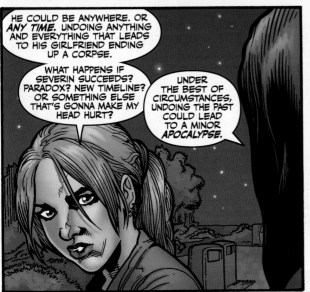

HE COULD BE ANYWHERE. OR *ANY TIME*. UNDOING ANYTHING AND EVERYTHING THAT LEADS TO HIS GIRLFRIEND ENDING UP A CORPSE.

WHAT HAPPENS IF SEVERIN SUCCEEDS? PARADOX? NEW TIMELINE? OR SOMETHING ELSE THAT'S GONNA MAKE MY HEAD HURT?

UNDER THE BEST OF CIRCUMSTANCES, UNDOING THE PAST COULD LEAD TO A MINOR *APOCALYPSE*.

I THOUGHT SHATTERING THE SEED MEANT I COULD DELETE THE A-WORD FROM MY VOCABULARY.

WE MUST HOPE THE COUNCIL STOPS THE SIPHON.

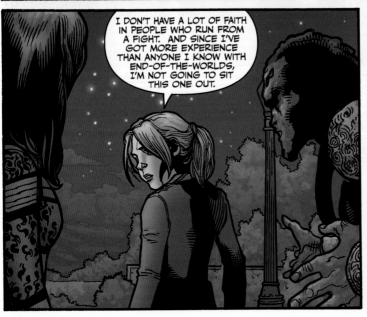

I DON'T HAVE A LOT OF FAITH IN PEOPLE WHO RUN FROM A FIGHT. AND SINCE I'VE GOT MORE EXPERIENCE THAN ANYONE I KNOW WITH END-OF-THE-WORLDS, I'M NOT GOING TO SIT THIS ONE OUT.

WE'RE GOING TO NEED HELP.

WHO WILL HELP US?

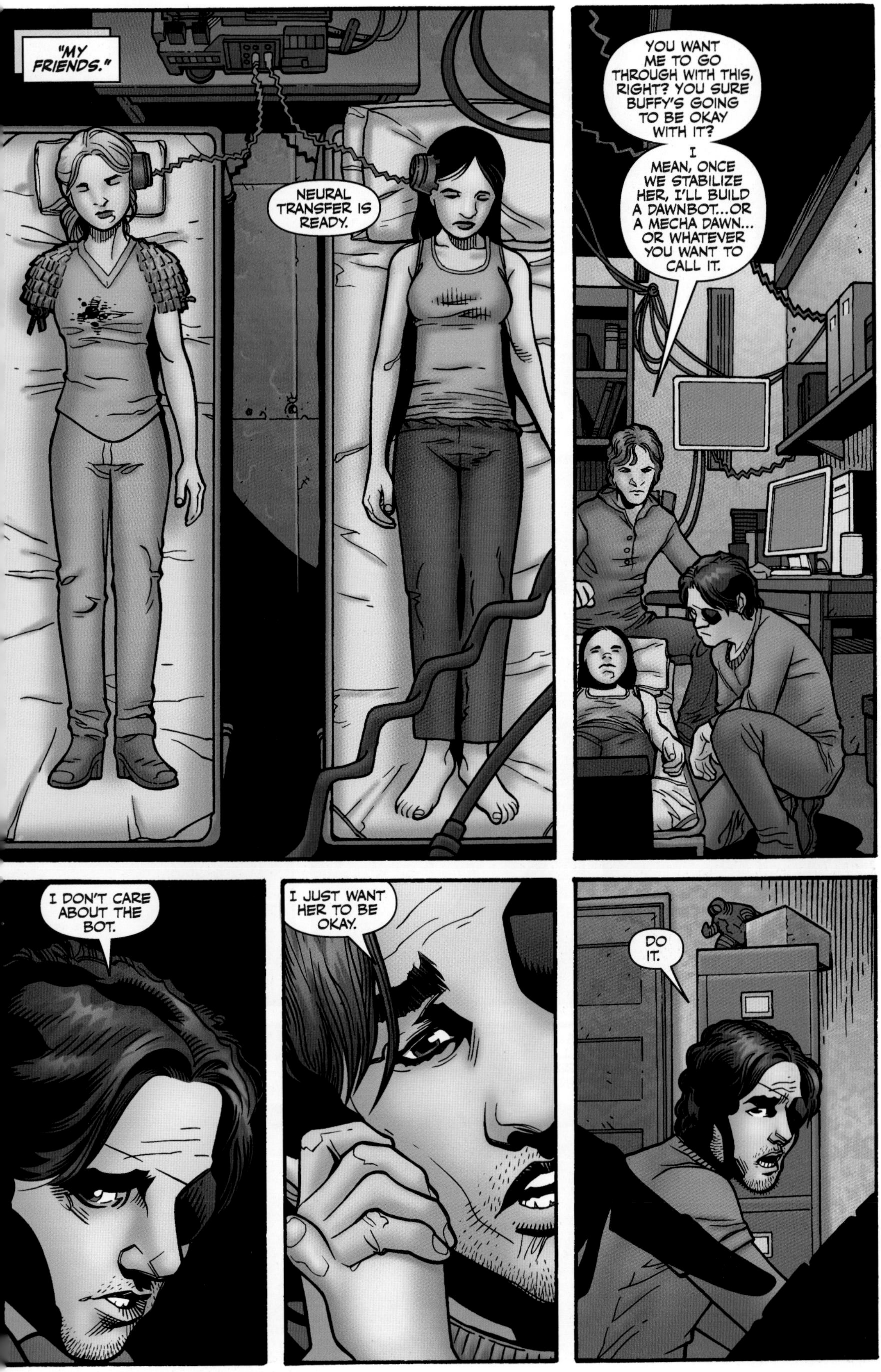
"MY FRIENDS."
NEURAL TRANSFER IS READY.
YOU WANT ME TO GO THROUGH WITH THIS, RIGHT? YOU SURE BUFFY'S GOING TO BE OKAY WITH IT?
I MEAN, ONCE WE STABILIZE HER, I'LL BUILD A DAWNBOT...OR A MECHA DAWN... OR WHATEVER YOU WANT TO CALL IT.
I DON'T CARE ABOUT THE BOT.
I JUST WANT HER TO BE OKAY.
DO IT.

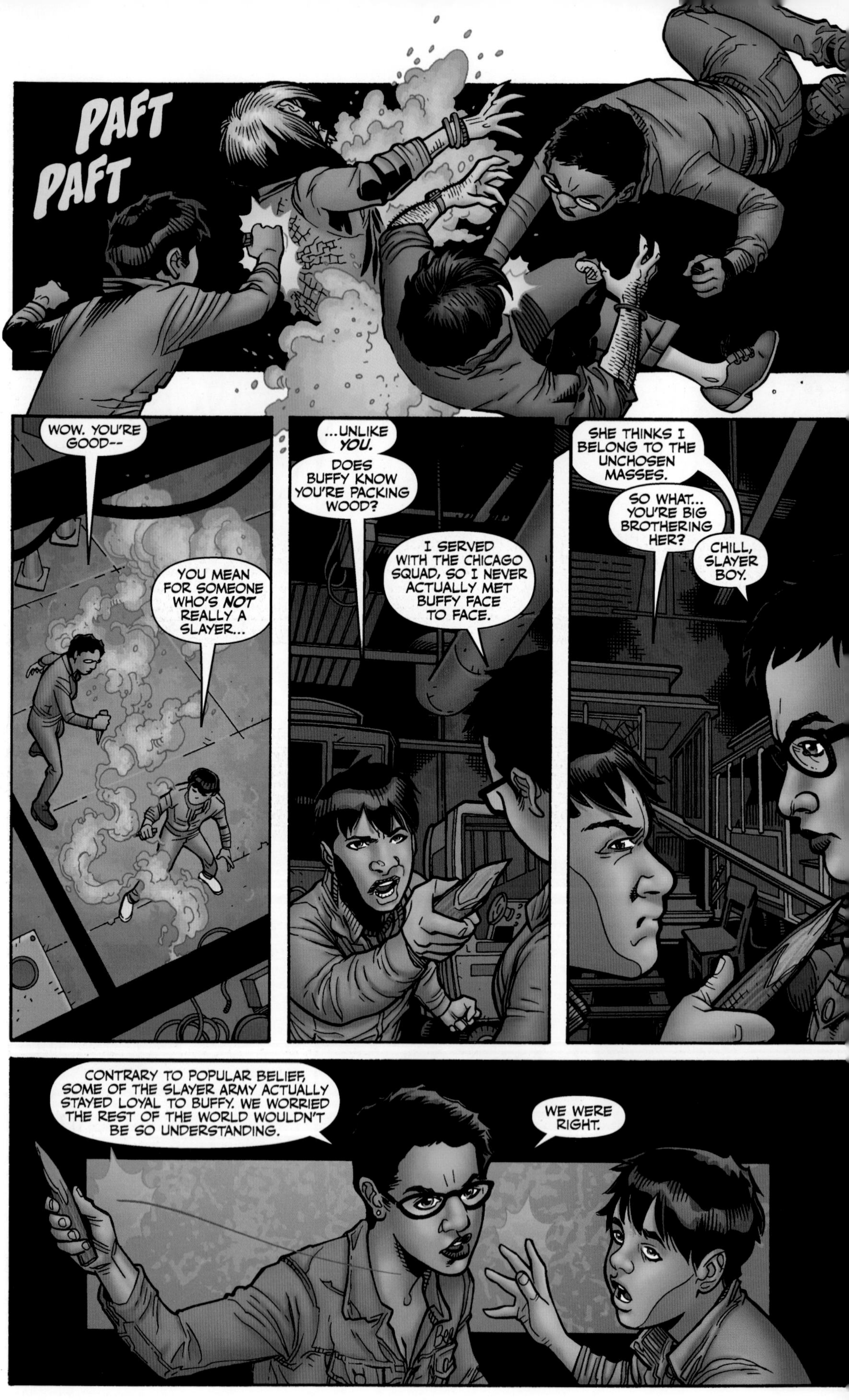
PAFT
PAFT
WOW. YOU'RE GOOD--
YOU MEAN FOR SOMEONE WHO'S NOT REALLY A SLAYER...
...UNLIKE YOU.
DOES BUFFY KNOW YOU'RE PACKING WOOD?
I SERVED WITH THE CHICAGO SQUAD, SO I NEVER ACTUALLY MET BUFFY FACE TO FACE.
SHE THINKS I BELONG TO THE UNCHOSEN MASSES.
SO WHAT... YOU'RE BIG BROTHERING HER?
CHILL, SLAYER BOY.
CONTRARY TO POPULAR BELIEF, SOME OF THE SLAYER ARMY ACTUALLY STAYED LOYAL TO BUFFY. WE WORRIED THE REST OF THE WORLD WOULDN'T BE SO UNDERSTANDING.
WE WERE RIGHT.

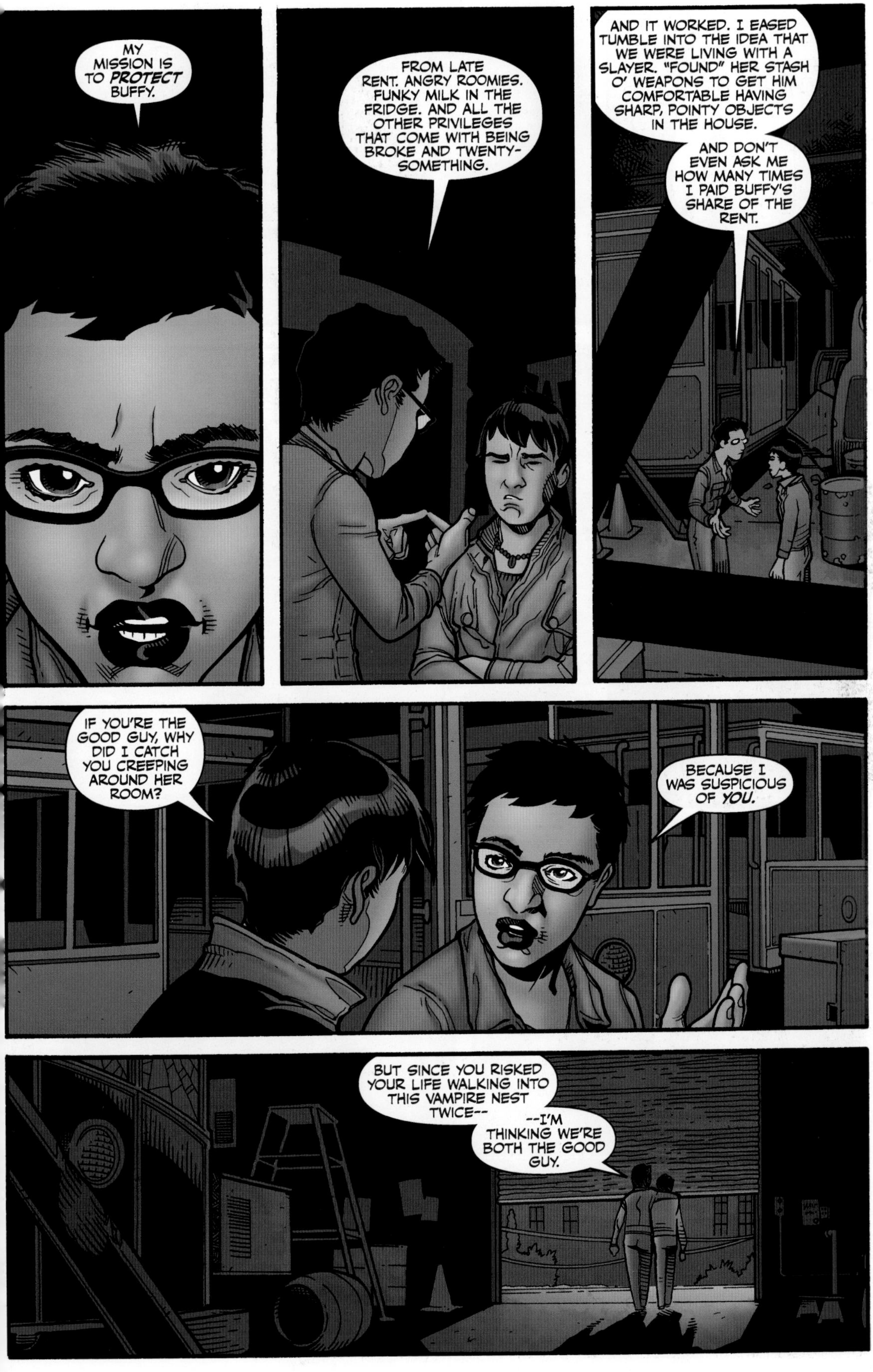

MY MISSION IS TO PROTECT BUFFY.
FROM LATE RENT. ANGRY ROOMIES. FUNKY MILK IN THE FRIDGE. AND ALL THE OTHER PRIVILEGES THAT COME WITH BEING BROKE AND TWENTY-SOMETHING.
AND IT WORKED. I EASED TUMBLE INTO THE IDEA THAT WE WERE LIVING WITH A SLAYER. "FOUND" HER STASH O' WEAPONS TO GET HIM COMFORTABLE HAVING SHARP, POINTY OBJECTS IN THE HOUSE.
AND DON'T EVEN ASK ME HOW MANY TIMES I PAID BUFFY'S SHARE OF THE RENT.
IF YOU'RE THE GOOD GUY, WHY DID I CATCH YOU CREEPING AROUND HER ROOM?
BECAUSE I WAS SUSPICIOUS OF YOU.
BUT SINCE YOU RISKED YOUR LIFE WALKING INTO THIS VAMPIRE NEST TWICE--
--I'M THINKING WE'RE BOTH THE GOOD GUY.

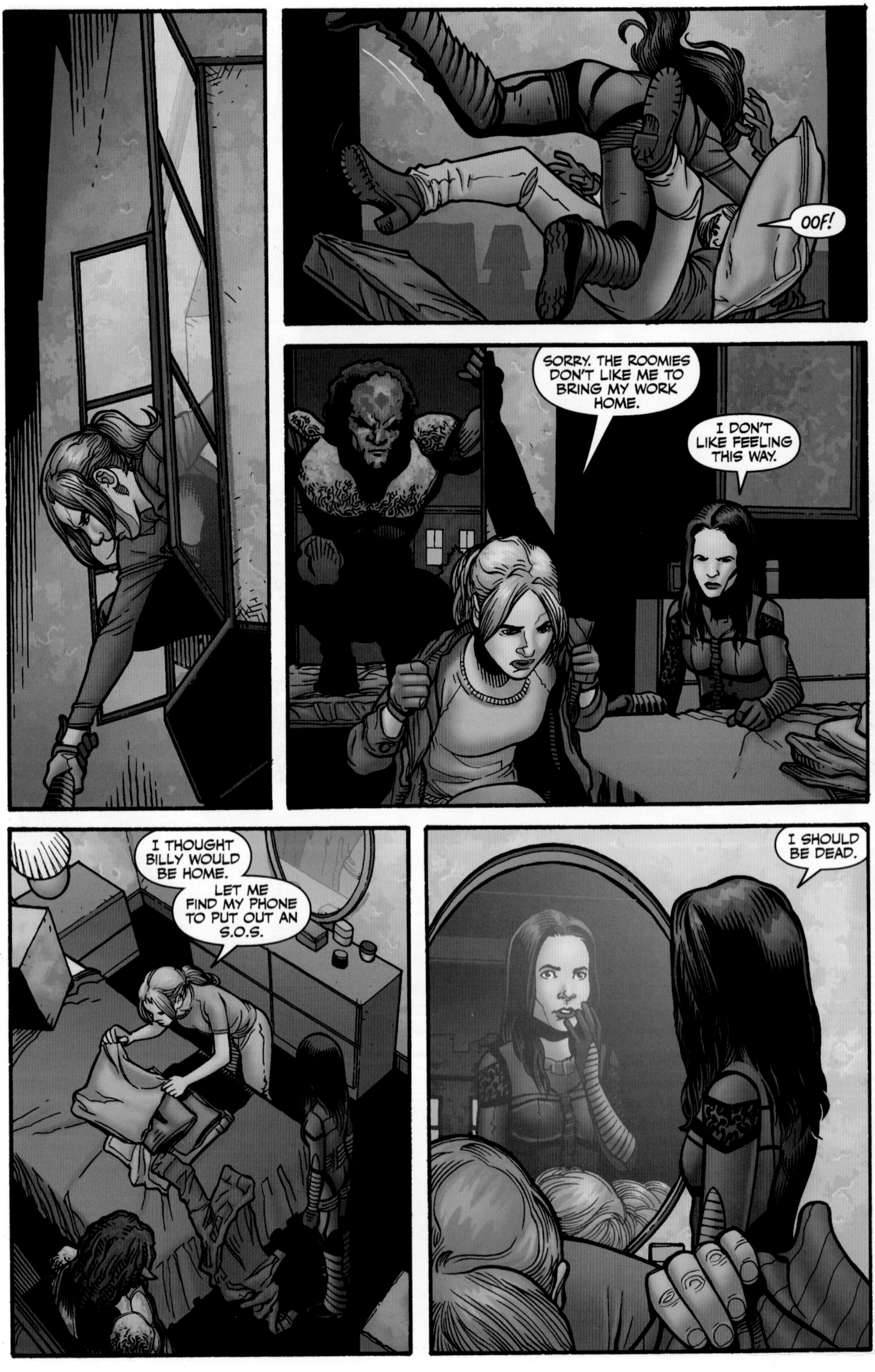
OOF!
SORRY. THE ROOMIES DON'T LIKE ME TO BRING MY WORK HOME.
I DON'T LIKE FEELING THIS WAY.
I THOUGHT BILLY WOULD BE HOME.
LET ME FIND MY PHONE TO PUT OUT AN S.O.S.
I SHOULD BE DEAD.

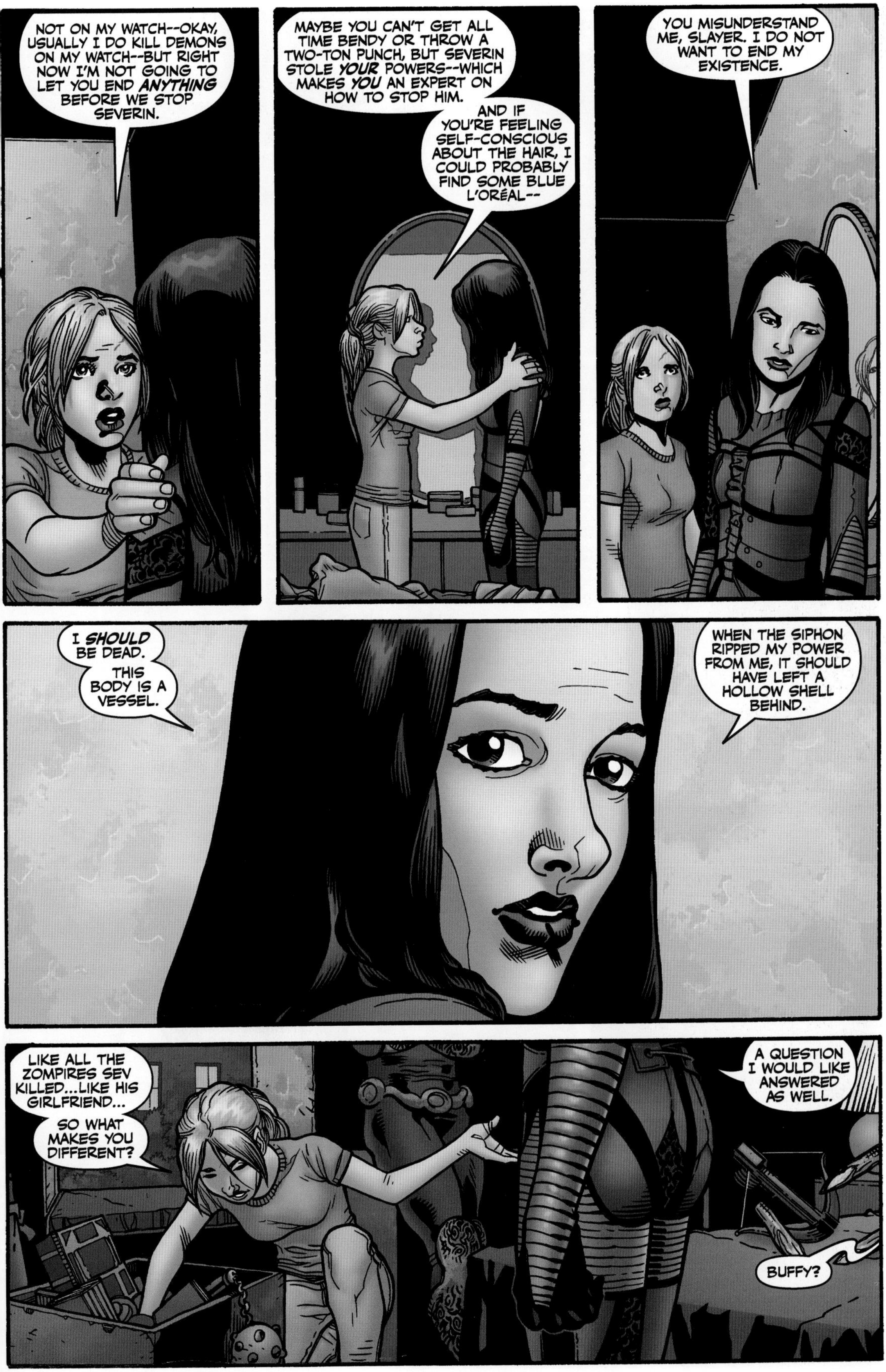
NOT ON MY WATCH--OKAY, USUALLY I DO KILL DEMONS ON MY WATCH--BUT RIGHT NOW I'M NOT GOING TO LET YOU END ANYTHING BEFORE WE STOP SEVERIN.
MAYBE YOU CAN'T GET ALL TIME BENDY OR THROW A TWO-TON PUNCH, BUT SEVERIN STOLE YOUR POWERS--WHICH MAKES YOU AN EXPERT ON HOW TO STOP HIM.
AND IF YOU'RE FEELING SELF-CONSCIOUS ABOUT THE HAIR, I COULD PROBABLY FIND SOME BLUE L'ORÉAL--
YOU MISUNDERSTAND ME, SLAYER. I DO NOT WANT TO END MY EXISTENCE.
I SHOULD BE DEAD.
THIS BODY IS A VESSEL.
WHEN THE SIPHON RIPPED MY POWER FROM ME, IT SHOULD HAVE LEFT A HOLLOW SHELL BEHIND.
LIKE ALL THE ZOMPIRES SEV KILLED...LIKE HIS GIRLFRIEND...
SO WHAT MAKES YOU DIFFERENT?
A QUESTION I WOULD LIKE ANSWERED AS WELL.
BUFFY?

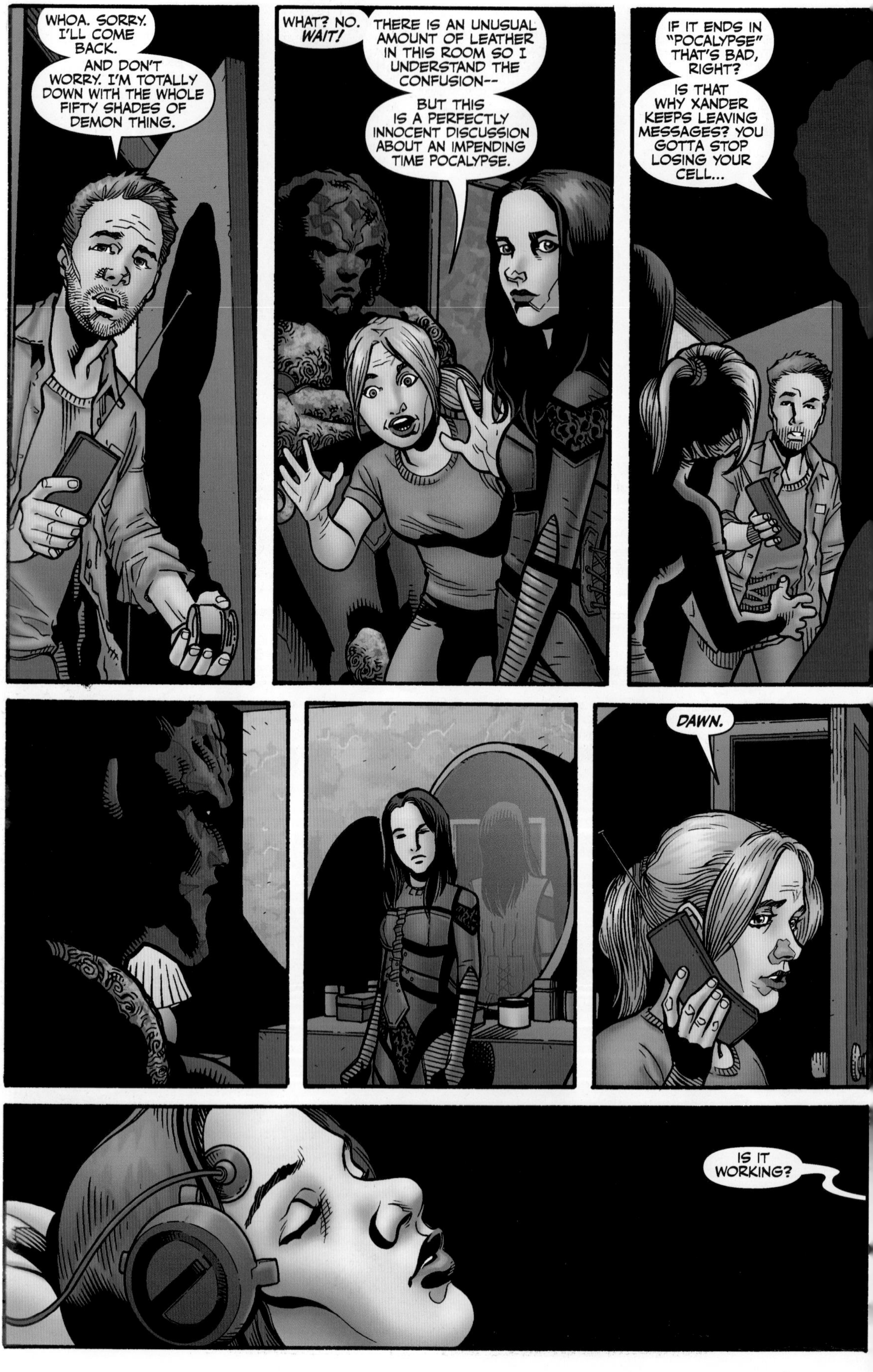
WHOA. SORRY. I'LL COME BACK.
AND DON'T WORRY. I'M TOTALLY DOWN WITH THE WHOLE FIFTY SHADES OF DEMON THING.
WHAT? NO. *WAIT!*
THERE IS AN UNUSUAL AMOUNT OF LEATHER IN THIS ROOM SO I UNDERSTAND THE CONFUSION--
BUT THIS IS A PERFECTLY INNOCENT DISCUSSION ABOUT AN IMPENDING TIME POCALYPSE.
IF IT ENDS IN "POCALYPSE" THAT'S BAD, RIGHT?
IS THAT WHY XANDER KEEPS LEAVING MESSAGES? YOU GOTTA STOP LOSING YOUR CELL...
DAWN.
IS IT WORKING?

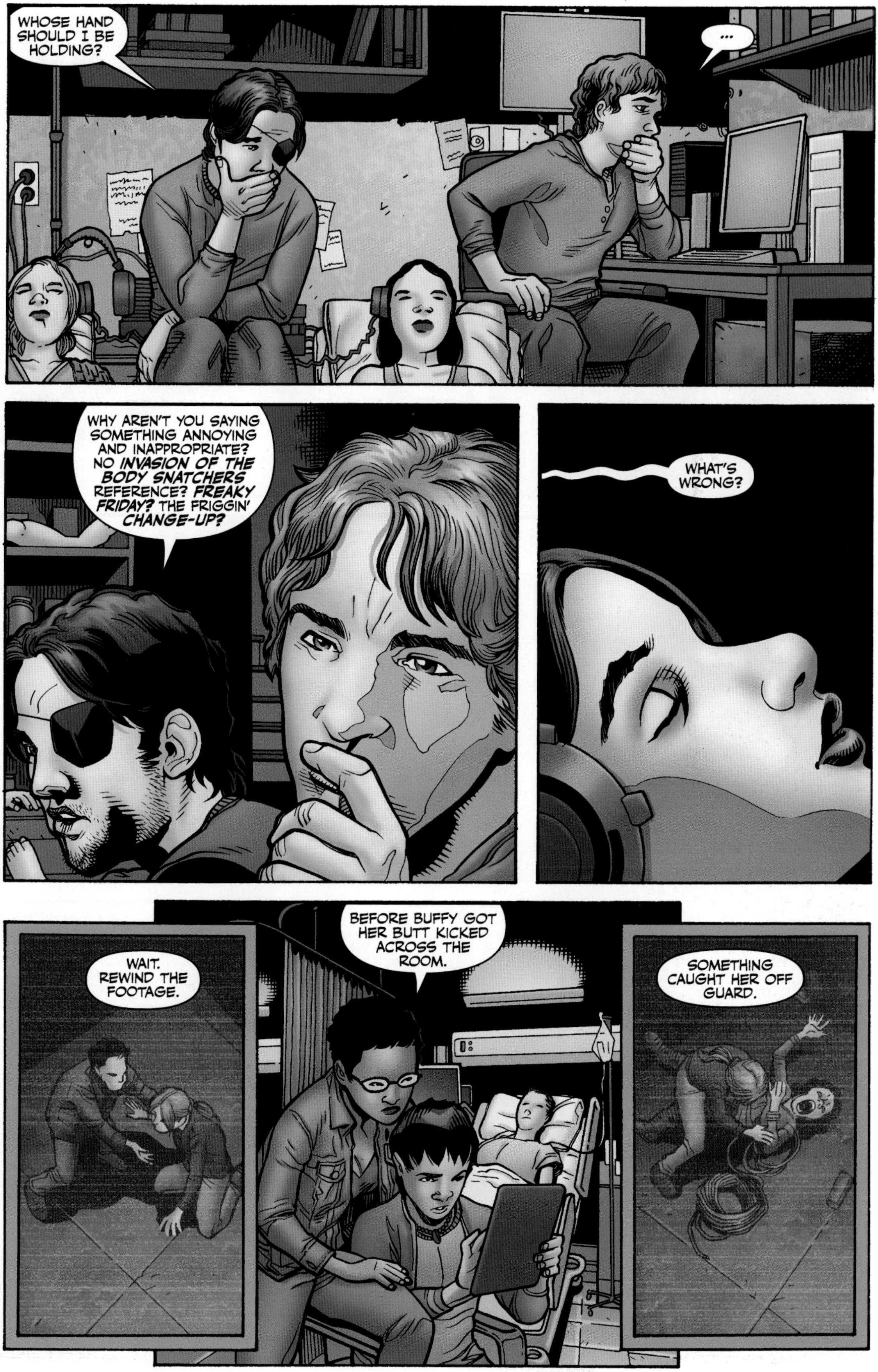
WHOSE HAND SHOULD I BE HOLDING?
...
WHY AREN'T YOU SAYING SOMETHING ANNOYING AND INAPPROPRIATE? NO INVASION OF THE BODY SNATCHERS REFERENCE? FREAKY FRIDAY? THE FRIGGIN' CHANGE-UP?
WHAT'S WRONG?
WAIT. REWIND THE FOOTAGE.
BEFORE BUFFY GOT HER BUTT KICKED ACROSS THE ROOM.
SOMETHING CAUGHT HER OFF GUARD.

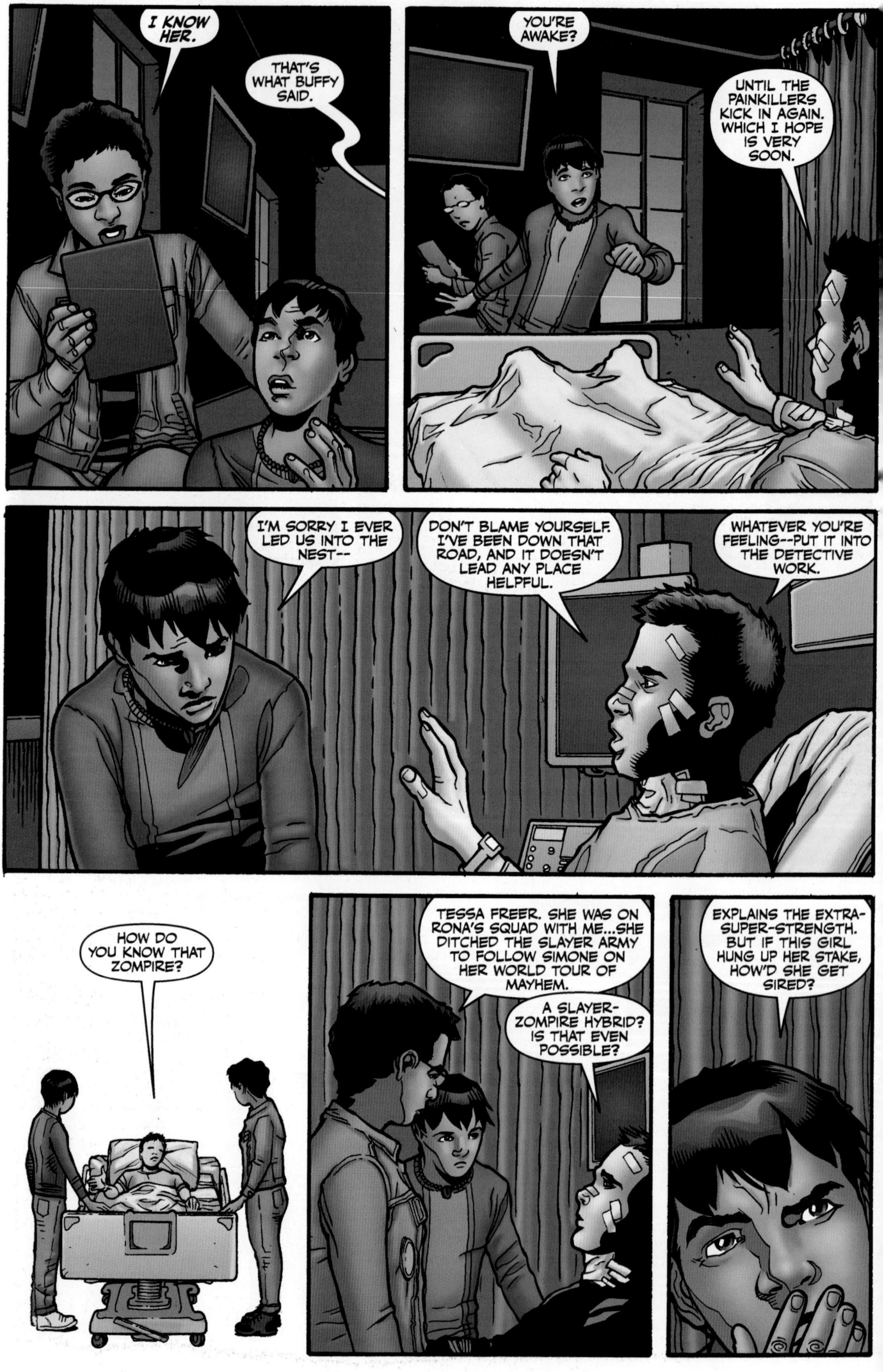

I KNOW HER.
THAT'S WHAT BUFFY SAID.
YOU'RE AWAKE?
UNTIL THE PAINKILLERS KICK IN AGAIN. WHICH I HOPE IS VERY SOON.
I'M SORRY I EVER LED US INTO THE NEST--
DON'T BLAME YOURSELF. I'VE BEEN DOWN THAT ROAD, AND IT DOESN'T LEAD ANY PLACE HELPFUL.
WHATEVER YOU'RE FEELING--PUT IT INTO THE DETECTIVE WORK.
HOW DO YOU KNOW THAT ZOMPIRE?
TESSA FREER. SHE WAS ON RONA'S SQUAD WITH ME...SHE DITCHED THE SLAYER ARMY TO FOLLOW SIMONE ON HER WORLD TOUR OF MAYHEM.
A SLAYER-ZOMPIRE HYBRID? IS THAT EVEN POSSIBLE?
EXPLAINS THE EXTRA-SUPER-STRENGTH. BUT IF THIS GIRL HUNG UP HER STAKE, HOW'D SHE GET SIRED?

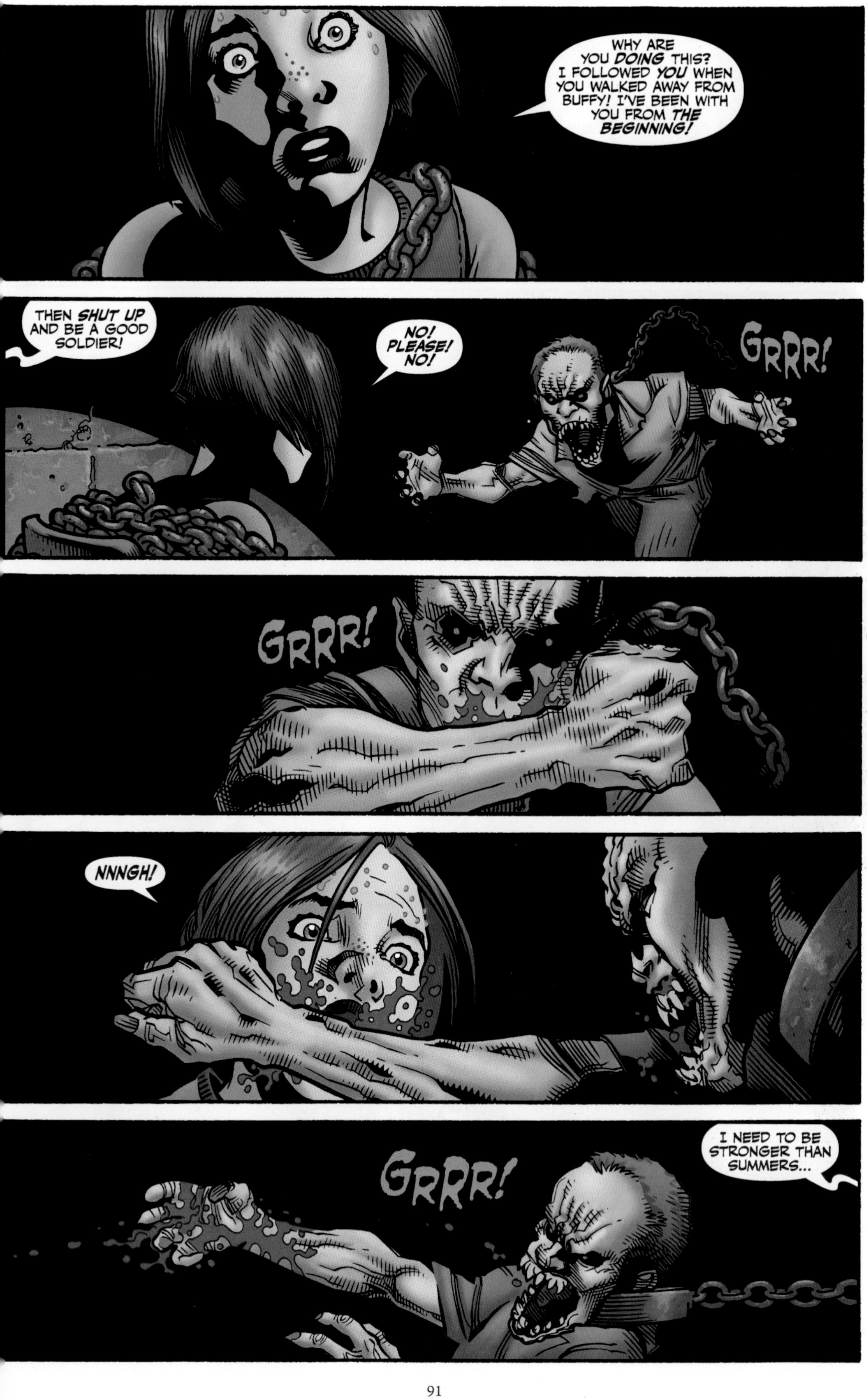

WHY ARE YOU DOING THIS? I FOLLOWED YOU WHEN YOU WALKED AWAY FROM BUFFY! I'VE BEEN WITH YOU FROM THE BEGINNING!
THEN SHUT UP AND BE A GOOD SOLDIER!
NO! PLEASE! NO!
GRRR!
GRRR!
NNNGH!
GRRR!
I NEED TO BE STRONGER THAN SUMMERS...

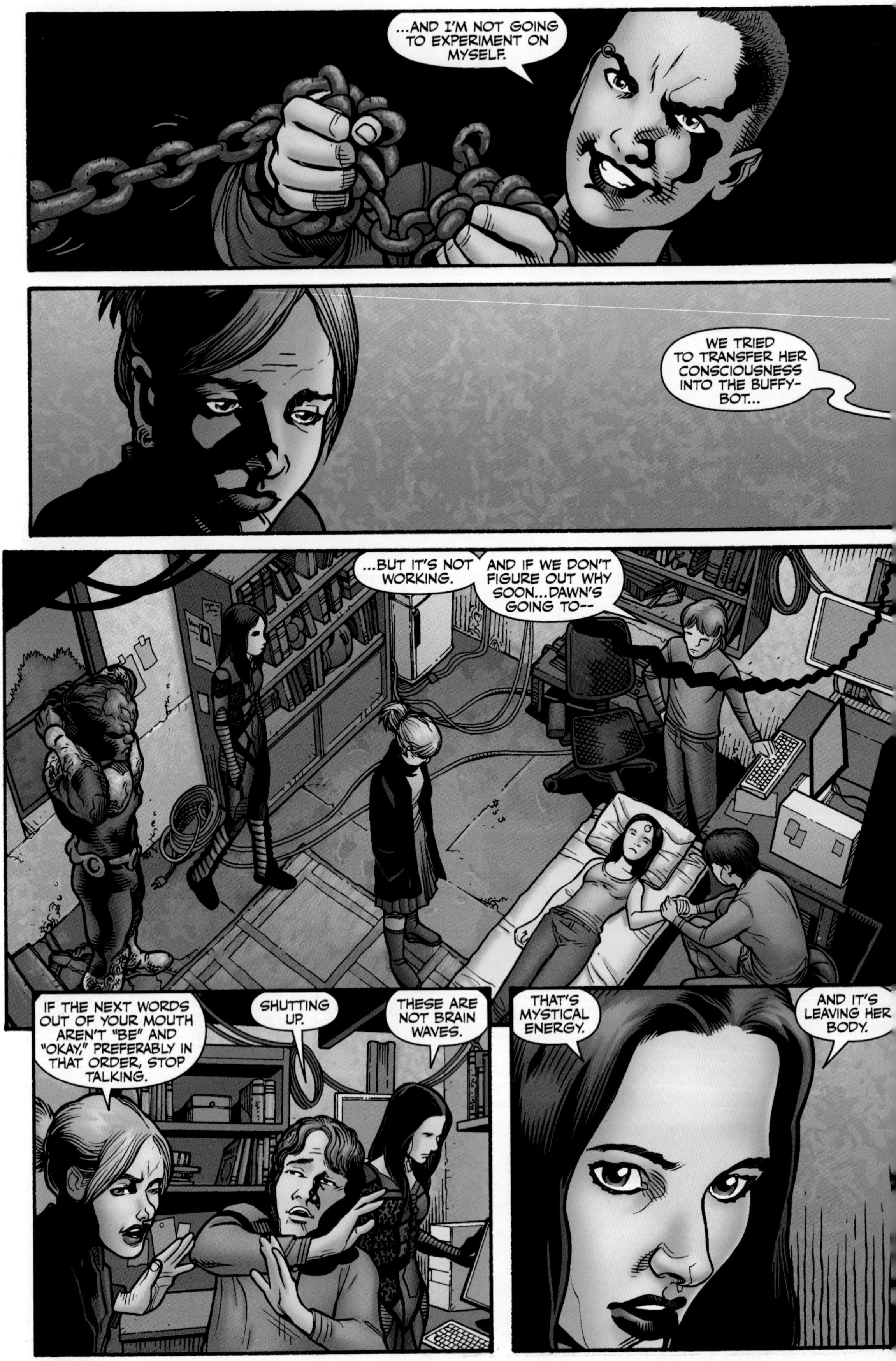

...AND I'M NOT GOING TO EXPERIMENT ON MYSELF.
WE TRIED TO TRANSFER HER CONSCIOUSNESS INTO THE BUFFY-BOT...
...BUT IT'S NOT WORKING.
AND IF WE DON'T FIGURE OUT WHY SOON...DAWN'S GOING TO--
IF THE NEXT WORDS OUT OF YOUR MOUTH AREN'T "BE" AND "OKAY," PREFERABLY IN THAT ORDER, STOP TALKING.
SHUTTING UP.
THESE ARE NOT BRAIN WAVES.
THAT'S MYSTICAL ENERGY.
AND IT'S LEAVING HER BODY.

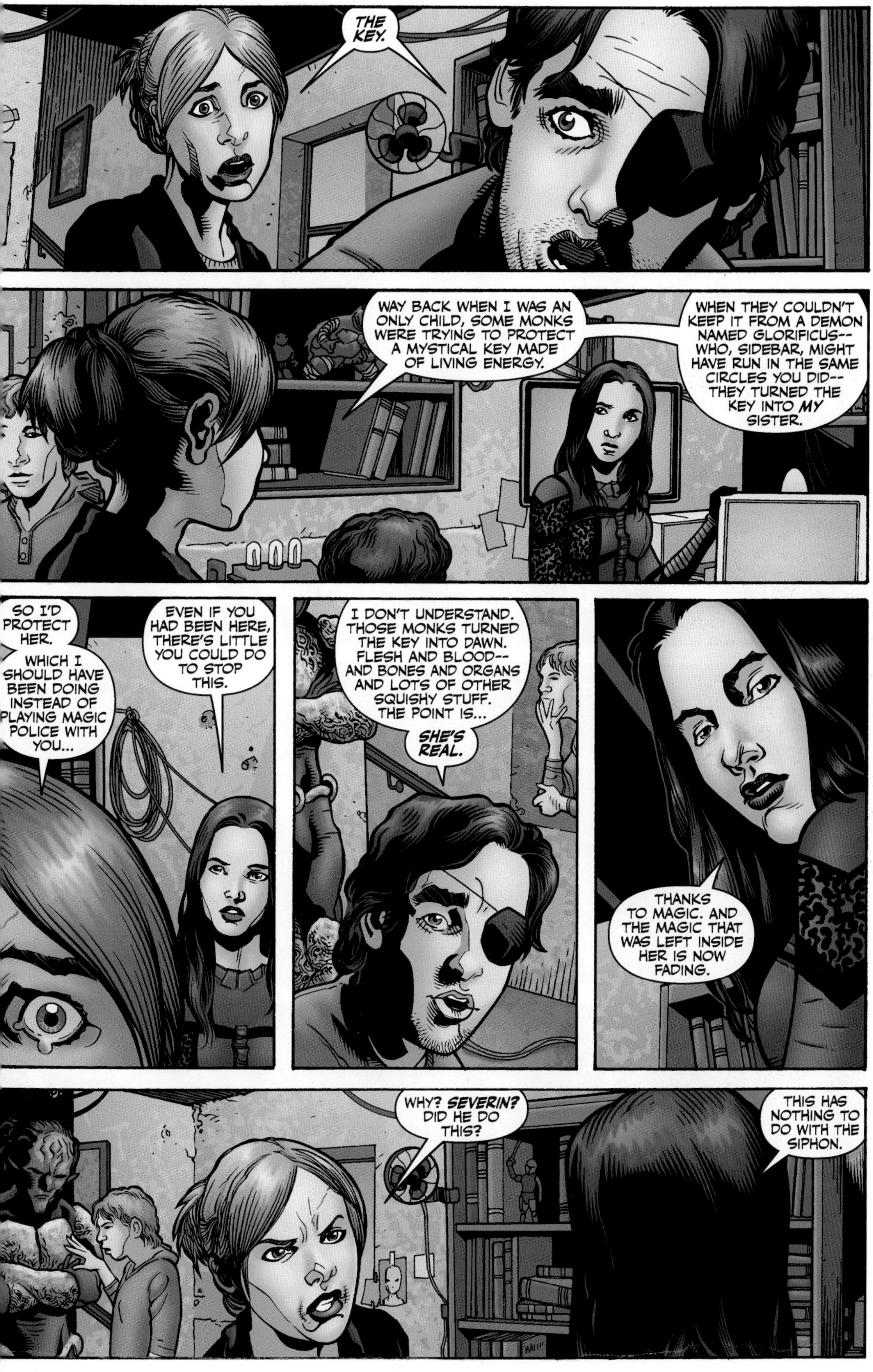
THE KEY.
WAY BACK WHEN I WAS AN ONLY CHILD, SOME MONKS WERE TRYING TO PROTECT A MYSTICAL KEY MADE OF LIVING ENERGY.
WHEN THEY COULDN'T KEEP IT FROM A DEMON NAMED GLORIFICUS-- WHO, SIDEBAR, MIGHT HAVE RUN IN THE SAME CIRCLES YOU DID-- THEY TURNED THE KEY INTO MY SISTER.
SO I'D PROTECT HER.
WHICH I SHOULD HAVE BEEN DOING INSTEAD OF PLAYING MAGIC POLICE WITH YOU...
EVEN IF YOU HAD BEEN HERE, THERE'S LITTLE YOU COULD DO TO STOP THIS.
I DON'T UNDERSTAND. THOSE MONKS TURNED THE KEY INTO DAWN. FLESH AND BLOOD-- AND BONES AND ORGANS AND LOTS OF OTHER SQUISHY STUFF. THE POINT IS...
SHE'S REAL.
THANKS TO MAGIC. AND THE MAGIC THAT WAS LEFT INSIDE HER IS NOW FADING.
WHY? SEVERIN? DID HE DO THIS?
THIS HAS NOTHING TO DO WITH THE SIPHON.

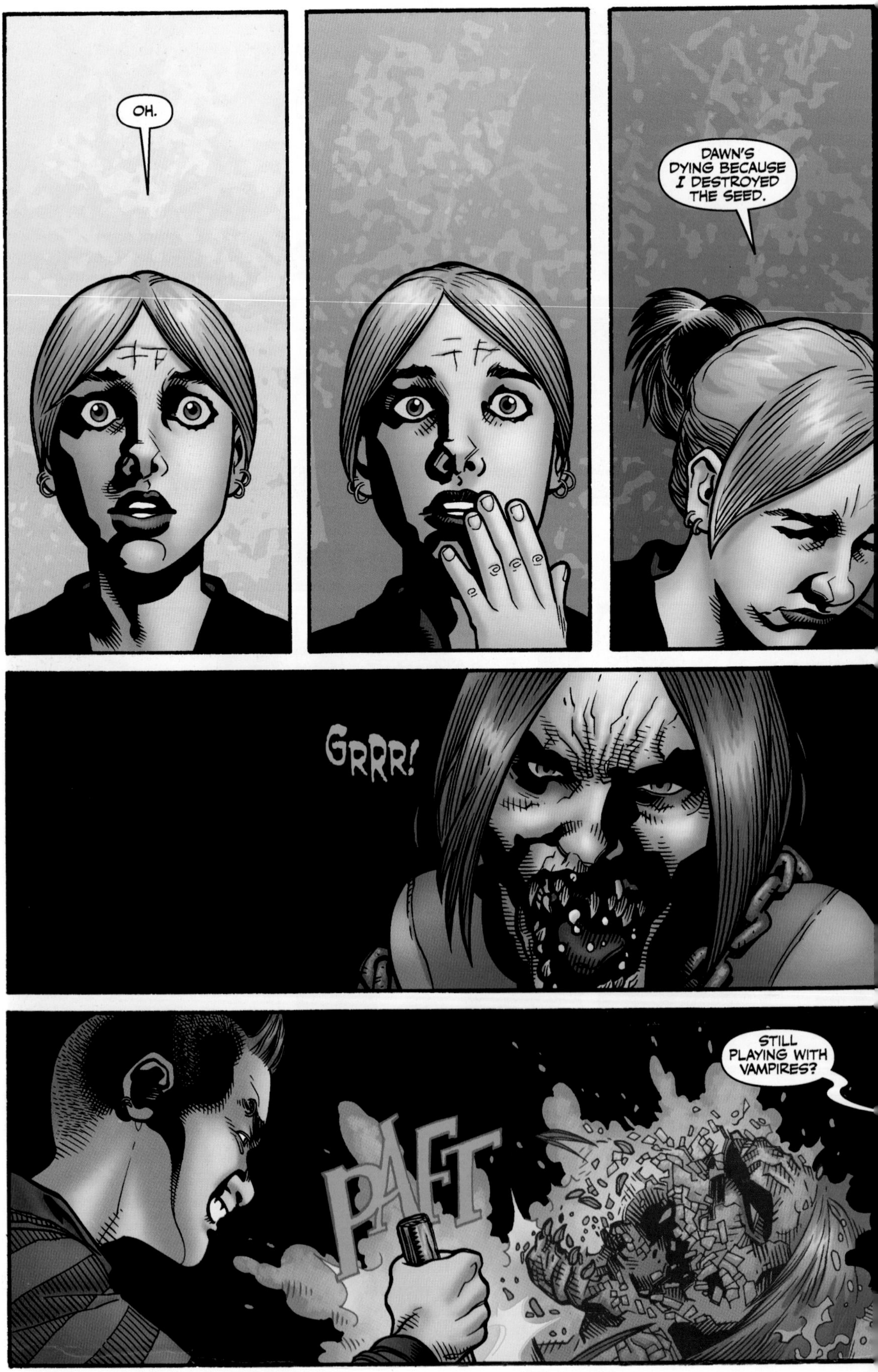
OH.
DAWN'S DYING BECAUSE I DESTROYED THE SEED.
GRRR!
STILL PLAYING WITH VAMPIRES?
PAFT

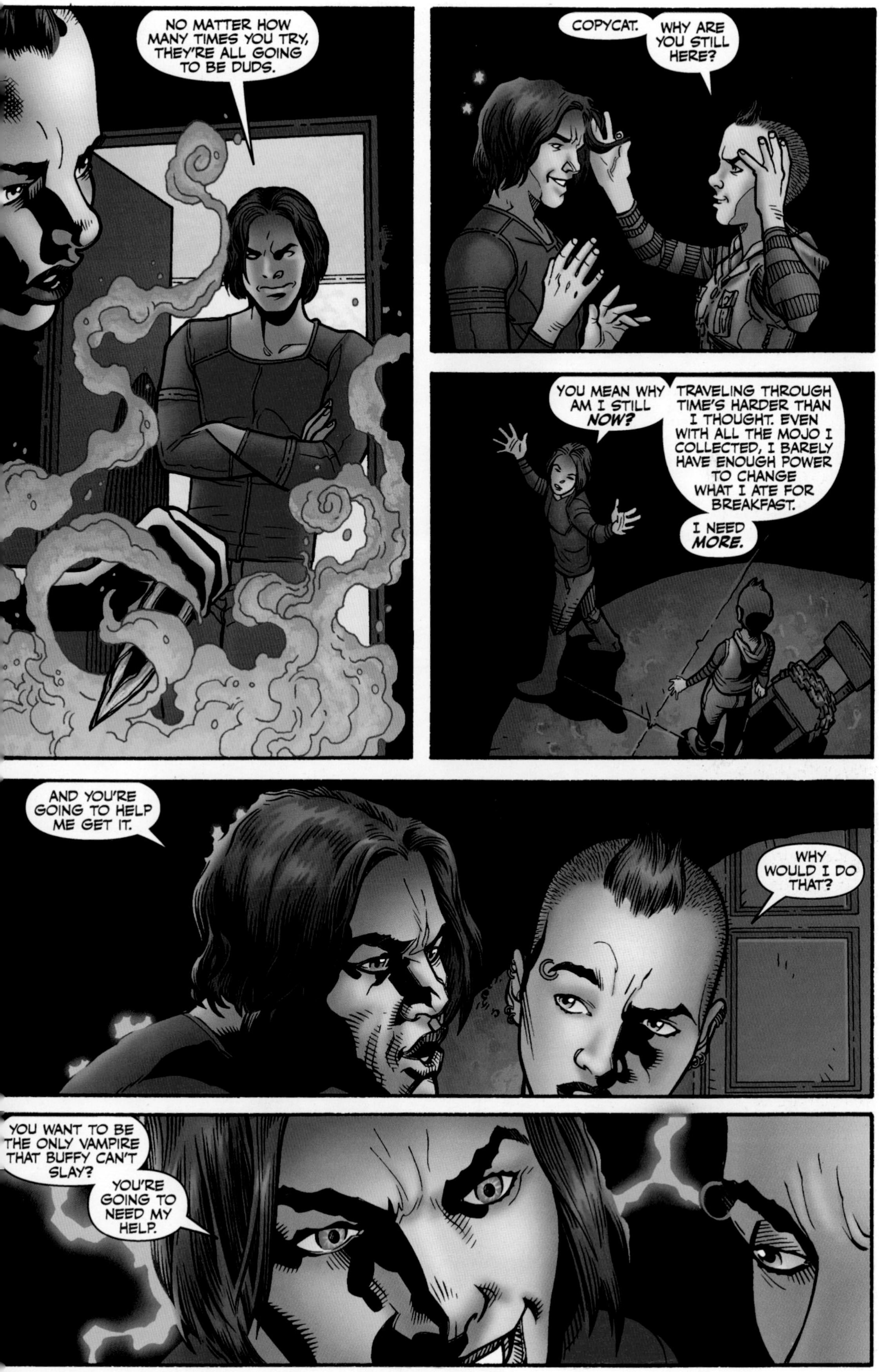
NO MATTER HOW MANY TIMES YOU TRY, THEY'RE ALL GOING TO BE DUDS.
COPYCAT.
WHY ARE YOU STILL HERE?
YOU MEAN WHY AM I STILL NOW?
TRAVELING THROUGH TIME'S HARDER THAN I THOUGHT. EVEN WITH ALL THE MOJO I COLLECTED, I BARELY HAVE ENOUGH POWER TO CHANGE WHAT I ATE FOR BREAKFAST.
I NEED MORE.
AND YOU'RE GOING TO HELP ME GET IT.
WHY WOULD I DO THAT?
YOU WANT TO BE THE ONLY VAMPIRE THAT BUFFY CAN'T SLAY?
YOU'RE GOING TO NEED MY HELP.

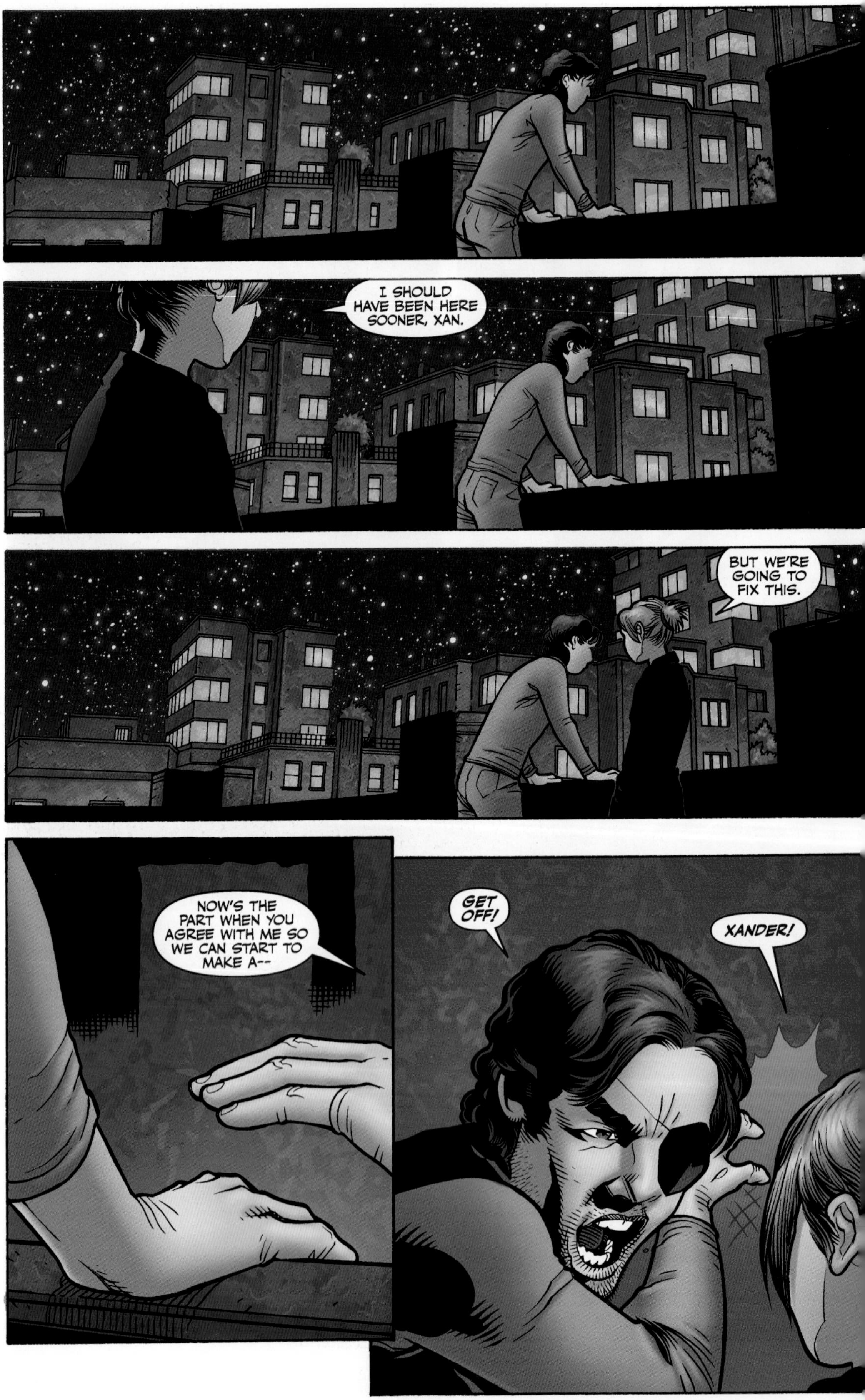
I SHOULD HAVE BEEN HERE SOONER, XAN.
BUT WE'RE GOING TO FIX THIS.
NOW'S THE PART WHEN YOU AGREE WITH ME SO WE CAN START TO MAKE A--
GET OFF!
XANDER!

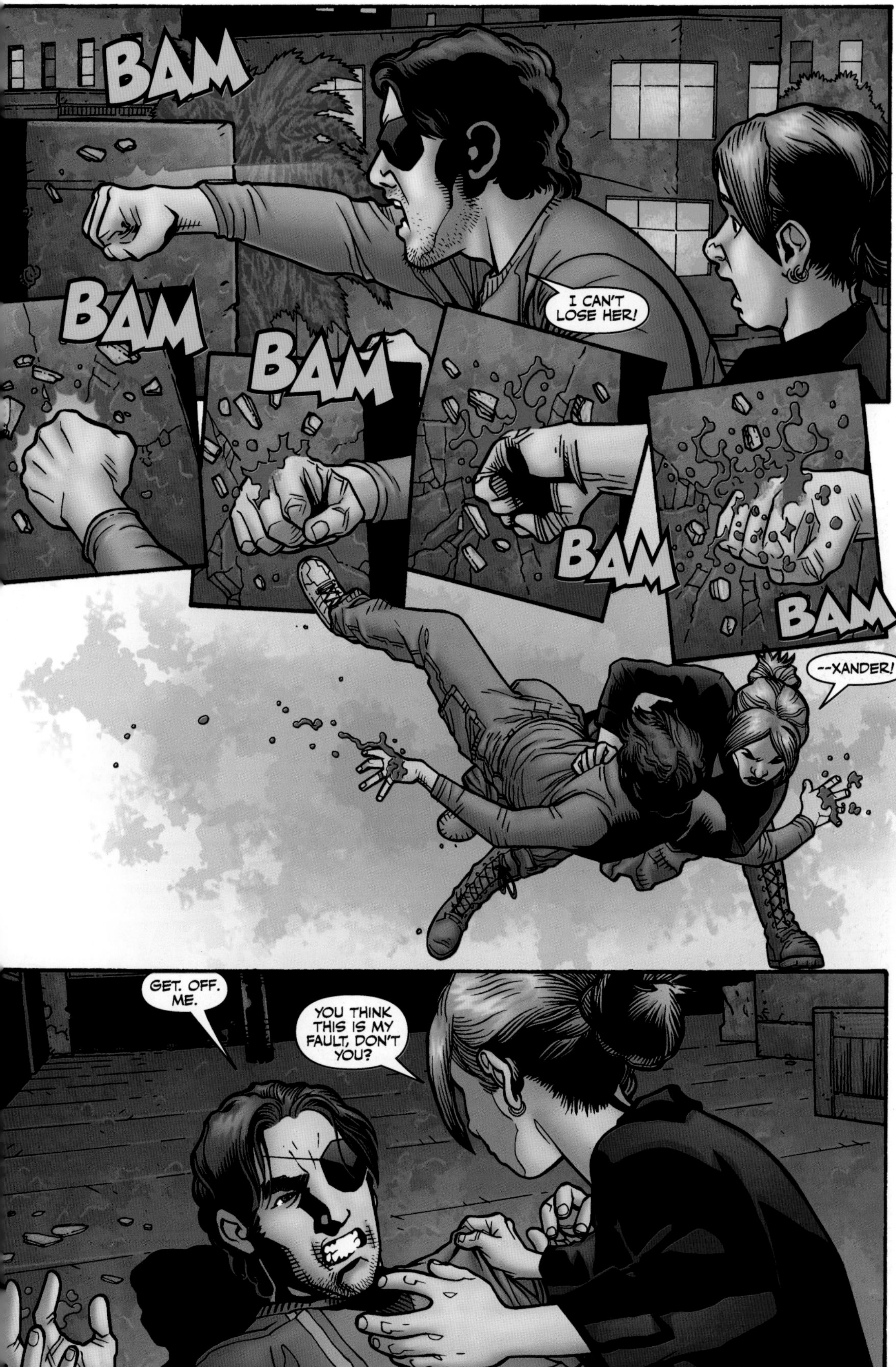
BAM
I CAN'T LOSE HER!
BAM
BAM
BAM
BAM
--XANDER!
GET. OFF. ME.
YOU THINK THIS IS MY FAULT, DON'T YOU?

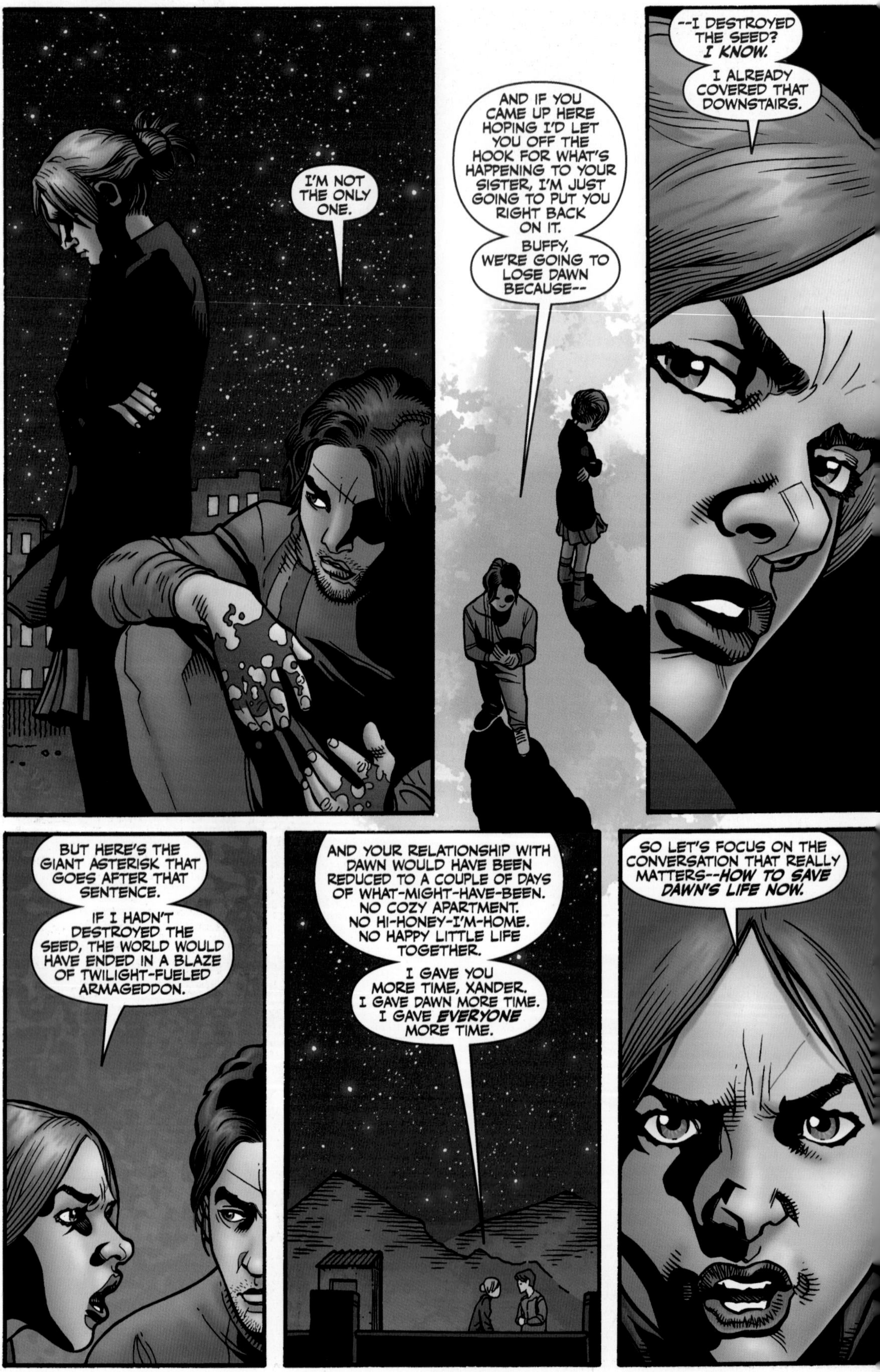
I'M NOT THE ONLY ONE.
AND IF YOU CAME UP HERE HOPING I'D LET YOU OFF THE HOOK FOR WHAT'S HAPPENING TO YOUR SISTER, I'M JUST GOING TO PUT YOU RIGHT BACK ON IT.
BUFFY, WE'RE GOING TO LOSE DAWN BECAUSE--
--I DESTROYED THE SEED? I KNOW.
I ALREADY COVERED THAT DOWNSTAIRS.
BUT HERE'S THE GIANT ASTERISK THAT GOES AFTER THAT SENTENCE.
IF I HADN'T DESTROYED THE SEED, THE WORLD WOULD HAVE ENDED IN A BLAZE OF TWILIGHT-FUELED ARMAGEDDON.
AND YOUR RELATIONSHIP WITH DAWN WOULD HAVE BEEN REDUCED TO A COUPLE OF DAYS OF WHAT-MIGHT-HAVE-BEEN. NO COZY APARTMENT. NO HI-HONEY-I'M-HOME. NO HAPPY LITTLE LIFE TOGETHER.
I GAVE YOU MORE TIME, XANDER. I GAVE DAWN MORE TIME. I GAVE EVERYONE MORE TIME.
SO LET'S FOCUS ON THE CONVERSATION THAT REALLY MATTERS--HOW TO SAVE DAWN'S LIFE NOW.

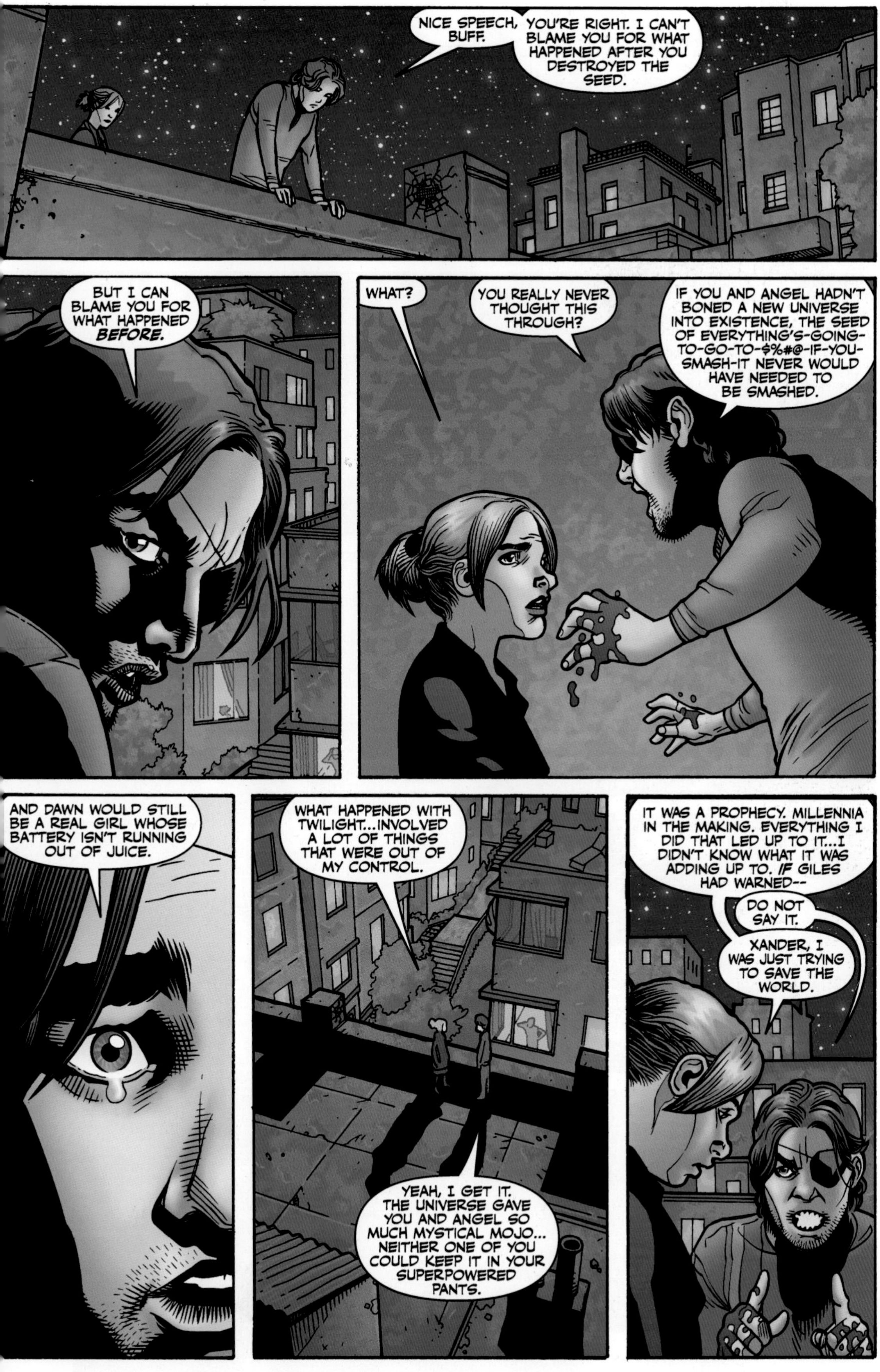
NICE SPEECH, BUFF.
YOU'RE RIGHT. I CAN'T BLAME YOU FOR WHAT HAPPENED AFTER YOU DESTROYED THE SEED.
BUT I CAN BLAME YOU FOR WHAT HAPPENED *BEFORE.*
WHAT?
YOU REALLY NEVER THOUGHT THIS THROUGH?
IF YOU AND ANGEL HADN'T BONED A NEW UNIVERSE INTO EXISTENCE, THE SEED OF EVERYTHING'S-GOING-TO-GO-TO-$%#@-IF-YOU-SMASH-IT NEVER WOULD HAVE NEEDED TO BE SMASHED.
AND DAWN WOULD STILL BE A REAL GIRL WHOSE BATTERY ISN'T RUNNING OUT OF JUICE.
WHAT HAPPENED WITH TWILIGHT...INVOLVED A LOT OF THINGS THAT WERE OUT OF MY CONTROL.
YEAH, I GET IT. THE UNIVERSE GAVE YOU AND ANGEL SO MUCH MYSTICAL MOJO... NEITHER ONE OF YOU COULD KEEP IT IN YOUR SUPERPOWERED PANTS.
IT WAS A PROPHECY. MILLENNIA IN THE MAKING. EVERYTHING I DID THAT LED UP TO IT...I DIDN'T KNOW WHAT IT WAS ADDING UP TO. *IF* GILES HAD WARNED--
DO NOT SAY IT.
XANDER, I WAS JUST TRYING TO SAVE THE WORLD.

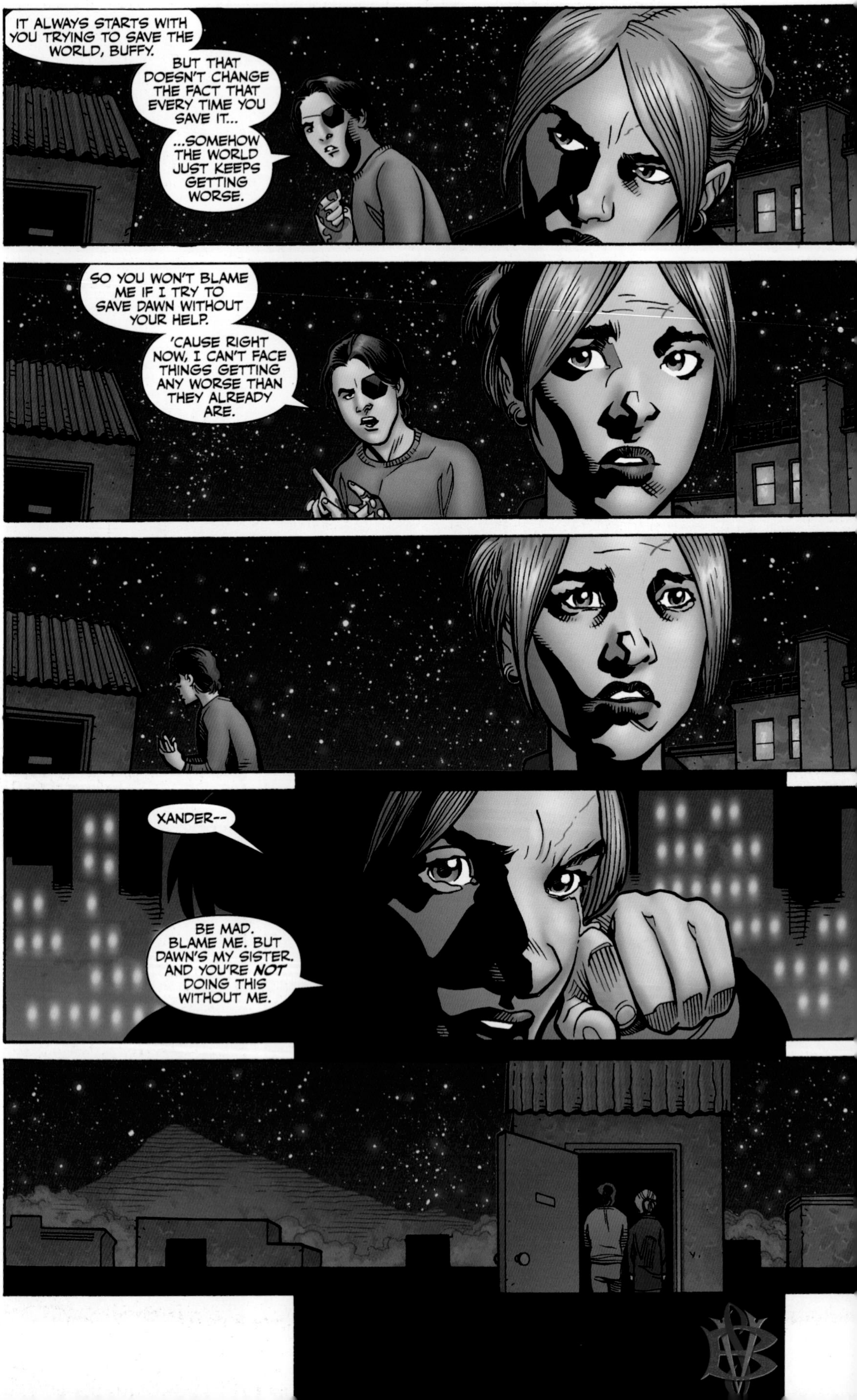

IT ALWAYS STARTS WITH YOU TRYING TO SAVE THE WORLD, BUFFY.
BUT THAT DOESN'T CHANGE THE FACT THAT EVERY TIME YOU SAVE IT...
...SOMEHOW THE WORLD JUST KEEPS GETTING WORSE.
SO YOU WON'T BLAME ME IF I TRY TO SAVE DAWN WITHOUT YOUR HELP.
'CAUSE RIGHT NOW, I CAN'T FACE THINGS GETTING ANY WORSE THAN THEY ALREADY ARE.
XANDER--
BE MAD. BLAME ME. BUT DAWN'S MY SISTER. AND YOU'RE *NOT* DOING THIS WITHOUT ME.

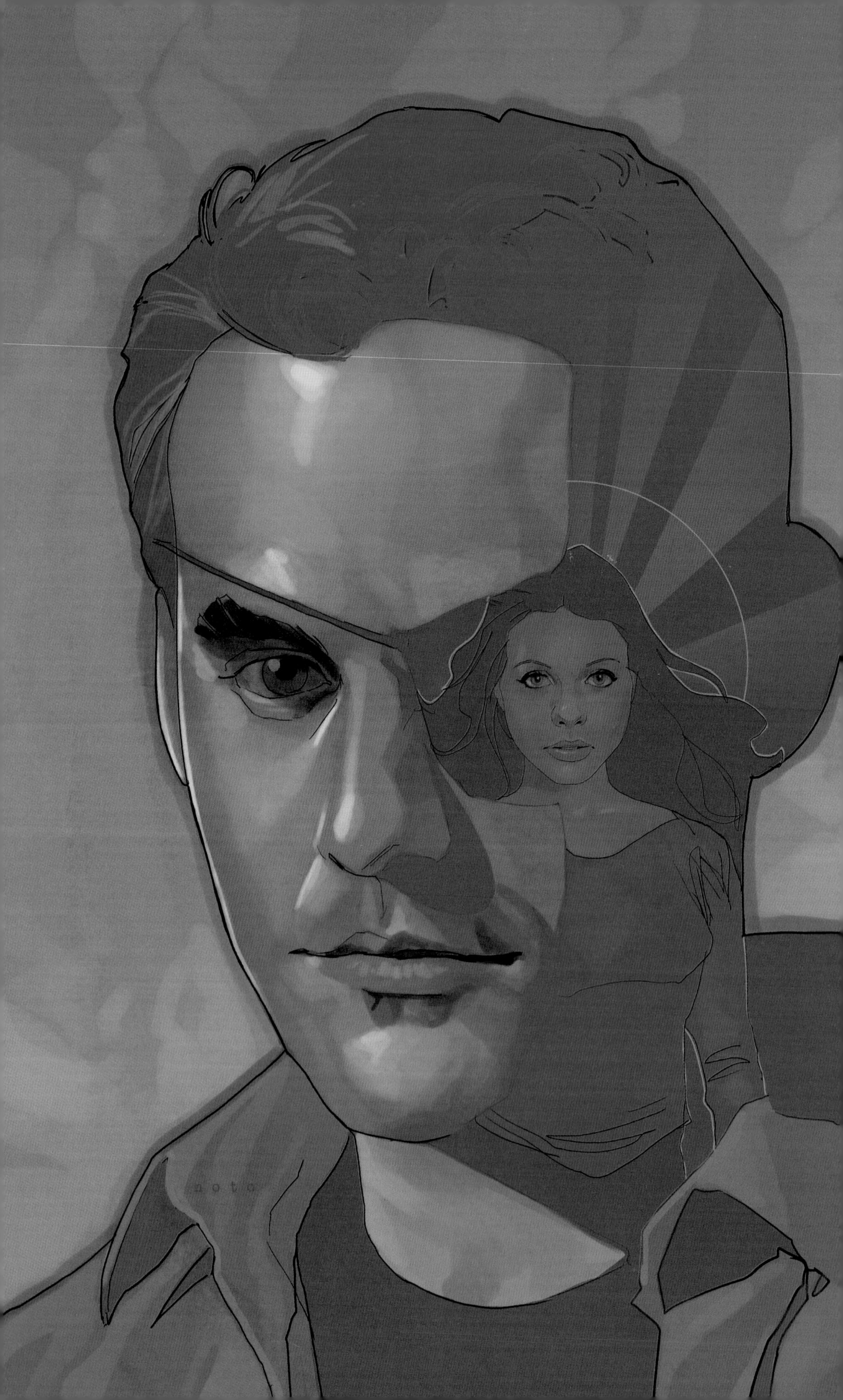
noto

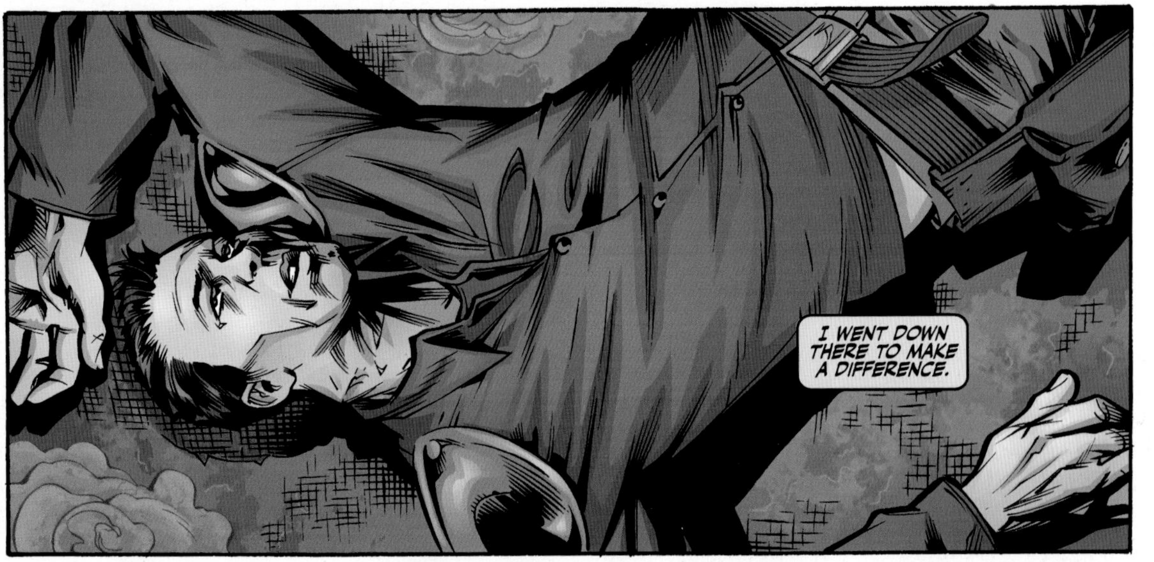
I WENT DOWN THERE TO MAKE A DIFFERENCE.

THE WATCHER

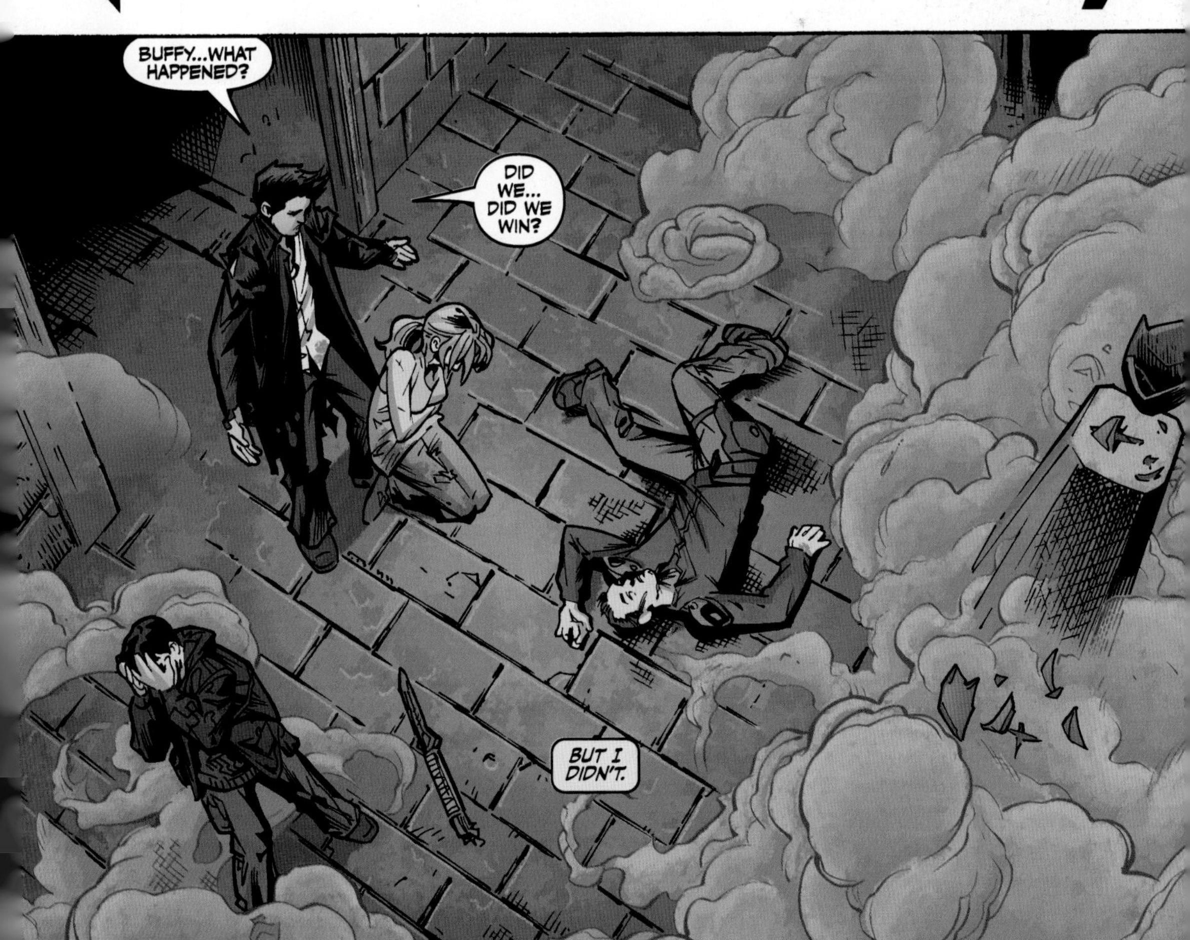
BUFFY...WHAT HAPPENED?
DID WE... DID WE WIN?
BUT I DIDN'T.

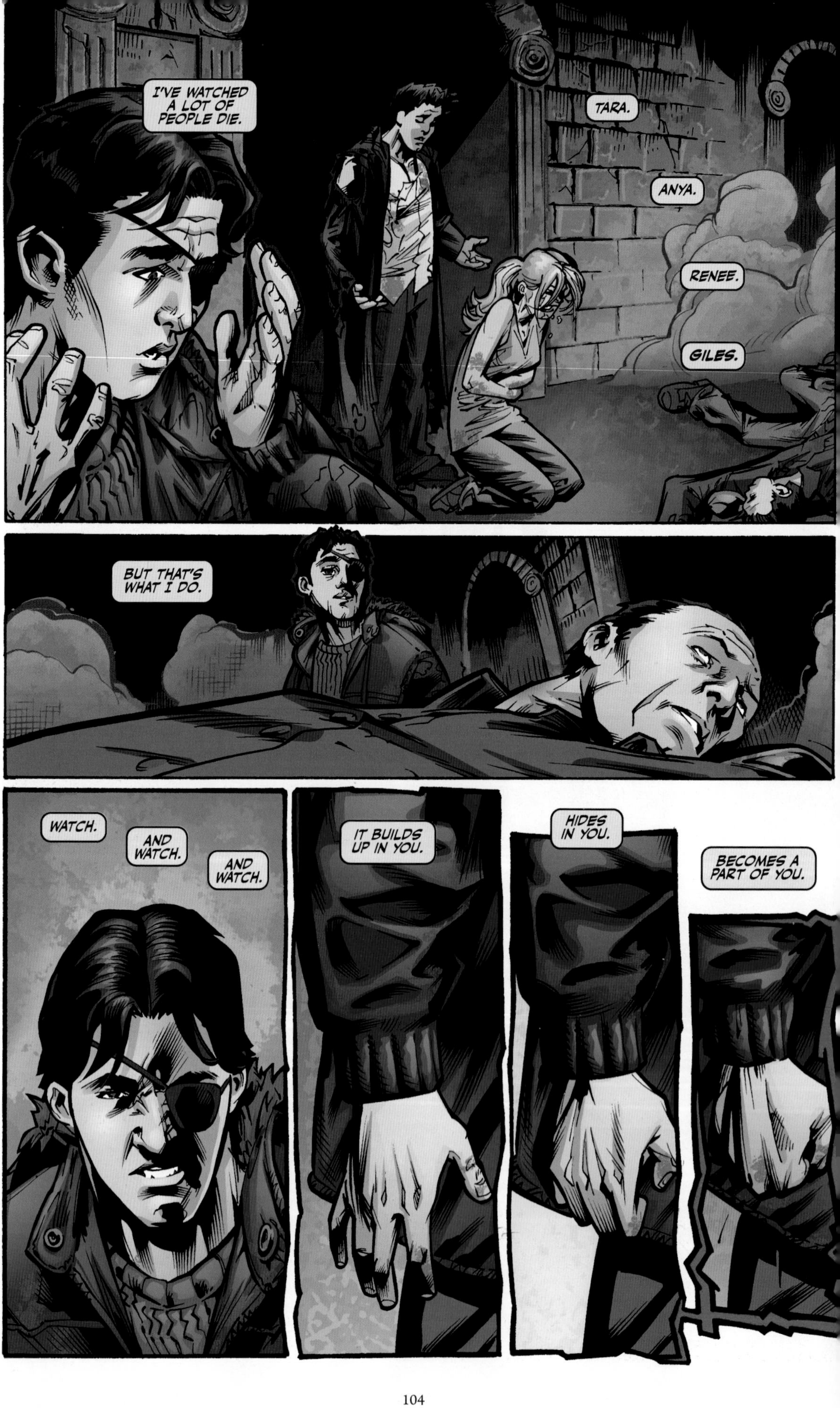
I'VE WATCHED A LOT OF PEOPLE DIE.
TARA.
ANYA.
RENEE.
GILES.
BUT THAT'S WHAT I DO.
WATCH.
AND WATCH.
AND WATCH.
IT BUILDS UP IN YOU.
HIDES IN YOU.
BECOMES A PART OF YOU.

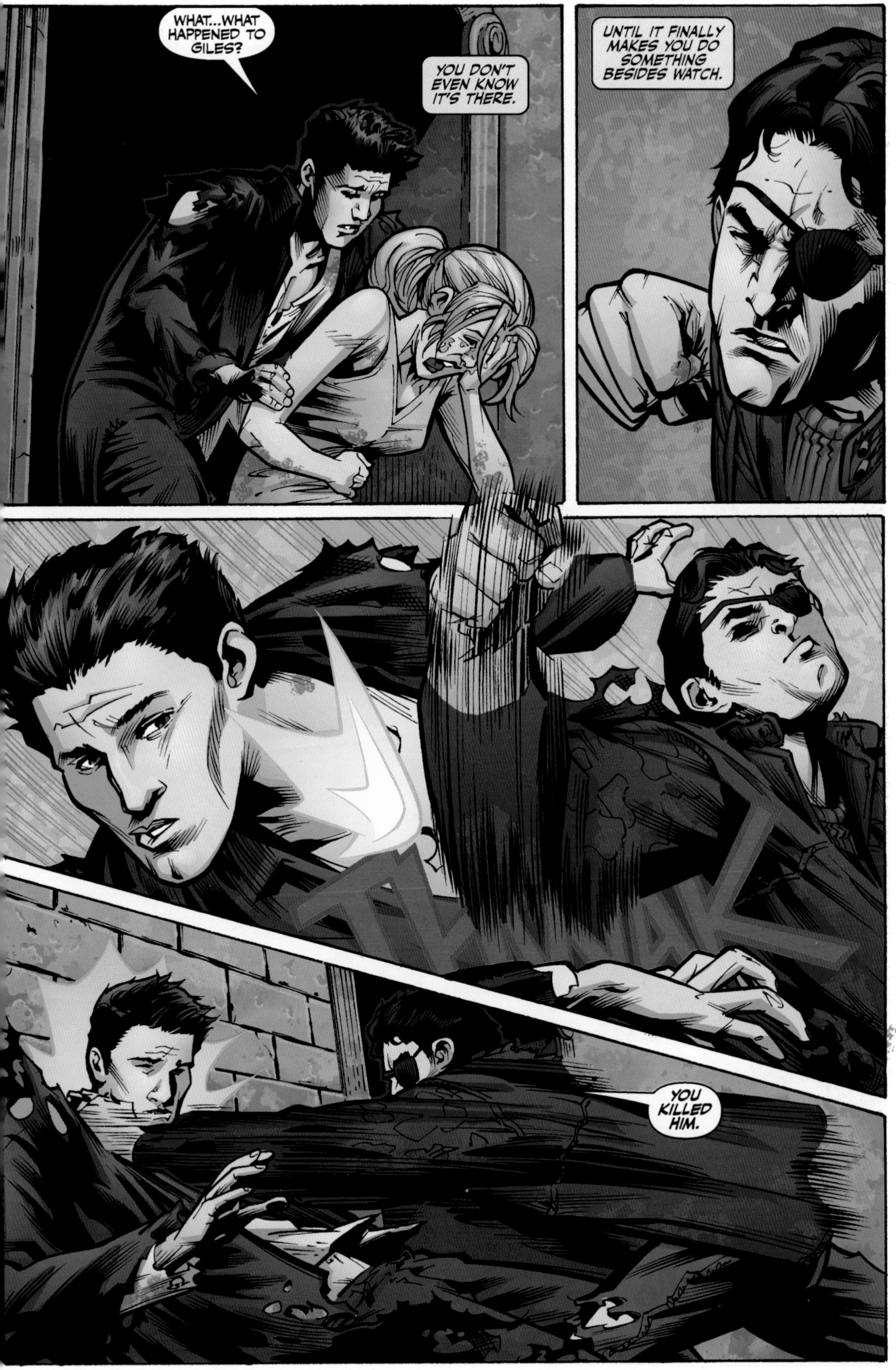
WHAT...WHAT HAPPENED TO GILES?
YOU DON'T EVEN KNOW IT'S THERE.
UNTIL IT FINALLY MAKES YOU DO SOMETHING BESIDES WATCH.
YOU KILLED HIM.

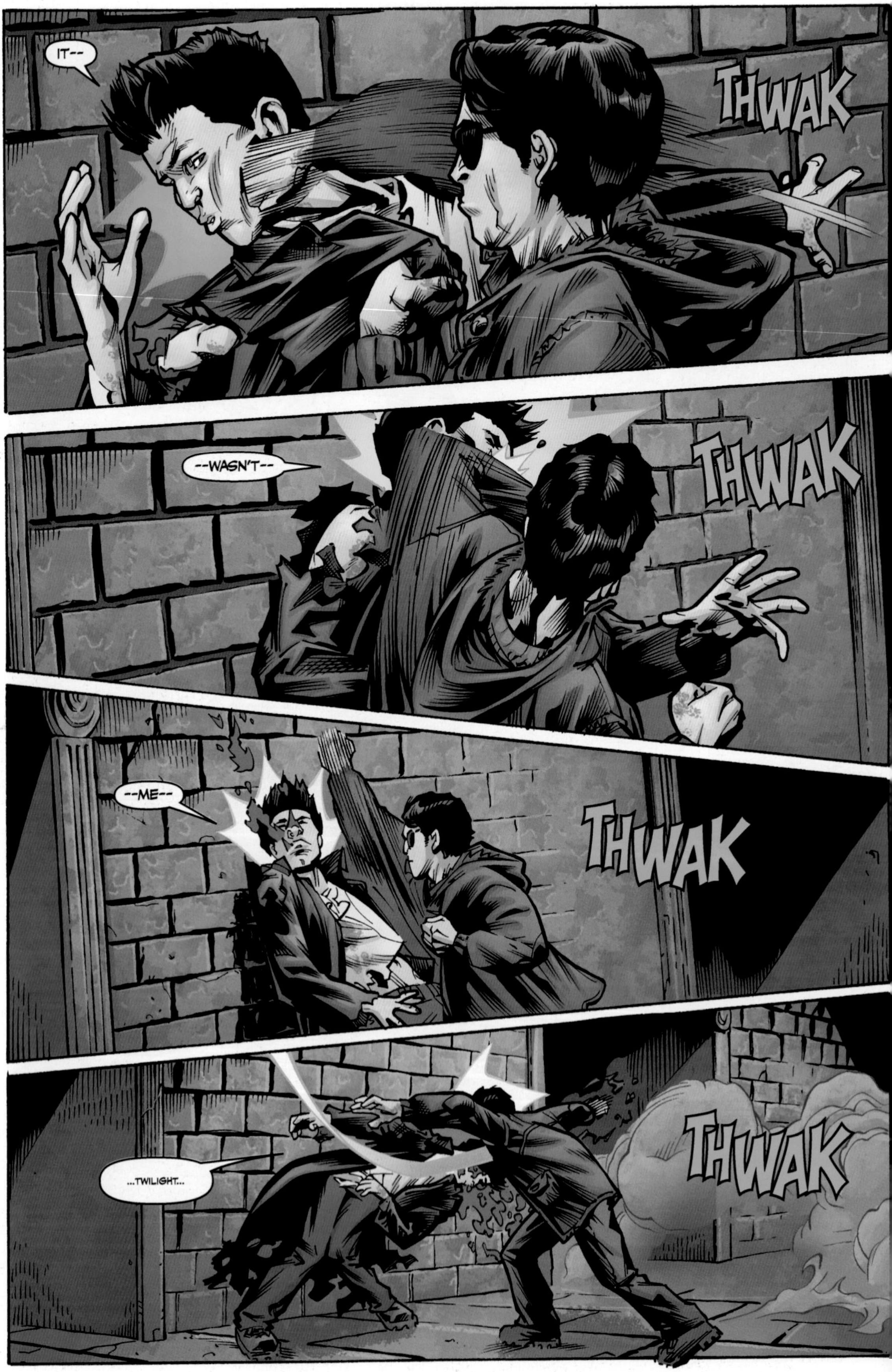
IT--
THWAK
--WASN'T--
THWAK
--ME--
THWAK
...TWILIGHT...
THWAK

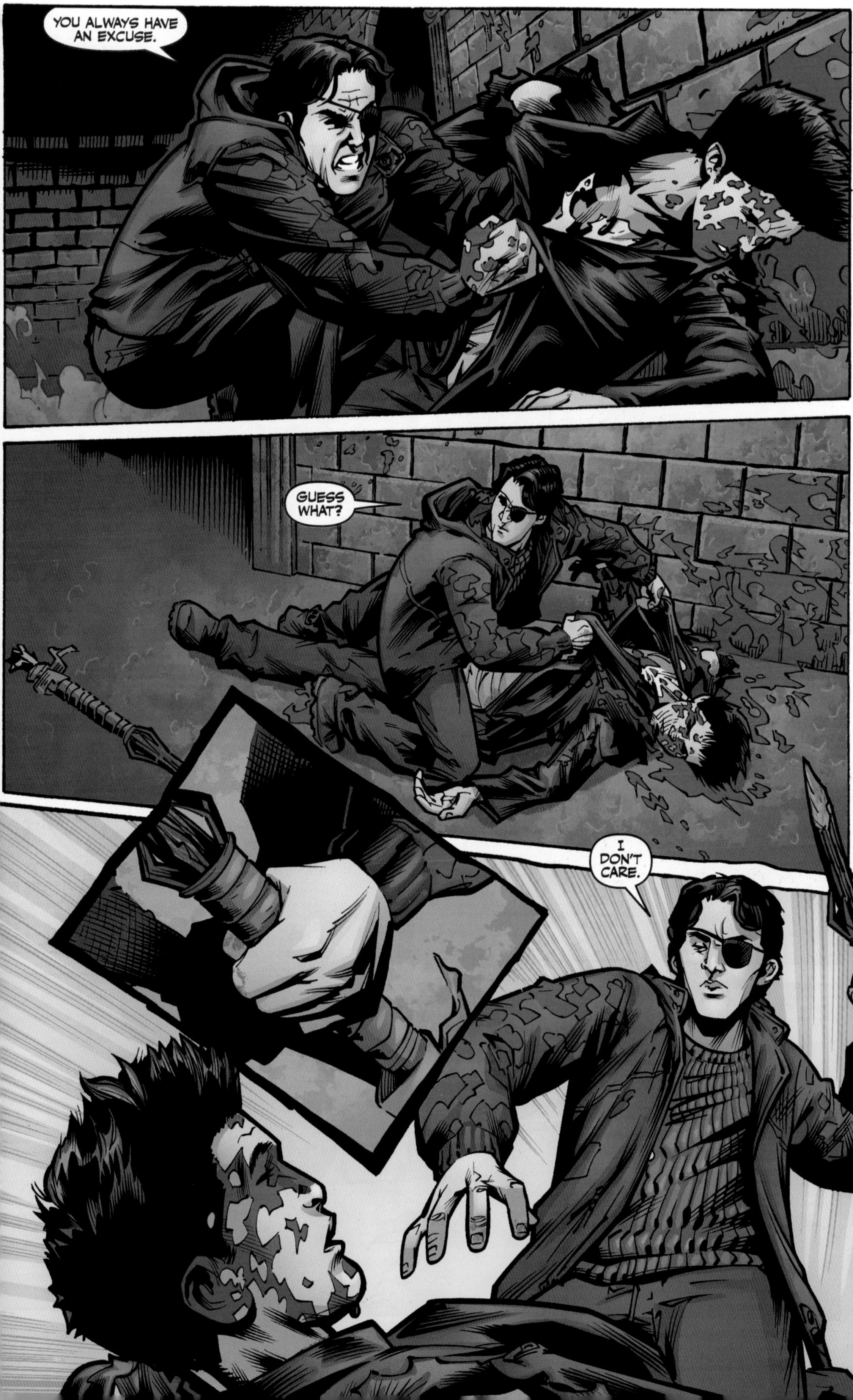
YOU ALWAYS HAVE AN EXCUSE.
GUESS WHAT?
I DON'T CARE.

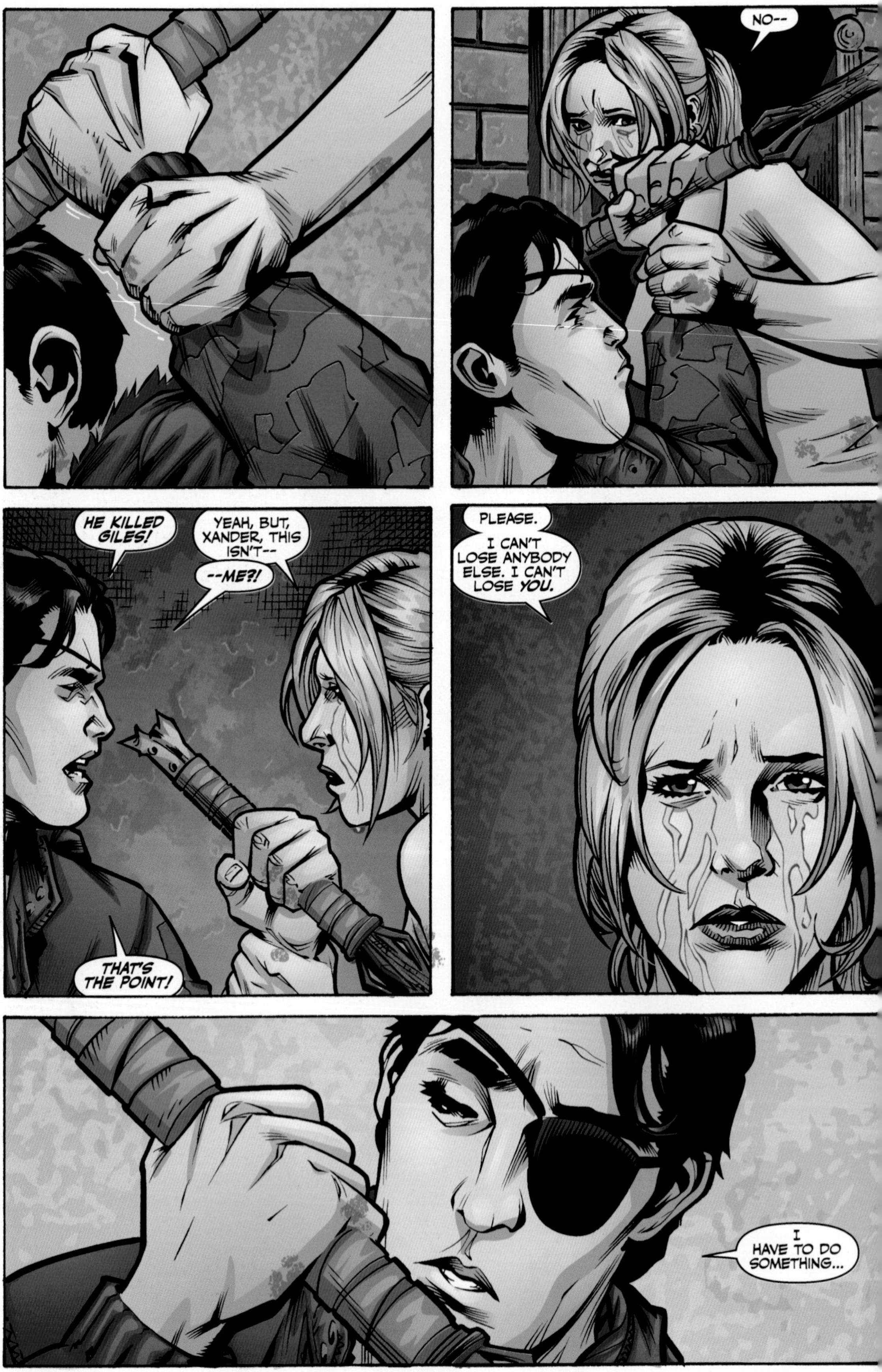
NO--
HE KILLED GILES!
YEAH, BUT, XANDER, THIS ISN'T--
--ME?!
THAT'S THE POINT!
PLEASE.
I CAN'T LOSE ANYBODY ELSE. I CAN'T LOSE YOU.
I HAVE TO DO SOMETHING...

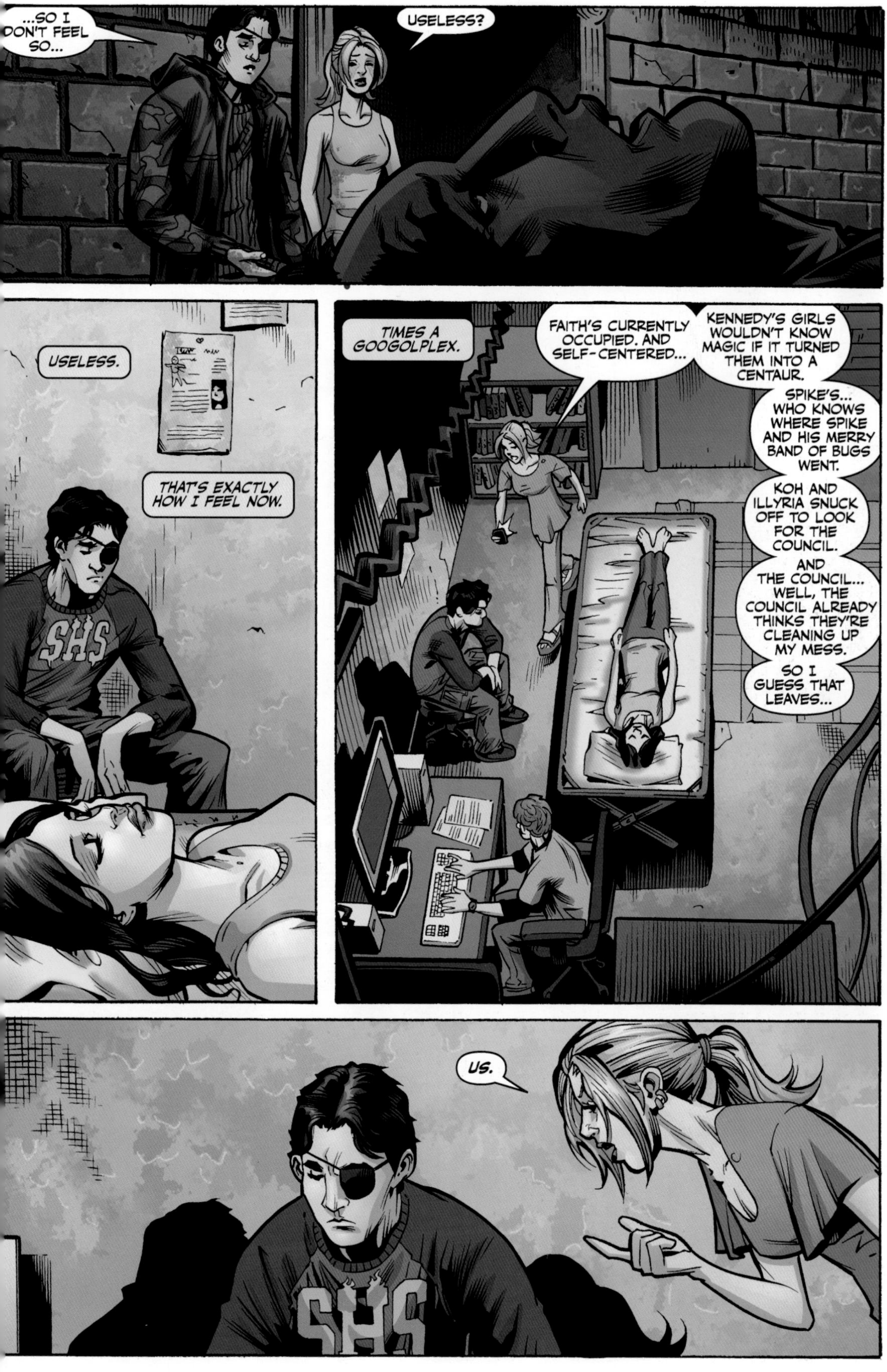

...SO I DON'T FEEL SO...
USELESS?
USELESS.
THAT'S EXACTLY HOW I FEEL NOW.
TIMES A GOOGOLPLEX.
FAITH'S CURRENTLY OCCUPIED. AND SELF-CENTERED...
KENNEDY'S GIRLS WOULDN'T KNOW MAGIC IF IT TURNED THEM INTO A CENTAUR.
SPIKE'S... WHO KNOWS WHERE SPIKE AND HIS MERRY BAND OF BUGS WENT.
KOH AND ILLYRIA SNUCK OFF TO LOOK FOR THE COUNCIL.
AND THE COUNCIL... WELL, THE COUNCIL ALREADY THINKS THEY'RE CLEANING UP MY MESS.
SO I GUESS THAT LEAVES...
US.

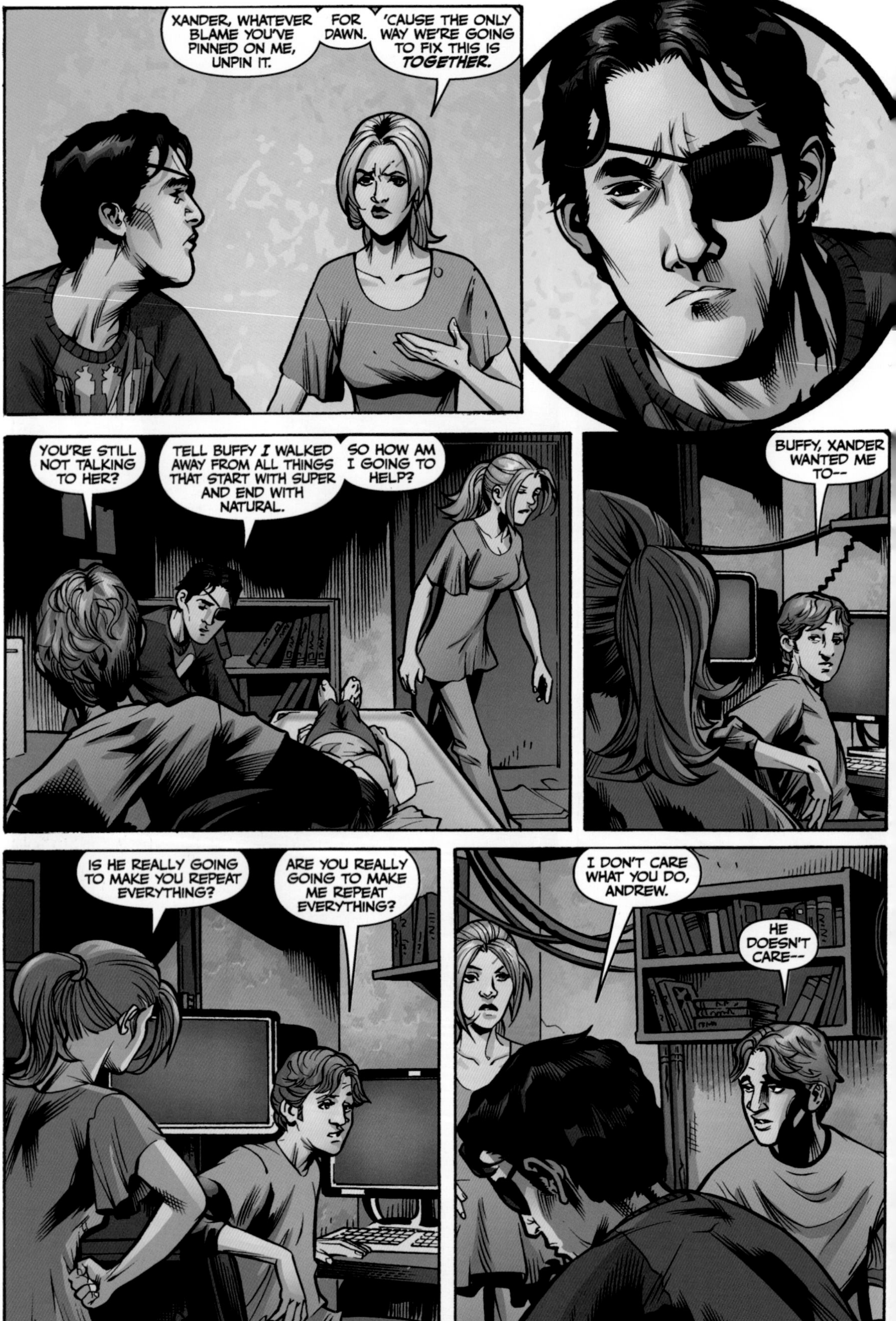
XANDER, WHATEVER BLAME YOU'VE PINNED ON ME, UNPIN IT.
FOR DAWN.
'CAUSE THE ONLY WAY WE'RE GOING TO FIX THIS IS TOGETHER.
YOU'RE STILL NOT TALKING TO HER?
TELL BUFFY I WALKED AWAY FROM ALL THINGS THAT START WITH SUPER AND END WITH NATURAL.
SO HOW AM I GOING TO HELP?
BUFFY, XANDER WANTED ME TO--
IS HE REALLY GOING TO MAKE YOU REPEAT EVERYTHING?
ARE YOU REALLY GOING TO MAKE ME REPEAT EVERYTHING?
I DON'T CARE WHAT YOU DO, ANDREW.
HE DOESN'T CARE--

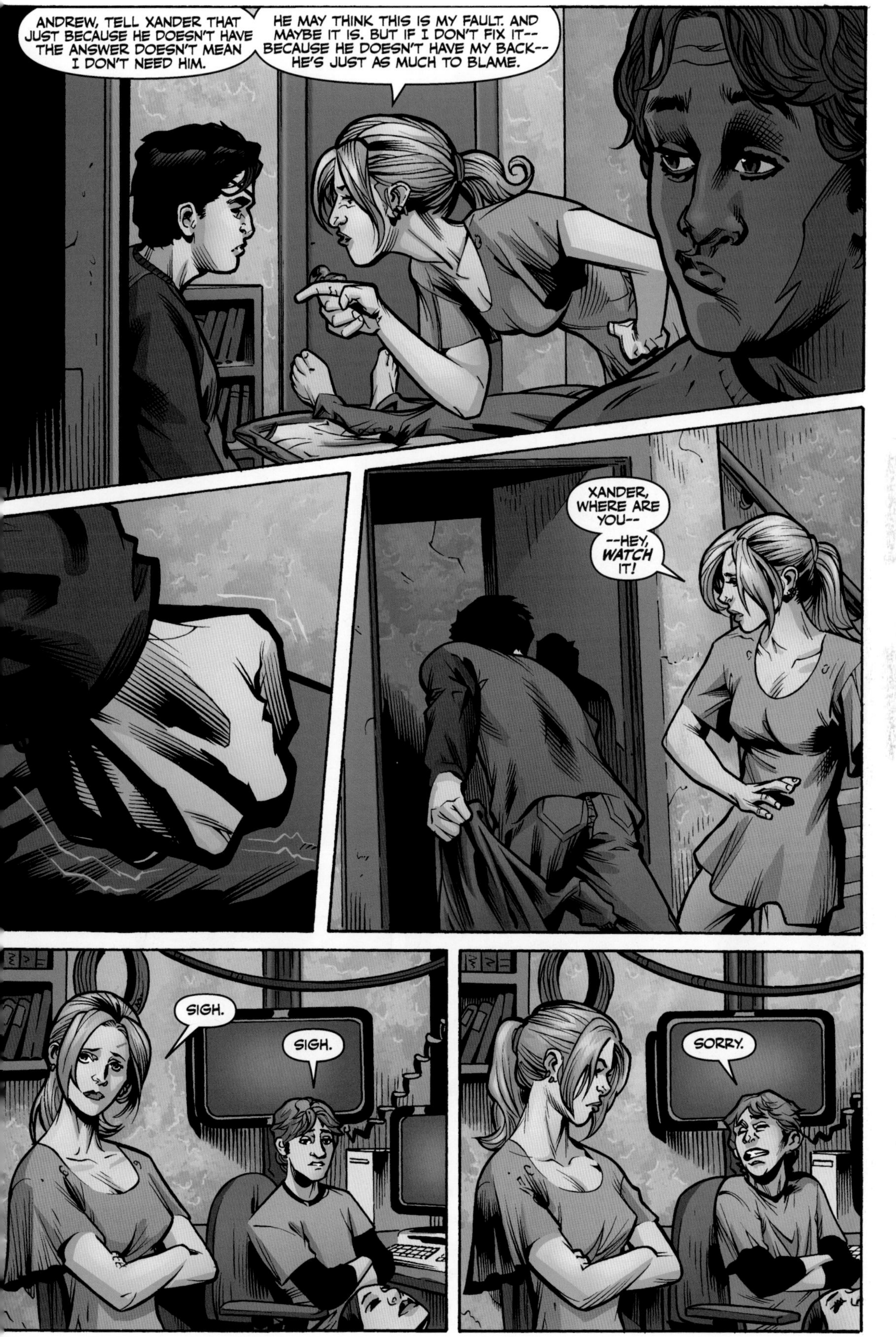
ANDREW, TELL XANDER THAT JUST BECAUSE HE DOESN'T HAVE THE ANSWER DOESN'T MEAN I DON'T NEED HIM.
HE MAY THINK THIS IS MY FAULT. AND MAYBE IT IS. BUT IF I DON'T FIX IT-- BECAUSE HE DOESN'T HAVE MY BACK-- HE'S JUST AS MUCH TO BLAME.
XANDER, WHERE ARE YOU--
--HEY, *WATCH* IT!
SIGH.
SIGH.
SORRY.

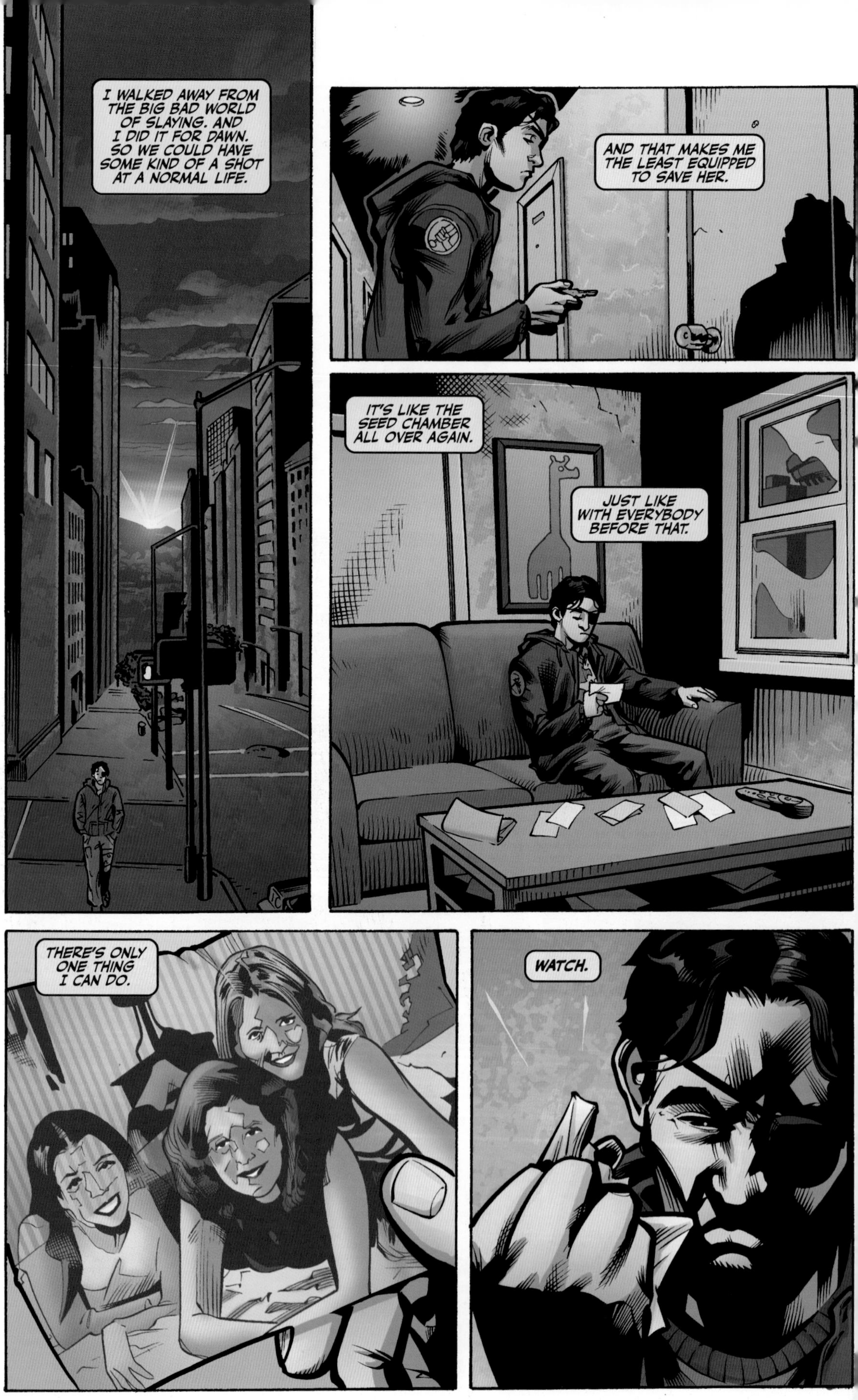
I WALKED AWAY FROM THE BIG BAD WORLD OF SLAYING. AND I DID IT FOR DAWN. SO WE COULD HAVE SOME KIND OF A SHOT AT A NORMAL LIFE.
AND THAT MAKES ME THE LEAST EQUIPPED TO SAVE HER.
IT'S LIKE THE SEED CHAMBER ALL OVER AGAIN.
JUST LIKE WITH EVERYBODY BEFORE THAT.
THERE'S ONLY ONE THING I CAN DO.
WATCH.

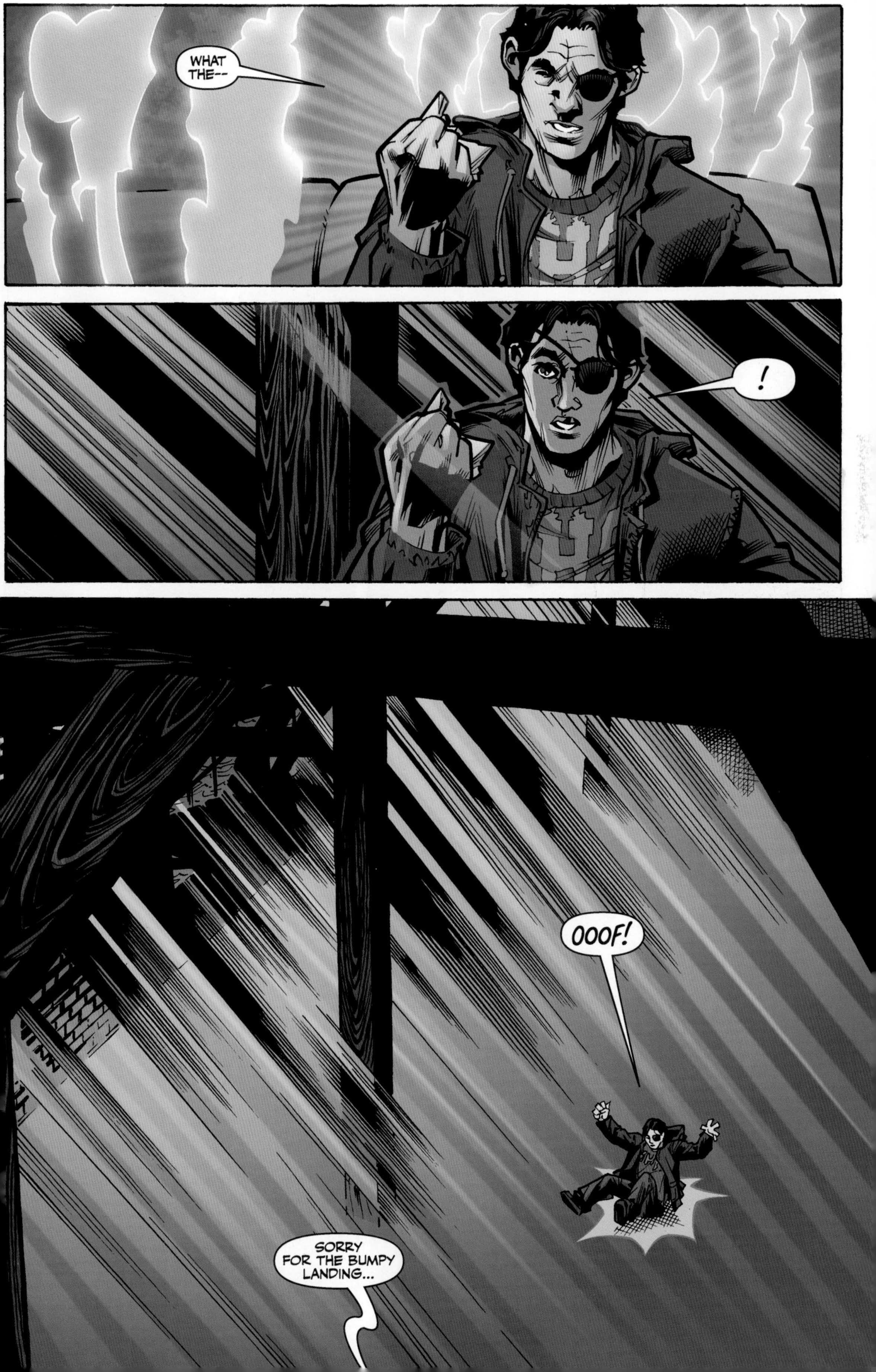
WHAT THE--
!
OOOF!
SORRY FOR THE BUMPY LANDING...

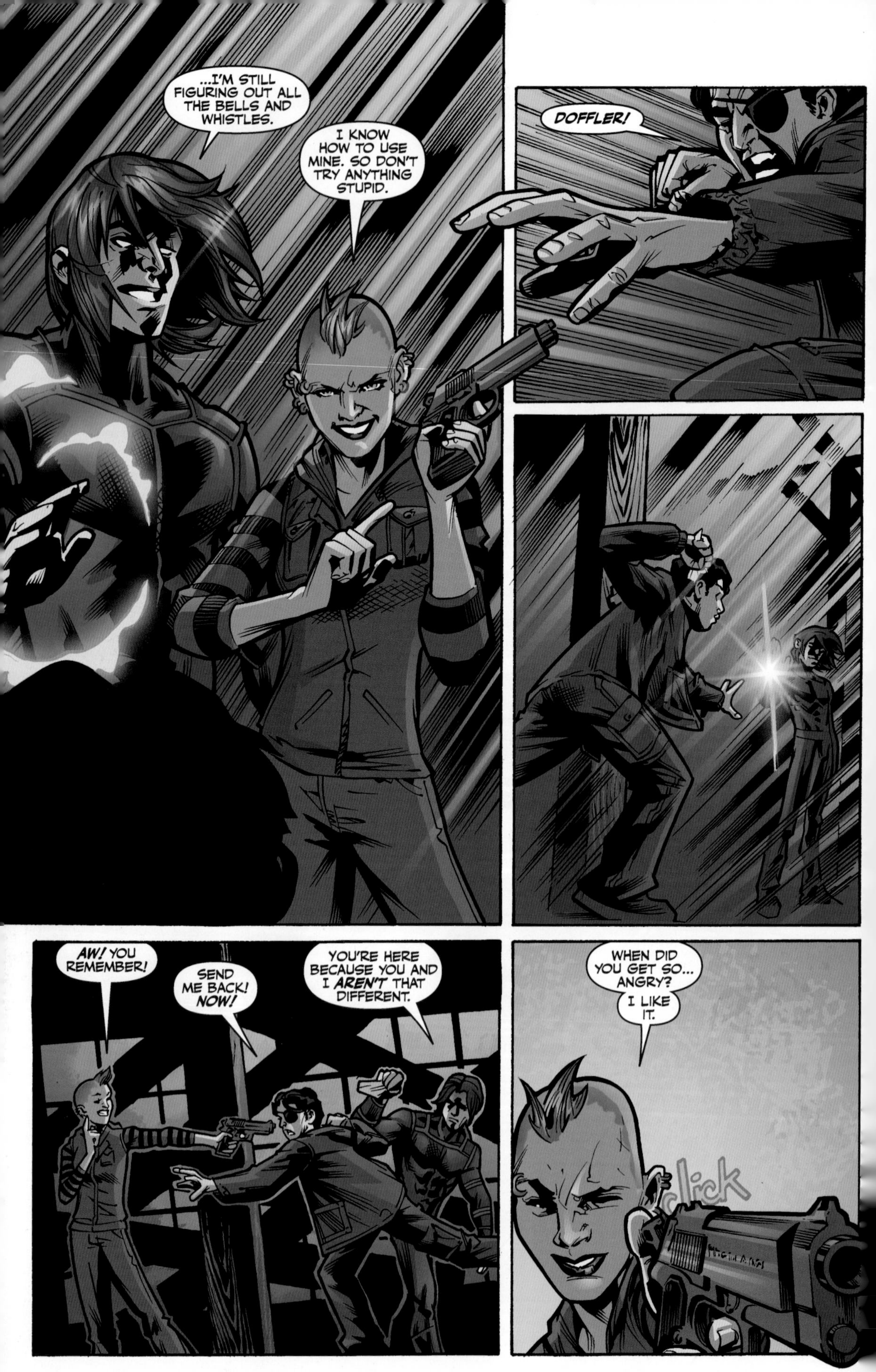
...I'M STILL FIGURING OUT ALL THE BELLS AND WHISTLES.
I KNOW HOW TO USE MINE. SO DON'T TRY ANYTHING STUPID.
DOFFLER!
AW! YOU REMEMBER!
SEND ME BACK! NOW!
YOU'RE HERE BECAUSE YOU AND I AREN'T THAT DIFFERENT.
WHEN DID YOU GET SO... ANGRY?
I LIKE IT.
click

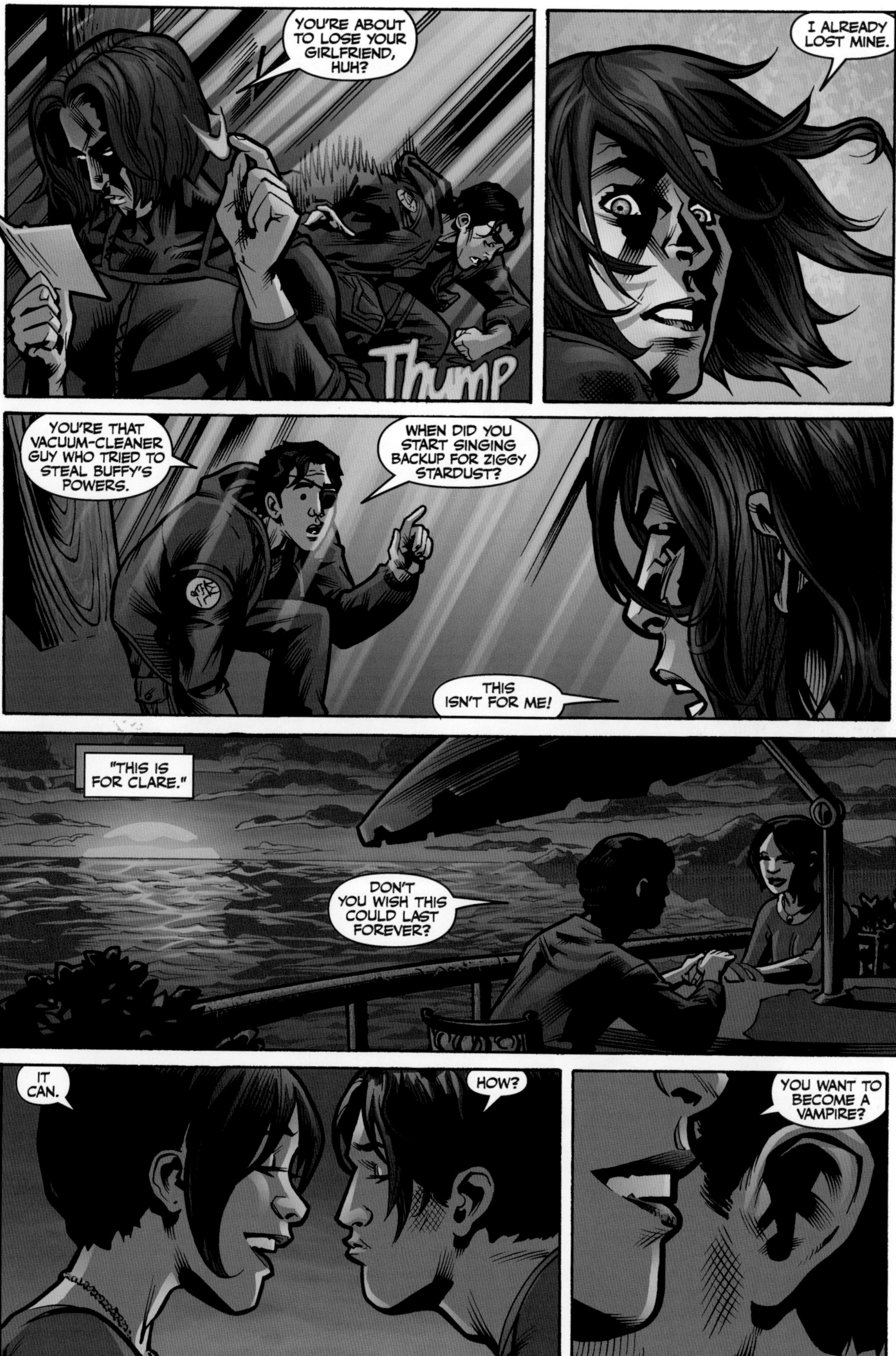
YOU'RE ABOUT TO LOSE YOUR GIRLFRIEND, HUH?
Thump
I ALREADY LOST MINE.
YOU'RE THAT VACUUM-CLEANER GUY WHO TRIED TO STEAL BUFFY'S POWERS.
WHEN DID YOU START SINGING BACKUP FOR ZIGGY STARDUST?
THIS ISN'T FOR ME!
"THIS IS FOR CLARE."
DON'T YOU WISH THIS COULD LAST FOREVER?
IT CAN.
HOW?
YOU WANT TO BECOME A VAMPIRE?

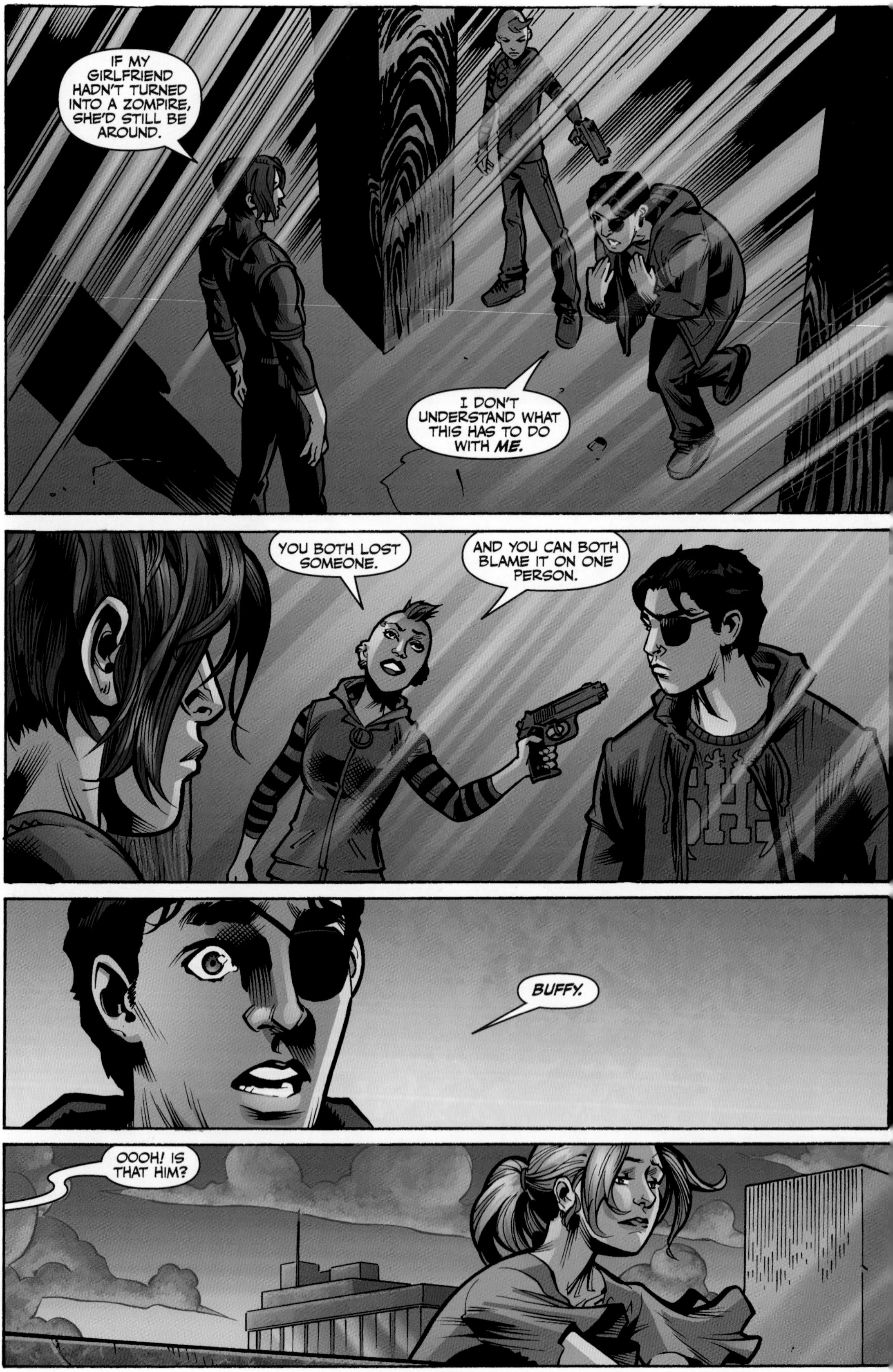
IF MY GIRLFRIEND HADN'T TURNED INTO A ZOMPIRE, SHE'D STILL BE AROUND.
I DON'T UNDERSTAND WHAT THIS HAS TO DO WITH *ME.*
YOU BOTH LOST SOMEONE.
AND YOU CAN BOTH BLAME IT ON ONE PERSON.
BUFFY.
OOOH! IS THAT HIM?

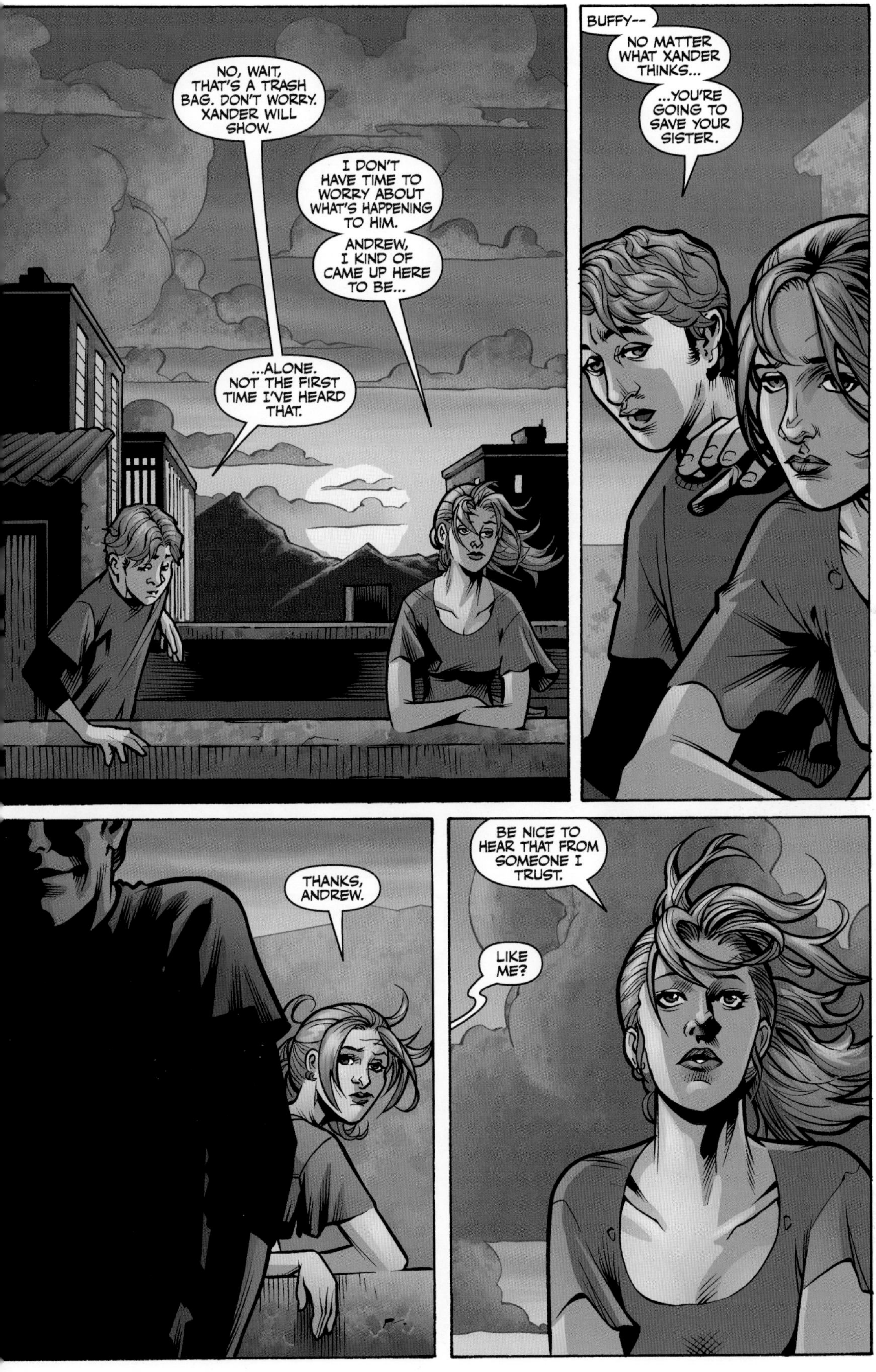
NO, WAIT, THAT'S A TRASH BAG. DON'T WORRY. XANDER WILL SHOW.
I DON'T HAVE TIME TO WORRY ABOUT WHAT'S HAPPENING TO HIM.
ANDREW, I KIND OF CAME UP HERE TO BE...
...ALONE. NOT THE FIRST TIME I'VE HEARD THAT.
BUFFY--
NO MATTER WHAT XANDER THINKS...
...YOU'RE GOING TO SAVE YOUR SISTER.
THANKS, ANDREW.
BE NICE TO HEAR THAT FROM SOMEONE I TRUST.
LIKE ME?

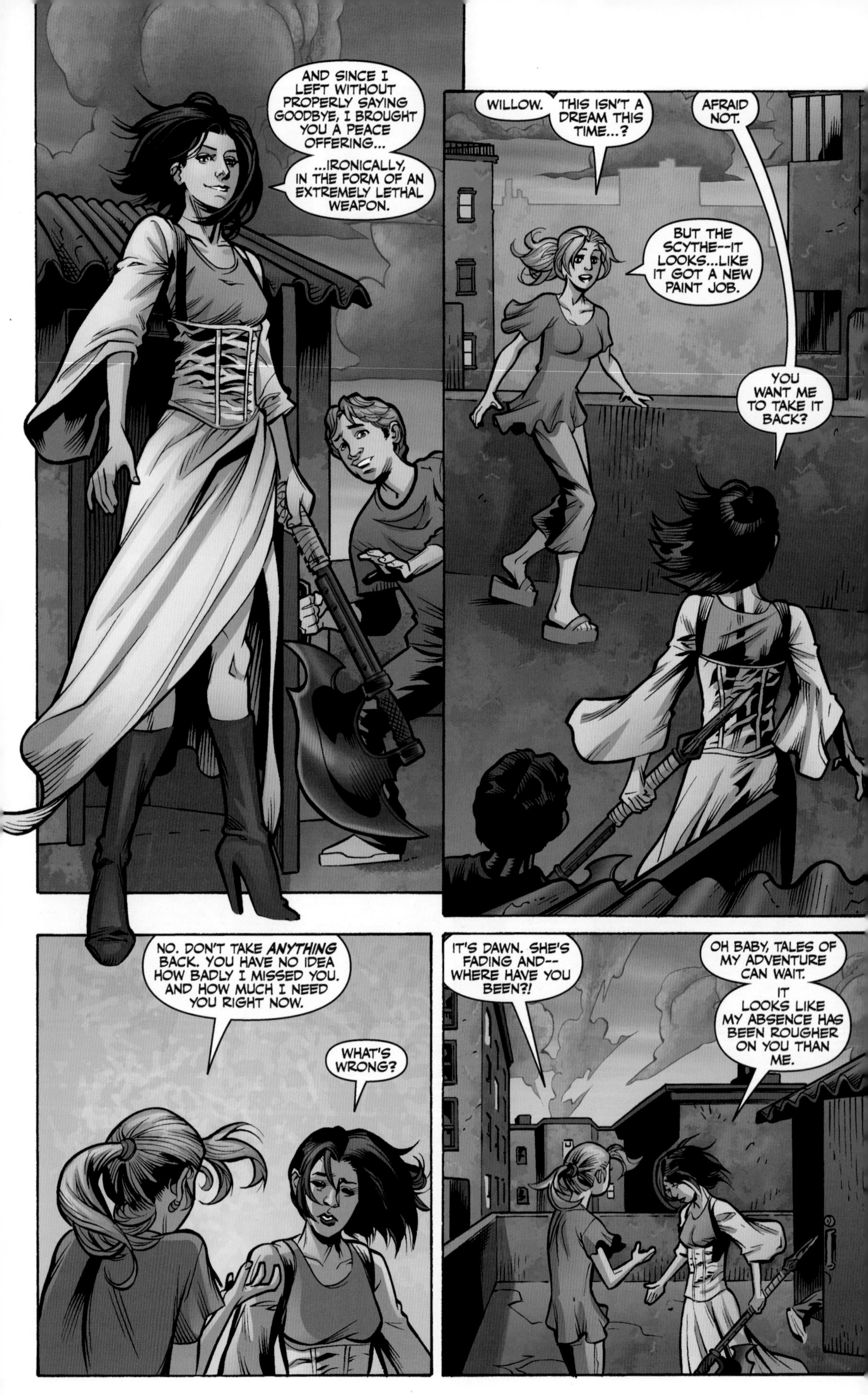
AND SINCE I LEFT WITHOUT PROPERLY SAYING GOODBYE, I BROUGHT YOU A PEACE OFFERING...
...IRONICALLY, IN THE FORM OF AN EXTREMELY LETHAL WEAPON.
WILLOW.
THIS ISN'T A DREAM THIS TIME...?
AFRAID NOT.
BUT THE SCYTHE--IT LOOKS...LIKE IT GOT A NEW PAINT JOB.
YOU WANT ME TO TAKE IT BACK?
NO. DON'T TAKE ANYTHING BACK. YOU HAVE NO IDEA HOW BADLY I MISSED YOU. AND HOW MUCH I NEED YOU RIGHT NOW.
WHAT'S WRONG?
IT'S DAWN. SHE'S FADING AND-- WHERE HAVE YOU BEEN?!
OH BABY, TALES OF MY ADVENTURE CAN WAIT.
IT LOOKS LIKE MY ABSENCE HAS BEEN ROUGHER ON YOU THAN ME.

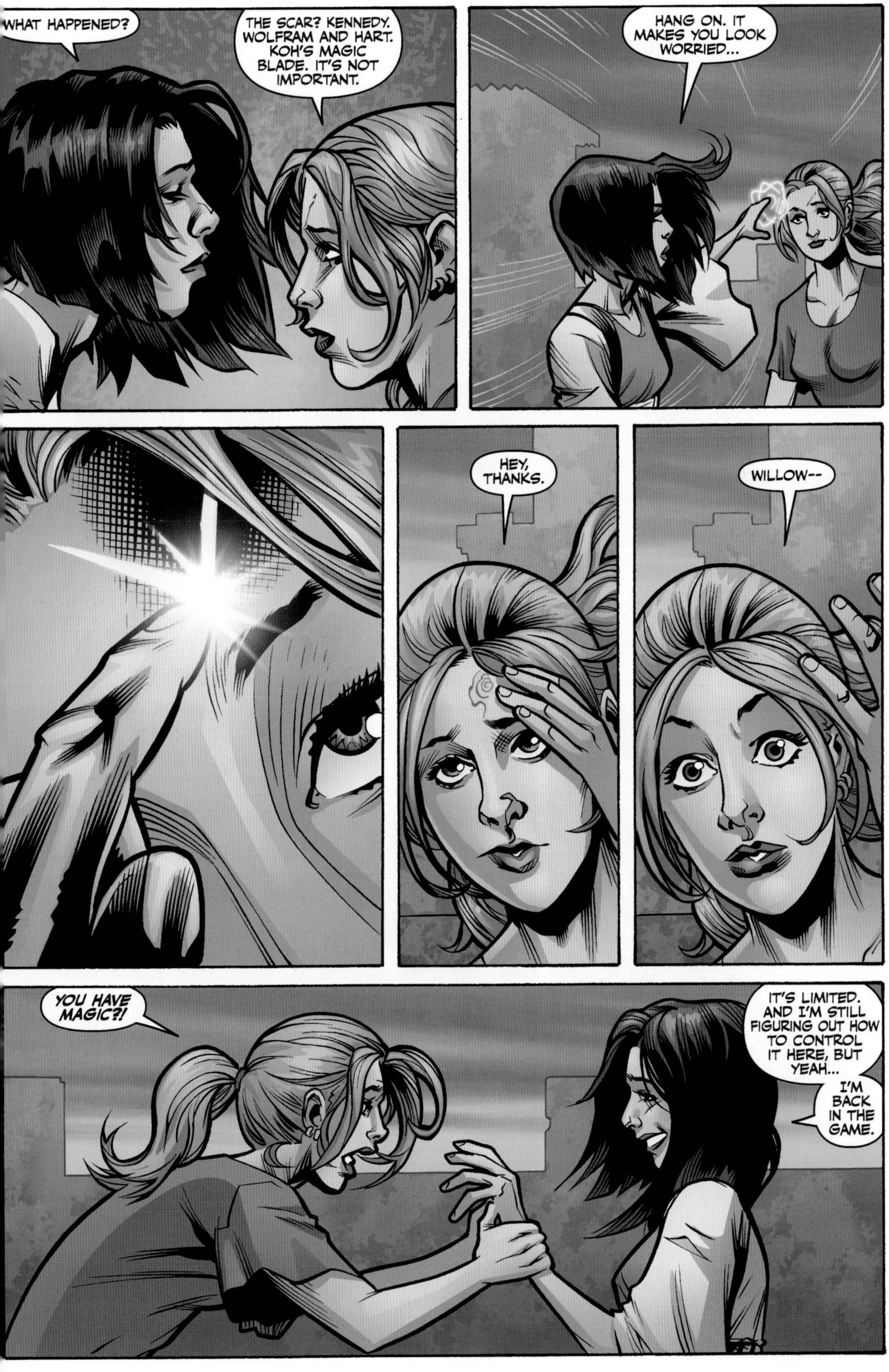
WHAT HAPPENED?
THE SCAR? KENNEDY. WOLFRAM AND HART. KOH'S MAGIC BLADE. IT'S NOT IMPORTANT.
HANG ON. IT MAKES YOU LOOK WORRIED...
HEY, THANKS.
WILLOW--
YOU HAVE MAGIC?!
IT'S LIMITED. AND I'M STILL FIGURING OUT HOW TO CONTROL IT HERE, BUT YEAH...
I'M BACK IN THE GAME.

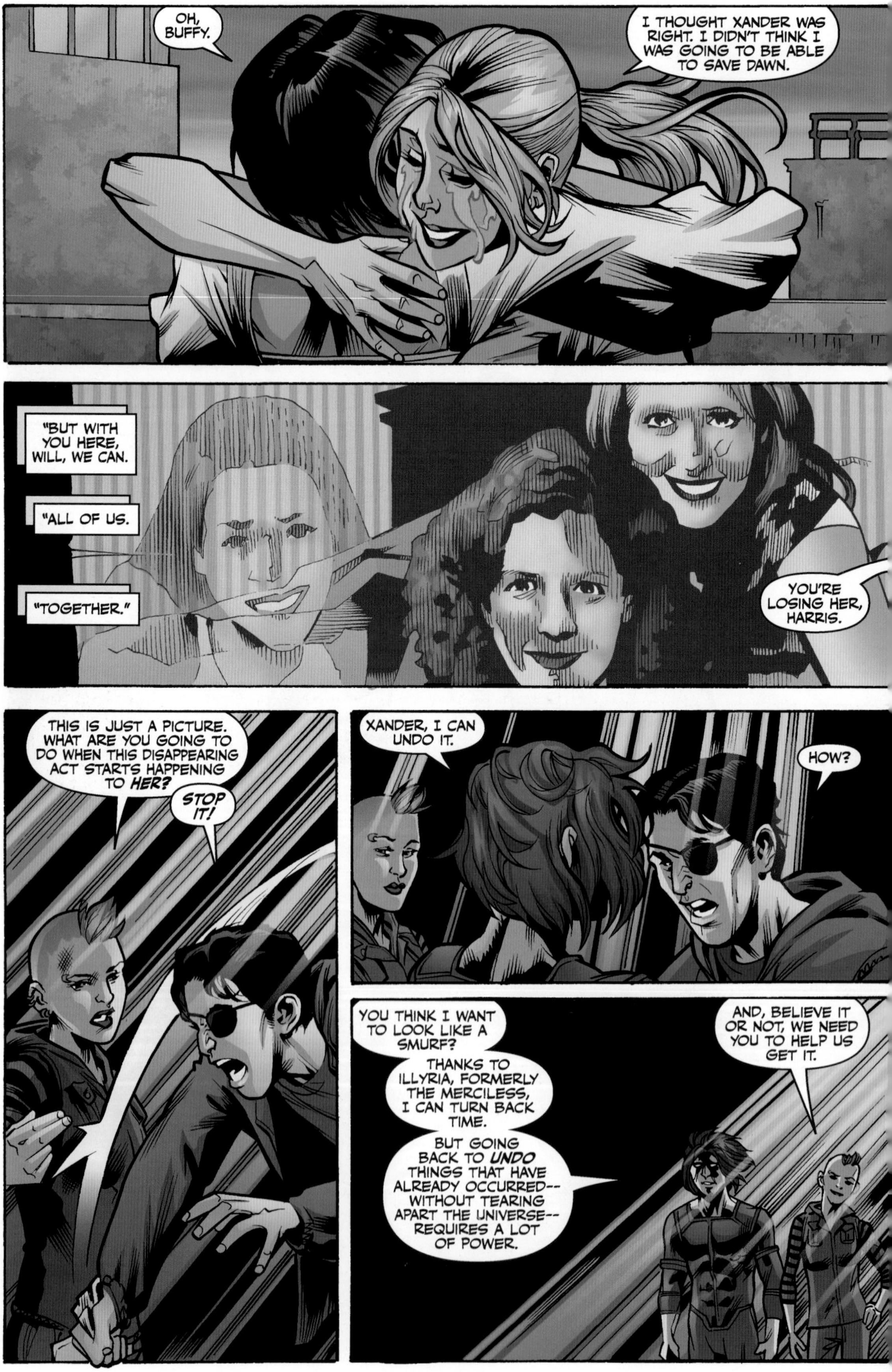
OH, BUFFY.
I THOUGHT XANDER WAS RIGHT. I DIDN'T THINK I WAS GOING TO BE ABLE TO SAVE DAWN.
"BUT WITH YOU HERE, WILL, WE CAN.
"ALL OF US.
"TOGETHER."
YOU'RE LOSING HER, HARRIS.
THIS IS JUST A PICTURE. WHAT ARE YOU GOING TO DO WHEN THIS DISAPPEARING ACT STARTS HAPPENING TO HER?
STOP IT!
XANDER, I CAN UNDO IT.
HOW?
YOU THINK I WANT TO LOOK LIKE A SMURF?
THANKS TO ILLYRIA, FORMERLY THE MERCILESS, I CAN TURN BACK TIME.
BUT GOING BACK TO UNDO THINGS THAT HAVE ALREADY OCCURRED-- WITHOUT TEARING APART THE UNIVERSE-- REQUIRES A LOT OF POWER.
AND, BELIEVE IT OR NOT, WE NEED YOU TO HELP US GET IT.

YOU WANT TO REWIND THE CLOCK AND KEEP YOUR GIRLFRIEND FROM TURNING INTO THE SPECIAL UNDEAD? I'M NOT GOING TO STOP YOU.

IT'S NOT THAT SIMPLE. SOMETHING TELLS ME SHE'S STILL GOING TO WANT TO BE A VAMPIRE. I NEED TO THINK BIGGER.

YOU'RE GOING TO STOP BUFFY FROM SMASHING THE SEED?

YOU REALLY WANT TO LIVE IN A DEMON-FILLED APOCALYPSE? 'CAUSE I DON'T.

NO, BUFFY NEEDED TO DESTROY THE SEED.

I NEED TO STOP TWILIGHT FROM EVER HAPPENING.

SO YOU'RE GOING TO...*KILL BUFFY?*

NO. I'M NOT A BAD GUY.

I'M OKAY WITH THAT LABEL.

THERE ARE OTHER WAYS TO STOP BUFFY FROM BIRTHING A NEW UNIVERSE.

WE JUST NEED TO STOP TWILIGHT.

I WAS ALL FOR KILLING HER.

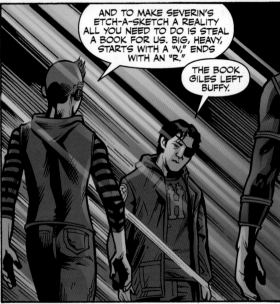

AND TO MAKE SEVERIN'S ETCH-A-SKETCH A REALITY ALL YOU NEED TO DO IS STEAL A BOOK FOR US. BIG, HEAVY, STARTS WITH A "V," ENDS WITH AN "R."

THE BOOK GILES LEFT BUFFY.

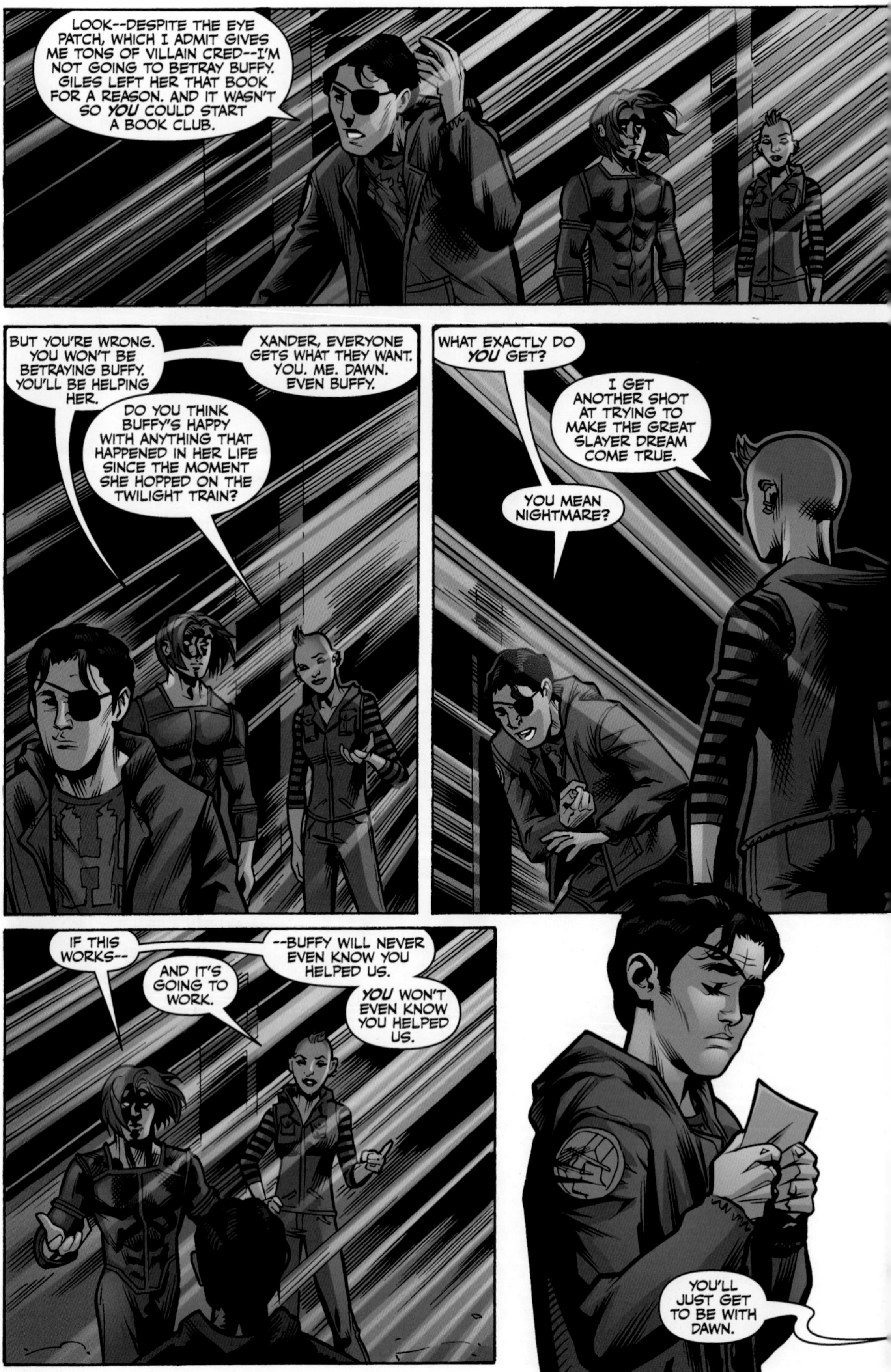
LOOK--DESPITE THE EYE PATCH, WHICH I ADMIT GIVES ME TONS OF VILLAIN CRED--I'M NOT GOING TO BETRAY BUFFY. GILES LEFT HER THAT BOOK FOR A REASON. AND IT WASN'T SO YOU COULD START A BOOK CLUB.
XANDER, EVERYONE GETS WHAT THEY WANT. YOU. ME. DAWN. EVEN BUFFY.
BUT YOU'RE WRONG. YOU WON'T BE BETRAYING BUFFY. YOU'LL BE HELPING HER.
DO YOU THINK BUFFY'S HAPPY WITH ANYTHING THAT HAPPENED IN HER LIFE SINCE THE MOMENT SHE HOPPED ON THE TWILIGHT TRAIN?
WHAT EXACTLY DO YOU GET?
I GET ANOTHER SHOT AT TRYING TO MAKE THE GREAT SLAYER DREAM COME TRUE.
YOU MEAN NIGHTMARE?
IF THIS WORKS--
AND IT'S GOING TO WORK.
--BUFFY WILL NEVER EVEN KNOW YOU HELPED US.
YOU WON'T EVEN KNOW YOU HELPED US.
YOU'LL JUST GET TO BE WITH DAWN.

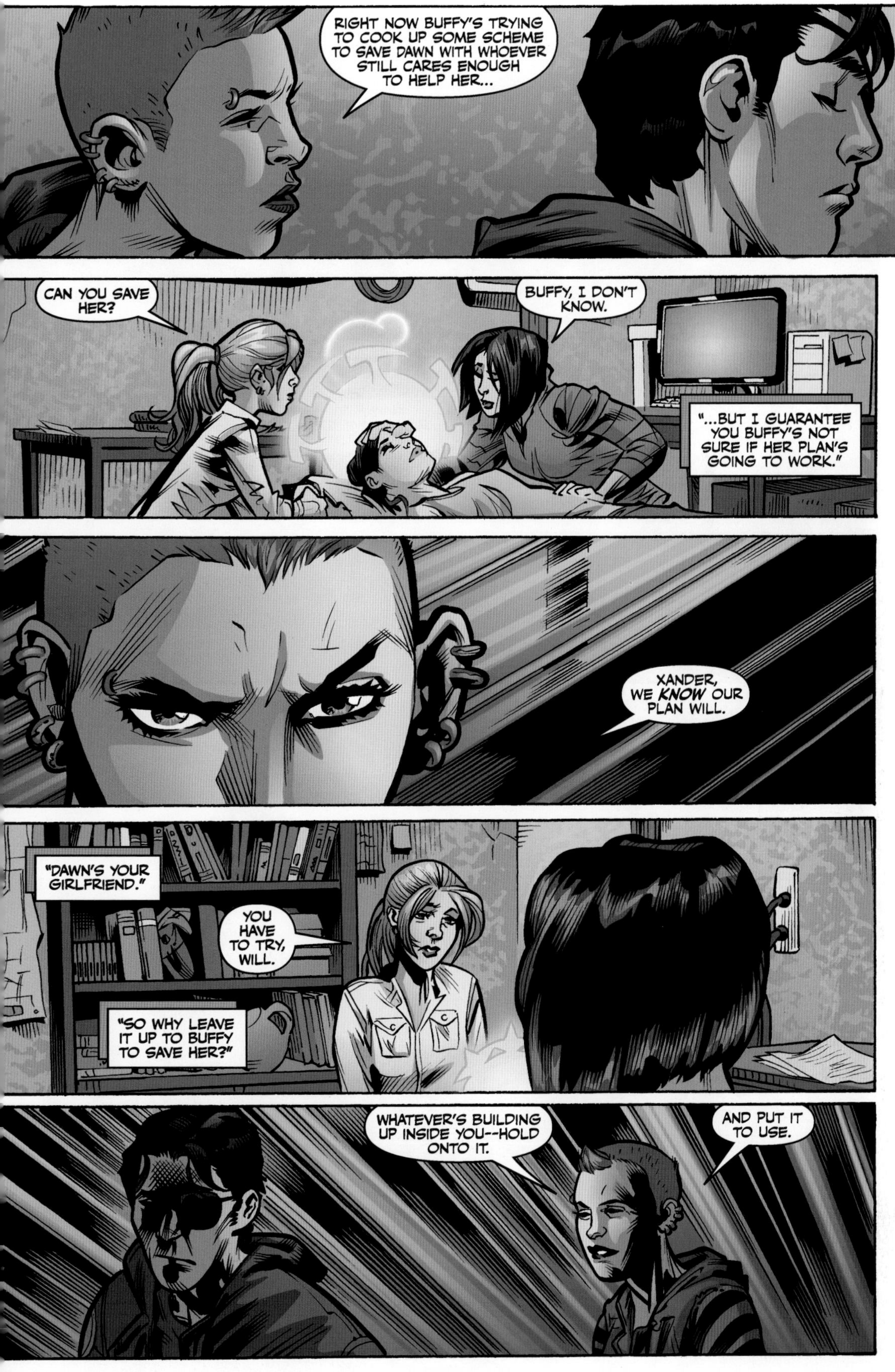
RIGHT NOW BUFFY'S TRYING TO COOK UP SOME SCHEME TO SAVE DAWN WITH WHOEVER STILL CARES ENOUGH TO HELP HER...
CAN YOU SAVE HER?
BUFFY, I DON'T KNOW.
"...BUT I GUARANTEE YOU BUFFY'S NOT SURE IF HER PLAN'S GOING TO WORK."
XANDER, WE *KNOW* OUR PLAN WILL.
"DAWN'S YOUR GIRLFRIEND."
YOU HAVE TO TRY, WILL.
"SO WHY LEAVE IT UP TO BUFFY TO SAVE HER?"
WHATEVER'S BUILDING UP INSIDE YOU--HOLD ONTO IT.
AND PUT IT TO USE.

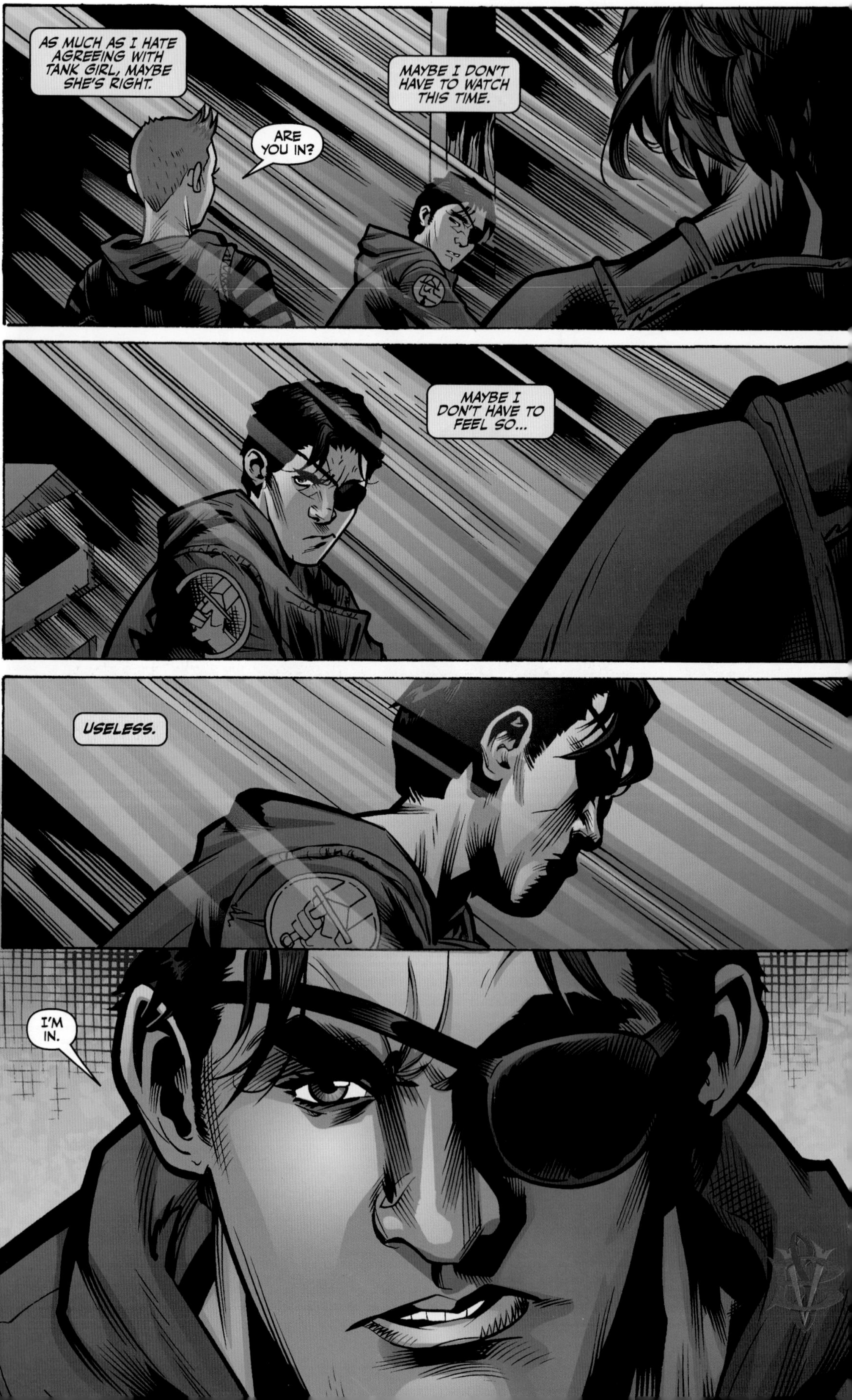
AS MUCH AS I HATE AGREEING WITH TANK GIRL, MAYBE SHE'S RIGHT.
ARE YOU IN?
MAYBE I DON'T HAVE TO WATCH THIS TIME.
MAYBE I DON'T HAVE TO FEEL SO...
USELESS.
I'M IN.

BUFFY *the* VAMPIRE SLAYER COVER GALLERY *and* SKETCHBOOK

VARIANT COVER ART BY
GEORGES JEANTY
with DEXTER VINES *and*
MICHELLE MADSEN

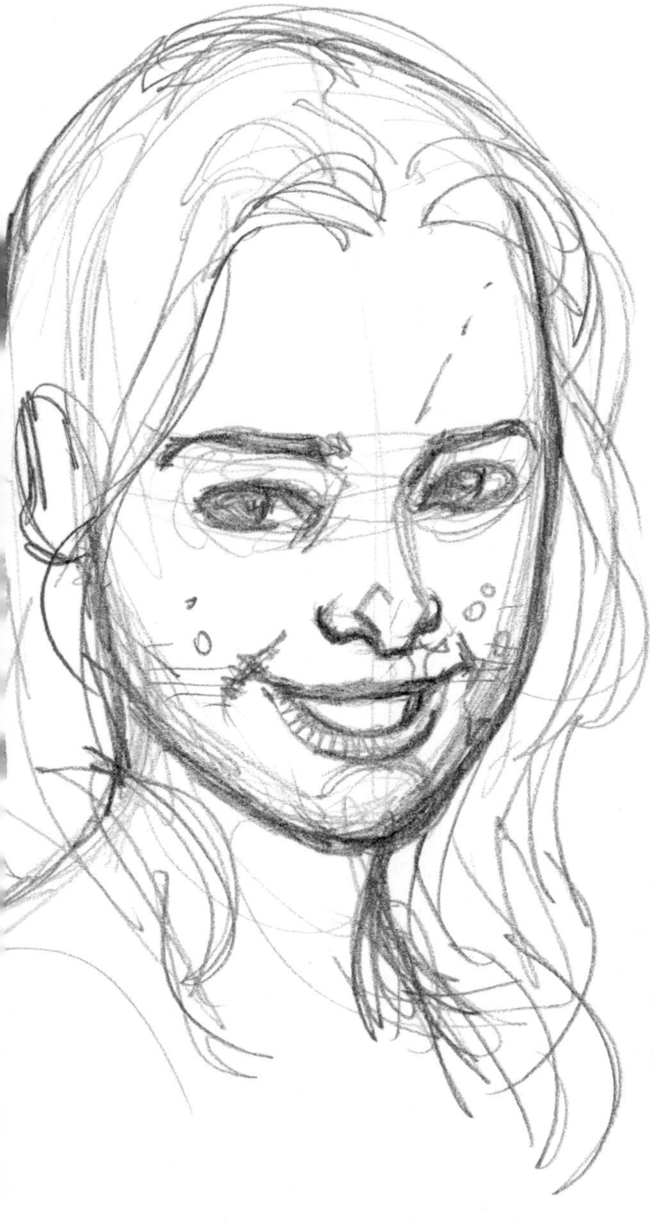

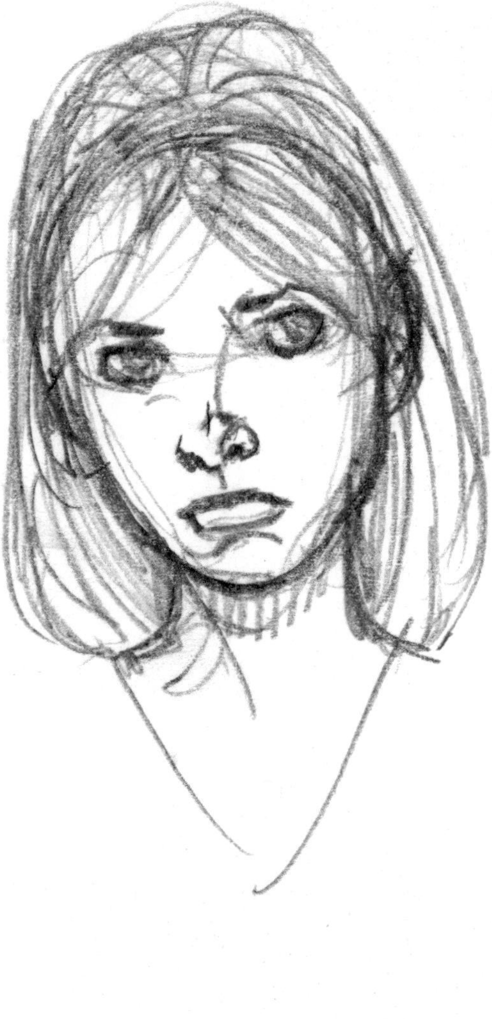

Georges warms up on Buffy's likeness for a scene in the first chapter of this book, with blood on her face and the scar on her forehead. Right, another warm-up for Buffy.

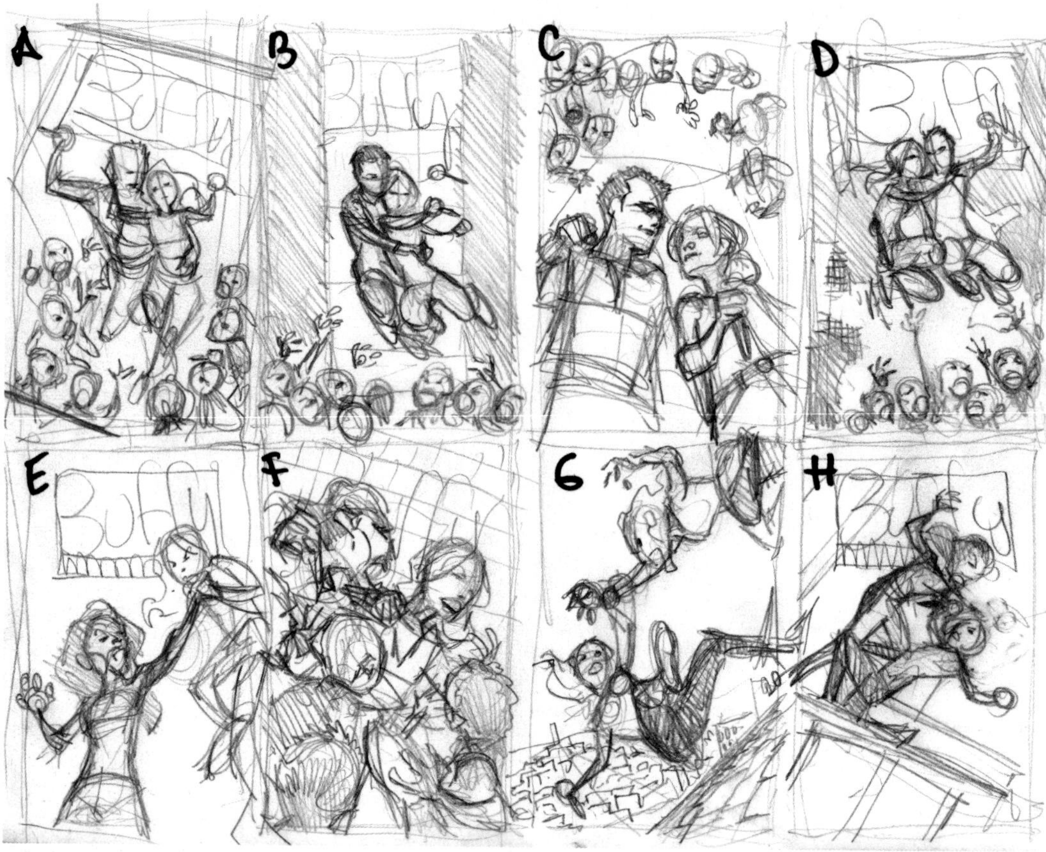
A
B
C
D
E
F
G
H

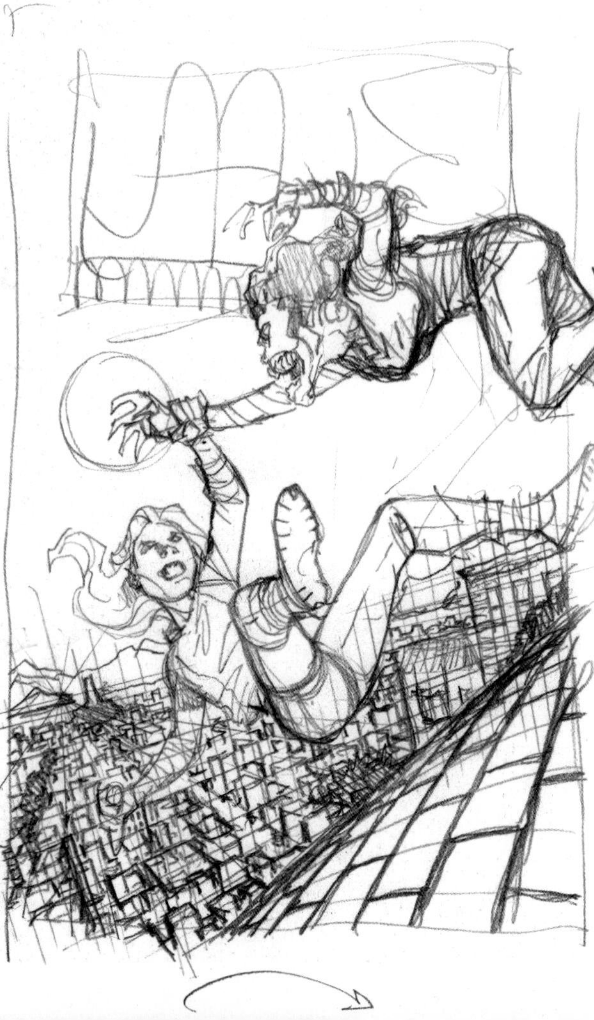

As usual, Georges offered a lot of cover ideas to choose from, then proceeded to do a tighter mockup (left), before going on to the finished pencils for the final piece, where he flopped the image, to take advantage of the natural movement from left to right. This cover became the central image for the Back to Basics ad campaign we ran in the middle of Season 9.

OPPOSITE: *Final variant cover for* Buffy *Season 9 #16.*

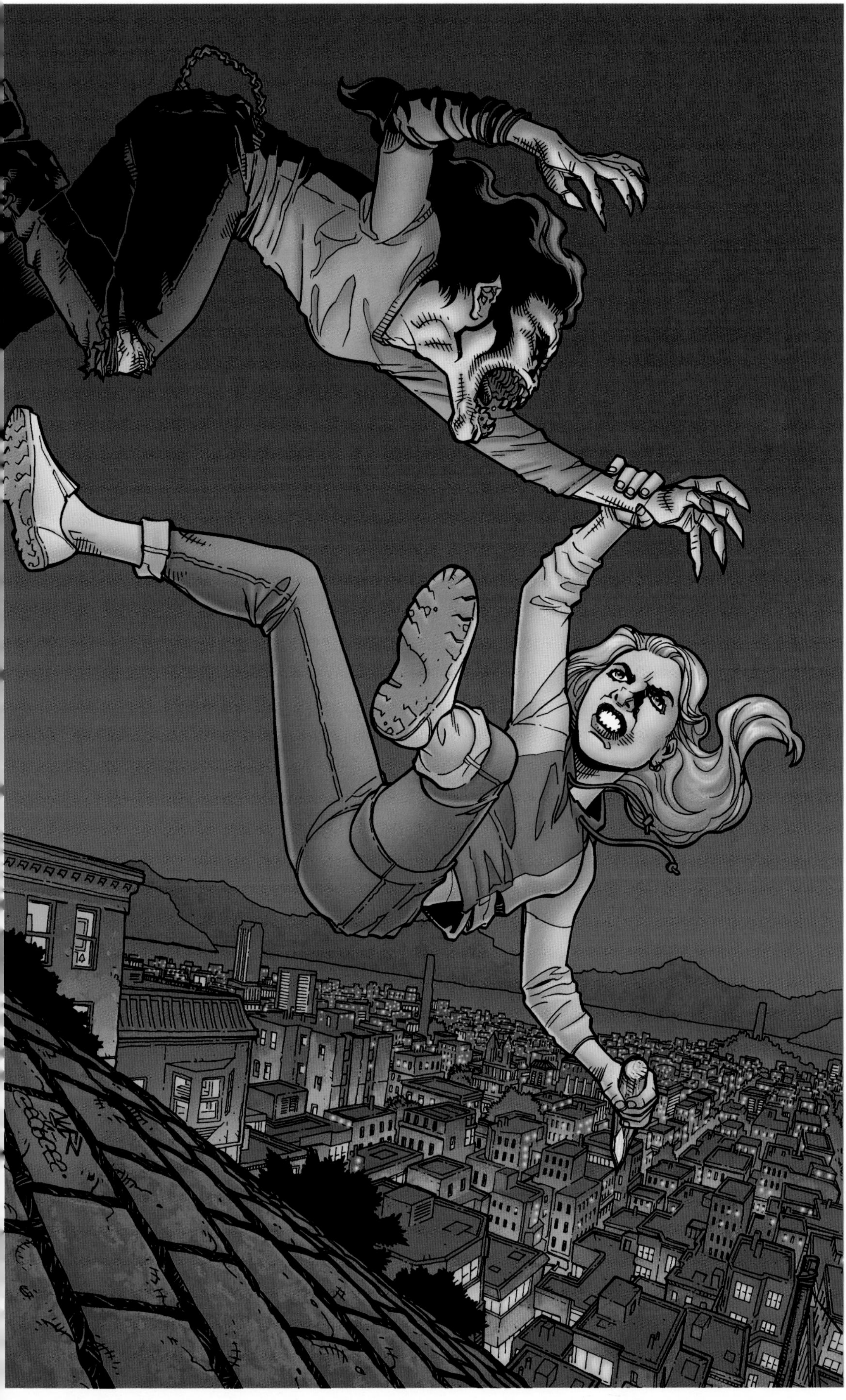

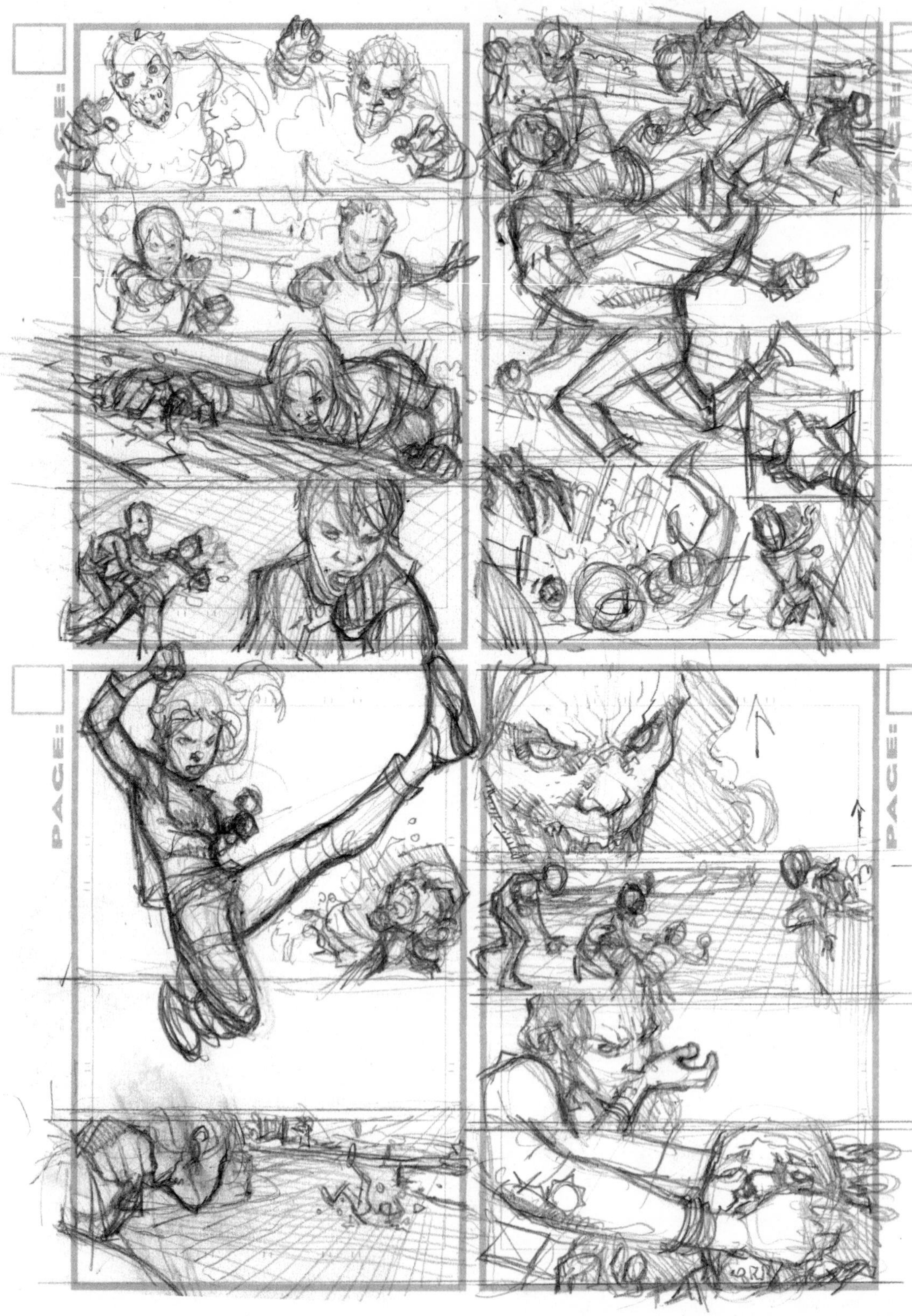
PAGE:
PAGE:
PAGE:
PAGE:

Rough layouts for the first chapter of this book. On the last of these pages, we decided to show the grisly way that zompires sire noobs.

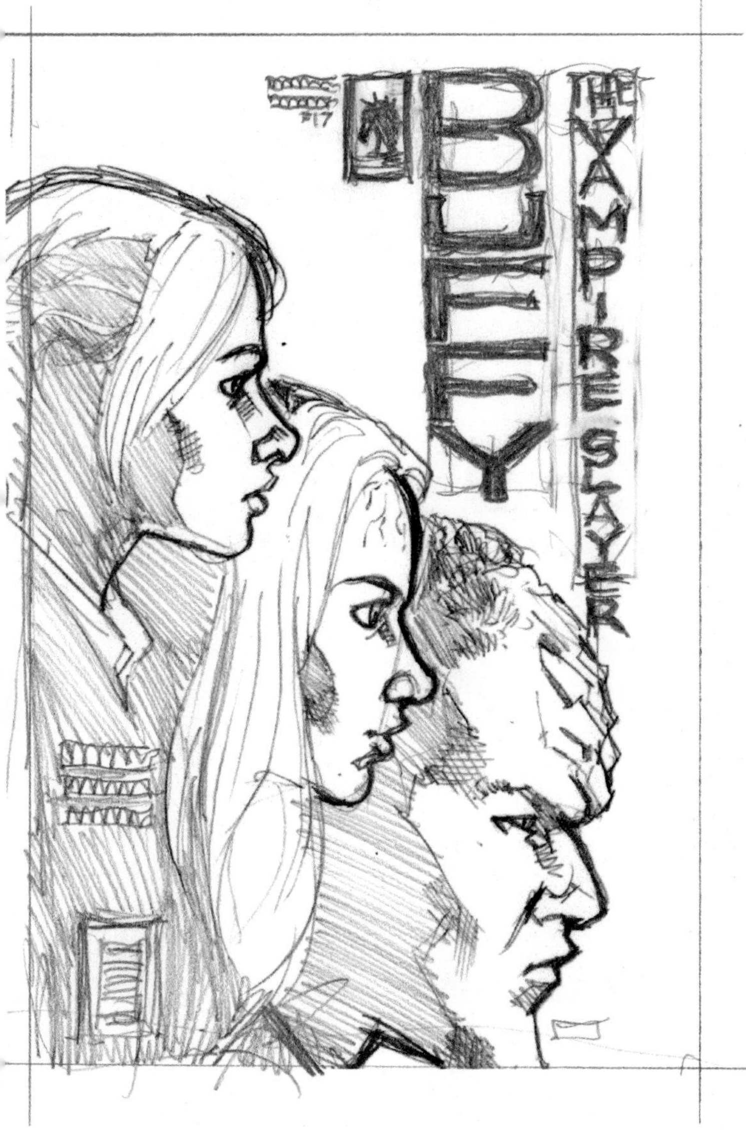
#17
BUFFY
THE VAMPIRE SLAYER

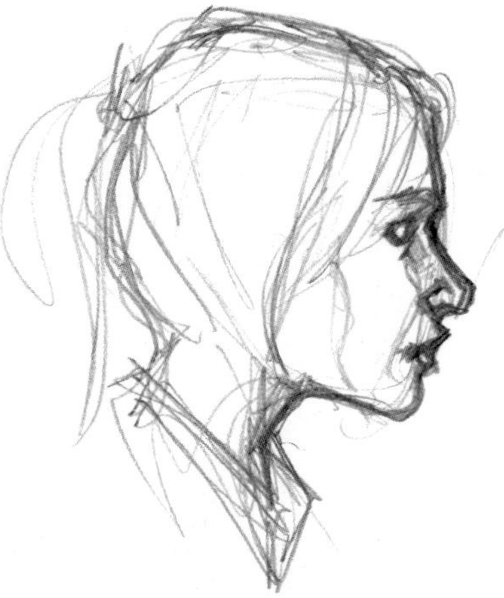

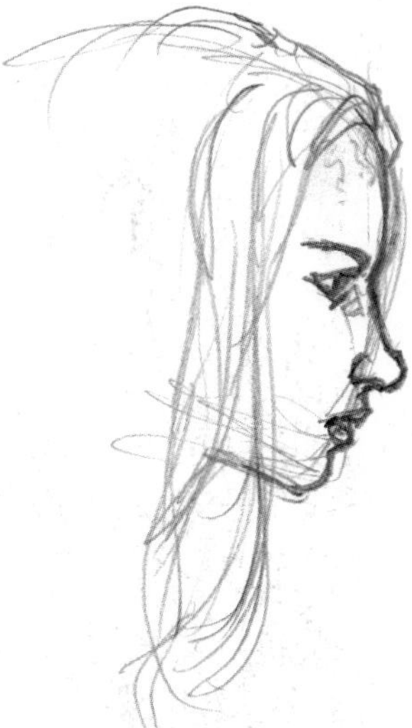

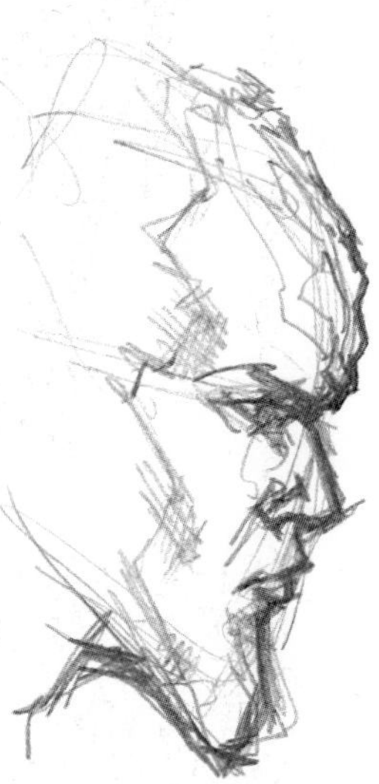

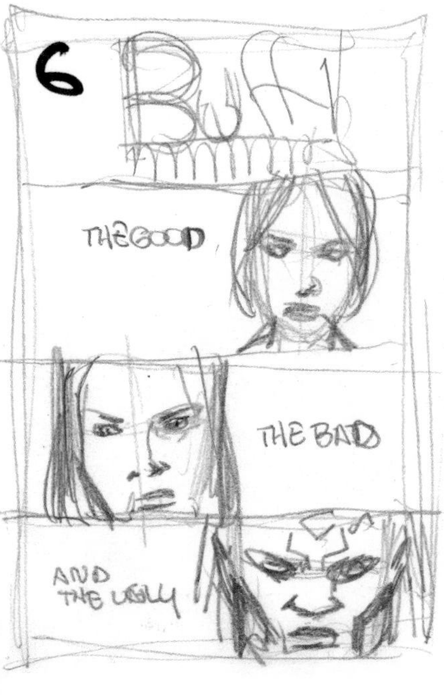
6
Buffy
THE GOOD
THE BAD
AND THE UGLY

LEFT: *One of at least seven ideas Georges presented for the issue #17 variant cover. Great idea, but we thought the profiles were more dramatic. Compare these studies to the final cover, on page 2 of this book.*

FOLLOWING PAGE: Buffy *Season 9 issue #18 final variant cover art.*

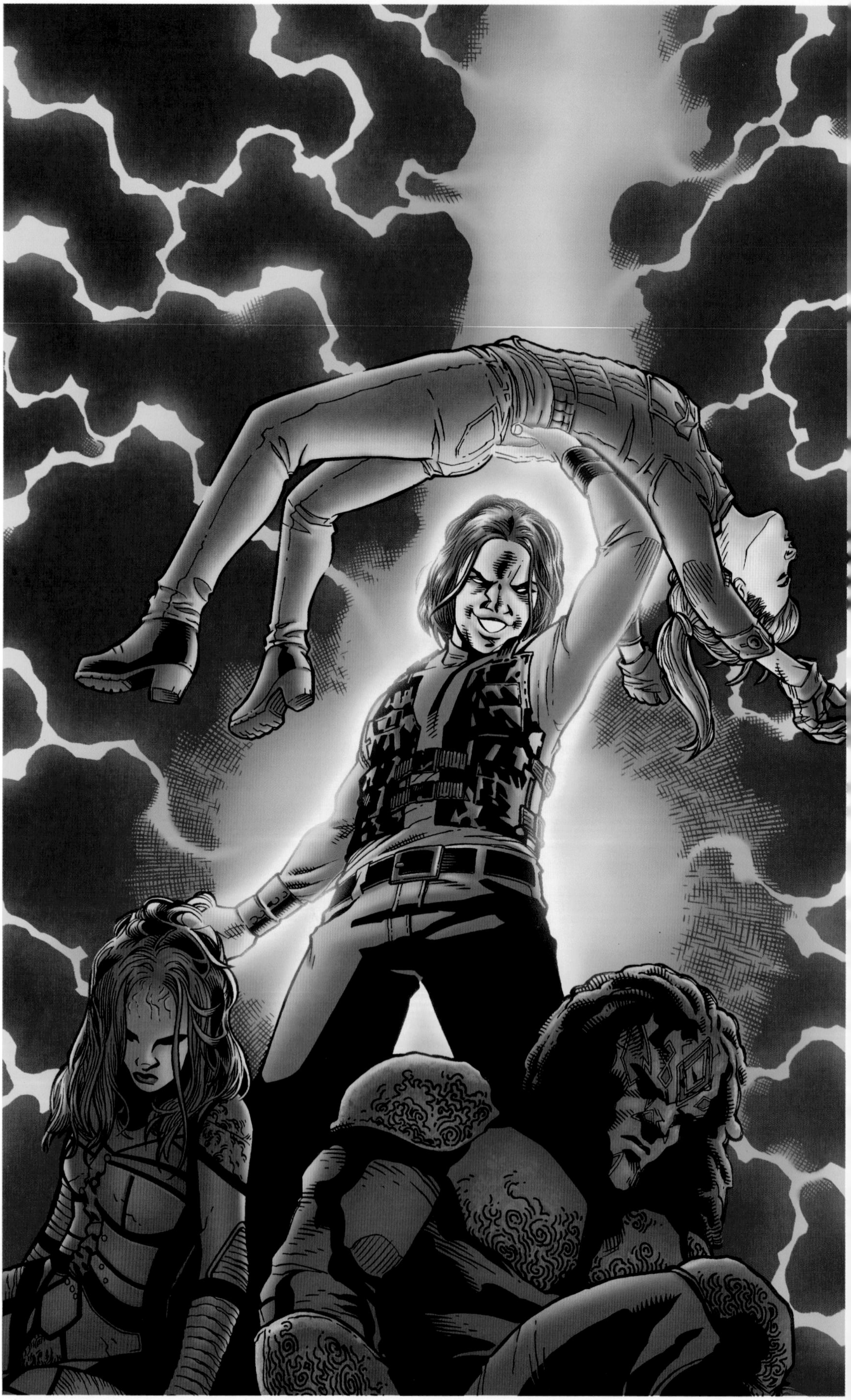

Buffy Season 9, #18
Draft 3, 7/3/12

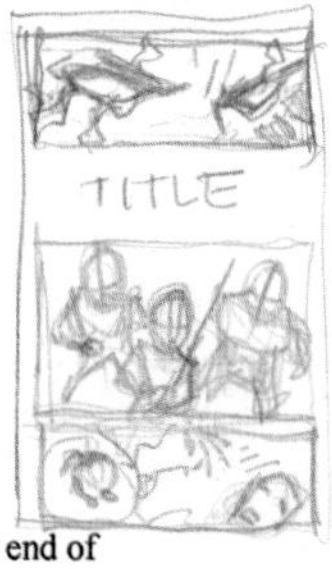
TITLE

PAGE ONE

PANEL ONE:

Close on Severin. His eyes glow with power. This is a direct pick-up from the end of #17. Severin still holds the burnt-out Matchstick Demon in his arms.

PANEL TWO:

Title: Welcome to the Team, Part 3

PAGE THREE:

Reverse so we see who he's facing off against -- Buffy, Koh and Illyria. Buffy is armed with a sword. Koh has his glowing blades. Illyria has her fists raised.

1/BUFFY
Drop the demon, Sev.

2/ILLYRIA
You are not worthy of the power you have stolen.

PANEL FOUR:

Back on Severin as he drops the Matchstick Demon's body to the ground. His hands charge with power.

3/SEVERIN
Really? Did "The Council" take a vote on that?

PAGE TWO

PANEL ONE:

Buffy, Illyria and Koh attack. Buffy is in the center, her sword raised above her head. Koh and Illyria are on either side. They all should look badass.

1/BUFFY
I'll let the sword answer.

PANEL TWO:

Severin sends sparks flying from his hands, knocking Koh, Buffy and Illyria through the air.

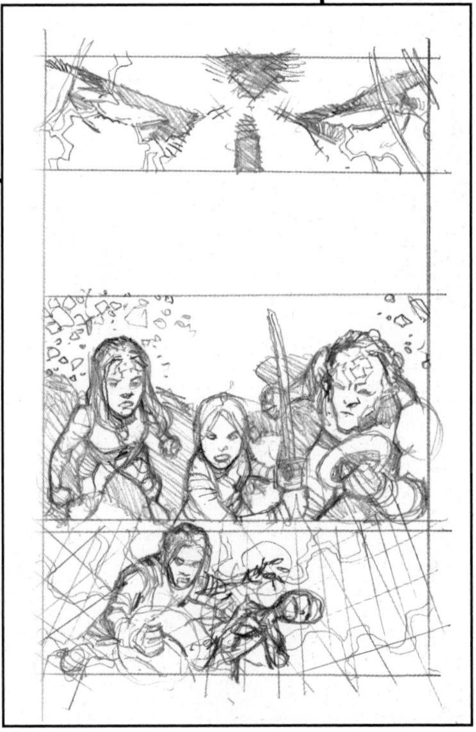

ABOVE: *The first page of script for* Buffy Season 9 #18*, with Georges's highlighting, as well as his initial thoughts on the page's layout.*

RIGHT: *Georges's rough layout for the first page. Georges blows up these layouts and copies them to the art board, so the initial rough tends to be extremely close to the final page, which you can see at the beginning of chapter 3.*

FOLLOWING PAGE: Buffy *Season 9 issue #19 final variant cover art.*

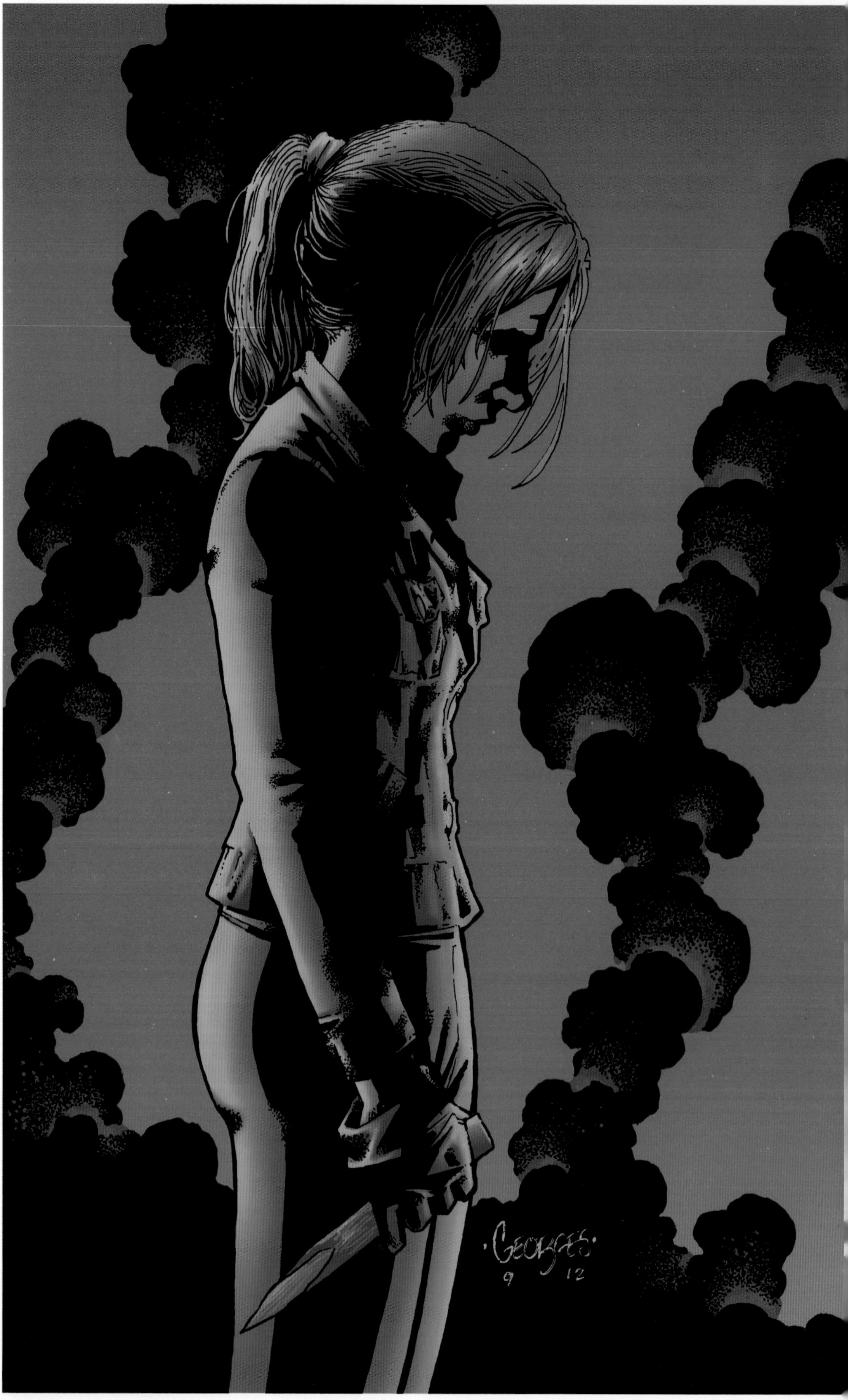
GEORGES
9 12

Georges's layout and Dexter Vines's final inks for the last page of Buffy Season 9 *#19. Georges's final pencil pages have much more elaborate grids than the one you see on the layouts for panel 1 here. Almost any panel with a background has a two- or three-point perspective grid to allow for Georges's sometimes meticulous backgrounds.*

FOLLOWING PAGE: Buffy *Season 9 issue #20 final variant cover art.*

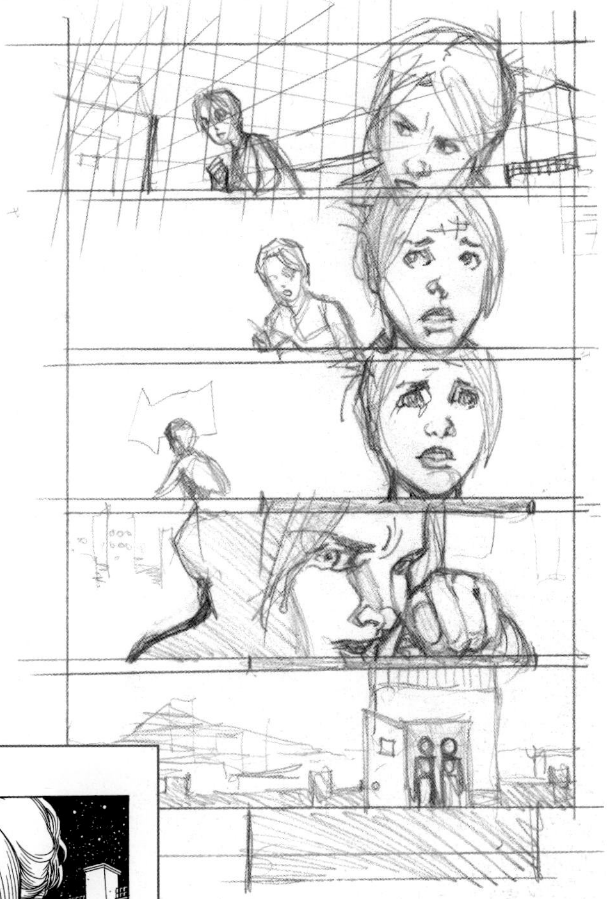

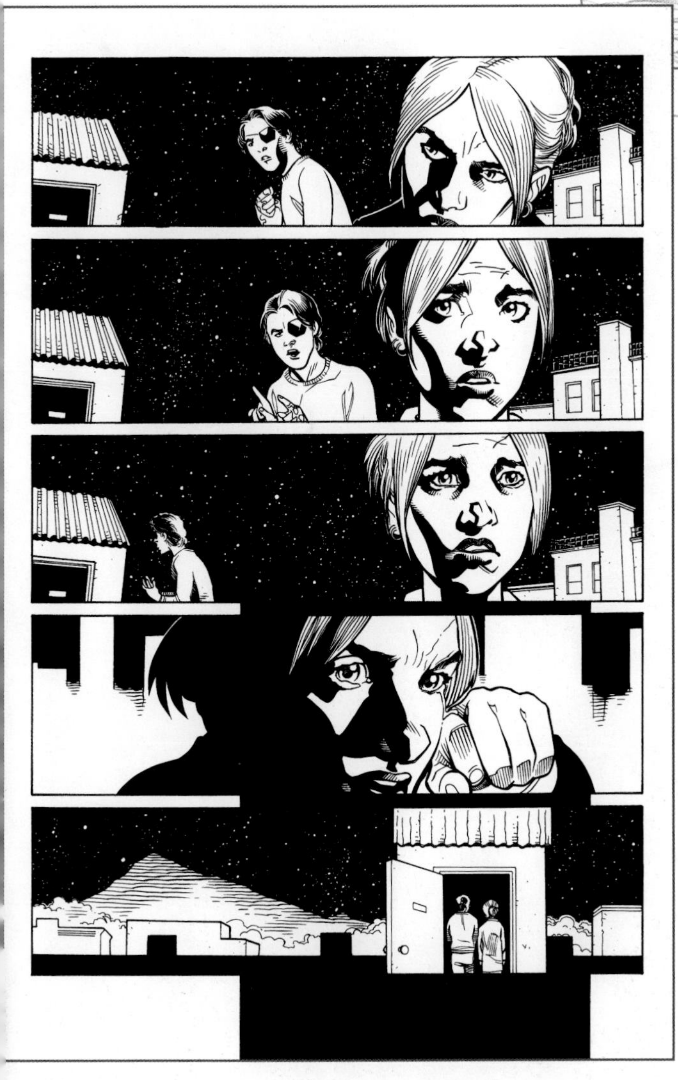

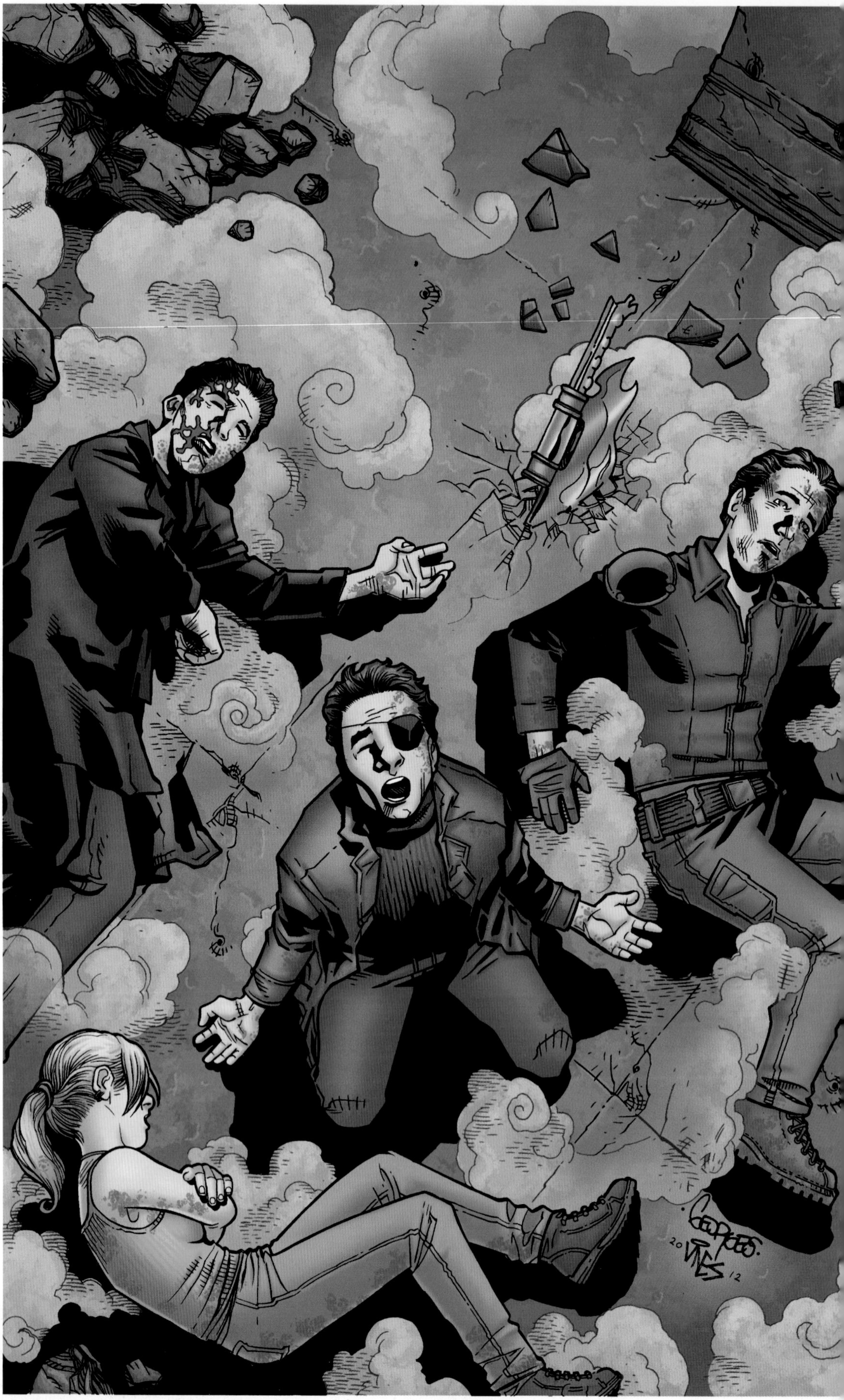

FROM JOSS WHEDON

Buffy the Vampire Slayer™

BUFFY THE VAMPIRE SLAYER SEASON 8

VOLUME 1: THE LONG WAY HOME
Joss Whedon and Georges Jeanty
ISBN 978-1-59307-822-5 | $15.99

VOLUME 2: NO FUTURE FOR YOU
Brian K. Vaughan, Georges Jeanty, and Joss Whedon
ISBN 978-1-59307-963-5 | $15.99

VOLUME 3: WOLVES AT THE GATE
Drew Goddard, Georges Jeanty, and Joss Whedon
ISBN 978-1-59582-165-2 | $15.99

VOLUME 4: TIME OF YOUR LIFE
Joss Whedon, Jeph Loeb, Georges Jeanty, and others
ISBN 978-1-59582-310-6 | $15.99

VOLUME 5: PREDATORS AND PREY
Joss Whedon, Jane Espenson, Georges Jeanty, Cliff Richards, and others
ISBN 978-1-59582-342-7 | $15.99

VOLUME 6: RETREAT
Joss Whedon, Jane Espenson, Georges Jeanty, Karl Moline, and others
ISBN 978-1-59582-415-8 | $15.99

VOLUME 7: TWILIGHT
Joss Whedon, Brad Meltzer, and Georges Jeanty
ISBN 978-1-59582-558-2 | $16.99

VOLUME 8: LAST GLEAMING
Joss Whedon, Scott Allie, and Georges Jeanty
ISBN 978-1-59582-610-7 | $16.99

BUFFY THE VAMPIRE SLAYER SEASON 8 LIBRARY EDITION

VOLUME 1
ISBN 978-1-59582-888-0 | $29.99

VOLUME 2
ISBN 978-1-59582-935-1 | $29.99

VOLUME 3
ISBN 978-1-59582-978-8 | $29.99

VOLUME 4
ISBN 978-1-61655-127-8 | $29.99

BUFFY THE VAMPIRE SLAYER SEASON 9

VOLUME 1: FREEFALL
Joss Whedon, Andrew Chambliss, Georges Jeanty, and others
ISBN 978-1-59582-922-1 | $17.99

VOLUME 2: ON YOUR OWN
Andrew Chambliss, Scott Allie, Georges Jeanty, and others
ISBN 978-1-59582-990-0 | $17.99

VOLUME 3: GUARDED
Joss Whedon, Jane Espenson, Drew Z. Greenberg, Georges Jeanty, and others
ISBN 978-1-61655-099-8 | $17.99

ANGEL & FAITH

VOLUME 1: LIVE THROUGH THIS
Christos Gage, Rebekah Isaacs, and Phil Noto
ISBN 978-1-59582-887-3 | $17.99

VOLUME 2: DADDY ISSUES
Christos Gage, Rebekah Isaacs, and Chris Samnee
ISBN 978-1-59582-960-3 | $17.99

VOLUME 3: FAMILY REUNION
Christos Gage, Rebekah Isaacs, Lee Garbett, and David Lapham
ISBN 978-1-61655-079-0 | $17.99

SPIKE

VOLUME 1: A DARK PLACE
ISBN 978-1-61655-109-4 | $17.99

WILLOW

VOLUME 1: WONDERLAND
ISBN 978-1-61655-145-2 | $17.99

AVAILABLE AT YOUR LOCAL COMICS SHOP OR BOOKSTORE!

To find a comics shop in your area, call 1-888-266-4226. For more information or to order direct:
On the web: DarkHorse.com • E-mail: mailorder@darkhorse.com • Phone: 1-800-862-0052 Mon.–Fri. 9 AM to 5 PM Pacific Time

DARK HORSE BOOKS

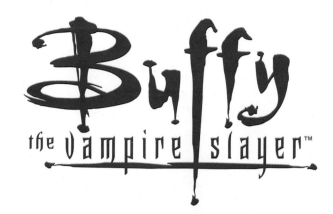

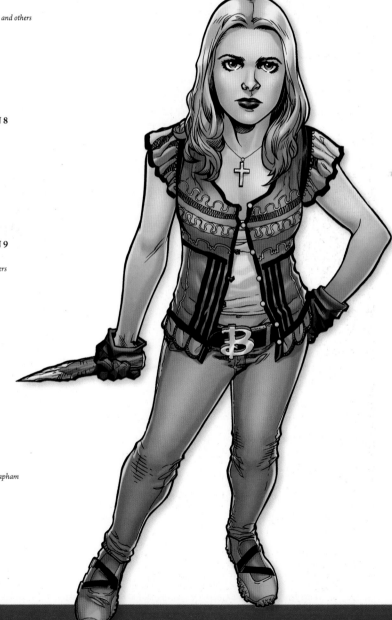

ALSO FROM JOSS WHEDON

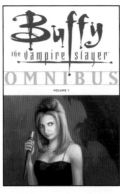

BUFFY THE VAMPIRE SLAYER OMNIBUS
VOLUME 1
ISBN 978-1-59307-784-6 | $24.99
VOLUME 2
ISBN 978-1-59307-826-3 | $24.99
VOLUME 3
ISBN 978-1-59307-885-0 | $24.99
VOLUME 4
ISBN 978-1-59307-968-0 | $24.99
VOLUME 5
ISBN 978-1-59582-225-3 | $24.99
VOLUME 6
ISBN 978-1-59582-242-0 | $24.99
VOLUME 7
ISBN 978-1-59582-331-1 | $24.99

BUFFY THE VAMPIRE SLAYER: PANEL TO PANEL
ISBN 978-1-59307-836-2 | $19.99

ANGEL OMNIBUS
Christopher Golden, Eric Powell, and others
ISBN 978-1-59582-706-7 | $24.99

TALES OF THE SLAYERS
*Joss Whedon, Amber Benson, Gene Colan, P. Craig
Russell, Tim Sale, and others*
ISBN 978-1-56971-605-2 | $14.99

TALES OF THE VAMPIRES
Joss Whedon, Brett Matthews, Cameron Stewart, and others
ISBN 978-1-56971-749-3 | $15.99

BUFFY THE VAMPIRE SLAYER: TALES HARDCOVER
ISBN 978-1-59582-644-2 | $29.99

FRAY: FUTURE SLAYER
Joss Whedon and Karl Moline
ISBN 978-1-56971-751-6 | $19.99

**SERENITY VOLUME 1: THOSE LEFT BEHIND
SECOND EDITION HARDCOVER**
Joss Whedon, Brett Matthews, and Will Conrad
ISBN 978-1-59582-914-6 | $17.99

**SERENITY VOLUME 2: BETTER DAYS AND
OTHER STORIES HARDCOVER**
*Joss Whedon, Patton Oswalt, Zack Whedon, Patric
Reynolds, and others*
ISBN 978-1-59582-739-5 | $19.99

**SERENITY VOLUME 3: THE SHEPHERD'S
TALE HARDCOVER**
Joss Whedon, Zack Whedon, and Chris Samnee
ISBN 978-1-59582-561-2 | $14.99

DR. HORRIBLE AND OTHER HORRIBLE STORIES
Joss Whedon, Zack Whedon, Joëlle Jones, and others
ISBN 978-1-59582-577-3 | $9.99

DOLLHOUSE VOLUME 1: EPITAPHS
*Andrew Chambliss, Jed Whedon, Maurissa Tancharoen,
and Cliff Richards*
ISBN 978-1-59582-863-7 | $18.99

[2]